NAILED IT!

J.R. Ripley

Beachfront Entertainment

First edition 2021

Kindle eBook ASIN: B08PC4F3HW
Trade Paperback ISBN: 9781892339461

Cover design by: StunningBookCovers.com

PRAISE

BOOKLIST
"Joins the growing list of Florida crime writers (Carl Hiaasen, Laurence Shames, Tim Dorsey) who mix capers with comedy...Readers will fall hard for this lovable loser as he struggles to stay alive while keeping his girlfriend from finding out what he is doing and his mom's pet pig from eating his stuff. Further adventures would be most welcome."

MIDWEST BOOK REVIEW
"...a darkly funny, rip-roaring novel about a fast-talking realtor who is quite possibly the world's worst judge of character....A wildly frantic novel about a ne'er do well whose bad deeds have caught up with him, and his wacky struggle to stay just one step ahead of the trigger, suspenseful to the very last word."

JUST PLUM CRAZY
"It's a comic thriller with a wacky plot...Lots of great characters...All kinds of bad stuff happens to Todd...But in the end everything seems to work out. Except the last sentence in the book is extremely clever."

NAILED IT!

1

"I don't get it, Jones." George Strange, Big George, to his employees, was no stranger to Florida. He and his wife, Imelda—no relation to the shoe lady—and sometimes his mistress, Christie, when his wife was busy with her charity crap, spent a lot of time in Florida, when he wasn't busy running his scrap business empire from that giant scrap heap that was Detroit.

Sure, he loved the town—he'd been born there—but it had seen better days. Hell, he loved the Detroit Lions—owned a premium suite at Ford Field and was a member of the MGM Grand Tunnel Club—and the team never even had better days. Not in his lifetime anyway.

Sure, Florida was weird. Everybody who's been here knew that. But this was the strangest thing he had encountered yet.

"How's that?" asked Todd Jones.

"We've been all over this property," George continued, his fleshy pink lips and tongue a sharp contrast to his mahogany tan. "And I'm sweating like a pig on a rotisserie." He yanked off his dark shades, wiped them on his shirttail then thrust them back on his squat nose.

"It *is* a beautiful day," remarked Todd, ever the real estate agent. Always show the client the good side of anything no matter how bad it really is. Always make a positive out of a negative. That was just basic good

1

salesmanship.

But inside he was sweating. Over the weather and over the deal. Dying to get out of this heat and indoors where he could wrap his hands around a chilled margarita.

"Yep. Gorgeous Florida weather." If you were an iguana. They thrived in this climate. Those midget dinosaurs were taking over the lower half of the state.

While George Strange, the client, was taking life easy in a loose cotton shirt that looked like an advertisement for Christmas candy canes, baggy blue shorts and leather sandals, Todd was all business, occupying a once-crisp, now soggy white button-down dress shirt, cuffed dress slacks and Hugo Boss shoes. In deference to the heat, his summer wool sports coat remained in the car.

The two men couldn't be more different. A real study in contrast. Todd, in his early thirties, stood just under six feet, possessed seagrape green eyes, bleached-blonde hair and a slightly bent roman nose earned from his days of college boxing. He was meticulous of both personal hygiene and dress.

George Strange, on the other hand, in his late fifties, stood maybe five-five, possessed very little hair and plenty of shiny dome covered in a close-shaven carpet of black hair. He had squinty brown eyes and a full goatee speckled with gray. His body type was pudgy going to fat and, if he had any sense of style at all, he kept it well hidden.

And that pig remark of his struck a little too close to home for Todd.

Todd's mom's pet porker, Mr. Squeals, was a permanent houseguest in his luxury condo. His once private sanctuary was now home to the pig, his mother and the stray his mother had picked up at the local grocery mart, a young Russian woman named Irina Sokolov.

Todd had tried, unsuccessfully, to get the condo board to ban the malodorous pig, Mr. Squeals, but his mom must have had something on a board member or two, because his request had been denied. Twice.

How he'd love to see that potbellied nuisance lazily rotating on a stainless-steel rotisserie over an open pit fire.

George Strange tugged at the cotton shirt sticking to his hairy chest. The Florida heat and humidity are a brutal cocktail. "Don't get me wrong, it's very nice and all but you advertised five point eight acres. I'm not seeing anything near that."

The house did have a great kitchen. The wife would like that. One wine fridge, two commercial ovens, two dishwashers. Not that she'd ever load the damn things. There were people for that. She loathed the scrap business he ran but loved the money it made them. And loved spending it even more.

Personally, George especially liked the forty-foot, outdoor, heated swimming pool and the exercise room, fully-equipped with every dumbbell and high-tech workout gizmo a body could yearn for. Not that he believed in exercise or even swimming.

Oh, he didn't mind standing around in the shallow end of the pool, slurping a fizzy pink piña colada through a plastic straw, but that was about it. What the pool was best for was seeing Christie splashing around in it.

With no close neighbors on either side, this

property offered plenty of privacy, except for the boats going by. But Christie wasn't shy, he could probably convince her to go topless. Ditto the exercise room, he could watch her work up a sweat in one of those skintight, sexy little leotard thingies that she was always buying with his money.

After her workout, he pictured them working up a little sweat together on the king-sized bed in the master wing overlooking the dark blue waters of the river.

"Is that what's bothering you? The missing land?" Todd flashed a smile. 'Trust me, George' it said. "Let's walk over to the edge of the river. Let me show what the lucky buyer of this estate gets."

The two men moved to the rear of the property and stood shoulder to shoulder at the edge of the slow-moving water. A warm breeze washed over them. "You get all this acreage here surrounding the house, plus all that." Todd waved his arm.

"Yer waving at water."

"Yep, all this beautiful, pristine water." Todd wouldn't so much as stick a toe in that water. He'd heard it was polluted beyond belief due to all the motorboats spewing fossil fuel and the homeowners' spilling pesticides into the river from the zealously manicured lawns every time it rained.

Runoff was one of Florida's many afflictions, be it pollutants or elections.

"Plus that property on the other side. See?" An impassable tangle of shrubs, grasses and palm trees stood on the opposite shore. Not even Tarzan could fight his way through that jungle.

"All I see is a lot of weeds." George tossed his cigar in the river and watched it float away. "I don't get it."

"Let's add it up, shall we? On this side, you've got about two acres give or take, figure another acre and a half for the river span, plus another two acres or so across the way. Add it up and you get—"

"Let me guess, five point eight acres." George took a step back. "I'll be damned. You mean to say, they count the water here?"

Todd shrugged. "It's deeded. It's all yours. Common practice." Truth was, Todd had sold worse. Up in Boca Raton, he'd actually been involved in the sale of some Intracoastal home lots that were completely underwater and offered at over a million bucks a pop. It was going to cost a lucky owner that much again to truck in enough landfill to get the property up high enough above water to then build their palace atop.

The lawsuits surrounding the deal still dragged on—and were dragging him down with them.

"Not yet it ain't." George dragged a fresh cigar from the cargo pocket of his baggy shorts and lit up.

"Why don't we step back inside? I can show you the actual boundaries of your property survey."

"*If* I buy the place," George said, ambling along behind his real estate agent. "And that's a big IF."

"You know, I probably shouldn't be saying this," Todd said, steering his client into the expansive kitchen, an explosion of marble and top-of-the-line restaurant-grade stainless steel appliances. The digital thermostat read a cool sixty-eight degrees. "But I feel honor bound to tell you, George, I do have a very interested client from up in Palm Beach. The wife wants to be closer to her mother. Can you believe that?"

"No." George Strange frowned. "Palm Beach, huh?" He hated Palm Beachers. So full of themselves. Stuck up bunch of asses. "Old money probably. Probably never worked a day in their phony lives or ever got their hands dirty."

"The oldest," Todd said as if that was a bad thing. In that ticking muscle called his heart, of course, he'd have given a kidney to have been born into Old Money. Instead he'd been raised in a two bed, one bath, single carport tract home by his cigarette- and pot-smoking, alcohol-swilling hippie mother. His father was out of the picture. Lucky him.

George tapped his chin with the damp end of his cigar leaving bits of tobacco leaf in his whiskers. "Three million, huh?"

That was a bit more than he'd paid for his two-level Book Cadillac condo and that was smack downtown Detroit. Close to his offices. It didn't hurt that the residences occupied the top floors of the downtown Westin none either. Always handy to have a hotel nearby when guests or the girlfriend were in town.

"That's cheap, trust me. The sellers are anxious. You get this 7,000 square foot house, four-car garage, 200 feet of river frontage, ditto on the opposite shore."

"The roof looks shot to me."

"I'll bring it up with the sellers. I'm sure we can get them to make an accommodation." He was representing both sides of this deal. Not quite ethical, perhaps, but it was quite profitable. "Besides, at the bargain price you're getting this one-of-a-kind estate for, what's one little roof?"

"Little? You could land a Cessna on top of this house!"

"Yes, isn't it magnificent? Like I said, nicest property in the area. By a long shot." Of course, it needed, at minimum, a half-million bucks worth of updates and renovations just to get it up to code but George could afford it. Todd had checked the man out thoroughly. Strange Scrap, Inc. did business all around the world.

"Well…"

"Don't forget, you're getting that state-of-the-art dockage."

"And the boat?" George licked his lips. He'd been drooling over that boat. A 48-foot Hatteras Convertible sport fishing boat. Twin staterooms, two heads. A real dream.

Any boat, actually. Imelda hated boats. Claimed she got seasick. That meant he wouldn't have to drag her along on any outings and she wouldn't even gripe about it.

"And the boat," Todd promised. "I'm sure I can work my magic."

"See that you do."

"Hey, I'm here for you. We Detroit men have to stick together, am I right?" Hoping to earn some brownie points with George Strange, he'd told him that he was from Detroit originally too. The funny thing was, it was true.

As for the Hatteras, at three million, he could eat a little of his commission. If the sellers balked at throwing in the boat, he'd offer to pay for it out of his own pocket.

Then again, the sellers had told him in confidence that they'd be happy to clear two-point-five for the house, so he didn't expect any complaints when he threw a full-price offer-to-buy at them and all they had to do was throw in a 30-year-old boat that they'd never miss. After all, the house and boat had been their mom and dad's. The kids just wanted their money.

Todd extended his right hand. "Do we have a deal? Or do you need to talk to your wife first?"

"You gotta deal, Jones." George stuck out his damp palm and the two men shook. "When can we close?"

Todd suppressed a grin. That crack about checking with the wife worked like a charm more often than not. "How soon do you need the place?"

"Yesterday soon enough for you?"

"I'll see what I can do to speed things along."

"You do that."

"Great." Todd rubbed his hands together. "I'll write up the contract and send it over for your signature."

"Oh, there is one little thing."

"Just name it." Todd folded up his paperwork and threw it in his leather briefcase resting open on the kitchen island. That island was a real monster. He'd seen smaller whales at the Miami Seaquarium.

"Imelda's gonna want one of her interior design freaks to do the place over on the inside."

"Sounds good."

"Sounds expensive. Ditto a landscape architect. You ask me, you throw down some grass seed, watch it grow then hire some schmuck to mow it once a week. Who needs landscape architects? Am I right?"

"You're right." Todd was only barely listening as he added up the dollars this easy sale was going to reward him with.

"I'm making you responsible for the roof." George thumped Todd in the chest with his middle finger.

"Me? What do I know about roofs?" Todd took a step back before the Neanderthal could thump him a second time.

"You're a realtor. You must know people."

"I suppose that's true."

"Of course, it's true. So you find me one of those people. One of those roof people. Not just anyone. The best. George Strange only gets the best. You get the best roofer in South Florida and you get him over here pronto. The day we close on this house, I want his ass over here on top my roof. Got it, Jones?"

"I'll do what I can." For six percent of three mil, Todd was prepared to put up with George Strange being a pain in the ass himself.

"What you can?" George's creased and well-fed face clouded over. "There's hurricanes brewin' out there, Jones. Get me my roof."

"Absolutely. You can count on me, Mr. Strange."

2

The South Florida sun raked over the green going brown St. Augustine grass and over the flesh of the two men standing next to each other on the driveway of a typical South Florida ranch house.

Hot and muggy. Count on it. Like the coming of the New Jersey-New York crowd each winter. There wasn't a suburb in South Florida that was exempt. Not from the snowbirds. Not from the *meat*.

Muggy plus heat equals meat—which was what a person would become if a person stayed out in the sun too long here. Meat. Medium rare.

Ronald Patton, Ron to his friends, Raunch to his best friend, was proud of that one. He'd coined the term himself.

Sadly, it had yet to catch on with the natives. Or the tourists, or the snowbirds. But what did they know?

Not much. But that was the way he liked it.

He was an Arizona boy himself.

And St. Augustine grass? Where did that one come from? Sorry, Augustine, the best we could do is name a grass after you? That cathedral you wanted? That mountain in the Alps? Not going to happen.

Sure, you had some good ideas, some excellent ideas but the human race is running out of things to name. There are only so many unnamed things to go around, you know, Augie?

Philosophy aside, and Augustine had some interesting ideas about things, Ron, himself, pretty much agreed with Augie that time was merely a human concept. Subjective, really.

How could it not be? Just look at the difference between him and his wife? Ready in a minute, dear? Sheesh. For him, that minute was more like time to watch six innings of a ball game. Which he'd been able to do on more than one such occasion. Talk about your proof of concept.

Speaking of time and waiting, Ron Patton softly closed his eyes. Why should eyelids be exempt from sunburn? He waited. Knowing that eventually, once his customer, Mr. Taderuski, got over the shock, he would speak.

"Fifty grand?" The fat man leaned back, scratched his belly, scratched his head. His belly was too big for his striped polo shirt and his flip-flops too small for his feet. His shorts were just plain ugly, like he'd skinned a bushel basket's worth of eggplant and sewn 'em together.

"That's how the numbers add up." Ron Patton tapped his pen against his tablet. This wasn't one of those fancy electronic gizmos. Those things cost too much and he found them finicky. Not good for fieldwork at all. No, this was an old-fashioned clipboard with a yellow legal pad clamped to it.

Ron swept back a lock of greasy black hair, practically melting in the sun. No matter what he did to try and rectify that hair, it always seemed to hold more grease than the rear axle of his van. He was well aware that his eyes were the dullest green imaginable. He was average height, average looks and average abilities—and he knew it too.

That was why he chose to make a living doing what he liked to call a non-average profession.

"I asked you to gimme a quote on repairing the roof. Not," Taderuski told the contractor, "build me the freaking Taj Mahal."

"Sorry," replied Ron. "That's the going rate. The best I can do."

"But fifty grand?" His mouth hung open big as his garage door.

"What can I say? Materials, labor. Prices just keep going up. Up and up and up. Know what I mean?" Ron aimed his eyes heavenward, well, at a passing cloud to be precise but he was sure Taderuski got the drift.

Mr. Taderuski, aka The Fat Man, pointed at his neighbor's house. "Wayne across the street got a quote for nineteen-five."

Ron thrust out his lower lip. "That's not bad. Not bad at all." He took a couple of steps sideways and pretended to compare the two houses. "Not quite the same configuration though."

"Not quite the same configuration? It's the same damn builder. Same damn house."

"Huh."

"Huh? Is that the best you can do?"

"'Fraid so."

"Fine." Taderuski's head shook so hard, so fast, side to side that Ron feared it might come unscrewed. "You take credit?" He unlocked the arms he'd been wrapping across his chest.

"'Fraid not."

"Why am I not surprised?" Taderuski whipped out his checkbook, signed furiously and tore out the check.

"I can't believe I paid you three hundred bucks and all I get is a crazy high estimate."

"Thank you." Ron looked the check over carefully. Everything seemed in order—one couldn't be too careful these days—then pushed it into his pocket. He wouldn't wait too long to deposit it though, maybe stop at the bank on his way home. Then pick up some takeout Chinese. He was in the mood for moo goo gai pan.

"I'll be honest with you, Patton, I won't be hiring you."

"Sorry to hear that." Ron tried to look sorry. He was shooting for dejected, downhearted, despondent. It was a face he'd practiced lots in the mirror but he wasn't very successful at it.

At least, that's what his wife, Elaine, told him. She told him at best he looked like he'd stubbed his toe on the corner leg of his La-Z-Boy chair. She told him lots of things. She was a real complainer. She'd be happy today though. He'd had a good day today. Over a thousand bucks good.

"I don't know how you can even begin to make a living!" Taderuski shouted as Ron backed his white van—with the blood red Ronald's Roofing name and telephone number airbrushed on its sides—out of his driveway.

Ron waved and drove off.

This latest hustle was working out great. Roofs were big ticket items, much bigger than the plumbing and electrical scams he'd run before. Those were peanuts compared to this.

What the hell did he care if Taderuski or anybody else hired him? He was making money, good money, thank you very much, charging for writing estimates.

If the roofing market ever fizzled out, he was considering becoming a pool contractor next. Another big-ticket item. And everybody in South Florida either had a swimming pool or wanted one.

One more stop and he'd be done for the day. This next place was supposed to be a big one, too. He'd GoogleEarthed it. One of those castles on the water. Ten million at least. That was a lot of shingles.

3

The silver Audi A6's tires screeched and shivered as Todd hit the blacktop and sped off. That George Strange was one strange bird. But, then again, the rich usually were. Coddling to them was a real pain in the butt. People complain about real estate agents and their commissions. As far as he was concerned, he earned each and every penny of his.

And then some.

And now he had to find Strange a roofer of all things. He'd have to ask around. While he had a file with numbers for a few willing-to-look-the-other way home inspectors and the occasional plumber or electrician, he'd had no experience with roofers. Maybe he'd ask Irina to call a few companies and send them out to the property. Line up some quotes. That ought to satisfy Strange.

Get him off his back until he had his signature on the contract. That was the only thing that mattered—a signed contract.

A white van with a couple of aluminum ladders strapped to its roof shot in front of the Audi from a cross street. Todd slammed on the brakes. "Watch where you're going, moron!" he called uselessly through the windshield.

The white van pulled into the forecourt of a whitewashed, Spanish-tiled palace, coming to a stop at the entrance. Todd made out the lettering on the side of the van: Ronald's Roofing.

"Well, well." Todd drummed his fingers across the steering wheel. "This is my lucky day." Any roofer working in this neighborhood had to be good.

He pulled off to the side of the road and killed the engine.

Ron Patton gulped down the last bits of a cheese, lettuce and mayo sandwich, dusting off the crumbs as he stepped down from the van.

Todd sauntered up the drive. "You got a card?"

"Is there a problem?" Ron squinted. Was this yahoo gonna call the cops on him for cutting him off? The rich could be touchy about such things. Liked to throw their weight around.

"I need a roofer."

"So?"

Todd nodded toward the van.

Ron turned and looked. "Oh, sure." He wiped a couple bits of cheddar from his lower lip. "This your place? Sorry, I'm running a couple minutes behind. Busy busy busy. You know how it is. When you're the best, it's hard to keep up with the requests."

"Right. No, this isn't my house." Todd stuck out his hand. "Card?"

"Sure thing." Ron opened the door to the van and dug around in the center console for a relatively clean business card. He handed it over. "You live around here?"

"No. I'm an agent. I've got a buyer lined up on a place down the street. 302 Vizcaya Lane."

"And he needs a roof?"

"Between you and me, the guy needs a lot of things.

His name is George Strange, and is he ever." Chuckle chuckle. Todd tucked the business card in his wallet. "Think you can handle it?"

"That's what we do." Ron Patton deliberately tossed in the word *we*. This gave customers the idea that he actually employed a real team of workers, diligently slapping down roof tiles in his wake.

"Great. I expect a quick closing. Ten days or so." George was a cash buyer. The best kind of buyer there was. "I'll give you a call and let you know the day of closing."

An elderly gentleman, and what appeared to be his wife, stepped off the portico of the home. "Mr. Patton, I presume?"

"Be with you in a minute!" Ron said with a supersalesman smile.

"Think you can get the matter taken care of right away? Strange is really anxious. Worried about hurricanes."

"You're not giving me much notice, but I'm sure we can squeeze him in."

"I'm counting on you." A wealthy man like George Strange could lead to more referrals to more wealthy buyers, so long as Todd kept the man happy. A bad word from Strange could wreak havoc on his reputation. And a real estate agent lived and died by his or her reputation.

"Don't worry," promised Ron. "I'm as good as my word. You can count on it."

Todd slogged down the drive.

Ron went to greet his newest customers, sizing them up quickly. They had to be pushing 85 or 90 and, despite the heat, dressed like it was winter in Buffalo,

New York.

In a hurry to get home, he quoted them sixty grand for the roof plus materials, with a ninety-day limited warranty on the materials only. Labor would be an extra charge.

The cheapskates balked, wasted about twenty minutes of his time as the wife struggled first to find her checkbook then even longer as she struggled to hold her Bic pen steady and fill out the check to pay him for writing the estimate.

Ron Patton folded the check and stuffed it in his pocket along with the others as he sped away.

Life's filled with suckers and he was licking them all —all the way to the bank.

Life was good.

4

Precisely ten days later, George and Imelda Strange pulled up to a somewhat dilapidated but exclusive South Florida home on the river, a 48-foot Hatteras Convertible sport fishing boat big enough to hold any fish he was likely to catch—and still have room left over for his mistress, Christie—and one leaky roof.

The closing had occurred two days ago and George and Imelda had flown into Fort Lauderdale International Airport this afternoon.

George Strange stared forlornly at the brown stains surrounding the two-tiered Lalique chandelier in what he'd described to Imelda as 'the grand entryway.' A pair of Louis Vuitton suitcases stood at attention on the ground beside him. Tomorrow, the movers would come hauling a truckload of furniture and personal belongings.

His assistant, Bogdan Kowalczyk, known familiarly as Bogs, followed the movers in Imelda's Jaguar XJ because she didn't want it hauled inside a transporter.

"It's not so grand now, is it, Georgie?" Imelda tapped the heel of her foot against the marble floor. "You promised me a mansion."

"It is a mansion. Ain't you seen this place? Wait'll you get a look around. It's humongous. You can host all those society charity things you always get so worked up about."

"In this dump?"

"We're gonna fix it up. What about that designer you hired?"

"That reminds me, Pamela's in town. She's dropping by with some sketches tomorrow."

"Can't wait," mumbled George. Pamela Watkins was Imelda's overpriced interior designer with offices in Beverly Hills and Miami. At her prices, she could have had an office on the moon. "We even own a piece of the river, remember? How great is that?"

Imelda rolled her eyes. "Right. This realtor of yours sell you the Brooklyn Bridge, too, Georgie?" She figured he must be good. Her husband wasn't usually taken in so easily.

"It'll look better in the daytime. A little patented Florida sunshine, that's all this place needs," he said, struggling to keep a straight face.

"Yeah, right. Bedroom's over there, correct?" Imelda pointed to the left. The realtor had sent them a link with a video and about a million photographs of the house and grounds. So far, Imelda stated she was withholding judgment.

No surprise there. Imelda withheld a lot of things.

"There's more leaks in here," Imelda pointed out, although pointing out to George the blotch on the twenty-two-foot bedroom ceiling was hardly necessary considering the rusty brown blotch had to be six feet in diameter.

Adding insult to injury, its ugly reflection shimmered across the shiny marble floor.

George frowned. That was bigger than it had been the day that dumb realtor had shown him around the place. "Where is that realtor, anyway?" He tugged at his Patek Philippe watch with its genuine alligator skin strap. "I'm gonna give 'em a call. He promised to get somebody working on this ASAP."

"Maybe he's taking you for *a sap*." Imelda looked at George in that cold, condescending way of hers.

"By the way, Georgie, you notice there's no bed here. There's no furniture. Period. Where are we supposed to sleep?"

"Crap. I forgot about that. I guess when the movers called to say they were running a day behind, I didn't think this through."

"No kidding." Their voices echoed in the emptiness.

It was all George could do not to ball up his fists and punch a hole in the wall. The house needed enough work as it was. If he had a sledgehammer in his hands, he would have gotten started on the demo right then and there.

"So where are we supposed to sleep? I'm tired. It's been a very long day. And there's lots to do tomorrow. Even more, now that I've laid eyes on this dump."

"Now, now, dear." George patted his wife's hand. "That's no way to think of this."

"Do you have a better way?"

"Don't think of it as a dump." Which it was beginning to look like.

"No?"

"No, think of it as a diamond in the rough." George spread his hands in the air. "Think what you can make this place. You and that wonderful imagination of yours." And his money. Lots of his money.

"I suppose you're right." Imelda rewarded him with a peck on the cheek. "But where *are* we going to sleep?"

George chewed on that a minute. He glanced out the

21

floor-to-ceiling bedroom windows. Nearly dark now.
"How about the boat?" he said, spying the Hatteras
nestled at the dock.

"The boat?"

"Sure, that baby's got everything. It'll be just like
home."

"I'm beginning to wish I was home."

"Come on, what do you say? Give it a try?"

"You know how I feel about boats, Georgie."

"It's only one night."

Imelda turned on her heels. "And I'm spending it
at the Ritz-Carlton. You coming?" she called from the
foyer.

"Yes, dear."

"Grab the luggage, Georgie."

George threw the suitcases in the back of the leased
Bentley and fumed. "I'm gonna kill that fuckin' realtor."

"Don't talk like that, Georgie. You know I don't like
it. It's crass."

Yeah, and it embarrassed her around all her high
society types, thought George. The type she, a girl from
the slums of Quezon City, wouldn't be hanging around
with if it wasn't for him and his money.

He backed the Bentley out of the garage and told the
Bentley to direct him to the Ritz-Carlton.

"Soon as we get to our room, I'm gonna give that
Todd Jones a piece of my mind."

"I'm very tired, Georgie. Can't we just relax tonight?
A nice quiet dinner and a bath?"

"Well..."

"You can give me a massage." Imelda rolled her
shoulders. "I'm tight."

George pictured a warm bubbly bath and his soapy

hands working their way up, down and all around Imelda's naked body. "Fine. First thing tomorrow, that realtor's gonna hear from me."

5

Todd rolled out of bed ready to start the day. Things were good. Life was good.

But instead of his feet hitting the soft lining of his comfy Rockport slippers, his toes alighted on Mr. Squeals' warm, clammy snout.

"Oink," said the pig, looking up at Todd with those big dumb black eyes of his. Eyes like the Devil's. Two black stones of death.

"Out!" barked Todd, wiping disgusting potbellied pig drool from his toes to the rug.

Mr. Squeals scrambled out and Todd shut the bedroom door, locking it. Crossing to the bathroom, he turned on the rain-head shower, letting the water build as hot as he could stand it, hoping to wash off the pig drool and drown out the noise.

That caterwauling leaking through the wall came courtesy of his mother, singing along to Fleetwood Mac's live concert version of Rhiannon, performed at the 1982 US Festival in San Bernardino, California—a concert which she claimed to have attended although her memories were vague at best. She also claimed to have slept with one of the Talking Heads that weekend. Which member, she couldn't recall.

Todd was convinced she'd bedded David Byrne. He was further convinced that Byrne's tune, Burning Down the House, planted some sort of subliminal message in his Mom's brain. That message had popped to the forefront of her impressionable cranium on at least two occasions. First, when she'd 'accidently' burned down her own condo. Second, when she'd nearly converted his condo to a pile of ashes too.

Rosalind Jones was fanatical for all things Fleetwood. She especially adored Stevie Nicks, whose looks she copied from the hair down to the clothes.

The only thing she lacked, seriously lacked, was the sultry voice. Todd loved his mom dearly but she sang like there was a siamese cat trapped inside her throat trying to get out.

After a healthy shower, Todd was glad to hear that the singing had stopped.

When he'd bought this twenty-second floor, luxury unit in Port Lauderdale Condominium Towers—one of Ft. Lauderdale's newest and ritziest condominium towers, with valet parking and an understated Italian-marbled entry, he never dreamed he'd be sharing it with his mother, a girlfriend he hadn't asked for, and a pig he desperately wanted rid of. Actually, being rid of all three would have been ideal.

Little chance of any of those things happening.

Todd supposed the fact that Irina had moved out of his office and into his bedroom could be considered a good thing. He had gotten his office back, which she'd been living in ever since Mom took it upon herself to invite her to stay.

Mr. Squeals shared the second bedroom with his mother. Both bedrooms looked out over the Intracoastal Waterway, the homes, offices and hotels beyond and the Atlantic Ocean beyond them.

Irina stepped barefoot into the en suite bathroom

doorway dressed in a skintight black one-piece leotard. He'd never seen her without the small white pearl dangling from a slender silver chain visible now against her pale skin due to the scooped neckline.

That explained the reason for the racket Todd had been hearing. Mom liked to workout with music. Irina was teaching his mom yoga and, in exchange, Mom was teaching Irina aerobics or vice versa. Todd couldn't remember exactly who was doing what and could not have cared less.

Irina Sokolov possessed black hair and her bangs cut sharply across a pair of bushy eyebrows. She viewed the world through pale green eyes, shiny as sea glass. She was skinny as a carrot. A carrot with breasts. A cute little tush too. Though Todd never would have suspected it the first time he'd laid eyes on her. "Telephone, Todd."

Todd wasn't surprised to see her there despite the locked door. She had a key. As for Mr. Squeals, how he always managed to unlock and enter was anybody's, certainly Todd's, guess.

"Who is it?" He splashed a dash of cologne under his collar and adjusted his silk tie. He had a good customer coming in today, flying down from Minnesota, looking to relocate with the wife and kids.

"Mr. Strange. I put him on hold." She held up Todd's smartphone so he could read the screen and see for himself.

"Strange?" Todd frowned at his reflection. "We closed on that deal a couple of days ago. I even sent him and his wife a basket of flowers and fruit. You did send it, didn't you?"

"Yes, Todd."

"Huh. Did he say what he wanted?"

"He said he wanted your ass on a stick?" Irina blushed. "I am sorry, Todd. Those were his words." She slid next to him and planted a kiss on his earlobe. "Good morning, my darling."

"Good morning." He was getting used to having her around. However, he still suppressed a shudder each time she added little words of affection.

Nothing personal, he just hadn't been ready for a relationship, let alone a live-in girlfriend. After all, he'd just broken up with his longtime girlfriend when she'd entered his life. But Irina's cousin, a pawnbroker by the name of Yevgeny Stalin, had done him a big favor concerning a not-quite-legal matter.

In return, Stalin—which was what he preferred to be called—and Irina had both somehow gotten the idea that he and she were a couple and that they were all in this crazy thing called life together.

This Stalin, like his namesake, was not the kind of guy you wanted to get on the wrong side of.

"What should I tell him?"

Todd motioned for the phone. "Good morning, Todd Jones here."

He winked at Irina, who left him to do his thing.

"My house. Ten minutes," demanded George Strange.

"Mister—" Through the wall, the hypnotic and pulsating drum beating of the song *Tusk* kicked in loud.

The line went dead. Todd stared at the phone. Strange had hung up on him.

"Damn." What was he so damn mad about?

There was only one way to find out. Todd stuffed his phone in his pocket and sailed out of the bedroom.

"Good morning, baby!" shouted Rosalind Jones, swaying sort-of-rhythmically side to side in a purple leotard that sagged at the ankles. A lacey purple skirt hung from her waist.

"Mom. Mom!" He twisted the dial on the stereo counterclockwise. "How many times have I asked you to keep it down?"

"I was keeping it down, baby." She leaned over the coffee table, bumped her coffee cup, sloshing cold coffee over the side, and reached for her open pack of cigarettes. "Whew, all that exercise has got me winded."

She picked up her lighter and lit up, puffing hungrily. "That's better." She wiped her damp brow with the back of her hand.

Irina called from the kitchen. "Would you like your coffee on the deck, Todd?"

"No time." Todd adjusted his tie once again. "I've got to go see George Strange, see what the trouble is. You know how these rich people are. Always complaining about the little stuff. Probably can't figure out how to work a light switch or something."

"But you must eat."

"Later. I'll catch something at the officer later. Speaking of which, can you check with the Buckminsters for me? They're flying in today and I've got an appointment with them at eleven." He glanced at his watch. "I may be a little late."

Irina smiled. "Do not worry, Todd. I will handle the Buckminsters."

"Great."

He started to the door.

"Uh-uh." Irina tapped her lips with her forefinger.

"Oh, sorry." Todd turned around and planted a kiss

on her lips.

"That's it?" hooted his mother from the living room. "Show the girl some sugar, baby!"

Todd cringed, picked up his shoes, tripped over Mr. Squeals, standing in front of the condo door hoping for somebody to take his fat butt for a walk, and ran to the elevator.

On the ride down from the twenty-second floor, he rang up Carlos the doorman and asked him to bring his car around.

6

Several smaller trucks flanked the big blue and white moving van blocking the length of the driveway at 302 Vizcaya Lane. Todd parked along the street and shambled up to the Stranges' new house.

"About time you showed up," grunted George Strange from the front door, directing two burly men holding up opposite ends of a yellow leather sofa. "Over that way. Near the fireplace."

"I see you're moving right in," Todd said with a smile. "Congratulations, again. This is a great place you've got here. A great place."

"What I've got is a money pit. And a leaky one at that." George grabbed Todd by the shoulder and pushed him inside. "You see that?" he said to Todd, pointing to the ceiling. "Water damage."

"Hmm." Todd scratched his neck. "What happened to that roofer? What was his name?" He snapped his fingers.

"That's what I want to know. I put you in charge of this, Jones." George thumped his damp cigar against Todd's chest. "Whoever he is, his name's mud if he doesn't show up soon."

"Tell him about the leak in the bedroom, Georgie." Imelda Strange strolled into the entryway from the kitchen where she'd been overseeing the arranging of the stemware. A wraparound seafoam-colored pareo dress danced around her slender ankles.

Todd was impressed. George's wife, while approaching fifty by his guess, was a beautiful woman. Maybe five-three, thick brown hair and soft brown eyes. Too much makeup. Filipino maybe. Not the woman at all he would have pictured for old George. He expected Mrs. Strange to be a female version of George himself.

"I think you just did, honey," grumbled George. "Where's Bogs? You seen him?"

"I asked him to help Esme carry her luggage to her room." Friends since childhood, Esme Ocampo served as Imelda's personal assistant.

"He's not your houseboy, honey."

Imelda shrugged and sauntered off in a swirl of perfume. Her voice carried from the billiards room. "Oh, Cuddles. Where are you, baby?"

"Cuddles?" Todd inquired. "You have children?"

A fawn and rust colored Doberman pinscher exploded through the front door, bringing down two men hauling some ultramodern painting in a four-foot long by three-foot tall frame. The men spilled to the tile in a tangle of limbs and curses. The painting skittered to the wall of the dining room and came to a stop.

The dog bounced off the side wall of the foyer, started up the spiral staircase then turned and shot back down them as Imelda Strange called "Oh, Cuddles!" once more.

With a clatter like a herd of horses, the Doberman shot through the house.

"Watch it, you clowns. I paid good money for that painting!" George hollered at the workers.

"Cuddles, eh?" Todd said.

"Yeah. Came down with Bogs and Esme in the Jag."

"That thing could eat a Jag."

"Tell me about it." George hated that dog. The dog hated him too. "About that roofer."

Todd scrolled frantically through his phone contacts. "I've got the number here someplace." Scroll, scroll. "Got it!"

Todd pressed *call* and was immediately put through to voicemail. "Ronald's Roofing, if we can't do it, nobody can. Leave a number."

"Ronald? Todd Jones here. You were supposed to come out to 302 Vizcaya. I expected you two days ago. The owner is very anxious. Call me back."

"Give me that." George yanked the phone out of Todd's hand. "Get your dumb ass over here, Ronald! *Muy* yesterday!" He cut the connection with his thumb and thrust the smartphone back at Todd. "That's the way you handle things."

"Right." Todd settled his phone inside his sports jacket. As for his shirt, it now boasted a wet brown cigar stain. He kept a spare shirt or two at the office and would stop in to change. "How's everything else? Anything more I can do for you?"

George's brow shot up. "You wanna dog?"

Todd opened his mouth but shut it again. What would be the point? Not even George Strange would be, could be fool enough to trade Cuddles for Mr. Squeals.

7

Ron Patton checked his phone messages while strolling the Hialeah Marina on the search for a good little runabout. Something he could go fishing in. By his way of thinking, not his wife's, he owed it to himself. He'd been working hard. He'd earned this.

He called Todd Jones back and immediately wished he hadn't. The asshole was shouting at him and carrying on like he was the only thing that mattered, and ordering him to drop whatever he was doing and hustle it on up to some dude named George Strange's house.

Ron would have told Todd to take a short hike off the roof of a tall building but that little bug in his ear—aka his nagging wife—would remind him that real estate agents were good for getting referrals from.

And Elaine would find out. Somehow. She always did.

So off he went. Without even bothering to change out of his cutoff shorts and oversized tank top. Not very professional but what did he care?

It had taken him practically an hour to get up here to Fort Lauderdale. He'd spent another forty minutes, forty *very scary* minutes, crawling around on Mr. Strange's expensive, multi-leveled roof.

Nobody had ever insisted that he actually get up on a roof before! He'd had to get his ladders out and everything. This place was tall!

It wasn't that he minded heights per se, he simply preferred looking up at them rather than down from them.

In case some yahoo asked him again, he might have to think about getting one of those drone gizmos. Send it up in the air and keep his feet on the ground where nature intended them to be.

"Okay." Ron yanked a ratty handkerchief from his butt pocket and patted his brow. He was getting too old for this. This was practically like real work. "I believe I've got everything I need." The heat radiating up from the driveway paving stones seeped up through the thin soles of his sneakers.

George, who'd been hovering the whole time, keeping an eye on him as best he could from the comfort and safety of the ground and a cold iced drink in his hand, said, "What's the bottom line?"

"Your roof is in pretty bad shape, Mr. Strange. Thirty years old, you say?"

"So I've been told."

"Hm-mm. You've had some storm damage, too. Wind, rain, hail—"

"I don't need a damn weather report," George snapped. "What's this new roof gonna cost me?"

Ron Patton ran the soggy handkerchief under his dripping chin. "By my calculations, we're looking at about two-fifty." He scribbled some numbers on his tablet to make it look like he was doing something. Carried some ones, multiplied by some twos.

"Two hundred and fifty grand?" George Strange whistled, low and deep.

Ron pointed to the peak over the entrance. "That's

imported Italian tiles you got up there. Those things don't come cheap. And with those new hurricane codes the county's come up with…"

Ron tried on a sympathetic face. "You know how it is." He left that statement dangling. Let the client work up his own ugly ending.

The way these things worked, any second now this too-rich rube would give him his three hundred lousy bucks—cash with a little luck—and he could get out of here.

"Nothing ever does," George replied. Imelda had already given him a bill for over a million dollars' worth of renovations before she'd even set foot in the place. And that was just for the inside. The landscape designer may as well dig a big hole in the ground for him to dump the rest of his money into.

"Amen to that," Ron could only say. "Am I right?" He braved a smile in Bogdan Kowalczyk's direction. It bounced off him without so much as leaving a dent in his thick skin.

George's beefy shadow, Bogs, hadn't said a word the entire time, just followed his boss around and gave Ron the stink eye.

Bog's wide fleshy face, decorated with green eyes, curly brown hair and a close-trimmed beard held all the animation of Teddy Roosevelt's granite bust on Mount Rushmore. Strange's lackey looked like a Mr. Potato Head on steroids. Probably spent his off hours at Gold's Gym.

He had big hands with short, thick fingers, all the better to grab him around the throat and squeeze, so Ron imagined.

A long scary silence filled the air.

Ron Patton began to fear, just a little bit, for his life. A limb, minimum, judging by the way that goon of Mr. Strange's was looking at him with cold, deadly and blood-thirsty black eyes.

Had he gone too far this time?

Had he crossed the line?

Ron's right leg trembled. He dug his heel into the ground to quell it. He'd never dared break the six-figure level before in one of his quotes, let alone go this high. The mark was suspicious.

The last thing he needed was somebody digging into his company's or his personal background and figuring out that he was nothing but a cheap huckster. *Come on, come on, Strange.* He sent ESP signals from his brain to Strange's. *Tell me to shove off and write me a check so I can get out of here.*

"Do it." George Strange crushed the stubby cigar under his foot, scrunching its hot burning embers with his bare toes.

"What?" Ron blinked, not quite believing what he'd heard. He twisted his pinkie in his left ear like it was a pipe cleaner.

"Do it, already."

"Do it? Do? It?" Ron didn't know quite what to say. He didn't quite remember how to breathe. It felt rather like some bull with opposable thumbs was whacking away at one of those big punching bags hanging on a chain that you always see big guys in boxing rings jabbing and throwing nasty hooks at. And he was the punching bag.

Punch. Punch.

Only in this instance, it didn't feel like punch.

It felt more like Wham! Blam!

A long scary silence followed because Ronald Patton was at a loss for words.

"You believe this guy?" George said to Bogs. Bogs heaved his shoulders. "Do it, Patton."

"Do it?" Ron finally managed to say yet again, realizing he was beginning to sound like some stupid mimicking parrot, but unable to come up with anything better at the moment.

"Somethin' wrong with your hearing, Patton? Spend too much time in one of those tanks spitting out mortars?" George grabbed his belly and laughed. "Get it? Tanks? Mortars?"

"What?"

"General George S. Patton, kid. Nobody ever tell you that your name reminded them of the general?"

Ron shook his head slowly side to side.

"No, I don't suppose they would. Not much of a comparison between the two of you." A history buff, George Strange revered General Patton. The General was a fighter. He, George Strange, was a fighter too.

One of his prized possessions was the Single Action Army Peacemaker with rare staghorn grips, once owned and carried by General George S. Patton himself. It had cost him six-figures and was worth every penny.

George sometimes tucked it into his belt and paraded around the house, much to Imelda's annoyance. This only made it all the more pleasurable an experience for him. He'd once stuck the pistol into his cummerbund and worn it to one of her stupid charity galas. That had created a stir all right.

"Come on, Bogs," George said with a wave of the hand. "We got things to do."

"But Mr. Strange!" Ron had his hand out. A hand that

should have been holding a three-hundred dollar check right about now. "About the roof—"

"You start tomorrow!" George Strange hadn't bothered to turn around or even break his stride.

Bogs, on the other hand, stopped, sneered, pumped and pointed an imaginary shotgun at Ron and fired. Twice.

Ron imagined eight or nine double-aught shot pellets slamming into his flesh.

Then, for the very first time since Ron had laid eyes on him, Bogs smiled a crooked smile.

8

"My cousin wants speak with you," Irina told Todd as he changed his shirt in the backroom of his downtown Fort Lauderdale office.

"I'll give him a call later." Todd handed her the soiled dress shirt.

"In person, he asks." She balled up the shirt and tucked it inside her purse. "What happened to shirt?"

"Strange thought it was an ashtray." Todd buttoned up a fresh white dress shirt and studied his reflection in the gold-edged mirror. "In person, eh? What's Stalin want? Is he planning a coup?"

"I do not think so," Irina replied in all seriousness, apparently not understanding he'd been joking. "He tells me he has present for you."

"A present? What sort of a present?" Moving to his desk, Todd riffled through his drawers for a tin of breath mints.

Irina found them first and popped open the tin for him, dropping one in his hand.

"Thanks."

"He didn't say. He's says is surprise."

"Okay, can't hurt, I suppose. What about the Buckminsters? Did you manage to get hold of them before they flew off?"

"Yes, they arrive around three. I told them somebody from office would be there to meet them."

"Perfect." Todd planted a kiss on her cheek without being asked or coaxed.

He headed up to Go For Broke, a squat windowless bunker, with solid bars protecting all the windows, located near the railroad tracks up in Lake Worth.

Todd parked in the dusty side lot. Go For Broke was your typical pawnshop, if typical included a shotgun under the counter and a muscled Latvian guarding the door who never said hello or come again soon.

Stalin wasn't a bad guy. And, except for the whole Irina situation and the Russian mob vibe, Todd liked him.

The Latvian was nowhere to be seen. Must be on his lunch break nibbling on hundred-pound weaklings, thought Todd, pushing through the front door.

He waited while Stalin wrapped up a transaction with some little old lady in a baggy emerald green tracksuit toting a brown and black cat on a leash.

Todd held the door open for her as she and her sidekick departed. Was it his imagination or did the cat look embarrassed and humiliated?

"What was that all about?" Todd asked Stalin.

A hideous necklace holding a green stone sat on the counter. Stalin tossed it in the trash. "Cheap. Imitation garbage." He wiped his disproportionately wide hands. Yevgeny Stalin was a fairly small man with a rugged yet pale complexion, thinning blond hair and the grace of a ballet dancer that belied his reputation as a cold and calculating killer. Wire-rimmed glassed rested on his nose like a permanent fixture.

As it turned out, the pawnbroker was also an acquaintance of another of Todd's friends, Steve Brezhinski, aka Surfer Steve, who knew him through his father, another Yevgeny—another coincidence. Surfer Steve's dad was a gun manufacturer residing in Boca Raton.

"I don't get it? Why did you buy it?"

"Mrs. Greenleaf comes in once a month. Needs money for cat food. Social security only goes so far. I like cats. I like Mrs. Greenleaf too. Reminds me of my tet-tet."

"Your what?" Todd wandered from the display counter to the other side of the store. A vintage Rolling Stones pinball machine caught his eye.

"We say *tetya*, aunt."

"Nice machine. Does it work?" Todd patted his pockets and came up empty.

"You see." Stalin tossed him a couple of quarters.

"Thanks." Todd inserted them in the coin slot and pulled the plunger. The steel ball shot up and he reached for the flippers. To his surprise, *It's Only Rock 'n' Roll* blasted from a hidden speaker. He chuckled. "Mom would love this."

"Plays thirteen Rolling Stones tunes," Stalin explained. "I be right back."

"Take your time."

Stalin went to the front door and locked it while Todd played. He returned with a small painting, no more than 20 inches on a side, in a scrolled wooden frame. "This is what I wanted you to see."

Todd turned. It was a surrealistic painting of a man seated on a blue sofa. "That's the ugliest guy I've ever seen. Who the guy?" Not Stalin's tetya, he hoped.

The steel ball clattered to the bottom of the pinball table. Todd was finished.

"I believe it is the artist's father." Stalin set the

painting down gently, propping it against an antique travel chest.

"Who's the artist?" Todd wasn't much into art. He had better things to do with money than to hang it on a wall.

"Magritte."

Todd whistled. Even he had heard of Magritte. "Why are you showing me this?"

"I want you to sell it for me." Stalin walked to his desk behind the counter. From a cabinet, he pulled out a bottle of Hammer + Sickle vodka and handed them each a generous glass.

Todd drank slowly. "Why me? Why not sell it yourself? I'm a real estate salesman not an art dealer."

Stalin sank into his leather chair and invited Todd to sit too. "I bought it recently from a woman cleaning out the attic of her mother's home in North Palm Beach. She found it in the garage attic."

"That's where I'd keep it," Todd said. "If I had a garage."

Stalin smiled patiently. "I pay her five hundred dollars for the painting. She was very pleased."

"Five hundred dollars? For a Magritte? Sure, it's ugly but that doesn't sound right." He studied the painting more closely, wondering if he was missing something.

Stalin's smile blossomed. "It isn't. It's worth possibly millions. Of course, I told her it was merely a reproduction, a good one, yes, but still a reproduction."

"And she bought that?"

"What can I say?" Stalin tipped the remainder of his vodka down his throat. "I have the trusting face and a reputation for honesty."

"And you'd like to keep that unimpeachable

reputation."

"Precisely. Good good. We understand each other." Stalin rubbed the edge of the frame. "I cannot afford to have word get out that I cheated a customer and misrepresented an item." Stalin waved a finger in the air between them. "Not good for business."

"Yes, I mean, no."

"Irina tells me you good man. All is good. So." Stalin clapped his hands and stood. "The store has been closed long enough. I must do business." He handed the painting to Todd. "You will sell the Magritte for me and I will pay you ten percent of the sales price. We are all winners, yes?"

Todd clutched the painting to his chest. "I'll do my best."

"Take nothing less than a million." Stalin slapped him on the back. "Wait. I almost forget! Stupid stupid. Come back. Come back here. We must look at rings."

"Rings?" Todd kept an iron grip on the painting. How was he going to get out of this?

From a glass display case bursting with jewelry, Stalin pulled up an assortment of expensive rings resting on a bed of satin. "You pick one."

"Pick one?"

"Yes, yes. Engagement ring."

"I don't understand." Todd gaped at the rings. There were some real beauties here, both antique and contemporary.

"This is my gift to you. What you say? Wedding present."

"Engagement ring?" Todd's forehead burst out in a wall of perspiration. "Wedding present?"

"For Irina! You plan wedding, yes? Irina's family,

they not be happy to hear you two shacking up." Stalin winked. "I no tell them but do not wait too long. Her papa very good with the rifle, if you know what I mean?" He winked a second time.

Todd began to get the drift.

"You make my cousin very happy." Stalin ran his hands up and down the rows of rings. "You pick ring. Any ring."

Todd flinched. The painting slipped from his sweaty fingers. He caught it between his shaky knees before it hit the ground.

"Careful, Todd. Which one do you like? You like this one?" Stalin pinched a beautiful platinum ring with a very large diamond between his fingers and waved it in front of Todd's eyes.

But all Todd could see were stars. "I-I couldn't."

"Ah." Stalin nodded. "I understand. You want Irina to choose with you. You are to be married." He slid the tray back into the display case and locked the case with a tiny silver key. "You must do this thing together. I will arrange with her a time. We make proper appointment."

Stalin was scooting towards the front door once again. A trio of customers stood waiting anxiously outside. He unlocked the door and invited them inside. "I be right with you, gentlemen," he said to the three Latino men.

Stalin grabbed Todd's arm. "Don't let this brokering take too long, Todd. I have expenses that must be paid."

"I understand."

"Good." Stalin released his grip and patted Todd on the shoulder. "You do good job with the painting and we do more business together in the future."

Todd walked uneasily to the Audi. Had those last

words of Stalin's been a promise or a threat?

9

It wasn't often Ron Patton had anything particularly special or interesting to say about how his day had gone. This day was the exception.

Normally, he hated when Elaine asked him about his day because really there was nothing much to talk about. He went to work. Did his job. Period. Let's eat.

Today, he couldn't wait to tell her in vivid detail about the day he'd had and the first thing he did when he parked in the driveway—there was no point even opening the overhead garage door because the garage was loaded to the gills with crap because this was the American way after all—was tell his wife about his day and the crazy Detroit scrap guy and his loony wife and her scary dog.

And their even scarier henchman.

"Sounds absolutely crazy," commented Elaine, spooning out the spaghetti she always overboiled.

She always used that angel hair pasta too. Ron hated that stuff because it was too skinny and slippery to stay on his fork.

He swore that stuff had a life of its own.

To counter this, he had to chop up his spaghetti into teeny bitsies that he could fit on the end of his fork. Made him feel like a toddler. All he needed was a baby bib and a high chair. "It was crazy. I couldn't wait to get out of there. You know, till this day, I thought henchmen only existed in the movies."

Elaine and Ronald Patton's American dream home was a three bed, two and a half bath, two car garage/junk depository 1,200-square-foot house on a seventy-five by one hundred foot lot, with state-of-the art appliances (circa 1968). The cost was roughly fourteen thousand dollars back in 1968 too. Prices have gone up since then.

A later owner had added the screened-in swimming pool, now a scummy green pond breeding fist-sized mosquitoes and ugly brown tadpoles because neither he nor his wife enjoyed swimming and both hated cleaning and maintaining pools.

Ron's house desperately needed a new roof. Elaine kept nagging him to call somebody. He kept putting it off.

"Did you at least get paid?"

Ron looked down at his plate.

"Ron?" She tapped the big serving spoon against her hip. "Look at me. Did you get the three hundred or not?" Elaine's passion was hair. She worked as a beautician and owned her own little shop in a tiny strip mall. Rents were astronomical and profits were slim. She counted on Ron to pull his own weight.

"Not, not exactly."

"What not exactly? We need that money. He owes you." Elaine had an inch on her husband height-wise and a good dozen inches on him width-wise. Her hair color was whatever she was in the mood for that week. Her eyes, kind of angry looking now, remained hazel no matter what her hair did.

"I know, Buttercup," Ron pouted forlornly. Overcooked spaghetti slip-slided left, right and everywhere but onto his fork and into his mouth.

"So why didn't you get the three hundred? What exactly is the problem?"

He dared to make eye contact with Elaine. "Exactly?"

She grabbed his arm and swung him around. He flew out of his chair—fork in hand—and hit the linoleum floor with a splat. Having seen and heard enough, the calico cat went skedaddling.

Ron landed on his butt and stayed there figuring it was the safest place to be at the moment.

"Well?" Elaine asked from the comfort and safety of her kitchen chair.

"He wants me to do it."

Elaine mouth hung open. "Do what?"

"The roof. Strange wants me to do his damn roof." Ron sat up and dusted his knees. "In fact, he was sort of insistent about that."

Elaine sat there a moment then broke out in raucous laughter. "Ha-ha. That's a hoot! He wants you to reroof his house? How dopey is this guy? You don't know the first thing about roofing. May as well ask you to give him a haircut or change a light bulb!"

"Hey!"

"What? Have you ever even held a hammer? Cuz I've never seen you pick up a hammer or a screwdriver or fix any damn thing around this house."

"I quoted him two hundred and fifty."

That elicited another round of laughter from Elaine. She leaned against the kitchen counter and sobbed. "I've never laughed so hard in all my life. I think I might've busted something."

Elaine gulped in some air then picked up the pot of green beans she'd forgotten on the stove and headed to the kitchen table. "Come on, let's finish eating. Food's getting cold. You do a roof." She snorted derisively.

Pushing himself to his feet, Ron scraped back his chair, sat himself down. "Can we drop this conversation, please? Talk about something else?" He stabbed at a knot of spaghetti.

"Sure." Elaine ladled a limp lump of green beans onto each of their plates and spooned the remainder of the sauce overtop. "Two hundred and fifty what? Shingles?"

Ron cringed. She says she's gonna let something go but does she let it go? Nope. "Two hundred and fifty thousand dollars."

Ron stuffed his mouth and chewed a wad of green bean and spaghetti slurry. Yep, overboiled again. At least the tomato sauce was decent. It came in a jar so there wasn't a lot she could do to mess that up.

She'd forgotten those little meatballs again too. The ones that come in a can. He loved those things but was too afraid to mention the omission considering the way his evening was going. And after the day he'd had too.

Life was so unfair.

Ron glanced at his wife who was looking like she'd just been introduced to that dame that turned everybody into stone with just one look. The ladle hung in her hand. Tomato sauce dripped slowly and steadily to the floor and she didn't seem to care.

That was different. Normally, she freaked out if he so much as smudged up the door of the fridge. "Elaine? You okay, Elaine?"

"Two hundred and fifty thousand dollars?"

Ron nodded but he didn't look happy.

Elaine fainted.

10

Todd wrapped the Magritte in a thick blanket and locked it in the trunk of the Audi for safety. The blanket was for emergencies, like when he and his last girlfriend, Holly, got in the mood to seek out a secluded beach and engage in some secluded late night groping and grabbing. This had occurred with greater frequency once his mom and Mr. Squeals had taken up residence in his condo.

He wondered what Holly was up to these days. Last he'd heard, she was dating a competitor of his.

Todd was half-tempted to hang the painting up in his office with a For Sale sign on it but he wasn't certain that what he was doing was all that legal. Better not to draw too much attention to it.

The last place he was going to keep it was at home. He couldn't see it lasting more than a day or two there, what with Mr. Squeals and his mother running amuck in the place. The pig was a walking-oinking-slobbering, four-legged, one-pig wrecking machine.

And his mother, well, she was a two-legged wrecking machine of another genus.

The only reason she was living with him now was because she had managed to burn down her own condo—that he'd been covering the rent on—in Naples, Florida, and then nearly did the same setting fire to his condo a couple of years back.

To the best of his knowledge, outside of Stalin, only Irina knew he had the Magritte. She had been surprised but did not seem overly concerned about her cousin's activities nor his dragging him into them.

Irina had suggested Todd sell it through an auction house. He had explained that doing so was too risky. If the last owner of the painting learned of it, she might create a stink.

Todd very much liked to remain stink-free and under the radar of any and all authorities.

As far as Todd was concerned, the whole situation stank. That was why he was on his way to see Surfer Steve. Being the indolent son of a gazillionaire has its perks. One of those perks was knowing lots of other gazillionaire types.

Maybe one of those wealthy types was an ardent art lover and collector. In particular, a Magritte lover. It couldn't hurt to ask and he dared not ask over the phone.

When conducting business of a dubious nature, paranoia had a way of kicking in.

The Brezhinskis dwelled in a well-staffed, well-armed estate in Boca Raton, a town filled with art lovers and collectors. How else to explain all those fancy art galleries filled with overpriced paintings, glass, stone and metal artworks?

In fact, the Brezhinskis lived across the street from those submerged, vacant lots Todd had sold to another sucker named Aristotle Constantine. That was where he and Surfer Steve had first crossed paths.

Those lots, he noticed, still sat empty.

That wasn't a good sign.

Last he'd heard, the land was tied up in

environmental impact studies ordered by the city and the Greek was not allowed to build so much as a tree fort on the property.

Not that there were any trees, as such, on the property. The land was underwater, after all. A few scrawny yet valiant black mangroves had sprouted up in the brackish water but that was the extent of it.

The Greek had been hurling lawsuits left and right at everybody in sight, including Todd.

The Brezhinski estate, a sprawling Tuscan villa, came into view. The idyllic property always struck Todd as the sort of place Mussolini might have lived out his retirement years in, had he gotten the chance.

Despite that idyllic appearance, Surfer Steve had told him that the place was bullet, bomb and hurricane proof.

A familiar man in khaki slacks and a red polo shirt, whom Todd only knew as Grant, answered the door. Like always, Grant was packing heat—a custom Brez-38 model handgun.

"Hello, Grant. Steve around?"

"Good afternoon, Mr. Jones. Steve is in the game room." He waved Todd inside. "I believe you know the way."

"Thanks."

Todd discovered Steve in his pride and joy, state-of-the-art, high-tech video gaming center. "Steve!" he shouted over the din erupting like a volcano of sound from the dozen or so speakers spread throughout the space, built into the soundproofed walls, no expense spared.

"Hey, dude!" Steve glanced up from some sort of surfing competition video game playing out on an 84-

inch screen.

Todd settled next to him in one of a half-dozen brown leather reclining loungers. "What's with the outfit?"

Todd had never seen Surfer Steve dressed in anything much more than a tank top and board shorts. Sandals optional. Now he was wearing a Brooks Brothers suit and black shoes, lace-ups even.

"Oh, this?" Steve paused the action—some bronze love god on his long board riding a no doubt gnarly wave—and tugged off a blood red necktie. He tossed it carelessly over his shoulder. "Dad wants me to take an interest in the biz. I go into the office three mornings a week now. What a buzz kill. This is how I work off the stress."

Steve was several years Todd's junior, with sun-bleached blond hair and a solitary, dime-sized, 18 kt gold loop earring dangling from his right earlobe. Up until what he was hearing now, the kid had never worked a day in his life.

Except at playing hard. The lay-about considered life to be a game and guns, drugs and alcohol to be his game pieces. Surfer Steve had a total disrespect for speed limits, noise ordinances, drug laws, well, all limits, ordinances and laws actually.

"Sure, sounds really stressful." Not.

"Grab a controller," Steve said enthusiastically. "You can be Goose."

"Goose?"

"That crappy surfer in the blue and yellow shorts. He sucks bigtime. I can't understand how he keeps beating me in the standings."

"Another time," Todd said, declining the controller

in Steve's extended hand. "Speaking of your dad, is he around?"

"The old man? Sure, we rode home together. Probably working in his office. That guy never stops working. Work work work. And for what?"

For this estate and that million-dollar car collection outside, the yacht, the vacation homes in Upstate New York and St. Maartens, maybe? Todd wanted to say but didn't.

And all of which his son, Steve, enjoyed to the fullest.

Steve shook his head side to side. "What a waste of time."

"Think he'd spare me five minutes?" Now that he was here, Todd realized it was the senior Brezhinski who was most likely to know a buyer for the painting of dubious provenance, not Steve. After all, this was a Magritte not a surfboard.

"C'mon, man." Surfer Steve threw down his controller, dusted the Fritos off his dress shirt. "Let's find out."

11

Situated about a mile away at the opposite end of the house, Yevgeny Brezhinski's home office boasted an unobstructed view of the Lake Okeechobee-sized heated swimming pool with the initials YB standing out big and bold in shiny gold letters at its fifteen-foot bottom. An eight-foot tall diving board, two waterslides and a twenty-foot rock waterfall provided distractions aplenty.

None of which the owner of the house made use of. But Surfer Steve and his friends more than made up for the senior Brezhinski's lack.

The pool also featured a swim-up bar. On party nights, a merman and mermaid served the drinks.

The office, a mahogany-lined, coffered-ceiling space the size of a modest house in the suburbs, smelled of Cuban cigars. The best ones. Three tall glass gun cases held polished weaponry of all sizes and manner. Take your pick. The cases remained unlocked. The entire Brezhinski collection on display. A well-stocked bar stood waiting in the far corner. Who said guns and alcohol don't mix?

The senior Brezhinski spoke softly on his smartphone, staring at figures on his laptop as Surfer Steve barged in with Todd in tow.

"Yo, Dad. Get off the phone. Look who's here, Todd."

Surfer Steve grinned. Todd cringed and tried to hide

behind Steve but the guy kept squirming.

Mr. Brezhinski said some quiet words into his smartphone then set it facedown on his desk. He stood.

The father of the creature Todd called Surfer Steve was by contrast an always elegantly dressed man, nearly six and a half feet tall. Everything about him exuded refinement from the manicured fingernails to the clipped gray hair. He had a richly-tanned and weather-lined face. A summer weight light gray suit and complementary blue tie hung from his lean frame. The tasseled leather loafers on his feet barely made a sound as he came forward.

A small red blemish under Brezhinski's left eye gave the appearance of a permanently tattooed tear drop. Like he was crying blood. Whenever Brezhinski smiled, he managed to look both happy and sad all at once.

"Hello again, Todd." He clasped Todd's hand. "Good to see you."

"Hello, sir. Sorry to interrupt your work." Todd shot a look at Steve meant to set the record straight that this interruption was not his idea.

"Nonsense. Have a seat." Mr. Brezhinski waved to a long leather sofa that matched his chair. "What are you boys up to today?"

"Todd's got something to talk to you about," Steve said. "Go ahead, Todd."

"Well…" Todd hesitated. He never knew quite where things stood between him and the senior Brezhinski. The businessman seemed to like him and he wanted to keep it that way. But there were so many gray areas involved here concerning the Magritte. Should he skate around the issue a bit? See how things went?

"Can I get you boys something to drink while Todd

finds his faculty of speech?" Mr. Brezhinski said with that happy and sad looking smile of his, which only addled Todd all the more.

Steve shrugged off the offer.

"Nothing for me, thanks." Todd clamped his hands over his knees and cleared his throat. "Here's the thing. I've got this friend."

"Yes?" Mr. Brezhinski leaned against his desk.

"And this friend has this painting, you see."

"Not yet I don't," chuckled Mr. Brezhinski.

"Right. He's asked me to sell it for him."

Mr. Brezhinski shrugged, reached into a hand-carved humidor and withdrew a cigar. He waved it at the boys. "Join me?"

Todd declined. Steve readily accepted.

"It's a Magritte, you see, and—"

"A Magritte, you say? René Magritte?" Mr. Brezhinski's eyes flickered with interest.

"Yeah, that's the guy." Todd had read up on the painter on Wikipedia. Now dead some fifty years or so, the artist was a renowned Belgian surrealist. What Todd found surreal was the crazy prices collectors were willing to pay for the crazy stuff.

"Tell me about this Magritte. What's it called?"

"Man On A Blue Sofa. I was hoping, what with all your contacts, you might know an interested buyer."

"Hmm. I don't believe I am familiar with that one. Let's see what we can find." Mr. Brezhinski strode silently across the Turkish rug to a wall of burled pecan bookcases.

After searching a moment, he pulled out a thick art book. He flipped through it slowly. "Yes, there is a reference to it here." He closed the book and returned it exactly where he'd found it. "It was lost during the war. World War Two, that is. How did you come across it?"

Todd hesitated then said, "Maybe it's best if we gloss over that part."

Mr. Brezhinski chuckled softly. "I understand."

Steve scratched his chin. "What is it, like stolen Nazi loot? How cool would that be?" He puffed on his cigar and blew smoke rings in the air over his and Todd's heads.

"You know, Todd." Mr. Brezhinski settled himself into a wingback chair near the bar. "Your name came up the other day regarding another matter."

"It did?" Todd's mind whirled, not liking the sound of this.

"Yes, Lawrence and I were talking."

"Roberts?" Alarms went off.

Todd had met Lawrence Roberts. He was Brezhinski's in-house attorney. Surfer Steve referred to him as his father's fix-it man. Was he about to be fixed for some reason?

Mr. Brezhinski nodded and continued. "As you may or may not know, Aristotle Constantine and I have been at legal odds for quite some time. We have history together."

"Yes, sir." Todd was well aware of that history. Some good. Some bad.

"The land has been tied up due to environmental impact studies the city was insisting on."

"Yeah, I know." Todd squeezed his temples to quell the headache those lots always gave him. "Constantine and his lawyers love reminding me of that."

Those underwater lots had been nothing but trouble since the first time he'd laid eyes on them. So to speak.

Being underwater, you couldn't actually see the lots in a strictly earthlike sense.

"Those studies are now over and I want that land."

"This is the first I'm hearing."

"I have heard through sources that Aristotle is having cash flow problems. I must have those lots. As you know, building a house of any size on that land would spoil my view. I would be forced to move. I do not intend to move. I will not be inconvenienced."

"Yes, sir. I understand how you feel."

"I know that Ari has been targeting you in these frivolous lawsuits, in addition to myself. I think, perhaps, I see a solution to our troubles." He tapped out his cigar ash in a crystal ashtray. "An end to all these tiresome lawsuits."

"Sounds good to me. How can I help?" Todd leaned forward. Steve's constant spewing of thick smoke was making his eyes tear up.

"This I gotta hear," said Surfer Steve. "Dad's great at this business biz."

"Sell me the painting and I will gift it to Ari."

"Gift it?" Todd gaped.

"Our friend Ari needs money but he is also a stubborn and proud man. I understand that. He is also an avid art collector, part of his weakness.

"I suggest the Magritte could help resolve things. I'm still willing to pay his asking price for the land. I believe throwing in the painting will sweeten the deal enough to put an end to our impasse. I'll have Lawrence reach out to his attorney but I am confident the answer will be yes."

"Let me get this straight, you're going to buy the Magritte from me—"

"At any price you and your friend deem fair."

"And then you want to just give this *million dollar* painting to Aristotle Constantine?" Todd wanted to be sure of what he was hearing and that Brezhinski understood the value of the painting he seemed so cavalierly ready to give away.

"I want to give him a *copy* of a million dollar painting," answered Brezhinski with a subtle smile.

"You mean a—"

"A forgery! That's brilliant, Dad." Surfer Steve crossed the room and slapped his old man on the back. "I told you he was good at this business stuff," Steve boasted to Todd. "I've got so much to learn from you, Dad."

"Thank you, I'm happy to hear you say that, Steven." Brezhinski mashed his cigar in the ashtray. "What do you say, Todd? Have we a deal?"

"And the original? What happens to that?"

"I keep it in my private collection."

"Dad's got a special room here at the house filled with the art he's collected," bragged Steve. "Can I show it to Todd, Dad?"

"Of course, but another time, Steven. This arrangement of ours will be our little secret, Todd."

"Mum's the word, Dad." Surfer Steve zipped his lip.

"In fact, I rather think that Magritte would have enjoyed our little charade, if he were alive today."

"How's that, Dad?" Steve swiveled his father's laptop around and checked the weather report.

"During the Nazi occupation of Belgium, Magritte is known to have made a living by forging Renoirs and Picassos. Marcel Mariën, a fellow artist and friend, arranged the sale of these paintings to discreet private collectors."

"Seriously?" said Todd.

"There are even whispers in the literature that he and, if I remember correctly, his brother, created and circulated forged banknotes."

"Wow, totally bogus," said Steve.

"Talk about surreal." Todd's mind whirled. "How are we going to find somebody to make a fake? I mean, a fake good enough to fool a guy like Constantine? If he's a serious collector like you say, he must know his stuff."

Todd didn't want to make the short-fused Greek angry. Not a second time. The first time had had bad enough consequences. Constantine had goons of his own.

"I'm sure if we put our heads together, we can come up with someone," assured Brezhinski.

"It's not going to be easy," replied Todd. South Florida was full of artists. It was also filled with persons with a certain deficiency of ethics. All he had to do was find somebody who embodied both of those strengths.

"I appreciate that. May I assume your friend is compensating you for your services?"

"Ten percent of the sales price."

"I will also pay you ten percent of the sales price out of my own pocket," Mr. Brezhinski said. "Nine hundred thousand for the painting." He held up his hand before Todd could say anything. "A small discount between friends, yes?"

Todd nodded. Stalin had wanted the million but, considering his total investment in the painting was a lousy five hundred bucks, Todd knew he'd be thrilled with the nine hundred grand.

"That's one hundred and eighty thousand dollars for

you. Cash, of course."

Surfer Steve whistled. "Wow, that's like almost enough to buy a brand new car, dude."

It was all Todd could do to keep himself from drooling.

"What do you say, Todd?" Mr. Brezhinski asked. "Do me a favor?"

Todd liked, no loved, the way Brezhinski said that. A favor. He would be doing Mr. Brezhinski a favor. That was a good, no, a great, position to be in. He pictured bright, lucrative days ahead. "I say things are looking up for all of us."

12

Here I am, thought Ron, sadly gazing upon the giant, sprawling nightmare that was George and Imelda's sprawling and intimidating Florida residence. It wasn't even ten o'clock in the morning and the sun was a boiling hot yellow blister in the sky.

He really wasn't cut out for this.

Ron had bought himself a belt full of tools. At the curb sat a truck full of fools.

But at least these fools were supposed to know what they were doing. They were supposed to be some of the best roofers in the county.

So one of them promised.

Truth was, they were a bunch of guys he'd picked up outside a temp agency waiting and hoping for an honest day's work. Some days roofs, some days lawns, some days pouring concrete. Work was work.

Ron didn't know honest from Einstein's Theory of Relativity, but the work part, that part was going to be true. That, this bunch would get and then some.

How he'd let Elaine talk him into this, he had no idea. Greed. That's what it was. His wife was just too damn greedy.

Although Ron had begged, George Strange nixed the idea of paying any deposit monies. Said it was insulting and that Ron would get payment in full upon completion of the job.

Ron took out an emergency home equity loan to pay the upfront costs for men and materials. Now he was really in deep.

Failure was not an option. Well, it was but he didn't relish the idea of losing the house he and Elaine had been living in for nearly fifteen years.

It was two days now since he'd first been ordered by George Strange to reroof his new house. Afraid to let the man down, Ron had come by yesterday and pretended to take some measurements.

What he'd really been doing was stalling. For time mostly. That and fervently praying that George Strange would have a heart attack and this whole insanity would come to a stop before somebody got hurt.

That most important somebody being himself.

"I'd like to see Elaine out here, crawling around on that damn roof," he muttered to the short, wiry man purported to be the leader of the men he'd picked up for the job. His name was Juan.

Juan smiled. He didn't understand more than a word or two of English. His crew apparently understood even less.

Toot-toot!

Juan yelled. "Truck!"

Yep, here came the truck from the roofing supply warehouse, its long, flatbed loaded down with tiles, tarpaper, flashing, mastics, cements, nails, lumber and a thousand and one other things that the salesman at Roofers Bargain Depot down in Miami had told Ron he absolutely was going to need if he was going to do this job and do it right.

Neither of which Ron was particularly interested in. But it was too late to back out now. If he did, George

Strange or that Bogs creature would murder him.

Then he'd go home and Elaine would murder him all over again.

Nope, he was stuck. No two ways about it.

The truck halted out there on the normally tranquil residential street, its diesel engine rumbling like it was late for its lunch. There was no way the monster hauler was making it in, let alone back out, of the driveway. Leaving the motor running, the driver popped his door and hopped down, electronic tablet in hand.

"Unload. Unload truck." Ron waved at Juan.

Juan, in turn, waved at his crew busy doing nothing, lounging around the battered off-white pickup truck and burgundy van they'd all arrived in. They started moving like ants on fire and didn't seem to mind the truck driver ordering them around.

The crew started piling everything up right there in the middle of the street.

"No. No!" Ron hurried down the driveway, waving his arms. "No street. There. Up there." The men looked at him blankly. "House! Casa! Over there!" He pointed to a relatively empty spot over by the four-car garage.

Ron turned to Juan and mimed carrying everything up to the house. To further pound home his point, he carried a roll of underlayment—who knew the damn stuff was so heavy?—up to the side of the garage and let it drop. Sadly, it rolled down the drive, unfurling as it went but they got the picture.

Juan, of course, smiled. Everything was funny to Juan. Run over a squirrel? Funny. Drop everything in the wrong spot, pick it all up and move it to the right spot? Hilarious.

Nonetheless, Juan soon got his boys moving things

and moving them in the right direction.

"And whatever you do, don't drop any of those tiles!" barked Ron at his crew. Those clay roofing tiles had cost him a pretty penny.

Ron was beginning to think that maybe he'd been quoting jobs too low all this time. How did anybody turn a profit installing a roof at the prices these tile manufacturers were charging for materials?

Ron had gotten a really good deal on some special roof tiles that a certain Caribbean island nation dictator had ordered for the new palace he was building himself high on a strategic hill with 360-degrees views of the Atlantic.

Unfortunately for the general but fortunate for Ron Patton, the general had been deposed before his new palace could be completed—the insurgents had come by jungle, not by sea.

According to the salesman, the general was now living out his years in Benin or someplace, where he'd had to settle for a previously-owned but gently used palace that he'd purchased for himself and his extended family and one hundred and twelve of his staunchest supporters—those who were lucky enough to escape with him and had thus avoided the firing squad in the capital square—along with their spoils.

Sensing Ron's nervousness and lack of confidence, the salesman at Roofers Bargain Depot had generously thrown in a copy of How-To-Install Clay And Concrete Roof Tiles, an instruction manual in a comb binding—retail value $29.95—free of charge.

Ron flipped through it the night before and flipped out. "How is anybody supposed to remember any of this stuff?" he complained to his long-suffering wife. "This here installing a roof is even harder than high school."

"Don't forget," Elaine told him, eyes never straying from Dancing With The Stars. "You're also gonna have to remove the old roof before you install the new roof. You did think of that, didn't you?"

"Of course, I did. You think I'm an idiot?" Ron had replied, and rather harshly too, considering he hadn't.

Later, after she'd finally retired to the master bathroom to do whatever it was she did in there—whatever it was, it took hours—he Google searched for one of those big, construction site-sized dumpsters to throw the old roof in. Cha-friggin-ching! Rental on those oversized trashcans didn't come cheap.

Seeing no alternative—George Strange, and maybe even the neighbors, would complain if he dumped all the old tile and underlayment and crap in the river—Ron ordered up a thirty-foot long Mess-Minder off the Mess-Minder website and scheduled a delivery for the next day.

This day.

This day that did not have a thirty-foot Mess-Minder in sight. Not even a Baby Mess-Minder, Jr.

"Where the hell is my Mess-Minder?" Ron asked Juan.

Juan smiled. "We no mind. We go work." Hilarious.

Ron frowned.

His crew scooted over to the van and began pulling down every length ladder imaginable from its roof. The burgundy van's sides, painted with bold, if wonky, lettering, read *Tlacoyos Today* and provided a telephone number if you wanted your tlacoyos. Today.

Ron didn't know what the heck a tlacoyo was but he knew what he wanted. He wanted his damn Mess-

Minder.
Like yesterday.

13

Ron dialled up the Mess-Minder folks from what little shade a fox palm along the edge of the driveway provided and said just that. The kid answering his call said "They'll get there when they get there."

That was real helpful.

Juan's crew extended the ladders, grabbed their tools and hurried up the scary and unreliable looking ladders like they were born to it.

Ron heard a bunch of hollering in Spanish. This was followed by the sound and sight of roofing tiles being pushed, flung and kicked haphazardly—emphasis on the hazard—off the roof and down to the lawn.

Crash crash crash.

Shards of clay tile flew in every direction. One striking Ron in the leg. He cursed and fled around the corner out of harm's way.

Juan, apparently smarter than the rest because he was still on the ground, urged Ron to climb up on the roof with him. "Inspect, yes?" The crew chief had one hand on a lower rung of the ladder and the other on Ron's wrist.

"Inspect, no." Ron shook his head emphatically. "You inspect. I wait for Mess-Minder."

As he had told Elaine, if there was one thing he was NOT going to do, it was go up on George Strange's roof. It was high and it was perilous. She might have talked him into taking this crazy job but nothing she could say was going to convince him to step foot on a ladder, let alone a roof.

Unless that roof was on the ground.

Leaving Juan to handle his men, Ron retired to his van, safe from flying tiles and the ever-growing cloud of dust their destruction created. He sat in the passenger seat and riffled through the thick how-to-install clay and concrete roof tiles instruction manual.

To say he had been too engrossed in reading up on the proper installation and securing of roof flashing in a valley would have been a lie but that was what he was going to tell Elaine he had been doing—rather than sleeping which he was doing—when the Mess-Minder slammed into the back of his van waking him.

"What the—" Ron's forehead bounced off the windshield. Reeling, he yanked open the door and spilled to the ground.

"Sorry about that, guy!" yelled a woman in blue and white vertically striped bib overalls.

"What the hell are you doing?"

"Delivering your Mess-Minder." The young woman stepped down from the truck, which she'd managed to squeeze up the drive with, Mess-Minder in tow. "Be right with you!"

Using a small forklift attached to the rear of the truck, she lowered the Mess-Minder to the ground.

"Guess it got away from me," the young woman said sheepishly as Ron frowned at the fresh dent and busted taillight of his van.

"Yeah, I guess it did. Maybe you should *mind* where you're going." He folded his arms.

"You're funny. I like that." She knuckle punched him

in the arm.

It hurt. Ron rubbed his upper arm. "You got insurance, right?"

"The company? Yeah, they must, I mean, right?" She returned to her idling forklift and called, "So where you want this tub?"

"You see that pile of rubble over there?"

"Yes."

"Park it right underneath that." Ron left her to do whatever the hell she wanted because, to his dismay, he saw Mr. and Mrs. Strange coming down from the front of the house.

Neither appeared happy. Both appeared strange.

"What the hell is going on out here?" demanded George Strange from twenty yards away, swaddled in a plush blue robe, some antique handgun stuffed in its thick belt.

His wife, Imelda, wore a robe too. Hers was silky and embroidered with pink flamingos. Wow, thought Ron, doesn't take long for the transplants to go local, does it?

"We're trying to relax and you yahoos are killing the mood." George stomped around the side of the house and stared at the waist-high pile of broken clay roof tiles. The empty Mess-Minder sat next to the heap.

Ron should have known she wouldn't have parked it underneath all that crap like he'd wanted.

That clunky forklift of hers had left a great gouging path in the lawn, two of them actually, one coming and one going. And there she went herself, the big flatbed truck rumbled down the road and he hadn't even gotten her insurance information.

Ron stepped back as the crew on the roof continued tossing old roof tiles—a few of which actually made it into the Mess-Minder. "Careful there, Mr. Strange." Ron pushed his customer out of harm's way.

Imelda coughed, bringing her hand to her mouth. "Is this disturbance going to continue much longer?"

"Sorry but you can't bake a cake without breaking a few eggs, right, Mrs. Strange?"

"I wouldn't know."

"Oh." That sorta put an end to things.

"Imelda doesn't bake." She didn't cook, clean or do much of anything else either but if George had learned anything from being married all these endless years it was to keep such thoughts to himself. And Bogs. He could tell Bogs anything.

"That's okay, I seem to be doing enough baking for all of us," Ron quipped, smiling and tugging at his sweat-soaked Ronald's Roofing polo shirt.

Neither Strange looked amused.

George asked him, "What do you do with the scrap?"

"Scrap?"

"All those busted tiles yer throwing away. Where do they go?"

"I really couldn't say. I fill the Mess-Minder and the Mess-Minder folks come pick it up. And dump it." He scratched the top of his head. "Somewhere."

Could be the Everglades for all he knew or cared.

"Hmm," said George. "I wonder if there might be some money in this. I'll have to ask one of my guys to look into it."

"Are these the new tiles?" Imelda ran her hand along an S-shaped clay roof tile sitting atop a pallet of its mates.

"Yes, ma'am," Ron said proudly.

"You can't use those things," George declared. The

gun lodged in the belt of his robe slipped free.

Ron caught it and handed it back to him. "Whoa, we wanna be careful with that."

"This?" George grabbed the handgun and aimed it at Ron's face. A too-close-for comfort six inches from his nose. "Not even loaded." George swung around, aimed at the pile of roof tiles and pulled the trigger.

Blam! Crack!

About twenty bucks worth of tiles exploded in the air.

Imelda swore.

Ron took a hasty step backwards. George squinted down the barrel of the gun. "Guess I missed one. She's empty now," he promised.

"Put the gun away, Georgie." Imelda sounded tired. "How many times must I tell you? Not everybody is impressed with your gun."

She certainly wasn't.

Ron certainly was. "I think it's quite a lovely gun." Could a gun be lovely? he wondered.

"Thanks." George, stuffed the deadly weapon back under the belt of his robe "Once belonged to General Patton."

"Hope he doesn't want it back," joked Ron.

"The General is dead," George Strange said darkly.

"Oh?" This was troubling. Had George Strange shot General Patton and stolen his weapon? This was South Florida, after all. Anything was possible in South Florida.

"Died in 1945," George Strange said.

Ron heaved a sigh.

"Now, about these here tiles." George hit the pallet with his big toe. "Like I said, they gotta go. You can't use 'em."

"Sure we can," assured Ron, not understanding George's problem. "Trust me. They'll work just fine. Great even. You should see the specs on these tiles. You wanted first class, Mr. Strange, and first class you're gonna get. First class all the way, baby." He patted the tiles lovingly.

"They're pink," complained George. "I hate pink. The old tiles were sorta orange. Like a, well, like an orange! Exchange 'em for orange tiles, Patton."

"Well, sir, I, uh…" Holy cowshit. "These tiles are nonreturnable."

"Nonreturnable?" George appeared never to have heard of the word nor come across the concept.

"Yes, sir." The salesman was quite explicit about that. Ron tugged at his damp collar.

"I don't like something, I get rid of it," insisted George Strange. "Or blow it the hell up." Being in the scrap business, he got to blow lots of things up. He liked blowing things up. And tearing things down. That could be practically as much fun as blowing things to smithereens.

Above them, Juan's men had already completely stripped the area over the garage and were working their way across the rest of the house with all the alacrity of a marching army of army ants. Like that old movie he and Elaine had watched on TCM, the one with Charlton Heston.

The Naked Jungle, yeah, that was it.

Ron could sense those soldier ants eating him alive now, his flesh, his bones, his clothing and even his brand new tool belt. How had everything gone so awry?

This was all Elaine's fault. And that jackass real

estate agent's fault. If that jackass Jones hadn't insisted he come to this jackass address—

"I like them" said Imelda. "We're keeping them. You men go right ahead with what you were doing."

What half of the men had been doing had been gawking at Imelda sunning herself earlier on the pool deck in her skimpy gold bikini but Ron understood what she meant. And yes, he'd been one of those gawkers.

Imelda took her husband by the elbow. "Come on, Georgie. We don't want to be in their way. Let's let the men do their work."

"Yes, Imelda."

Ron had dodged a bullet there and he knew it. Physical, literal, figurative, whatever.

Returning these butt-ugly Caribbean dictator castoffs and replacing them with some pricy new tiles would have been disastrous. The loan officer had been adamant. This was absolutely the last time the bank would be lending him any money until he caught up on his payments.

Ron would have been forced to take out a third mortgage on the house from some huckster private banker and that was the last thing he wanted to do. There are a lot of crooks in the world, a guy has to be careful.

Crisis averted, Ron retired to the relative safety and comfort of his van to contemplate his forthcoming wealthy and early retirement.

14

Alone in his home office, Todd sulked at his desk. The view from the window, which he usually found so calming, did nothing for his mood. He stared at the hideous *Man On A Blue Sofa* propped against the wall on the corner of the desk.

Despite his concerns, he couldn't keep leaving the expensive painting in a car trunk so he had sneaked it into the condo. He didn't dare mention its existence to his mom. She'd want to see it. And somehow, someway, she'd mess it up.

Or set fire to it.

He sipped his second martini and pondered. He'd been searching the Internet and asking around, making subtle inquiries about painters in the local area.

A soft knock on the door startled him.

"Yeah?"

"Is me, Todd. I come in?"

"Sure." Todd stood, stretched out the kinks and unlocked the office door. "What's up?"

Irina peeked in wearing a lace-trimmed black chemise, hair loosely knotted behind her neck. "You no come to bed?"

Todd ran his hands along his tired face. "In a minute. This whole painting thing is going to be a lot harder than I thought."

"This is the painting Stalin gives you to sell?" Irina

lifted the canvas. This was the first time she was actually seeing it. "Is good, yes?"

"Is good, no. At least, that's my opinion." He took the painting and set it back down. "Let's be careful with this. It's worth about a million bucks."

"Yes," Irina whispered.

"Remember," Todd said, taking Irina's hand. "Mom can't know about this and porker isn't allowed anywhere near it. If he eats this thing, I'll eat his butt." And he would.

"Yes, I will not let Mr. Squeals harm the painting. I will talk to him."

It sounded ridiculous but Irina really did have a way with that damn potbellied moocher. In fact, Todd was convinced that Mr. Squeals had a crush on Irina.

"Have you no luck finding someone to purchase this painting? You went to see Steve's father, yes?"

Todd rubbed his teeth across his lower lip. He hadn't known Irina long and he certainly didn't know her well. How much could he tell her? How far could he trust her?

"Todd?"

Todd took a deep breath. "Here's the thing." He led her to the leather loveseat and sat her down next to him. "Can I trust you?"

"How you say this?" Tears pooled in the edges of Irina's eyes. "You my everything."

Scary as that was, Todd took that for a yes.

"Steve's dad wants me to sell the painting to him."

"This is wonderful news, Todd!" Irina beamed. "Why you not seem happy?"

"Because there is a condition attached."

"What do you mean condition?"

"I mean Mr. Brezhinski wants me to do him a favor.

Actually, it would be doing both of us a favor." Todd explained about the four home lots up in Boca Raton and Aristotle Constantine's lawsuits.

"I do not like this Mr. Constantine. A nasty man."

"He can be," agreed Todd.

"What does Steve's father ask you to do in exchange for which he will buy the Magritte?"

"He wants me to find someone who can make a copy of the Magritte, something that will fool the experts."

"For why?"

"He plans to give it to Constantine."

"Why would Mr. Constantine want a copy of this painting?"

"That's the thing. He wouldn't. In fact, if he knew it was a copy, the shit would hit the fan."

"I do not understand this." Irina frowned at the *Man On A Blue Sofa* resting on the desk across the room like a puzzle in search of a solution.

"Brezhinski is willing to pay nine hundred thousand for the Magritte. He intends to keep the original for himself and give Aristotle Constantine the phony. To sweeten the deal. With the Magritte and a few million bucks, the Greek is willing to part with the land and drop all legal action."

"Ah." Irina leaned back against the sofa. "I understand this."

"Think Stalin will mind if we create a forgery?"

"No. Not if we do not tell him. Why would we do tell him?"

"That's my girl." Todd patted her knee. Her skin was surprisingly soft.

Irina smiled up at him and pressed her face into his shoulder. "See? All worries over. You tell Irina troubles.

Troubles go away." She ran her fingers across his chest. "We go bed now?"

He detected the scent of Lancôme Climat, Irina's favorite perfume. Despite the stirring between his legs, Todd's quandary remained foremost in his thoughts. A lot was at stake here.

"The trouble is," he said, "I'm having trouble finding a qualified artist. And by qualified, I mean somebody who can pull this off and keep their mouth shut. Brezhinski and I have agreed. We're willing to pay fifty grand to the right person."

Irina rose and picked up the Magritte. She studied it for several minutes under the glow of the desk lamp, turning it this way and that.

Todd yawned. Maybe Irina was right. Maybe he should go to bed, get some sleep. The answer might come to him in the morning.

Irina pressed the painting to her chest. "Why you no let me do it?"

15

Todd leaned forward, elbows on his knees. "You?"

"Yes. I do this for you. I do for free. You keep fifty thousand." She set the Magritte reverently on the desktop.

Todd stood and crossed to the desk. He stared at the hideous painting. "Do you really think you can do this?"

"Yes. I can do this." Irina lifted his martini glass, swirled the tiny bit of liquid at the bottom and drank.

"I don't understand. I mean, no offense but this job has to be done right. It's got to be good enough to fool Aristotle Constantine and Aristotle Constantine is no fool."

"I fool him. We fool him."

"I don't know, Irina…"

"Come. I tell you story." Irina led him back to the loveseat. They sat. "I know you do not know me well. I was art student at university."

"You were?" He'd had no idea. "When Mom brought you home, she said you were working as an au pair or something and lost your job.

"I was. Yes. But I graduate from Saint Petersburg Academy of Arts. Very famous school. I took job as au pair so I come to America."

"An art student, eh? Do you really think you can make a legit-looking copy of a Magritte?"

"I think so." There was hesitation in her voice. "My

80

training classical, not like this. Still..." Irina tugged at her necklace and rolled the tiny pearl between her slender fingers. "My papa, he painter too. Not famous, but very, very good. I very good too." She blushed. "I can make, what you say, legit?"

Todd laced his fingers with hers. "If you really think you can do it..."

"If you not happy with results, you find somebody else, yes? I think I make you happy."

Todd stood, crossed to the window and gazed at the panorama. He turned to Irina with a smile. "I think you make me happy too."

Irina grinned ear to ear, leapt to her feet and kissed him hard.

"I think it's bedtime," Todd said, finally coming up for air.

"I think it is time Irina make you happy." She pulled him to the rug.

16

The following morning, enjoying a quiet breakfast for two out on the patio overlooking the Intracoastal —Mom was out taking Mr. Squeals for his morning constitutional, which included pooping, sniffing and scaring all the cats and dogs in the neighborhood— Todd and Irina made plans for the job of producing the forgery of the Magritte.

Tossing back his pulp-free orange juice, Todd cleared the dishes from the outdoor table to make room for a spiral notebook. "Let's make a list of what we need and get you to an art supply store. The sooner you get started, the better."

"Yes, Todd, I am happy to."

While the coffee brewed, she pulled up photos on her smartphone of some of her earlier artworks. All originals, of course. Even though Todd was far from being an expert, he could see that they were really good and told her so.

Irina Sokolov seemed to be a woman of many secrets. And so far, those he was discovering, he liked.

Talking everything over, they compiled a list and, like Santa, checked it twice. He tore the sheet from the notebook and folded it in two.

Todd handed Irina his Visa card and told her to take the Audi. His mom's car was an unreliable deathtrap. Todd wasn't taking any chances. He needed Irina alive and well for this.

He walked her to the door and pressed the list into her hand.

"I'll be back soon," promised Irina, grabbing her purse and sunglasses.

"Terrific, oh, and you'd better get double of everything."

"Double of everything?" She rested her sunglasses atop her head. "I do not understand."

"Double brushes. Double paint. Double canvases and frames. Double whatever."

"Double whatever." Irina mulled this over. "I think I understand." She opened her purse and dropped Todd's keys inside. "But why we do this?"

"Two." Todd held up two fingers.

"Two?"

"I'd like you to paint me two copies of Man On A Blue Sofa." He kissed her fingers. "Can you do that for me, darling?"

Todd shivered every time he thought of the weird painting. What had Magritte been thinking, or smoking, when he drew the guy sitting on a sofa in a formal black suit, white shirt and black tie, and black bowler hat with a yellow banana running out of his nostrils and into his right ear?

Todd had half a mind to tell Irina to nix the banana in her version. But that was his own personal prejudice doing the talking.

If some too rich, too blind art lover wanted a tasteless painting of a man sitting on a blue sofa with a yellow banana growing out of his ear—or was it growing out of his nose and into his ear?—Todd wasn't going to argue.

Not with a million bucks on the line, he wasn't.

And why was it called Man On A Blue Sofa rather than Man With A Banana Stuck Up His Nose?

Irina let her fingers dangle in his hand. "You want me to paint two Magrittes?"

"I do."

"Exact same thing?"

"Exact same thing." He kissed her fingers some more. One. Two. Three. Four. Five.

Unfortunately, kissing her fingers reminded him of Stalin and his offer of the engagement ring. He hadn't mentioned that little discussion with Irina yet. And wasn't sure he planned to. Had Stalin mentioned it to her? Was she waiting for him to bring it up?

"Why?" Irina's question pulled him back to the current situation.

"Have you heard the expression 'save something for a rainy day?'"

Irina scrunched her brow. "Umbrella?"

Todd shrugged. "Okay. Let's think of this second painting as our own little umbrella. Our *secret* umbrella."

"Secret umbrella." Irina mulled Todd's words over.

"Just between you and me. We don't mention it to Brezhinski, Stalin, nobody. Can you do that? Keep it a secret, Irina?"

"Of course, Todd. I keep secret." She crossed her heart.

"That's my girl." Todd kissed her. This time on the mouth. "Off you go now. If you need me, I'll be at the office. I'll call for a ride. You can always reach me by phone. I've got a few showings today."

"Yes, Todd." She reached for the door handle.

"There is one little thing." Todd placed his hand on her shoulder. "Actually, it's a big thing."

"Yes, darling, Todd?"

"This Magritte must be fifty years old. How are we going to make our copy look that old?"

Irina mulled this over too before replying. "There are ways to do this thing. I have read about this in art study books. I examine problem. We find way to do this."

"Are you sure? I mean, no offense but it's got to look good. It's got to look great. It's got to look—"

"Authentic?"

"Yeah. Precisely."

"Trust me. I make you happy last night?"

"Oh, yeah."

"Good. I make you happy with painting." She kissed him passionately, said goodbye, and slipped out the door.

Funny, thought Todd, watching her disappear into the elevator, because he really did trust her. How strange was that?

17

George Strange was on his way to Orlando, pretty much smack dab in the middle of the state and as far from the beaches on either coast as a person could get.

Christie not only pointed that out to him, she complained loudly about it. She said she wanted to see the water. "Hell," he told her, "you got the Detroit River and a Great Lake or three back home. What do you need to see water for?"

Her reply was to call him insensitive. Him, insensitive! There was absolutely no figuring women.

What he was heading up to Orlando for was to check out an abandoned six-hundred room motel just begging to be turned into scrap. Situated out near Disney World, the failed motel was a tear down. Somebody was going to put up another, bigger hotel, and try again.

A sucker truly was born every minute. And a scrap dealer to pick up the pieces and sell them for a hefty profit when that next sucker inevitably failed.

Good luck to 'em, thought George. All he cared about was tearing this joint down. And he wasn't charging the owners a nickel. His payment would be all that lovely scrap. He'd sell it for millions.

To make up for his 'insensitivity', George promised Christie they could hit the Magic Kingdom tonight. His mistress was nuts for Cinderella. The girl had begged and begged until he found himself agreeing to some stupid dinner at Cinderella's Royal Table.

Sometimes he felt like he was dating a child.

His phone rang and he answered over the Bentley's speaker. Miro Frankowski was on the line. Miro was Bogs' twenty-four year old nephew from Hamtramck.

Hamtramck was pretty much under siege, surrounded as it was by the city of Detroit. Not that it wasn't a lovely little burg, but the biggest thing to come out of the town, as far as George was concerned, was Mitch Ryder. And he called himself Mitch Ryder and the Detroit Wheels NOT Mitch Ryder and the Hamtramck Wheels. George figured that pretty much said it all.

Christie loved dancing to *Devil With The Blue Dress On* and George loved to watch her move.

Which got him thinking, maybe he could book Mitch for Christie's next birthday bash. She'd dig that and a happy Christie was a happy George.

"What's up, Miro? Get off, okay?"

"Yes, Big George. I'm at the airport now. Shuttle's taking me to the rental center."

"Great," barked George, always thinking you had to yell if you were talking in a moving car. "Meet you at the site in forty-five."

Miro was the offspring of a Polish father and Bangladeshi mother. Hamtramck is now more like a Bangladeshi and Yemen town than anything else. That made for some interesting cuisine. George's stomach rumbled just thinking about it. Maybe he'd pull over for a bite to eat before meeting up with Miro.

"No problem," replied Miro. "I've got the address on my phone. Anything else you need?"

The kid was a real go-getter and George pictured him moving up quickly through the ranks of Strange Scrap,

Inc.

George considered the question. "Pick me up some roses. Yellow ones." Christie loved roses.

"Sure, Big George."

George liked that. The kid asked no questions. Did what he was told. Yep, he'd go far.

George fished around in his pockets until he came up with a cigar. Plenty of time to take care of business, then pick up Christie at the airport later.

He had a reservation at Disney's Animal Kingdom Lodge resort. Christie loved to look out over the African savannah from the comfort of their suite and watch all the animals cavort.

Personally, he thought duck looked best with a little orange sauce.

18

"My people are in a hurry," said the profusely sweating man following after George Strange and Miro Frankowski in the high-pitched whiny voice of his that, unbeknownst to him, was grating like the Gates of Hell on George's ears. "They are quite anxious to begin construction."

"And I'm ready to begin *destruction*. My people will have this shithole," he crushed a fallen piece of sheetrock underfoot as he walked, "and keboodle down and out of here in under a week," vowed George, coughing as he wandered down through another empty corridor. "Right, Miro?"

"Right, Big George." Miro stretched his ropey arms, stiff from the flight and the car ride. He had a jutting jaw, long, thin sideburns, a dark complexion, eyes the color of slate—and just as lifeless looking—and a sheet of thick brown hair that swept from right to left.

The whiny geek wiped his sweaty brow with the back of his arm. Served him right, thought George. What was the fool thinking wearing a suit in this sweltering heat?

"Papers are in my car," said the man.

They trudged out to the guy's Ford. He slid a brown leather briefcase out, opened it and handed George a packet.

"I don't want those." George swatted the packet

away like he was swatting a pesky horsefly.

"Fax 'em or pdf 'em or whatever the hell it is you do up to my office. They'll take care of the paperwork."

"Right." The man threw the papers back in the briefcase. "The minute I return to my office." Which couldn't be too soon. "Are you worried at all about the weather, Mr. Strange?"

George glanced at the thick white clouds blocking his view. "I dunno. Why, you thinking it's going to rain? They won't close the Magic Kingdom, will they?" Christie would be pissed. And somehow she'd find a way to blame him for it.

"Uh, no. I mean about the hurricane coming."

"Hurricane? I thought that damn hurricane skirted up the west coast of Florida and fizzled out somewheres around Panama City?"

"Yes, it did. That was Hurricane Nita, I believe," said the company representative. "But there's another stirring up trouble—Hurricane Oscar—and this one looks like a doozy. My bosses are hoping you can get the land cleared before the hurricane hits us."

"You think it might hit Orlando? I thought those storms preferred the coast?"

"They can hit anywhere, Mr. Strange. Hurricanes can be quite unpredictable, no matter how much predicting the folks at NOAA and the weather people like to do. They tend to bounce around." He made bouncy hand motions.

George presumed he meant hurricanes, not weather people. "You don't say? Well, this the first I'm hearing of it. Still, no problem."

George assured the corporate stooge, "If Hurricane Oscar does come bowling through here, he just might save my guys a ton of work. All we'll have to do is pick up the pieces. Get finished even quicker. Let's go, Miro."

Miro followed Big George to the Bentley. "What should I do, Big George?"

"First thing, send all those notes and pictures up to the office. Whoever's free, one of the supervisors, they'll handle it from here." Miro had been taking diligent notes and scads of pics with his cellphone as they'd toured the property.

"You want me to fly home?"

"Nope. I want you to drive that rental car you got down to Fort Lauderdale. You got the address of the new house, yes?"

"Yes, Uncle Bogs provided it."

"Great. You hustle on down there but no speeding tickets, mind you." George had already had to pay his lawyers twice to clear the boy's license. Miro was quick tempered and heavy footed. "When you get there, you tell Imelda that I've been held up for a day or two. Business."

"Yes, Big George."

"That's my boy. No point flying off to Detroit when I might need you back on this Orlando job. You stay down at the house for a few days. Enjoy a nice Florida vacation. I know I'm going to," he added, thinking of the next couple of nights with Christie.

There's nothing a bad boy needs like a good alibi, George was thinking as he slid his butt down in the luxurious Bentley, started the engine and cranked up the AC.

"And enjoy the pool!" George hollered out his window as the two cars passed each other going in opposite directions on the way out of the deserted parking lot.

19

Ron gazed up at George and Imelda Strange's new roof. Their sparkling new pink roof. At least what he could see of it. Which, admittedly was very little from the ground.

Wow, it really was pink. Row after row of pink.

Those acres of tile looked a hell of a lot pinker up there in the mid-day sun than they had sitting in that dusty Miami warehouse.

He really ought to get one of those drone gizmos. Not that he ever expected to do another insane job like this again, although it had gone rather smoothly. And Elaine had been hinting that he might want to make a real go of it.

Juan had implored him to at least climb one of the short, shaky ladders leaning against the gutter over the garage and take a peek at the finished product but Ron was having none of it.

Juan could smile all he wanted to. Ron Patton was not climbing any ladders and he was definitely not stepping foot, let alone walking across, any roofs.

Still, they were finished and it looked pretty damn good. Ronald's Roofing, after nearly four years in business, had actually done it. They'd actually completed their first roofing job!

Ron could barely believe it. That roof actually looked like it might have been done by a crew of professionals.

And, miracle on top of miracle, they even had a bunch of left over supplies. Tons of tiles, flashing, underlayment and glue. That salesman at Roofers Bargain Depot must have grossly miscalculated the materials needed for the job. What an incompetent rube.

But no real harm. Ron figured this extra stuff could fetch hundreds, if not thousands, of dollars more cash profit. He could sell it all on Craigslist or maybe over at the Fort Lauderdale Swap Shop.

Hell, he could hold a yard sale, sell it out of his garage...if he could fit it in his garage.

Elaine, by far the better bookkeeper between the two of them—she kept the accounts at her beauty salon, whereas Ron had never had any actual business to keep actual track of—had run the numbers last night using some program on her PC.

After deducting the cost of materials and labor, Ronald's Roofing stood to make a tidy little profit. And he'd barely lifted a finger.

Now this was the American Dream.

"Good. Bueno," Ron assured Juan and his crewmen huddling around them. "Finito. Bueno."

"Time to pay." Juan smiled and held out his hand, palm up.

"Right, right." This could get a little tricky. "I need to get a check. They pay me. I pay you." Ron smiled. It seemed to be the only thing Juan really understood.

Sure enough, Juan smiled and bobbed his head. He relayed some words, apparently Ron's, to his crew and they smiled and bobbed their heads too. It was a regular Smile & Bob Fest.

"Be right back." Ron headed for the front door.

Imelda was in there somewhere, gabbing with her designer, who'd shown up earlier in a matte black Mercedes-Benz S-Class.

Ron was thinking he might pick up one of those for himself. Secondhand, probably, but still. A Benz is a Benz.

He was about to knock on the mahogany and etched glass door when Miro threw it open. "What do you want? I don't hear any work going on."

Ron frowned. The kid was half his age and all attitude. Spent half his time frowning at Ron, asking him why he wasn't up there working with the rest of the guys and generally making a nuisance of himself.

He spent the other half of his time wandering the property, taking potshots at the alligators or whatever else he found interesting, with that damn shotgun of his that he strutted around with on a nylon shoulder sling.

"We're finished." Ron forced himself to remain civil. Miro rubbed him the wrong way. "You can tell Mrs. Strange that we're done."

Ron peeked past the snotty kid. He could hear the murmuring voices of the ladies deep in the bowels of the house. "Mister Strange still out of town?"

He hoped.

George Strange was going to absolutely hate that shocking pink sitting on top of his house looking like scoops of pink bubblegum-flavored ice cream.

"The boss got back late last night." Miro knew this because Big George had arrived with Christie in tow and asked him to get her settled in at the Ritz-Carlton.

Now it was Miro's turn to frown. "Maybe I should wake him."

"Your call." Ron shrugged like he could care less. "Maybe somebody wants to go up and inspect the roof. You know, like a final inspection."

Ron couldn't help noticing Miro's shotgun leaning against the wall inside the door.

Miro knitted his brow. "Doesn't the county have somebody whose job it is to do that?"

"Done and done. See?" Ron waved a form in front of Miro's face. "Good to go. So as soon as somebody pays me what they owe me, me and my crew will be out of here."

Truth was, nobody had inspected the roof, county or otherwise. Turned out the inspector the county had sent out didn't like heights any more than Ron did.

He'd been happy to take Ron's word for it that the roof was sound. He'd been even happier to take the fifteen hundred bucks they'd finally settled on as a payment for his signing off on the work.

Shutting the door in Ron's face and leaving him to stew, Miro apologized for interrupting Mrs. Strange and her lovely guest.

Why bother Big George with something so petty?

Imelda wasn't happy to be interrupted. Least of all, by one of George's employees. She and Pamela Watkins were busy coming up with new ways to spend George's money.

She knew all about his affair and also knew damn well that those nights spent in Orlando were spent frolicking with Christie Campbell. If they'd had a brain between the two of them, the model wouldn't be tweeting and Instagramming pics of their dinner with Cinderella and Prince Charming.

The more he cheated, the more of his money she was determined to spend.

"Bring me my purse," she commanded. "I believe you'll find it in my closet." Her closet was the size of the average American bedroom and outfitted with wall-to-wall built-ins, a marble-topped island and two floor-to-ceiling mirrors.

Miro carried the pink Hermes purse to Imelda and waited while she drew out a checkbook with matching cover and wrote out a check for a quarter of a million dollars as nonchalantly as if she was paying the gardener for the month.

"Thank you." Imelda handed the check to Miro.

Miro nodded and returned to the front door, opened it and found Ron leaning against the wall snacking on a pack of salted sunflower seeds.

"Got it?" Ron asked.

"You're done." Miro flicked the check at Ron. "You got everything cleaned up?" He'd been constantly ragging on Juan and his crew about leaving their trash everywhere. And not just roofing refuse, lunch trash, beer cans, toothpicks and cigarette butts.

"Sure. Nothing to do but pack up the trucks. You want to check?"

Miro shut the door in Ron's face.

Ron took that for a no.

Ron waved the check in the air but not so close that Juan and his crew could see the actual number written there. He was no idiot. They'd only ask for more.

All smiles, Ron stuffed the van with as much of the leftover roofing supplies as he could. Removing his tool belt, he set it on the passenger seat. The belt still looked remarkably new and retained that new leather smell.

Ron ordered his crew to load up their vehicles with the rest and follow him to his house to unload it all.

He had a check in his pocket for two hundred and fifty thousand dollars. What would the bank say? Would they even deposit it coming from him?

They damn well better.

20

Irina returned to Port Lauderdale at the end of a very long day, tired and depressed. She removed her shoes at the door—Todd was fastidious about that—leaned against the wall and rubbed her sore feet.

She'd failed Todd before she'd even started. Unable to find anything appropriate to the task.

"What's wrong, honey?" asked Rosalind, adorned in an ankle-length purple dress that looked vaguely like something she'd once seen Stevie Nicks wearing in a picture. She'd picked it up in a thrift store and liked to think that Stevie herself might have cast it off.

"I fail Todd."

"What? Failed? Don't talk silly. You're the best thing that ever happened to that boy of mine. Well, besides me and Mr. Squeals."

"Thank you."

Rosalind Jones laughed. "That's better. You're smiling." She pinched Irina's chin. "Come on, let's wash those sorrows away. I'll get the drinks and meet you on the patio."

Todd's mom carried two glasses of chilled chardonnay out to the patio and handed one to Irina.

"Thank you," Irina said, idly rubbing Mr. Squeals warm nose.

"You're welcome. Now, tell Mama what's eating you."

"I look all day for—" Irina caught herself in time. She had promised Todd she would not say a word of their little project to anyone, not even his mother. "Some special supplies for Todd. I could not find them anywhere."

"What are you looking for exactly?" Rosalind set her drink on her lap and her feet up on an empty chair.

"I'm sorry. This I cannot say." Irina blushed. She didn't like keeping anything from Rosalind. Todd's mother had been so good to her. If it had not been for her kindness, she wouldn't be here now.

"Oh, a surprise is it? A little something for my birthday maybe?" Rosalind chuckled, nudging her with a bony elbow. "I'm amazed Todd even remembered."

"You have birthday? I mean, birthday soon?"

"Okay, okay. Play it that way." Rosalind pulled out a cigarette from the pack tucked down a hidden pocket of her dress and lit up. Mr. Squeals grunted his disapproval. "Quiet, Mr. Squeals. You have your vices, I have mine."

Mr. Squeals harrumphed once more then settled down on the sun lounger he'd long ago claimed as his own personal property.

The way it currently smelled, Todd had no problem letting him keep it.

"I'm sure you'll think of something," Rosalind said. "Smart girl like you." She flicked ash from the tip of her cigarette. It landed on Mr. Squeals' nose and he sneezed. "I don't own a copy of that new fifty-year anniversary, five LP collection of Fleetwood Mac's, if that helps you any."

Irina stiffened. "Collection!"

"Like that, do you?"

Irina handed Rosalind her wine glass. "Thank you!"

"You're welcome." Rosalind slurped up the few remaining drops at the bottom of Irina's glass and slapped Mr. Squeals across the rump. "C'mon, Squeals. Green Acres starts in five minutes. Don't want to miss it, do you? Arnold? Go see Arnold?"

Mr. Squeals barreled off to the living room, throwing himself on the sofa with a loud thud. The old sitcom about a city lawyer turned country farmer featured Arnold the pig. Whenever Arnold made an appearance, Mr. Squeals riveted his eyes to the high-def screen.

A light bulb had come on in Irina's head and Mrs. Jones had been the one flipping the switch. Sure he wouldn't mind, she used Todd's home computer to check a few things.

Satisfied, she waited eagerly for his return, spending her time and nervous excitement cooking a hearty meal that included lasagna, homemade garlic rolls, fresh peas and a peach pie she made from scratch. She bought a quart of vanilla ice cream because Todd liked his pie with ice cream.

"How did your day go, darling?" Irina asked him as he came through the door, wrestling with his necktie.

She helped him remove it and hung it with his jacket.

"Got a nibble on a townhouse. I think they'll make an offer." He sniffed the air. "Is that peach pie I smell?"

"Wait and find out," Irina teased.

"What about you?" he asked, leaning closer. "Any luck?"

"No, but your mother, she gives me idea."

Todd frowned. There was love behind it, but a frown it was. "Mom gives me ideas too, but I probably shouldn't share them. Or act on them." He followed Irina to the kitchen. The dining table was set.

Rosalind Jones pulled out her chair and sat. Mr. Squeals assumed his position under the table. Ever ready for a handout.

"So what's this idea?" Todd asked after the main course, pleasantries, and the small talk were officially out of the way.

Irina dished out thick slabs of warm peach pie and plopped a scoop of ice cream atop each. "Maybe we should wait until after dinner?" She nodded in Rosalind's direction.

"Huh!" Mrs. Jones snatched up her plate and a spoon. "I'll take this in my room. You two can discuss your *secret*."

Todd narrowed his eyes and watched his mother disappear down the hall. "She doesn't know, does she? You didn't tell her?"

"No." Irina licked a soft blob of vanilla ice cream off her spoon. "I am careful."

"Good." Todd dug into the pie.

"What I try to do today, I learn this is impossible."

"Impossible?" Todd's fork hovered over his plate.

"I could find no place and no one who could sell to me paints and canvas correct to the time period."

"Damn."

"Yes. Also, it is difficult to be discreet. They wonder why do I ask."

"Maybe I'd better tell Brezhinski that it isn't going to work. He'll have to come up with another plan."

"No. This plan could work still. And it is so much money. I have another idea."

"Let's hear it."

"I have a friend, a dear friend from art school. Her name is Yulia Krylova. Like me, she attended the Academy to be an artist. However, she developed a passion for restoration and reconstruction."

"We don't need someone who can fix up an old painting, Irina. We need someone who can paint us a copy of an old painting."

"Yes, I finish."

"Sorry."

"Yulia very, very good. She works at KMSKA."

"What's that?"

"The Royal Museum of Fine Arts in Antwerp."

"Belgium?"

"Yes. She, I think, will, if not have access to what we need, know someones who could get these things for us."

Todd scrapped his fork across his plate, mulling over Irina's words. "I think you might be on to something. Have you asked this, uh…"

"Yulia."

"Yeah, have you spoken to Yulia about this?"

"No." Irina picked up the dessert plates, carried them to the kitchen, and rinsed them in the sink. "I did not want to contact her until I get your permission. I did check on your computer. I have not spoken with her in quite some time. But her address is the same there as in my address book and she is still listed as working with museum."

Todd moved the glassware to the kitchen counter. "Care for a brandy?"

"Yes, please." Irina loaded the dishwasher. "What shall we do?"

"Think it's too late now to call her?" Todd moved to

the bar and filled snifters for each of them.

Checking the time, Irina was happy to see that it wasn't too late to make a transatlantic phone call. "It's late but not so late."

"Okay, let's take our drinks in the office. You can telephone her from there. I hope she's in."

In the study, Irina picked up the telephone and dialled the number in her tattered address book. "Is ringing," she said after a moment. "What do I tell Yulia?"

Todd made himself comfortable on the loveseat. "We need to feel her out. Tell her you have a friend who's an artist and who's looking to get his hands on some oils and canvas from Magritte's time. Think that might be okay?"

"Yes, I think so."

"We have to be careful not to say too much on the telephone. Somebody might be listening."

"KGB?" Irina's eyes widened in fear.

Todd grinned. "Something like that."

"Do we tell Yulia our secret?"

"No, but we can't stop her guessing. I suppose that's a risk we'll have to take."

"You trust her, don't you?"

"Absolutely."

"Good enough for me." Todd stood and paced to the window. "Tell her in general terms what we are looking for. If she thinks she can help us, we'll talk about the details in person."

"Oh, hello, Yulia? Is me, Irina." Irina cupped her hand over the telephone. "In person, Todd?"

"How would you like to spend a few days in Antwerp?"

Irina jumped up and down and began speaking a mile a minute in Russian with her friend.

Todd pulled his smart tablet from the middle drawer of his desk and began checking the airlines. Last minute flights weren't going to be cheap but since things were going his way for once, he could afford to splurge a little.

21

Todd was exhausted. By the time their flight, the third in their journey since departing Miami, ended at the surprisingly small Antwerp International Airport, he was regretting the trip.

The flight was long, the food horrible and the weather on arrival cold and dreary. "This is supposed to be summer," Todd complained, hauling his and Irina's suitcases into the back of a silver and green hybrid Antwerp Taxi while the driver resolutely remained safe and warm inside the cab.

Then again, this was the sort of business transaction that required the personal touch. And a whole lot of discretion.

He slammed the trunk and they climbed inside. Irina gave the driver directions. Todd shivered. "I should have packed a coat."

"Would you like my sweater?" Irina wore a fluffy green sweater over a pair of denim slacks and leather boots.

"No, thanks. I'll pick something up." Todd had settled for a short-sleeve shirt, jeans and loafers. "Good thing we're only in town for a couple of days."

"Maybe we could come back another time?" Irina stared out the window, watching the beautiful old buildings go by. "We could go to Russia. I show you my home. After—" She stopped suddenly.

"After what?"

"After this business finished," she said finally.

"Better still, we could go to Cannes and I'll show you the beaches." Todd had always wanted to visit Cannes.

The taxi took them northwest, by Todd's reckoning and before long the center of Antwerp loomed.

Deep in the heart of the Flemish Region, also known as Flanders, Antwerp grew on the shores of the Schelde River and was predominantly a Dutch-speaking region. Todd had read up on Belgium in a slender guidebook he'd picked up in the airport. The country was largely divided into three regions, the Flemish Region, the Brussels Capital Region, and the Walloon Region; and two distinct cultures, the Flemish and the French.

He didn't know a word of Dutch. Neither did Irina. However, her French was passable and he knew a word or two. This would have to suffice.

Antwerp was also the diamond capital of the world. But that wasn't what he was here for.

The driver seemed to know the best twists and turns and to have a fear of direct routes. Nonetheless, the cabbie eventually announced they'd successfully arrived at the proper address with all the pride of a man who's just announced that he's successfully and singlehandedly landed a man on the moon.

Todd hopped out, was forced to claim their suitcases from the trunk as their driver once again resolutely remained seated in the cab with his hands on the steering wheel.

Todd paid the driver off and lifted their suitcases to the cobbled sidewalk.

Yulia Krylova lived on a narrow street near the Royal Academy of Fine Arts, a kilometer or two from the museum. Her compact third-floor apartment, made all the smaller by the vast array of books, paintings, paint supplies and clothing scattered about in disarray, was warm and inviting.

Two bushy white cats seated at the window ledge watched them calmly. This was the only window.

"Welcome!" Yulia wore a thick cotton sweater under which a white shirt with scalloped sleeves peeked out. Paint stains colored her snug blue jeans. She and Irina hugged. "And you are Todd." She wrapped her arms around Todd then released him. "You have good trip?"

"Lovely," said Irina. "Your apartment is very homey."

"Thanks. Hungry? Thirsty? I'll get us a beer. Have a seat." She threw some clothes and canvases from the futon sofa to the floor. "Be right back."

Not that she was ever out of sight. As tiny as the apartment was, the kitchen was practically microscopic. Yulia carried three open bottles of Jupiter. "One of our most popular beers. Maybe not the best but, if there is time, we will sample some others."

Todd inspected the bottle's unfamiliar red and white label featuring a pivoting black bull.

"Or you prefer slivovitz?"

"No, this is good." Todd and Irina thanked her for the drinks.

"You have not changed since art school," said Irina, seated beside Todd.

"No true, I think!" Yulia Krylova's cropped black hair gave her an almost boyish appearance. She had green eyes, and a rosy complexion, and was on the short side.

"Not quite the same. I gain many pounds." Yulia patted her tummy fondly. "I blame it on L'Atelier des Frites."

"I noticed that sign when we drove up to your building," replied Todd. The restaurant occupied the ground level of the four-story building. "What is it?"

"They sell the pommes frites. What you call french fries, like McDonald's?"

"Right."

"Whenever they are frying the french fries, I cannot resist buying some. And they are always frying the french fries. A grand cornet with curry catsup." She kissed her fingers and smacked her lips. "Delicious!"

"We must try this," proclaimed Irina. Todd agreed.

Yulia sat cross-legged on a worn rug on the wood floor. One of the cats thumped down from the window ledge to join her. She stroked its head. "This is Cha-Cha. Her brother is Coussi."

"Cha-Cha?" Todd asked.

"I named her for Marc Chagall, the painter, you know? He painted lots of cats. You can see them in many, many of his paintings."

"Maybe you should insert pigs in everything you paint," joked Todd. "That could be your thing."

"Very funny." Irina pinched him in the side. In response to Yulia's look of confusion, she explained. "Todd's mother. She lives with us and has a pet potbellied pig named Mr. Squeals."

"How adorable!" Yulia gushed.

"You don't have to live with him," Todd replied.

"If I remember, you are from the same town as Chagall, no?" Irina asked.

"Yes." Yulia's eyes seemed to fill with fond memories. "Vitebsk. This was Marc Chagall's childhood home. His small house on Pokrovskja Street, built by his father, is a museum now.

"Vitebsk? Sorry, but where is that?"

"Belarus," Yulia explained. "Between Minsk and Moscow, if that helps."

"Not even a little bit," confessed Todd.

"No matter." Yulia grinned. "We must finish our introductions." She pointed to the window, which looked out on a slash of slate gray sky visible between buildings. "He is Coussi. Coussi is named after one of Henri Matisse's pet cats."

Coussi fell from the window on hearing his name and came to inspect the newcomers, rubbing against their legs.

"So, tell me, Irina, are you painting and what is this mysterious project of yours?" She stretched her legs and propped herself up with her hands.

Irina glanced at Todd who nodded for her to continue. They'd talked it over plenty before landing.

She folded her hands in her lap. "A friend has asked me to make him a copy of a Magritte. He is a fan but cannot afford the real thing."

Yulia laughed. "Who can!" She wrapped her lips around her beer bottle and sucked. "So your friend wants this copy to have all the appearances of an authentic Magritte."

"That's the idea," said Todd, trying to gently nudge the cat away without insulting their hostess. "Think of it like building a reproduction of a classic automobile and using as many period correct pieces as possible."

"I understand." Yulia leapt to her feet and returned with a plate of green grapes. She placed the plate on Todd's lap because Cha-Cha was now lying in Irina's lap. She plucked off a handful of grapes. "And you will paint this, Irina? Yes, there is no one better."

Yulia ruffled her friend's hair. "You always were a masterful painter. Not like me, Todd. My skills lie in restoration and reconstruction."

"I think your work is lovely," replied Irina, her eyes alighting on Yulia's work scattered throughout the room.

"My teachers and the critics didn't agree with you." Yulia plunked herself back down on the floor. She appeared comfortable there. "No problem. I paint to amuse myself. And I love my work at KMSKA. You know, we have a Magritte or two in the museum. Maybe you like to see them? Museum is closed for renovations but I can take you. It's only a couple kilometers from here."

"Another time," Todd said before Irina could suggest otherwise. "We're in sort of a hurry."

In fact, he'd turned his phone on after landing in Antwerp and both Brezhinski and Stalin had texted him to see where things stood with their projects.

"We have a deadline. And I'm not so sure we can make it as things stand." Aristotle Constantine had given Brezhinski ten days to turn over the painting.

While Irina assured him she could finish the oil painting in that time, he had his doubts. Then again, the fake Man On A Blue Sofa wouldn't have to fool anyone other than Constantine because there was no way he'd ever show it or even acknowledge its existence to anyone else for fear of legal consequences.

Fortunately, Todd happened to know Constantine struggled with macular degeneration. That would make fooling him all the easier. The guy was no Mr. Magoo but he was heading in that direction.

Todd leaned towards Yulia. "Can you help us?"

"Yes. I have a friend." She grabbed another handful

of grapes from the plate on his lap. "Nico. He is living in another friend's apartment while she is away. It is near the university."

"Is it far?"

"No. We walk. Shall we get something to eat first? Many wonderful restaurants and bars nearby."

"No offense," replied Todd. "But how about if we take care of business first?"

"Ah, you Americans." Yulia slapped his calf. "Always the business. "Bien. Let's go."

22

Yulia held out her hand—a gold band speckled with paint and holding a large amethyst stone adorned her ring finger—and Todd pulled her to her feet.

She grabbed a sweater from a beat up wardrobe against the wall and offered an oversized gray sweatshirt to Todd. "I notice you've been shivering since you arrived. Sorry, no heat in the apartment. This should help."

Todd held the wrinkly sweater in two fingers and studied it dubiously. The collar was tattered and paint splattered across the chest and up each sleeve. Not exactly his cup of tea but neither was freezing to death in Antwerp. In summer, no less.

Todd pushed it over his head. The arms were a bit long. He tugged the sleeves up. "Thanks."

"Where are you staying? Have you a hotel? You can stay here, of course."

"I booked us in at the Hilton Antwerp," Irina replied.

"Ah, very nice. It is in the heart of Old Town and overlooks Old Town Square and the Cathedral of Our Lady. Good choice. You will love it."

"Irina's a woman of many talents," Todd replied.

"We'll come back for your luggage. The Hilton is not far. Cha-Cha! Coussi!" The two white fur balls came running. They leapt on the short, narrow kitchen counter. Yulia fed the two cats there, dumping a can of moist cat food onto a dinner plate, and the three departed.

"Nico is a painter and a sculptor. But he earns his living working in De Grotes. It is an art supply store," Yulia explained as they strolled up the narrow street. She and Irina held hands. Todd followed behind.

"He will be there now, I think. In the basement, they have supplies going back many, many decades. He will find what we need. But," Yulia turned her head around to Todd, "this, he says, will not be cheap."

"Don't worry. I brought cash and plenty of it." Todd patted his wallet. "I hope American money's okay?"

"No problem, I'm sure."

Todd's smartphone chirped. "Hold on." He stopped on the sidewalk and fished out his phone. "It's a text from Mom. I forgot I was supposed to text her that we'd arrived safely." He typed out a quick note to let her know all was well then buried his phone in his pocket.

Hopefully, Port Lauderdale Condominium Towers, and his condo, in particular, would still be standing and in one piece when they got home.

He'd gone over and over the house rules with her before leaving and left her a list of do's, DO NOT DO'S!, and emergency contact numbers—the fire department being first and foremost on that list.

It wasn't that he didn't trust his mom when she promised to be careful and not burn down the house while he and Irina were in Antwerp but, as a precaution, he bought half a dozen brand new fire extinguishers and placed one in every room in the house. He also showed his mother how to use one. She seemed to understand the basic principles—aim, pull, squirt—and everything had been going great until Mom decided that showing wasn't enough and she wanted to give one a try.

Rosaline Jones had been standing in his luxe kitchen when she'd made that unilateral decision.

She aimed, pulled, squirted, squealed—like a pig, of course—got frightened and spun around. This guaranteed not an inch of the kitchen, from floor to ceiling, would be spared. Screaming and the fire extinguisher squirting and foaming like a rabid dog, she tossed the canister in the refrigerator. "To contain the damage," so she said.

Contain the damage, his Sub-Zero refrigerator did. The ten thousand dollar refrigerator now contained nothing but damage.

His mom promised to have all the foam out of the refrigerator by the time they got home. Off the walls and out of the refrigerator.

Todd brushed his worries aside. He had more important, or at least more pressing, things to deal with now.

De Grote's art supply shop spread across several storefronts. Easels, canvas, wooden artists' manikins, and just about anything else the artist, starving or otherwise, could need in the pursuit of their preferred art, filled the dirty display windows.

"I warn you," Yulia said, pulling open the door to let Irina and Todd inside. "Nico can be quite extravagant."

"Extravagant?" Todd asked her.

"You'll see." Yulia winked at Irina.

The ceilings hung low and the crowded aisles squeezed close together. What didn't fit on the tottering shelves spread across the floor. The atmosphere was a complicated blend of charcoal, clay, linseed oil, paint, turpentine and a unique smell referred to by the locals as l'odeur des artistes.

"There he is! Yoo-hoo!" Yulia stood on tiptoes and waved to a gangly young man in baggy, cuffed black trousers, ankle-high, lace-up boots, a green military shirt of some sort with yellow epaulets, and a matching beret. His grin was wide, his teeth big and his moustache even bigger.

Nico dropped what he was doing, cutting a slab of rich brown clay with a string for a customer, and raced over. "Yulia, my Yulia!" They squeezed each other so hard, Todd heard the air rushing out their lungs.

"And these are your two special friends from America." Nico took a step back to assess Todd and Irina. He twisted the ends of his moustache. "Well, well, well. I am Nico. Nico Berchem." He curtsied. "A direct descendant of the venerated artist." He struck a pose, hand beside his ear, hip thrusting outward. "Perhaps you see the resemblance?"

"Nico claims to be related to Nicolaes Pieterszoon Berchem, a popular seventeenth century Dutch painter of pastoral landscapes."

"A claim I can substantiate," Nico pointed out.

"I am Irina Sokolov." Irina extended her hand. Rather than shaking it, Nico gently twisted her arm over and kissed the back of her hand.

"And you," he pointed. "Are Todd."

Todd extended his hand. "Hi, it's a pleasure to—"

Without warning, Nico leaned closer, grabbed Todd's cheeks between his hands and kissed him on the mouth.

Todd fell back. "What the—"

"Now we are friends," exclaimed Nico.

Irina and Yulia tittered.

"I think we're more than that now." Todd blushed and wiped his fingers across his lips. "Do you do that to everybody you meet?"

"Isn't he precious?" Nico asked Irina. "Are you planning to keep him because, if not…" He wriggled his brow and the two ladies giggled some more.

"Stop teasing, Nico," Yulia told him. "Todd is here on business, remember?"

"Oui, oui. Business. Yulia gave me the grand brushstrokes but what exactly do you need, my friends?"

Lowering his voice, Todd explained how they were trying to duplicate a Magritte.

Nico grinned. "Duplicate. I must remember this word. It sounds so much nicer than…well, other words. You are a naughty boy, I think." He pinched Todd's butt.

"Hey!" Todd jumped forward, smashing into a display of charcoal pencils.

Nico winked at Irina. "I like naughty boys."

"Me, too," Irina replied.

Nico howled.

Todd rubbed his rear. "Can we focus here, people?"

Yulia made a face at Nico.

"Okay, okay." Nico swung his head around the shop. "Hey, Henri! I'm heading to the catacombs."

A blunt-headed scarecrow hovering near the register, looking bored, waved desultorily.

"Come." Nico hooked his arm through Todd's and led them toward the center of the store where a narrow stairs, surrounded on three sides by a flimsy wooden railing, penetrated downward. Countless names had been scratched into its worn surface. Todd noticed one set of initials dating from 1932.

"Watch our heads," cautioned Nico.

Todd shot Irina a questioning look which she returned with a shrug and a smile. They plunged deeper and deeper, down one stairway and then another. Each level they descended, the ceilings got lower and lower and the light dimmer and dimmer.

If this kept up much longer, they'd be falling straight down in the dark.

Dust covered rows and rows of boxes and a jumbled assortment of materials and supplies.

Todd coughed "What is all this?"

"De Grote Père never threw anything away. It's been a family tradition ever since," explained Nico, still holding on to Todd and leading him down yet another rickety stairway constructed of narrow treads and high risers.

"Karl De Grote, grandson of Père, keeps up the tradition but never ventures down here. As far as I know," he paused to face the ladies, "only I dare descend these frightful steps that lead us to the depths of Hell itself."

"Very funny." Yulia sneezed and rubbed her nose. "De Grote's has been here for over a hundred years."

Nico turned his gaze on Irina. "Some say the De Grotes even save the bones of dead artists who had refused to pay their outstanding balances." He kicked a long rectangular box on the bottom of a rustic wooden shelf. "Who knows what or who's inside these things, eh?"

Irina gasped.

"He jokes," said Yulia.

"Maybe," allowed Nico. "But we are here." He clapped

his hands as they rounded a tight corner. "Voilà! I believe we can find everything in this section. I am quite familiar with Magritte. Yulia is the expert, however. I will leave all the final decision-making to you." He bowed to his friend.

The four of them spent more than an hour scrounging around in moldy old boxes and crates, and lifting dry old tarps.

It was dusty, dirty and smelly. They stumbled on three desiccated rats. Big ones, too.

"This is almost worse than living with Mr. Squeals," Todd whispered in Irina's ear.

"At least they are dead rats and not dead artists." Irina paused to inspect several tubes of paints which Yulia had brought her. They had quite a small pile now, canvas, framing, paints, brushes. All period correct.

"What do you think?" Todd asked Irina. "Will this work? Is it the right stuff? And is it enough?"

"Well…"

"Remember," he whispered, "we only have to fool Constantine. And, even then, maybe only for a short time."

"What do you mean?"

"I'll explain later. Well?"

"Yes." Irina nodded. "This is everything I could need to paint Man On A Blue Sofa."

"Three times over?"

"Yes. I am certain."

"Great." He did not want a return visit to this place. He rose, dusted off his trousers and helped Irina to her feet. Nico and Yulia were squealing with delight over some latest find. They'd been doing that nonstop since they'd arrived. "Hey, you two. I think we're done here."

"Wonderful!" Nico said. "We can put everything in these boxes."

"Okay." They got busy filling two wooden crates. Todd wasn't looking forward to carrying all this stuff back up those stairs. "Let's talk money, Nico. What do I owe you for all this?"

"Mm-mm." Nico tapped a finger to his cheek and twiddled his moustache. "Everything here is quite rare. Very valuable."

Todd held his breath.

"You have cash?"

"US dollars."

Nico shot a look at Yulia. "I don't have much of a head for money. What do you think, Yulia?"

Yulia appeared taken by surprise. "Under the circumstances...Nico is taking a chance helping us...is twenty-five hundred too much?"

"Dollars?" Todd wanted to know.

"Yes, if this is not too much."

"I think this is fair," Irina put in, taking Todd's hand.

"Right." Todd's first instinct was to try to haggle him down but he didn't want to insult Irina's friends. They might prove useful again someday. "Twenty-five hundred it is." He held out his hand to Nico. "Deal?"

After a moment, Nico shook his hand. "Deal. However, if you would pose for me, in the nude, of course, I could accept fifteen hundred." He raised his eyebrow in question.

Todd whipped out his wallet and quickly counted out twenty-five one-hundred dollar bills into Nico's open hands.

23

The four of them hauled everything up the stairs and straight out the back door into a De Grote's delivery van. Todd didn't care that Nico had avoided running their little exchange of cash for art supplies through De Grote's cash register. In fact, he preferred it that way. There would be no record of this transaction.

Paper trails were for future jailbirds.

Nico drove them to Yulia's first to retrieve their luggage. From there, he dropped them at the Hilton.

A porter wheeled their suitcases and the wooden crates up to their room.

Giving them all some time to freshen up, it was agreed that Yulia and Nico would return for them in two hours so they could go out and celebrate the completion of a successful expedition into the catacombs of De Grote's and the making and renewal of friendships.

Once a department store called Grand Bazar, dating from the late 19th century, Todd and Irina were pleased to discover that beyond its Old World ornate fin-de-siècle façade, the five-story Hilton was a modern and luxurious four-star hotel.

Irina drew open the pale gold curtains. "Is not the view beautiful?"

"Sure, I guess so."

The 500-year-old Cathedral of Our Lady, towering

over 400 feet above the ground and occupying approximately a hectare of city space on the ground, filled their view. Generations of workers had toiled almost two centuries—with construction starting in 1352—and left behind a whole lot of blood, sweat, and tears to build the Gothic cathedral, the largest in all Belgium. Since then, Our Lady had survived Protestants, French revolutionaries, wars, fires, vandalism and more.

"I remember reading in art history class that Our Lady has in its possession several major works by Rubens."

"Anything they'd care to part with? Cheap?" teased Todd.

"I think not. Would you like to bathe first?"

"You go ahead."

While waiting for Irina to finish showering, Todd flipped on the television in their room. An item came up about Hurricane Oscar. "Hey," he called through the open bathroom door. "The weathercasters are saying that Hurricane Oscar's heading for Miami."

Irina turned off the shower, plucked a plush white bath towel from the chrome rod and wrapped it under her arms. "When?" she asked, poking her head through the doorway.

"A few days, maybe." Todd seated on the edge of the king-size bed, ran a hand along the side of his head. "I know you were hoping to stay a little longer to visit and do some sightseeing, but I think we'll need to get back, with it looking more and more like this hurricane will be heading our way." They had booked four more nights at the hotel.

Irina stood beside him now, running a comb

through her wet hair, watching the full-color satellite images on the TV screen.

"I don't want to get stranded here, or detoured to another city, if MIA gets shut down." Todd looked at Irina. "I suppose you could stay a couple extra days, if you really wanted to."

"No. I go with you. Besides, you need me to begin the work on the Magritte right away, no?"

"Right away, yes." Todd pulled her down on the bed. "But not right this minute." He uncinched her damp white bath towel.

24

Yulia and Nico came knocking on their hotel room door as Todd was scrambling into clean clothes and Irina was finishing her makeup.

The foursome went to Cafe Quinten Matsijs, a small tavern reputed to be the oldest in the city—circa 1565, for beer. The tavern sat on a cobbled and narrow pedestrian street and held tall stained glass windows. The interior was all rich wood rafters, beams and lattices, and plenty of historic atmosphere.

"The tavern is named after the painter Quinten Matsijs, a well-known painter in the late fifteenth to early sixteenth century. He is credited with founding the Flemish school of painting," explained Yulia.

Nico continued with the history lesson. "Matsijs was born in Leuven. He specialized in portraiture of all social classes. Perhaps you have heard of the Grotesque Old Woman?"

"Is that the name of one of his paintings or the name of his evil stepmother?" Todd joked.

"Your Todd is very amusing, Irina." Nico had swapped his green military jacket for a plaid shirt and braided black sweater and matching black beret. "A British painter by the name of John Tenniel—"

"*Sir* John Tenniel," Yulia corrected.

"Fine. *Sir* John Tenniel drew his inspiration from the Grotesque Old Woman for his portrait of the Duchess in

Alice in Wonderland."

"Whose baby is transformed into a pig." Yulia suddenly realized. "Hey, maybe your Mr. Squeals used to be somebody's baby!"

"She's definitely my mom's baby," Todd said, wishing she'd let him transform Mr. Squeals into luncheon meat. He accepted a second bottle of Maredsous Blonde. The tangy partial loaf of Maredsous cheese they were complementing the beer with reminded him of a brie or camembert.

Todd found the fruity Benedictine beer surprisingly good. He thought Nico stroking his thigh under the table the whole time was not so good.

From there, it was dinner and more beer a short walk further at Grand Café De Rooden Hoed, the oldest restaurant in Antwerp, established in 1750 or so.

Yulia and Nico seemed determined to take them to the oldest that Antwerp had to offer—from its deepest, dustiest cellars to its cafés. Todd held his tongue for Irina's sake but, personally, he'd have preferred the newest and hippest.

Yulia insisted on a table in the back of the restaurant with a view of the Handschoenmarkt and the cathedral. They ordered mussels served in big-lidded pots served with french fries because it was the Antwerpen thing to do.

Over too much food and even more alcohol, Nico regaled them with stories, some lewd, some crude and all colorful.

While Nico caught his breath and refilled their beer glasses, Yulia explained that the Handschoenmarkt had a story of its own.

"On the wrought-iron crown above the Matsijs Well

near the cathedral, you can see the artist's depiction of Brabo holding aloft Droon's hand in victory."

"The same Grotesque Old Woman guy?" Todd asked.

"The very same," replied Yulia.

Nico cleared his throat to gain everybody's attention. "According to Flemish legend, to cross the Scheldt River, one had first to pay a toll to a terrifying giant living along its riverbank. This giant was named Druoon Antigoon." He stopped and fingered the sharp tips of his moustache for effect. "Those who invoked his wrath and refused to pay his toll, he punished them severely by chopping off their hand."

Slam!

Nico slammed the side of his hand into the table like a mighty ax, rattling the dishes and glasses. Irina gasped loudly and paled.

"Until one day, Silvius Brabo, a brave Roman soldier slayed the evil giant, cut off its hand."

Slam! went Nico's hand once more.

A nearby waiter shot them a nasty look.

"Brabo tossed the dead giant's hand into the Schelde River." He rubbed his hands together. "End of giant. End of story."

"This is where Antwerp derives its name," added Yulia on a somewhat less gruesome note. "Hand werpen is to hand throw, so throw hand, you see, in Dutch. This now becomes Antwerpen in Flemish, Anvers in French, and Antwerp as you American's say.

"Is that what all those hands I keep seeing are about?" asked Todd. In the short time since arriving, he'd noticed hands on the town flag, its coat of arms and even hand-shaped cookies and chocolates.

"Yes, the hand is a symbol of Antwerp."

"I am only reminded of the terrible chopping off of hands."

"Kind of ruins the appetite, doesn't it?" agreed Todd. "Maybe we shouldn't mention that story to Mom."

"Agreed."

The two boxes of assorted chocolates they'd also purchased would go to his mom and Irina's cousin Stalin. These held no such unpleasant reminders and the sales girl assured them the chocolates were true Belgian classics.

"My cousin been so good to me," said Irina. "To us both, yes?"

Todd wasn't about to disagree though, despite the small fortune he stood to make on this little caper, he still wasn't happy with the predicament that the pawnbroker had put him in.

And that was just concerning the painting.

What was he going to do about this whole marrying Irina thing?

That was the real predicament.

26

Ron Patton punched the kitchen wall with his fist and immediately regretted it, both the hole in the kitchen wall—Elaine was going to murder him—and the subsequent excruciating pain that began in his knuckles and ran all the way up to his elbow.

But could Elaine really blame him for his frustration?

Well, yeah, but still...The stinking lousy bank had stuck a five to ten business days hold on his check from Strange. Juan and his crew weren't happy about that. There was no way Ron could pay them until that check cleared. To get them off his back, he'd promised them each a hundred dollar bonus for the inconvenience.

"But who's paying me for my inconvenience? That's what I'd like to know!" Ron had hollered for the ninety-third time to his wife in the past twenty-four hours. But who's counting?

Here he had enough money to live like a king and he couldn't even touch it. Well, maybe a prince or a duke, because Elaine was gonna want her share. Probably make him stick it in some boring bank in some boring savings account.

Banks! He was sick of the lot of them and itching to get his hands on all that money.

He ran his fingers along the edges of the hand-shaped hole. Who did he know who could repair drywall quickly and on the cheap?

27

Christie knew she had promised George she'd stay far away from his house but her curiosity had gotten the best of her and she simply had to see it. George's new house sounded wonderful, palatial. She was tired of being cramped up in a hotel room, Ritz-Carlton or not.

Besides, who knew? Maybe one day this house would be her house too. So she took one of those sightseeing cruises, the Fort Lauderdale River Queen, which promised a two-and-a-half hour tour of all the mansions that Fort Lauderdale and the vicinity had to offer.

As the double-decker tour boat chugged its way slowly past what Christie recognized from a couple of phone pics George had shown her as his new home, she gaped and took pics of her own.

The young tour guide, dressed in some costume shops idea of a proper white sailor suit, spoke with authority into the microphone attached to various low-quality speakers mounted throughout the boat, and stated that the house belonged to some tycoon and his wife.

Then she saw the Hatteras sport fishing boat moored at the dock, which George had rechristened Imelda, and that boiled her blood.

28

It was another rainstorm and it was a doozy. George and Imelda Strange didn't have to look out the windows of their new Florida home to see it, or strain with their ears to hear it. Because water was falling—like rain—from their bedroom ceiling.

And that wasn't the only place water was falling from.

"I'm gonna kill that roofer." George yanked open a dresser drawer and pulled out the Colt.

"How about trying to telephone the roofing company before you go shooting first and asking questions afterward, Georgie?"

Reclining royally on a plush turquoise chaise in the sitting area of the bedroom, away from the drips coming from the ceiling and the drip now venting his rage, wearing a silk robe and languidly skimming the pages of some glossy interior design magazine, Imelda gave her husband a hard look.

George gave the idea some thought while stroking the barrel of the gun. "I suppose," he said begrudgingly, "that your way does have some merit." He dropped the Colt among his socks. "Hard to talk to, let alone get work out of, a dead man."

George had learned that lesson the hard way, having been a little too impulsive in his youth. He slowly slid the drawer closed once more.

"Look at it," he groused, himself staring at the wet hearth of the stacked rock fireplace in the bedroom. "Only fireplace in South Florida where the water comes down rather than a fire goes up."

"Call Bogs," suggested Imelda. "He'll make it right." Bogs had a way of making everything right, especially when Georgie was out of town.

29

Bogdan Kowalczyk didn't mind the rain. Not today. In fact, he found it rather cozy. He spent the morning helping Esme settle into her new quarters over the garage. A brand new bedroom set had arrived.

Six months younger than Imelda, Esme had dark brown eyes and darker hair, the color of kamagong, a rare Philippine iron wood, so she'd told him. She was shorter than Imelda too, barely reaching his shoulders.

Esme had been sleeping on a sleeper sofa temporarily, which was being relocated to a guest room. Bogs had offered his services—both in the new bed's assembly and the breaking in of its mattress.

Bogs and Esme enjoyed each the other's company and neither took their relationship too seriously. If at all.

While his nephew Milo sloshed happily around the grounds in the rain—that boy seemed to enjoy nature and its hardships—Bogs and Esme enjoyed themselves, having sex, drinking sweetened coffee, watching the rain fall on the slate-colored, slow-moving river. It was quite romantic, actually, thought Bogs, lying naked atop the bed, ankles crossed.

And then his cellphone on the nightstand buzzed. It was Big George.

Of course.

It was inevitable.

30

George stalked to his office to wait for Bogs.

George was madder than ever. Mad enough to stomp on something or someone. The new roof was leaking all over. It was like that jackass Ron Patton had stuck a sieve on the roof rather than a quarter million dollars' worth of fancy imported roof tiles.

Pink tiles for chrissakes!

And with all the rain, the lucrative demo and scrap job up in Orlando had been put on hold. Between the current rains and the goddamn hurricane, who knew when that job was going to get done? That meant no sneaking away to Orlando for him and Christie.

And what was with her anyway? She'd been acting cranky for days.

To top off the sour cherry that was his life, he hadn't yet been able to take out his new boat for her maiden voyage. Sure, he'd rechristened her the *Imelda*, but that was just to keep his wife happy and off his back.

What he really wanted to do was christen that master stateroom belowdecks—with Christie. Yet, there *Imelda* sat, bobbing in the water like so much useless scrap.

How ironic was that? Here he owned a chunk of riverfront and even a liquid chunk of freaking river and he couldn't even leave the dock in this weather.

Something had better change and change soon.

"Heads are going to roll," George vowed, knuckles planted on the marble windowsill as he gazed glumly out at the gray skies hanging over him, hearing the thunder thunder, watching the lightning lightning and the drizzle drizzle, forced to listen to the rain fall from his ceiling.

"Nobody takes advantage of George Strange," he proclaimed to the God of Storms looking down on him from above.

"Not that jackass roofer or that jackass of a real estate agent who sold me this dump." He groped around in his pockets for a cigar, snatched his lighter off his desk and lit up, knowing full well that Imelda had forbidden him to smoke anywhere indoors. "Heads are *definitely* going to roll."

"What's up, Big George?" asked Bogs, strolling through the open mahogany door into his boss's office dressed in leather moccasins, jeans and a flannel shirt. The Stranges' liked to keep it a chill sixty-eight degrees indoors no matter what the cost.

"What's up?" spat George, seated behind his massive, ornate desk, which he'd had custom built by a metalworker out of bits of scrap metal taken off his jobs. "I'm up. I'm up to here!" He settled his hand around his chin. "The damn house is leaking like the Titanic. We're up to our necks in water."

"Have you called the roofer?" Bogs remained standing, half turned to Big George, half turned to the view.

"No, I'm a moron."

Bogs reddened, recognizing he'd made a huge blunder.

"Of course, I've called the roofer. A hundred damn

times I've called the roofer! He ain't answering." George pushed himself up from his chair. "That's why I want you to go deliver a message to him in person. One he can't ignore. Know what I mean?"

Bogs managed a small smile. "It will be my pleasure. Never did like that guy."

George smiled too because, knowing Bogs, it definitely would be his pleasure.

"Know where I can find him?"

George riffled through his desk. "Got his card here someplace." He latched onto a cheap business card. He frowned. "Fat lot of good this will do you. Nothing but a post office box number for an address."

Bogs took the card. "You leave it to me, Big George. You mind if I take Miro along? The boy could use the exercise."

"Let's keep Miro here for now. I might need him." Like to drive Christie down to South Beach for him for a quiet rendezvous. Maybe a special dinner at one of those fancy, overpriced restaurants would help her get over whatever it was that was making her so touchy lately.

George puffed and puffed at his glowing cigar. "I want that damn realtor, too. Whatsisname? Todd Jones. I've been calling him too. All I get is some office secretary who swears he's out of town. Out of town, my ass."

The landline phone on George's desk jangled. "That's the office. I gotta take this." He waved Bogs away and picked up the phone.

"Yeah?" he barked into the receiver. "Hold on." He cupped his hand over the phone. "You get Patton and Jones over here pronto. I want this roof fixed immediately. Or else. You got that, Bogs?"

"I got it, Big George."

"Good. You see that those two clowns get it too."

31

Ron paced. He didn't know what to do. It had been raining practically nonstop for days and George Strange had been telephoning nonstop ever since it had begun. Two inches, four inches, he was up to his neck in rain and phone calls.

Then that creep, Bogs, had started calling. Calling and threatening.

And now, finally, Bogs had shown up at his house!

"I don't get it," he whispered to Elaine, as they huddled in the kitchen. "How did he find me?"

"Like I told you," Elaine said, busy fixing coffee for their guest. "He told me he went to your PO box and they gave him my address. The beauty shop address. The one you insisted we use as the address of record for the PO box."

Ron rented a box at one of those mail store franchises for all his many "businesses." Being located in the same strip mall as his wife's shop, it was convenient. Apparently that had made it convenient for Bogs too.

Elaine poured hot water from the pot on the stove into three mugs. One was practically an antique that had once belonged to her mother, the second was a gift from a client. It read Don't Forget To Rinse on the side. Ha. Ha.

The third mug had been left in the dark corner of an

upper kitchen cupboard by a previous homeowner. And once she rinsed the dead bugs, dirt and unidentifiable debris out of it, it really wasn't a bad mug at all.

Of course, she'd give that one to Bogs. After all, she and her husband knew its history.

Ron gripped the edge of the counter. "So you had to lead him here? To me? And now you're making him coffee?"

Elaine pulled down a bag of generic Oreo-style cookies. The manufacturer should have called them Okay-O's or So-So's, rather than Crēm-D-Lites, because that was how they tasted. But they were nearly half the price. "It pays to be nice."

"Not to people like George Strange. Not to animals like that guy out in our living room."

Speaking of which, with great apprehension and an ounce or two of sheer terror, Ron followed her out to face Bogs.

"Hello, Ron." Bogs stood in front of the curtains. His Wranglers were damp. The navy blue raincoat kept most of the rest of him reasonably dry. "Some weather we're having, ain't it?"

"Here's your coffee, Bogs." Elaine smiled and handed Bogs the brown mug. Next, she offered the bag of cookies. He thrust a hand inside the bag, withdrew two cookies.

"Dear?"

Ron took a second mug from his wife who then returned to the kitchen for her own mug.

She returned to find Bogs making himself at home in Ron's favorite chair and her husband settled on the far end of the sofa. She took a seat in the middle and helped herself to a cookie.

Bogs wrapped his fist around his two cookies, crumbled them and dropped them into his coffee mug. Plop. Plop. Plop.

Ron sipped and waited, alert.

"Sorry to bother you folks at home," Bogs said, nodding to Mrs. Patton. "But it seems we have a bit of a problem."

Ron cleared his throat. Or tried to. He poured some hot coffee down his pipes and tried again. "Argh-hrm." That was better. A little better, anyway. "What sort of a problem?"

"Well, I notice your little place here, it's got no leaks. I mean, look at yer ceiling." Bogs did so.

Ron and Elaine did so.

"Right, no leaks." Elaine was relieved to see it. Roofs can be terribly expensive.

"Mr. Strange's house, on the other hand, has got leaks. Lots of leaks. Lots and lots of leaks."

"Really? I'm sorry to hear that." Ron's knees shook, forcing him to move his coffee from his kneecap to the side table, which was another kind of dreadful because Elaine yelled at him whenever he set a glass or a can of beer down on one of her precious end tables.

"You're a hard one to reach, Ron. Mr. Strange's been calling and calling. I guess you never got his messages?"

"Messages?" Ron's voice came out like a mouse squeaking. A mouse on helium. "Messages? No, I don't think so." Time to cast some attention on the wife. "Elaine, did I get any messages?"

She jumped as if snake bitten. "N-no. Not that I know of." She kicked Ron in the shin bone, inadvertently, or so she would claim once Bogs was gone from her house and hopefully her life because really this guy scared her. Really scared her!

"Yeah, I figure something must've happened," Ron said. "I have been having trouble with my phone lately. Didn't I say that, Elaine? Trouble with my phone."

The best she could manage was to nod. It was such a dumb excuse. And a bald lie. Anybody could see that. Who did her husband think he was fooling? Not Bogs, that was for certain.

Feeling abandoned, Ron tried another tack. "Tough to get good work these days. I blame it on a shrinking manual labor pool. And what can I say? That crew. They were terrible. Had such good references too. I'm sorry I ever hired them."

"Sure." Bogs drained his coffee in one gulp and rubbed his neck. "So what I need you to do is fix that roof."

"Huh? Excuse me?"

"Fix Mr. Strange's roof."

"Why, ah, sure. I mean, sure." Ron looked at Elaine but Elaine was looking at the carpet.

"Great." Bogs stood and zipped up his rain jacket. "Let's move."

"Now? You want me to go now?"

"That's the idea."

"Really, Mr. Bogs, it's going to take some time. I'll have to fit you into the schedule. Put together a crew."

Bogs turned to Elaine. "What do you think, ma'am?"

Elaine glanced at her husband, sipped her coffee, wished she were single, then said, "Ron's right. Not much sense him going right this minute. If he goes up on that roof now, unprepared, he just might make things worse."

Ron privately vowed to get even with Elaine later for

that little crack. Not that she was wrong. But still, did she have to say it out loud? To this clown?

"No. It wouldn't help," Elaine went on, ignoring the all too familiar and too clear signals that Ron was irritated with her. "Let's say day after tomorrow. That will give Ron plenty of time to bring in the right supplies and put together a plan of action."

"That's what Mr. Strange needs to see," said Bogs, in a voice that sounded deep as a bellowing diesel engine buried in the hot bowels of some tramp steamer churning its way across the South China Sea. "Some action."

"Ron will make this right," Elaine promised. "Ronald's Roofing stands behind its work." Amazing, how a person can lie in the face of fear. "You have my promise. *Our* promise."

Ron seemed speechless and capable only of staring slack-jawed at the damp outline of Bogs that now occupied his favorite chair.

"We'll see you in two days." Bogs strode two steps to the front door and threw it open. "Oh, and thanks for the free trim, Elaine."

Ron turned on his wife as Bogs slogged down to a black F-150 pickup out on the street. "You gave him a haircut?"

"What can I say?" said Elaine, picking up the dirty mugs. "The man was looking a little shaggy."

32

The minute Todd and Irina returned to Florida, Todd's smartphone began sending him messages. "What the hell?" He studied the screen as they waited for their luggage at the international arrivals carousel.

"Something is wrong?"

"It's George Strange. Remember? The guy I sold that house on the river to."

"What is problem?"

"I dunno. He wants to see me. Sounds mad." Todd scrolled through the rest of his messages. "Whatever it is, it will have to wait. Looks like I've got some deals waiting at the office. I'll drop you and our luggage off at the condo then head downtown."

He didn't know or care what George Strange's latest problem was. He had problems of his own.

33

Two days later, Todd stood outside George Strange's home, ringing the doorbell. Right on time. He promised the man four pm and it was four on the dot. A warm mist filled the air, yet the sun peeked around the edges of the sky, promising that sunny days may yet come.

George Strange hadn't ceased calling. According to his mom and Carlos, the Port Lauderdale doorman, that employee of Strange's, Bogs, had even shown up at the condo inquiring of his whereabouts.

The lout later had the gall to turn up at the office when Todd was out on a showing and had scared his receptionist so badly that she was in tears on his return and threatening to quit. It was all he could do to calm her down.

So here he was. Wasting valuable time. Time he could be selling more properties, not hand holding a fussy customer that he'd already closed a deal with.

Remember, Todd told himself, rich customers have rich friends. Anyone of those could be a future customer of his.

Meanwhile, all was going well on the Magritte front. Irina, with his blessing, had turned his home office into her art studio. Thick drop cloths covered the furniture and floor. A large easel stood in the corner and held the painting in progress.

He'd hung a Do Not Disturb sign on the office door.

Neither Rosalind Jones nor her sidekick, Mr. Squeals, were to be allowed in under any circumstance.

So far, things were looking good.

A stranger answered the door to George and Imelda Strange's house. A foreign-looking young man with a blunt demeanor.

"Hi, Todd Jones here to see Mr. Strange."

The dour man folded his arms over his chest. "You the real estate dude?"

"That's right." In the distance, he heard Cuddles bark. Probably to mislead the world into thinking that he was a dog rather than the missing link between Dobermans and diplodocuses.

"I hope you have life insurance, pal." The man smiled—or was that a snarl? Todd couldn't be sure.

Todd wiped his feet at the door and followed the young man to George's newly-furnished office with commanding view of the river.

"Well, well," said George, rising from his desk and tossing some boring paperwork aside. He hated paperwork. What he loved was blowing things up and turning them into scrap. Paperwork was for losers and suckers. "Look what the cat dragged in."

"Hello, George." Todd smiled. "I see you and your wife are making yourselves right at home. Looking good. Looking good." Normally, he'd dress up before visiting clients but, in this case, he hadn't bothered, opting to keep things casual in white Ralph Lauren jeans and a pale yellow polo shirt.

"That'll do, Bogs. Why don't you go see if there's some lizards whose heads you can blow off or spiders needing their little legs pulled."

"You sure, Big George?"

George cut his eyes at the man. He didn't like being second guessed. Bogs departed.

"Nice fellow, that Bogs." Todd ran his hands along George's unusual desktop. "Hope you got a leash for him. Nice desk too, by the way. Custom made?"

"Shut up, Jones."

That got Todd's attention.

George Strange gestured for Todd to sit. He did. In a chair that looked like it had been built out of hubcaps, a boxy old IBM computer, several pieces of rebar of varying lengths, and rusty auto transmission parts. At least the seat was reasonably well-cushioned.

"Looking good, huh?" George fell back in his own elaborate desk chair. Something like a Mad Max version of a royal throne. "I don't supposed you noticed the leaks?"

"Leaks?"

"Leaks! The whole fucking house is leaking." He pointed a damp cigar ceilingward. "From the top down!"

"Hmm. Sorry to hear that. Why didn't you get the roof replaced? You know, like we talked about."

George's cheeks swelled and colored like ripe plums. "I got that damn roof replaced. Didn't you notice the fucking pink roof tiles when you drove up?"

"Really? Pink? Can't say that I did."

"A quarter million dollars' worth of new roof and what do I get—"

"A quarter of a million?" interrupted Todd. "For a roof?" He fell back in his seat and immediately regretted it. Something sharp poked him in the back. He turned. Was that a nail? "I don't know," he said, turning back to George. "A quarter million for a roof. That sounds a bit excessive."

"You think so? You think so, Jones? He's your pal. *Your* roofer."

"He's not my—"

"You recommended the incompetent sonofabitch and look what it gets me!" George rose, banging his knees against his desk. He threw his cigar at the window and watched it fall to the carpet.

"Call him back. What was his name?"

George gulped in some air. "You know what I do, Jones?" George threw his cold eyes on Todd and picked up a golden putter some charity had given him to thank him for his hundred grand donation. They'd engraved its head with his name.

"You're in the scrap business."

"That's right. I buy scrap, I sell scrap. I blow things up and I turn those things into scrap."

George slammed the putter into the floor. "Then I sell that heap of scrap by the pound. Like this nice little job I got lined up in Orlando, the Orange Blossom Resort. Another sucker's failure that's gonna be my fortune. Six hundred rooms are soon going to be nothing but a pile of rubble. A pile of rubble that I'm gonna turn into money in my pocket!"

George took a whack at the soggy cigar on the floor with the putter. Whatever he'd been aiming for, he'd missed, leaving a nasty looking streak of brown goo and broken cigar bits all over the rug. Which he ignored.

"You need an up close and personal lesson? You need me to turn *you* into scrap and sell *you* by the pound?"

Todd stood. The chair was killing him anyway. "Mr. Strange, George, there's no need to get mad. No reason to resort to threats—"

"Bogs!"

The muscle-bound Pole stepped into the room, folding his hands under his armpits, making his biceps look even bigger. "Yes, sir?"

"Mr. Jones here would like to learn about the scrap business. I'm thinking maybe you're just the guy to teach him a thing or two."

For the first time since he'd laid eyes on the goon, Todd watched Bogs smile. "Really, that won't be necessary, Bogs, George. I've got this under control. Trust me."

"I trust you to get *your* roofer up on *my* roof and finish the job I paid *you* for."

"Actually, sir, it was Ronald's Roofing that you paid —"

"I don't care if I paid George W. Bush!" bellowed George Strange. "I paid a quarter million dollars for that lousy pink roof and another three million bucks for this house and, so far, it looks like I'm gonna have to spend another three mil just getting this place up to living standards!"

George savagely wiped the spittle from his jowls then grabbed Todd by the collar of his shirt, popping two buttons in the process. "Now, you get your pal, Patton, up on that roof. You get a whole army of men up on that roof. And," he squeezed tighter, "*you* get up on that roof."

"Me?"

"Yes, you."

"I don't know a thing about roofs."

George hooded his eyes. His breath blew hot in Todd's face. "Then I guess your buddy Patton's gonna have to teach you. Of course," his grip eased but only barely. "I'm a reasonable man, Mr. Jones. You do have a choice. So maybe you'd like me and Bogs to teach you about the scrap business instead? Get my drift?"

"Yessir." Red-faced and gasping for breath, Todd nodded. He got the drift.

"Good. Good. And to see that you do, Bogs here is gonna be up on that roof with you. Supervising." He turned to his flunkie. "Got that, Bogs?"

"Yeah, Big George."

"Excellent. And you don't let them down and off this property until the job is done." George didn't bother asking Bogs if he could handle the job because, if anybody could handle a job once he'd been assigned it, that anybody was Bogdan Kowalczyk.

He'd come up through the ranks, starting as a fifteen-year-old kid sweeping up scrap at Strange Scrap, Inc.'s Detroit yard and had worked his way up the corporate ladder from there. Bogs may not be spelling bee championship material, but the man was strong, resourceful, loyal and didn't have an ounce of morality in his over-muscled body.

George twisted the alligator band of his Patek Philippe. "Where is that lousy excuse for a Patton, anyway? He was supposed to be here an hour ago. Is there a problem?" He asked this question of Bogs.

"No. No problem, Big George. Miro is bringing him along now. They should be here any minute."

"Can't be soon enough." George looked at his watch once more. "I gotta freaking charity ball to attend and you gotta roof to attend to. Get busy."

George Strange pushed Todd aside and went to put on his monkey suit. The crap he put up with to make his wife happy. Or at least as happy as she ever got.

34

Bogs escorted Todd outside.

"So where's this roofer?" Todd wanted to know. No way he was going up on that roof by himself. Probably break his neck. "I don't even have a ladder," he said aloud, for Bogs' benefit.

"I sent my nephew to get him. He was behaving rather reluctantly."

Todd could imagine. What a piece of luck, all rotten, that he had to recommend the worst roofer on the planet to George Strange.

"Your nephew?"

"Miro."

"We've met." Unfortunately.

"They should be here soon."

"Fine." Todd studied his practically new white denim jeans. Four hundred bucks a pair. Not a speck of dirt on them. "Mind if I run home and change clothes first?"

"You can change when you're done, hot shot." Bogs shoved Todd off the porch. "Here they come now."

Sure enough, coming up the street, the Ronald's Roofing van, loaded down with an assortment of ladders on its roof, turned slowly up the drive. A black Chevy Suburban with tinted windows followed close behind.

Miro jumped down from the Suburban and

swaggered over to his uncle.

"Any trouble, kid?"

"Nah. Not really," Miro replied. "I found him hiding in his wife's hair salon."

Todd, Miro and Bogs looked at the Ronald's Roofing van in which Ron remained seated. Unknown to them, he was hastily reading his sweat-stained copy of How-To-Install Clay And Concrete Roof Tiles. There wasn't a single chapter, not even a lousy paragraph, devoted to how to repair a botched roof job.

Bogs walked over and banged on the hood of the van. "Let's go, Ron!"

Ron glanced out the windshield, swallowed hard, tossed the manual to the footwell on the passenger side, and exited. "Who's this guy?" He pointed to Todd.

"I'm the idiot who recommended you to Mr. Strange."

A smile of recognition broke Ron's nervous face. "Oh, sure. I remember you. Thanks. For nothing."

"Enough talk. Jones here has offered to be your helper. Now get to work." Bogs waved to the ladders on the van's roof.

"Sure thing." Ron appeared puzzled but that didn't stop him moving. "Give me a hand, would you?" he asked of Todd.

Together, they grappled with one of the longer ladders and managed to lean it up against the stuccoed side of the house. Unfortunately, it had to be at least a half-dozen feet shy of the roof slanted along the lower side of the garage.

"Where's your crew?" Todd wanted to know.

"They refused to come," grunted Ron, trying to figure out how to make the ladder go up.

No crew. That was why he'd been hiding. How could they expect him to repair a roof by himself?

Ron gripped the rungs and tugged. Nothing happened. Well, the ladder fell down but he managed to right it again.

"I don't get it. Why won't this thing extend? I must've seen those guys do this a hundred times." He kicked a side rail hard. "You think it's defective?"

"I think you're defective." Todd flipped a couple of doohickeys on the ladder and slid it upward. The top of the ladder cleared the roof by a good two feet.

"Thanks," Ron looked up with admiration. "Truth is, Juan, my crew chief, said no pay, no work. Now what kind of attitude is that? I ask you."

"So pay them, already and let's get them out here. Strange told me he paid you a quarter of a million dollars for this botched job."

"Sure, but the damn bank's put a hold on the check." Ron jiggled the ladder. It seemed secure. At least as secure as a ladder that wasn't permanently bolted down could be. "So those stinking bums abandoned me. Scattered like New Yorkers in the spring time."

Todd leaned closer despite the fact that Bogs and Miro had retreated to the garage from which George and Imelda Strange were now backing out in a Bentley. "So, what's the plan?"

"The plan?"

"Yeah, how are you going to fix this roof so we can get Strange off our back and get the hell out of here?" Never to return again, no matter how many times George Strange called, Todd vowed to himself.

"Start pluggin' holes, I guess." Ron jiggled the ladder once more. Just to be sure.

"Start plugging holes?" Todd craned his neck. "This roof's huge. We could be here till Christmas. Where do we start?"

Ron frowned. "Fine. I guess we could check inside the house first. You know, inspect the ceiling. See what the problem areas are." The manual had mentioned something about that.

"Now that's a plan." Todd yelled at Bogs. "Hey, we need to check inside the house first. Figure out where the leaks are."

"I guess that makes sense." Waving for Todd and Ron to follow him, Bogs entered the house through the garage, Miro at their heels. The kid picked up a shotgun pointing barrel down in an umbrella stand in the mudroom and slung it over his left shoulder.

The more they wandered, the more depressed Todd became. George was right. The house seemed to be leaking more than ever. "What did you do?" he whispered to Ron as they marched along the upper floor hallway, "drill a bunch of holes in the roof?"

Ron merely stuck out his arms and shrugged. "I don't know. Juan assured me they knew what they were doing."

"Didn't you check their work?" Dumb question. Clearly, Ron Patton had not.

"I figured I could trust them." He wasn't going to tell this yahoo real estate peddler that he wouldn't have known what to look for even if he had gone to the trouble of checking up on the crew's work.

Todd shook his head in disgust.

"Seen enough?" Bogs asked them as they descended the grand staircase. They made an odd parade, a realtor, a roofer, a musclebound corporate fixer of sorts, his shotgun-toting nephew, and Cuddles the let-me-weave-in-and-out-of-your-legs-a-million-times-and-see-if-I-can-make-you-trip-and-fall-on-your-ass-again Doberman.

Todd was on the verge of grabbing that shotgun from that shotgun-slinging Pole-Bangladeshi and giving Cuddles a twelve-gauge enema.

"Yeah, I've seen enough." And the more Ron saw, the more depressed he got. "Let's get to it," he replied. Still having no idea what 'getting to it' would involve.

"You got this, kid?" Bogs rested a hand on his nephew's shoulder. "I got something to take care of." He shot a wink to Esme, visible in the kitchen washing out some pans in the sink.

"Sure, Uncle." He gripped the sling of his ever-present shotgun. "I can handle this."

"Good. Call me if you need me. I might go out back and check on Big George's boat. Make sure she's secure. Every time the wind kicks up, I see her bobbing around like a bronco at the rodeo. We're in for a doozy of a storm."

With the Stranges off to their charity ball in Palm Beach, Bogs and Esme planned to steal aboard the good ship Imelda for a little alone time. It was going to get noisy up on the roof what with Patton and Jones working up there. On the Hatteras, they could get some privacy and make some noises of their own.

Besides, Bogs had a bad knee and didn't like climbing ladders. It only made the pain flare up. Miro could go babysit the two babies up on the roof while he and Esme plied the high seas in their own fashion.

35

"Why don't you go up on the roof?" Ron suggested to Todd. "I'll stay down here." Safe on the ground.

"What?"

"Yeah, I'll hold the ladder for you. And I can hand you up anything you need."

"Are you out of your mind?" Todd gaped at the idiot roofer. "I don't know anything about roofs. You're the roofer, you get up there and I'll stay here on the ground. I'll hold the ladder. I'll hand you whatever you need."

Miro pointed his matte black shotgun at the pair. "How about you both get your asses up the ladder and get busy." He hadn't been asking a question.

"Right. What are we arguing about?" Ron said readily. "Sounds good." In a life-threatening sort of way.

"After you," Todd said, waving at the ladder, one nervous eye on the gray and purple sky. The sooner this was over, the better.

Ron turned to Miro. "We're going to need some tools and materials. It's all in the van." He'd loaded up everything he hadn't yet been able to sell that had been left over from the job.

Miro assented.

"Gimme a hand," Ron said to Todd.

The first thing Ron did was grab his like-new tool belt. If one good thing came out of this, it was that he'd finally get a chance to wear it with purpose, rather than merely for looks and the feeling of male pride wearing all that leather gave him. He strapped it on.

"Got one of those for me?" asked Todd.

"Sorry, no. But here's some tools." Ron handed a rusty toolbox to Todd then turned his attention to opening up a brand new pair of kneepads. He velcroed these around his knees the way he'd seen Juan and his men do it.

"What about kneepads?"

"Only the one pair."

"Great."

"Hey, what are you griping about? How'd I know you were gonna be here? Besides, a good roofer has his own tools."

"I'm not a roofer. And you aren't a good one."

"Oh, yeah?"

"The roof's up there!" hollered Miro, pointing the barrel of the shotgun upward.

"Let's get this over with," said Todd.

Making several scary trips, they managed to carry roofside the toolbox, a case of caulking, glues and adhesives, a cordless nail gun and plenty of stuff that neither Todd nor Ron knew what the stuff was good for. They also struggled to hoist up several rolls of underlayment and some extra pink roof tiles.

Miro helped by watching and snickering at their struggles.

"Now what?" Todd gazed down at the ground far below, felt dizzy, and instantly regretted it. The wind was blowing. If it blew any harder, it was going to lift him right off the roof.

Miro, shotgun slung over his shoulder, appeared at the top of the ladder and jumped onto the roof like he was part mountain goat.

Maybe he was.

"We'll start near the master bedroom," Ron decided. Plenty of leaks existed there and, if he could fix those, maybe, just maybe George Strange would calm down some. Get off his back.

"Fine."

Trembling from the knees downward, Ron and Todd moved toward the back of the house, facing the river. Miro followed at a distance.

Ron knelt and inspected the area where the master bedroom fireplace chimney poked through the roof. Todd joined him.

"Even I can see what a crappy job you did," Todd said. "Look at this. Bare plywood. No tarpaper, no tiles. No tar. Nothing."

"Hey, I'm not responsible for this," Ron whispered. "This is all that Juan's fault."

"He works for you. I don't get it," Todd settled on his haunches.

"What?"

"You're a roofer. Own your own company. But look at this! He picked up a cracked, loose tile and tossed it over the side of the house.

"Hey!" complained Ron. "Those fucking things are expensive!"

"It's like you've never done a roof in your life."

Ron glanced at Miro to make sure he was out of range. "Maybe I haven't," he said slowly.

"Huh?" Todd said. "Haven't what?"

"Maybe I haven't ever done a roof," Ron replied, failing to make eye contact.

Todd furrowed his brow. "What do you mean you

haven't ever done a roof?"

Ron sighed, picking at a shard of pink tile with a fingernail. "All I've ever done is give quotes."

"Give quotes?"

"I give quotes. You need a roof, I give you a quote. Get it?"

"No. I don't get it." Todd shook his head. "Enlighten me."

"I give you a quote, it's high, too high. So you hire somebody else. They do your roof."

"And how exactly do you expect to stay in business? How can you possibly make any money if all you do is give quotes and never actually do the work?" He was stuck on a crazy high rooftop with a couple of lunatics. One of whom carried a loaded weapon. How had his life gone so wrong?

Ron motioned for Todd to slide closer. "I charge a few hundred bucks for the quote."

"You charge—" For a moment, Todd was confused. Then he understood. It was genius. Really genius. Show up at a customer's home, get paid to give them a quote and...Never. Do. The. Work.

No equipment, no material, no expenses except for gas money. Absolute genius.

Except...

"You really don't know anything about roofs?" It was Todd's turn to glance nervously at Miro.

"Not a damn thing."

"So we're in trouble here. If Strange finds out—"

"If Miro finds out," interjected Ron. "I've been around that kid. He can't seem to go more than an hour without feeling the need to pull the trigger on that shotgun attached to him like a third arm."

Todd grabbed Ron's collar. "Miro can never know."

Ron gulped.

"I don't see no work!" hollered Miro, proudly straddling the peak of the roof. Growing bored, he took aim at a lazily passing laughing gull and fired off an imaginary round. "Pow! Got you, bird." He'd save his real ammo for these losers he was babysitting.

"We're talking about the best way to attack the problem," shouted Todd. Turning to Ron, he said, "Come on. We're going to have to do the best we can."

"This is never going to work," Ron said glumly.

"It's got to," Todd said firmly. "Besides, it's not like George is going to check. And I'm guessing Miro doesn't know a damn thing about roofing either. We can do this. All we have to do is make this look good. We'll throw everything at this roof. Underlayment, nails, glue, whatever. We can fool him. No problem."

"Yeah," Ron felt suddenly uplifted. "You're right. Let's do this." He slapped his lucky leather tool belt. "Let's get busy."

36

The wind howled around them like a disturbed specter searching for someone or something to take out its anger on.

The sun, what little there had been of it, was swallowed up by the dark, threatening clouds. Light rain fell, making the surface of the tiles dangerously slick. Several times, Todd and Ron fell, slamming into the roof hard, breaking more and more tiles in the process, as they worked frantically, and ineptly, to cover the endless holes.

Todd shivered. His fingertips were raw and numb. The two men were totally exposed. It was cold and windy on the steeply pitched roof.

If he didn't fall off the roof, he stood a good chance of being hit by lightning and electrocuted. Maybe both.

This was everything Todd imagined a Florida version of Hell to be like.

"Don't you think we ought to quit for the day?" Todd hollered at Miro, still standing guard from the apex of the roof, despite the wind, despite the rain.

"Work!" Miro shouted, clutching his stupid shotgun.

"That guy think he's Superman or something?" complained Ron. He and Todd crouched on one of the master bedroom peaks, pulling back loose tiles and gluing down paper and more tiles. "Look at us, soaked through and shivering from the cold and there he stands."

Todd sneezed and wiped his runny nose against his wet shirt. "Yeah. I don't know how much longer he can expect us to work in the dark."

"I say we shoot some nails in this underlayment and tell him we'll be back first thing in the morning." Ron slowly straightened. He was never going to get used to standing on a rooftop for as long as he lived. Not that he ever intended to stand on a rooftop again no matter how long he lived.

In fact, the first thing he was going to do when this nightmare was all over was to throw away all his ladders.

Then he *couldn't* climb up on any more rooftops.

"Works for me. Let's hope it works for him." Todd nodded towards Miro while he scrambled to his feet.

"Time to pull out the big gun." Ron snatched up the portable nail gun in his right hand. He'd always wanted to try this thing. It looked mean. It looked nasty. It also looked complicated.

But the guy at the big box store assured him it was a cinch to use. "Point and shoot," the salesman said. "Simple." He'd even helped him out by showing him how to load up a coil of inch-and-a-half nails in the chamber thingie.

And it looked so cool when he watched the guys on Juan's crew shooting their nail guns. He'd be like Clint Eastwood but up on a roof, not a horse. If only Elaine could see him now. "Step back."

"You sure you know how to use that thing?"

Tat! Tat! Tat!

"What the—!" Ron flinched. The gun in his hand jumped with a life all its own.

"Careful!" Todd jumped backwards, slipping and clutching at the slick tiles in desperation to keep himself from falling to the hard ground far below.

Tat! Tat! Tat!

Tat! Tat! Tat!

Dozens of sharp steel nails skipped off the hard tiles and went bouncing in every direction.

Todd yelped as one buried itself in his thigh. A bright red spot rose on his wet white denim jeans.

"What the hell are you doing?" demanded Miro. He pumped his shotgun and aimed it menacingly at Ron.

"What?" Ron's brain seemed to have gone on the fritz. The nail gun seemed to have more self-awareness than he did at the moment. All he could think was "How do I stop this thing?"

Tat! Tat! Tat!

Tat! Tat! Tat!

"Hey! I'm talking to you!" Miro stomped closer, busting tiles with every heavy-booted step.

"What?" Ron spun around. The nail gun was still nailed to his hand. It wouldn't let go.

Wind gusted.

Rain streaked.

Ron bobbled.

Nails flew all around, whizzing dangerously with deadly potential.

Todd covered his head with his hands and curled into a ball on the roof.

Tat! Tat! Tat!

Tat! Tat! Tat!

Six perfect shots landed in Miro Frankowski. Four in his chest. Two in his throat.

Miro opened his mouth, clutched his throat. The

shotgun slipped off his shoulder and clattered as it struck the tile.

Miro lurched once. Lurched twice.

Then he reached the edge of the roof.

And went over.

37

Todd gaped. "Are you mad, Patton? What the hell did you do that for?" Todd struggled to his knees, wincing in pain as he extracted the sharp nail from his left thigh and tossed it aside.

Rain pelted them.

The gun had stopped. Empty.

Ron gulped, staring in horror and fear at the nail gun. "It wouldn't stop. It just wouldn't stop. I-I couldn't...it wouldn't..."

"Drop that damn thing." Todd waved his hands in a downward motion. "Before you do any more damage."

"Yeah. Yeah." Ron slowly bent his knees. "Don't worry." The gun shook in his hand. "Out of nails."

Rain smeared Ron's vision as he concentrated on releasing the nail gun from his uncooperative hand. After several excruciating and tense moments, he was finally able to uncurl his fingers.

The nail gun fell.

Thunk.

Todd breathed a sigh of relief.

"Where's Miro?" Ron asked. "Do you see him? Is he okay?"

The shotgun had clattered down the roof and lodged in the rain gutter. But where exactly was Miro?

"Shut up a minute and let me look." Todd forced himself to crawl to the edge of the roof. He laid down on his stomach, gripping the gutter, and slowly, carefully peeked down.

"Is he dead?"

Todd ignored Ron. Between the darkness, the wind and the rain, he could barely see anything. Nothing but wet and shadows.

Miro had taken a header off the back of the roof, overlooking the patio pool deck. Todd saw no sign of him. "I don't see—"

And then he did see. Miro was floating in the unlit swimming pool. Head down.

"He's in the pool."

Ron blew out a breath. "That's good. That's good, isn't it? In the pool."

"Not necessarily," Todd said, wiping his hands as he slowly ascended the roof to join the roofer. "He's face down."

"You think he's dead?"

"We're going to have to check. Come on, let's get down there."

Crouching and tiptoeing across the roof like Evil Santa's helpers, Todd and Ron scampered down the ladder to the lawn.

Todd led the way.

Ron stopped him with a hand on his shoulder. "What about Bogs?"

"Right." Todd paused. "I saw him going out on the fishing boat a while ago with that woman. "He's probably still out there." It wouldn't do to be seen by him.

"Maybe we should leave," suggested Ron, whose feet were itching to go in the opposite direction. "Scram."

"And then what? We've got to check. See if Miro's

dead or not. If he's okay, we've got to get him some help."

"He's gonna be mad," warned Ron.

"We're wasting time," Todd said, starting forward once more. "He could be drowning."

Ron followed against his better judgment. When they reached the corner of the house, the pair reconnoitered.

"All's quiet," Todd said. "Miro hasn't moved a muscle." The body drifted slowly across the surface of the pool.

"I see a light on in the boat," Ron said.

The wind whistled past their ears.

"I see it. Stay close to the ground." Todd crawled on hands and knees across the pool deck. Ron was right behind him.

Scuttling along the side of the pool, Todd made out the dark, wet form of Miro floating a couple of yards out of reach.

Suddenly, the door to the stateroom on the Hatteras blew open. Bogs stepped out on deck.

"Duck!" whispered Todd, flattening himself to the marble-tiled patio. Ron followed suit.

They held their breaths as Bogs took a turn around the boat. He paused, stared back at the house a moment.

Was he looking towards the roof? Was he going to come looking for Miro? For them?

Todd shivered and it wasn't from the cold.

A woman's voice called out from inside the stateroom. Bogs took a final look around then returned to the cabin.

Todd scrambled to his knees. "I can't reach him. Grab that pole in the corner." They'd passed a blue aluminum pole with a leaf catcher attachment on one end leaning against the side of the house on their way to the pool.

"Right." Ron hurried across the patio and returned with the pole.

Grabbing the handle of the pole, Todd leaned forward, balancing on his knees and extending the leaf catcher at the other end, trying to net Miro, who wasn't showing any signs of life.

Ron noticed that too because he said, "He's dead, isn't he?"

Todd didn't bother to answer. What was the point? He focused on the body in the pool, keeping one eye on the Hatteras. If Bogs came out for an encore, they were dead meat.

His first two tries failed miserably and only succeeded in pushing the body further out of reach. Cursing, Todd twisted the pole, extending it to its full length, and tried again. On his third attempt, Todd managed to get the net end of the pole over Miro's back and slowly, ever so slowly, managed to drag the body closer to the coping.

"Grab him," Todd ordered Ron.

Ron latched onto Miro's waterlogged trousers.

Todd took a breath to settle himself, then turned Miro's head around.

Ron groaned.

It wasn't a pretty sight. Miro's throat was a mess. His dead eyes glared balefully at Todd and Ron.

Ron bolted.

"What are you doing?" Todd whispered loudly. "Where are you going?"

Ron stopped behind a patio table. "I'm getting out of here. If you're smart, you'll get out of here too!"

"Not without him," Todd replied.

"What? You mean, Miro?"

"Yes, Miro. We can't very well leave him here, can we?"

"Why the hell not?"

"Because when Bogs or George or the police find his dead body floating in the swimming pool, who are the first two people you think they are going to be looking for?"

Ron's shoulders sagged. He clutched the back of a wrought iron patio chair to keep from totally collapsing. "What a fucking nightmare. I don't feel so good."

It was only the simple fact that he hadn't had any solid food in five hours that kept him from vomiting all over himself.

"How do you think Miro's feeling?" Not that he could feel anything at all now.

Ron glanced nervously at the boat. He didn't want to think about what Bogs might do if he saw what he'd done to his nephew, Miro. "What are we going to do?" he asked, pulling at his hair.

"We're going to move him."

38

"Move him? Move him where?"

"I don't know yet. We'll figure that out later. The first thing to do is get him out of this swimming pool before Bogs comes out again or George and his wife come home."

"I hate this," said Ron, returning and grabbing Miro by the legs while Todd pulled on a flaccid arm.

Heaving with exertion, they flopped Miro's lifeless body out of the warm pool and onto the cold deck.

All the while, Todd had this eerie sensation of being watched, followed. He'd had it while they'd been toiling up on the roof and it wasn't merely Miro's lurking presence that had been the cause of it.

It was as if some evil presence had been watching him.

Todd hated that feeling of being observed.

Todd grabbed Miro under the shoulder blades. "We'll haul him out to your van."

"My van? What's wrong with your car?"

"My trunk's full of golf clubs," Todd lied. He did not want a corpse in the Audi. "And we can't very well dump his body in the backseat where anybody could see him, can we?"

"I suppose not."

"Besides, you've got plenty of room in that van of yours."

Moving awkwardly, they lugged Miro's corpse around the side of the house.

"Set him down here," Todd said. Sharp stabbing pains shot through his back and thighs. Of course, who was he to complain? He was in better shape than Miro.

"Behind this hedge so he can't be seen from the street," grunted Todd.

"Right."

They laid the body on the ground at the edge of the driveway. Ron looked this way and that. It was dark and miserable and rainy. No nosy neighbors out walking their pooches in this weather.

"We can wrap him up in some of that underlayment in your truck," Todd suggested.

"Good idea." Ron pulled out a roll of leftover black underlayment and cut off a good length with the razor blade knife he'd tucked into a slot of his tool belt.

Spreading the fabric out on the ground, the pair began rolling Miro on to it, both careful to avoid looking at his bloody chest and neck.

They hurriedly rolled him up and shoved him unceremoniously inside the rear of the Ronald's Roofing van.

"I can't wait for this nightmare to be over," Ron grumbled, anxious to be done with this and eager not to have to look at Miro's bloody corpse ever again—especially since he did feel sort of responsible for what had happened to him. Not that he was ever admitting that to anyone. Not even Elaine.

"This is all your own damn fault, Patton." Todd slammed the doors tight.

"You still harping on that, Jones? Let's worry about what we do next," snapped Ron. "I can't exactly keep a dead body in my van forever." What would Elaine say?

"Shut up and let me think." Todd leaned against the van, catching his breath.

They had to do something. And fast. Bogs could appear any minute. George and Imelda could come rolling up the driveway.

"The first thing we've got to do is go back up on the roof."

"The roof?" Ron gaped. "What the hell for?"

"We've got to go back for Miro's shotgun. Get the ladder. The *nail gun*," Todd emphasized. "Think about it. You don't want to leave *that* lying around, do you, Ron?"

"Uh, no."

"Exactly. We'll leave the rest of the stuff up there to set the scene, make it look like we were coming back in the morning."

"Are we?" Ron chewed his fingernails.

Todd grunted. "I suppose we have to. If we want to make this look good."

"What do we tell Strange? That guy's got a temper and a short fuse. Not to mention, he likes to strut around with a Colt .45 strapped to his hip."

"We tell him nothing. Play dumb." That shouldn't be too hard for Ron the incompetent roofer, thought Todd.

"He's going to ask questions—"

"And we're going to answer them all the same way. We. Don't. Know. We don't know where Miro is, where he went or where he might be now. We only know that he said to call it a night, so we did. Came back first thing in the morning to get back to work. Hell, we can offer to help look for the kid," he ended with a chuckle.

"What about the blood? On the roof, the grass, the driveway." Ron wished he had a cigarette but Elaine had forced him to quit when they got married.

"I don't see any on the driveway and, anyway, the rain will wash any blood away," Todd told Ron. At least he hoped so.

"Someone's coming!" Ron cried as the hiss of wet tires on pavement grew louder. He hid behind the front of his van.

"It's just some neighbor driving home. Relax," Todd ordered. "This is no time to fall apart, Ron."

Ron peeked over the hood, trembling. All he wanted to do was to get home, sink into his favorite chair, even if it had been forever soiled by the one-time occupancy of Bogs.

Maintaining a calm demeanor for Ron's sake when what he really wanted to do was kick the guy in his stupid ass, Todd said, "Like I said, we'll go up on the roof, take care of things there, come here in the morning and act like everything is normal and we don't know a damn thing about Miro. Not even that he's missing." He grabbed Ron. "You got that?"

"I-I suppose."

"Fine. Then we've got to dispose of the body."

"We could toss him in the river."

"The river?" Todd repeated skeptically.

"Sure, maybe the alligators or some shark will eat him. Get rid of all the evidence."

"And maybe they won't. And maybe Miro's corpse will wash up in front of somebody's mansion or get caught up in some yacht's propellers. Then what?"

"You got any better ideas?" Ron said testily.

"First things first," Todd answered, because he really had no idea of the best way to dispose of a corpse. Yet he had no doubt that if he didn't come up with a way, he just might end up a corpse himself. "Let's get up on that roof before the weather gets any worse. And I want to be gone before the Stranges return."

"Me, too." Ron hustled after Todd.

They ascended the ladder, scooped up some materials, organizing them under a plastic tarp near one of the chimney stacks.

Todd picked up the nail gun before Ron could get his hands on it. It might have been out of nails, but he didn't trust the idiot roofer with it in any case. He handed Ron the toolbox figuring the guy couldn't do much damage with that.

"I'll get the shotgun." Holding the nail gun at his side, Todd inched down the steep roof to the gutter, grabbed the shotgun by the sling and tugged. The gutter rattled. The weapon was lodged and refused to budge.

"That you, kid?" boomed Bogs.

Todd froze. Two dark shapes stood on the deck of the Hatteras. Bogs and Esme.

"What is it?" asked Esme, the wind carrying her voice. She carried a tote that they had fetched from the kitchen filled with sandwiches and a bottle of George's favorite Italian wine.

"I thought I heard something on the roof."

"Probably just the storm, a branch or maybe a squirrel."

"Yeah, probably. I guess Miro must've sent those two losers home for the night and gone inside where it's warm and dry." Bogs took Esme's arm. "Let's get back inside too."

Todd waited until the door to the stateroom shut. This time, he took the shotgun by the barrel, turned it sideways and pulled—hoping the damn thing didn't shoot him in the face.

The weapon shot free.

He sighed with relief, slung it over his shoulder and started down the rain-slick ladder. Ron was already on the ground. "Help me lay the ladder down," ordered Todd.

"Why not leave it?"

"Because I don't want to make it too easy for Bogs or anybody else to get up on the roof and start poking around."

"Right." Ron grabbed a hold of the ladder and they eased it to the lawn. "Now what? I've still got Miro in the back of my van, genius."

"What the hell's your problem?" snapped Todd. "You're lucky I'm helping you. I mean, shit, this is murder we're talking about. It's bad enough you fucked up the guy's roof, now you've murdered one of his employees!"

"I didn't murder anybody," roared Ron. "It was an accident."

"Yeah, an accident, Ron? You want to tell Strange that? You want to tell Bogs that? Do you, huh?" Todd prodded the roofer in the chest.

"Oof!" Ron staggered.

"You know what George will do if he finds out? Do you want to know what Bogs is going to do when he finds out? That's his nephew in there!" Todd pointed at the van.

"And sticking him there, in my van, was your stupid idea!"

"You really want to talk about stupid, Ron? You're the stupid man who shot him."

"I keep telling you it was an accident," hissed Ron.

Todd folded his arms across his chest. "So tell George that."

The two men glared at one another.

"Personally, I'm sick of this entire thing. I'm cold, wet, tired and hungry. I have half a mind to get in my car and leave you to face Strange and Bogs alone."

"Oh, yeah?" Ron smiled a devilish smile. "You know what I'm gonna tell George, if you do?" He was not waiting for an answer. "I'm telling him *you* killed Miro."

"It was your nail gun that killed him."

"Which your fingerprints are now on."

Shit, thought Todd. Ron was right. His prints were on the nail gun. And the shotgun.

Todd's mind raced through various scenarios. "Fine, here's what we're going to do. But first," he threw open the back of the van, "we give Miro his shotgun back."

Todd unwound the underlayment and stuffed the weapon between Miro's dead legs. "Better it should disappear with him." He started to close the door.

"Good idea. Now tell me, smartass, how do we make this—" Ron slammed his hand against the van's rear door, "disappear?"

39

Christie Campbell plucked a tissue from the travel pack in her purse and blew her nose. She used a second tissue to wipe the sheet of dampness on her forehead. It was so muggy inside the closed up car. She tossed both wadded up tissues to the footwell on the passenger side.

A fitted navy-blue Detroit Tigers baseball cap with floral accents and a pair of bejeweled Gucci sunglasses with dark lenses hid her distinctive blond hair and blue eyes

Not that she was famous or anything, at least not outside Detroit—which was just about the only place cheap George bothered to run his ads—but she didn't want Imelda, or one of George's employees or even George himself spotting her here, hunkered down in a rented silver Honda Accord with steamed up windows, parked in front of a deserted dog park several houses down from George and Imelda's new house.

Growing up in Monroe, Michigan, Christie had always dreamed of following in the footsteps of Christie Brinkley, who, despite her parents' insistence to the contrary, she claimed to be named after. They claimed they had named her after her great-grandmother. But that was such a boring story in comparison.

Christie dreamed of emulating the successful model/entrepreneur too. How she was going to go about that, that was the question.

And a tough one, too.

Especially since George Strange was proving to be so unhelpful. He'd promised her the moon and here she sat, sneaking around behind the wheel of a ho-hum rental car while George and Imelda hobnobbed with the rich up in Palm Beach in some swank luxury hotel ballroom.

She was tired of George's excuses and his broken promises. She wanted more and she wanted it NOW.

If only her parents had moved to California when she was a girl, like Christie Brinkley's had, maybe she'd have met some real celebrities. Maybe be a real celebrity herself now.

But no, her parents had to stay in Monroe, teaching middle school of all things. How ho-hum was that?

Grabbing another tissue, she rubbed her nose again, careful not to rub too hard lest she make her nose too red. Not a good look.

Being the spokesperson/model for Strange Scrap wasn't half as fun as George had told her it would be. Mostly, she hung around in her suite at the Westin Book Cadillac in Detroit waiting for George to telephone. At least she had access to the spa and 24-hour fitness center.

Looking out the car window, Christie couldn't believe her eyes. What were those two men doing now?

She rubbed her palms across the inside of the windshield to clear the condensation.

First, one of them shot Miro. Then, they had dragged his body to the Ronald's Roofing van in the driveway and tossed him inside. Now they were arguing in George's driveway over something. What?

She was so glad she'd decided to stick around and

keep an eye on the house rather than tailing George and his wife up to Palm Beach as she had originally intended.

This was lots more interesting.

At first, she thought she might just slip inside the house and cause a little mischief, rip up some of Imelda's clothes, or George's or leave an incriminating love note for George on his pillow so his wife would see it when they returned.

That would teach the bastard.

How could he say he loved her, wanted to spend eternity with her—like Cinderella and Prince Charming—and then go and name his stupid boat after his wife?

The two men separated. The guy with the tool belt got in the van. The other went in the Audi.

Christie clipped on her seatbelt.

The Audi pulled slowly down the drive. The van followed soon after.

"Crap." Christie fiddled around with the knobby things on the steering column until landing her fingers on the windshield wipers.

Thwack-Thwack.

The Audi drove off, heading south on Vizcaya.

Should she follow? Or wait and see where the van went next?

The van did have Miro's corpse inside. It might be interesting to see what these two killers planned to do with it.

Smiling at the thought of the adventure and what opportunities it might hold for her, Christie cranked up the motor.

She decided to follow the van and waited for it to pass. She performed a U-turn and began trailing it at a discreet distance.

40

Todd stopped short of the Port Lauderdale Towers entrance, rolled down his window and waved for Ron to pull up beside him.

Ron leaned over toward the passenger side and rolled down its window. "Yeah?"

"I'm going to park in the garage. I can't go through the lobby looking like this."

Grass stains, mud and blood streaked his clothing. The doorman on duty might ask questions. Questions he didn't want to answer. "Wait for me at the end of the drive. I'll run up, change clothes and meet you back here in fifteen minutes."

"You still haven't explained what this plan of yours is." All he'd said so far was to follow him to his place and that they'd then go dump the body someplace where nobody would ever find it.

"You aren't planning on ditching me, are you? Because if you are..." Ron left his threat unfinished because he had no idea how he'd exact his revenge on the realtor.

"Relax. I've got an idea. Trust me. Fifteen minutes."

"I'm giving you ten," Ron said, switching on the radio for something calming.

Todd rolled up his window and headed to the parking structure, slotting the Audi in one of his two assigned spaces. His mom's ancient bronze Camry

—from the Bronze Age maybe—was only bronze in memory. As a birthday present to herself, she'd had the car painted lavender on her sixty-fifth birthday.

Checking himself in the rearview mirror, Todd adjusted his collar and combed a hand through his wet locks.

He ran into a couple who looked like they'd been out celebrating. The woman eyed him with suspicion. "Some night, eh?"

"Are you a resident?" asked the woman's companion, a tall man in a dark suit.

"Yep. See." Todd dangled his keys. "Oh, you're looking at my clothes. I had a flat. Had to change the tire on I-95, of all places. Can you imagine?"

The elevator came to a stop. Casting looks over their shoulders, they scooted off.

"I guess you can't." Todd chuckled and pushed the button again for his floor.

Mr. Squeals greeted him at the door with a grunt. Todd nudged the animal aside. Inside, lights blazed and music blasted.

"What the heck is going on here?" Todd gaped at his living space. A bare-chested Mick Jagger swaggered and flaunted himself in the middle of his living room.

The pinball machine last spotted at Go For Broke. The back glass of the classic Rolling Stones pinball machine featured Mick and his bandmates.

His mother stood at the base of the glowing, pulsing, throbbing and music pounding wood, glass and metal beast that was now his burden, stabbing the flipper buttons on each side. Her feet danced to the beat of the music.

Irina, standing on the opposite side of the pinball

machine, smiled on seeing Todd. Her eyes grew wide when she saw the state he was in.

"What's this doing here?" Todd asked, forgetting his own rule about taking off shoes at the entrance, as he hurried closer. His mom, he'd grown accustomed to. Irina, he was getting used to. The pig he was tolerating, barely.

But a pinball machine in his living room?

"Aren't you happy?" Irina gave him a kiss. Her slacks and T-shirt bore paint stains. "What happened to your clothes?"

"I'll explain later. About this machine—"

"Yes, Cousin Yev brings it. He called to ask how selling painting is coming. I tell him not to worry. And he knew how much you loved this game, so he makes a gift of it to you!"

Ding! Plunk! Ding! Plunk!

I Can't Get No Satisfaction blared from the pinball machine. The thing looked so much bigger here in his condo. And noisier.

"Mom!" Todd shouted. "Could you stop for a minute, please? That thing's giving me a headache." He clutched his head.

Rosalind looked over her shoulder, letting the steel ball clunk to the bottom where it momentarily disappeared only to reappear in the chute, ready to go again.

"Hi, baby." She reached for a Belgian hand-shaped cookie from the open box on the pinball machine's tabletop and waved it at him. "These are good!"

"You don't like?" Irina asked, tapping Todd on the shoulder.

"No, no," Todd said quickly. "It's great. Great." He

didn't dare insult Stalin, even if it was merely Yevgeny and not Joseph. The man had a pawn shop loaded with weapons. "I'm just wondering if the living room is the best place to keep it."

"You are unhappy with me." Irina hung her head.

"No, it's simply that—"

"Cousin Yev told me how much you enjoyed the game and asked if I thought it would make you happy and I said yes."

"It makes me happy," said Rosalind. "The only thing that would make me happier is if your cousin has a Fleetwood Mac pinball machine. Now, that would be something, wouldn't it? Hey, baby, how about asking him next time you talk to him?"

Rosalind swirled in a circle, arms extended. Her flowing purple skirt caught on Mr. Squeals' nose and he snorted.

"Sure, Mom." When hell and pigs freeze over.

Missing or ignoring Todd's sarcasm, Rosalind returned to her game.

Asking Irina to join him, Todd retreated to his office and closed the door. This helped with the noise, but only barely. The drapes had been pulled shut and the dimly lit room smelled of paint and turpentine.

"Everything is okay?" Irina asked. "You seem unhappy. Is it the game? Do I do something wrong?" She took his hands.

"No, everything's fine. It's just that something has come up. I have to run up to Orlando overnight. Business."

"Tonight? Must you?"

"Yes, it's very important."

Irina curled her lip. "Shall I keep you company?"

"No, you can't. I've got an associate. In fact, he's waiting for me downstairs."

"What is this on your slacks?" She ran her fingers along his thigh. "This is blood?"

"What? Yeah, scratched myself on a nail at a home construction site I was touring with a client."

"We must wash wound. And you need clean clothes. You are wet. Are you not freezing?"

"Actually, yes. But I don't have time to shower. I'll change clothes then I've got to go."

"Not before I clean wound. Come." She opened the office door and led him to their en suite bathroom. "Take off these pants." She rummaged under the sink and came up with a first aid kit. She cleaned the wound using alcohol and a cotton swab and then applied a bandage.

Todd kept looking at his watch. It had been fifteen minutes already. Had Ron driven off?

Did he care?

Todd threw open his closet and selected a pair of jeans and a chambray shirt. He had a denim jacket and a pair of trainers in the entry closet. He put these on.

"I'm leaving, Mom!" he called.

"What?"

Mr. Squeals leapt off the sofa, popped his leash in his mouth using his tongue, and looked up at Todd with hope in his beady little eyes.

"No, Porky, we are not going for a walk."

Mr. Squeals frowned a piggy frown, spat out the leash and retreated.

"One minute," Irina said, as Todd opened the front door. She returned in less than a minute with a paper bag holding several bagels and a bottle of water.

"For the trip." She thrust them in his hands.

"Thanks. You going to be okay?"

"Yes. I will see you in the morning?"

"Absolutely. Promise. And if George Strange calls, you don't know where I am."

41

Irina kissed Todd goodnight and picked up the three damp paintbrushes resting in an empty jelly jar she'd set at the edge of the kitchen sink. The new Sub-Zero fridge Todd's mom had charged to his credit card in his absence shined like a silver jewel. She'd had the old one hauled away. Rosalind figured this was far better and far less trouble than trying to clean all the goop out of the old one.

Irina had rinsed the camelhair brushes out earlier, along with an assortment of palette knives. All provided by De Grote via Nico.

With Todd being gone overnight and their bed big and empty, perhaps she would work on the Magritte.

"I'll be in the studio," Irina told Mrs. Jones.

"Okay." Rosalind banged her fist against the side of the pinball machine. "Damn machine." A steel ball clattered to the bottom. "What's the big secret, Irina? What are you painting? Is it a surprise for me? My birthday present?"

"Maybe," Irina told her with a wink.

And that gave her an idea.

Two, actually.

She had several extra canvasses, including some modern canvasses she had purchased locally to practice on. They had brought back a limited number of vintage canvases for the actual paintings.

Irina chose a two-foot by three-foot canvas and began sketching out her idea. Todd's mother would be so surprised. Todd, too!

42

Christie couldn't believe her good luck. She hadn't had to choose at all. The guy in the van followed the guy in the Audi to a condominium near the port. The Ronald's Roofing man sat there now near the porte-cochère with the engine idling.

Pulling up a browser on her smartphone, she googled the firm. They didn't have a website or even an address that she could find.

However, googling the Ronald's Roofing name, a bunch of complaints popped up from irate customers saying how Ronald Patton—so that was his name—had conned them. They all sang the same tune: Ronald Patton was nothing more than a cheap con artist, a hustler, a fake, a fraud. "Beware!" they proclaimed.

Had Ron Patton murdered before? She googled some more but found no results to indicate a murder conviction, not that that was conclusive one way or the other.

"Wow," Christie said aloud. "I can hardly believe George hired such a flake. What was he thinking?" Then she giggled. Because, really, it was funny and George did deserve it.

As for Miro, yeah, he was dead and that was too bad but, really, he'd always sort of icked her out. The dude was creepy and always spying on her for George. He'd gotten her in hot water with George on more than one occasion. At least, his spying and tattling days were now over.

As for his killers, what were they up to? The guy driving the Audi had disappeared into the two-story private garage. Parking at the far end of the visitor parking lot, she had ventured inside the structure on foot and discovered the Audi parked and empty.

Who was he?

Using her smartphone, she took a photo of the Audi's Florida license plate. Phone in hand, she strolled along the side of the tower and through the lobby entrance into a soaring marble-floored space with gold-toned furnishings and a stone lion head on the wall from which water burbled, and gurgled into a stone fountain bowl.

Christie smiled at her target. The fellow in a crisp white short-sleeve shirt and blue tie seated at a small modern desk between the main doors and the elevators.

"Hello, I'm afraid I have a confession," Christie smiled and leaned into his personal space. The guy was middle-aged and average looking. He looked lonely and bored too. This was going to be a piece of cake. She left her sunglasses in the car. Now, she tossed off her ballcap and shook out her long hair.

"A confession?" The doorman blinked as if he might be dreaming.

"Yes," Christie purred. "I'm afraid that, when I was backing up in the garage, I put a small ding in this car." She held up the smartphone shot of the Audi's rear end.

"Hmm." The doorman lifted a pair of reading glasses from his shirt pocket, pressed them to his face, and took a look, mostly at her, she noticed.

"I feel terrible. If you could tell me who the car

belongs to, I'd love to apologize. And offer to pay for any repairs, of course."

The doorman stood, inhaling the scent of Christie's perfume. "I wouldn't worry, if I was you." He tapped her phone screen. "Must be a real small dent. You can hardly see anything." In fact, he didn't see anything at all but wanted to be nice.

"Oh, it's there, alright. I'd be so grateful if you'd help me." She let her fingers fall on his forearm and saw the goosebumps rise on his flesh. "I don't know how I could possibly sleep tonight until I've made this all better."

The doorman ran his tongue over his upper lip and gulped. "What unit did you say you were in?"

"I'm visiting my aunt. I'm afraid I don't remember her unit number."

"What floor is she on? I can look her up."

"My name is Christie, by the way. Christie Campbell. Like the soup. You didn't tell me your name."

"Call me Jeff."

"Jeff, that's a nice name. Can you help me, Jeff?"

Jeff returned to the desk. "Let me fire up the computer and see what we've got."

A minute later, he smiled up at Christie. "Todd Jones. Here's a phone number for him, plus the unit number." He scribbled the information on a Port Lauderdale Condominium Towers branded scratchpad and handed it to her.

"Thanks, Jeff." Christie stuffed the paper down the front of her shirt, knowing that that was exactly what some sexy seductress would do in a Hollywood movie.

Christie could see that Jeff appreciated the move. She started for the exit.

Jeff jumped up and got the door for her. "Where are

you going? Aren't you heading upstairs?"

"I just remembered one teensy little thing I need to do. But I'll be back. Hope I see you again."

"Me, too," said Jeff.

Hurrying back to the rented Honda, Christie sat waiting. Whatever was going to happen ought to be happening soon.

After all, how long did those two intend to keep Miro's body in the back of that van?

Christie smiled. This wasn't exactly the life she dreamed of, but it wasn't ho-hum now, was it?

43

"It's about time," complained Ron, twisting the key in the ignition as Todd jumped inside the van on the passenger side.

"So what's the big plan, hotshot? We gotta get this over with. I heard on the radio there's a hurricane on its way."

"Relax," said Todd, clipping his seatbelt. "The forecasters have been saying that for days."

"Yeah, but tonight they're saying it's going to hit us and hit us hard. Right here in good old South Florida."

Todd smiled.

"What's so funny about that?"

"It's a good thing we're driving to Orlando then." Fortunately, hurricane impact glass secured his Port Lauderdale condominium. Mom and Irina would be perfectly safe.

"Orlando?

"Yep."

"Hell of a long way to go to dump a corpse." Only recently, the weather predictors figured Hurricane Oscar was going to zig, maybe hit the Florida Keys and then drop its wrath on the Tampa Bay area, scoot up the west coast along the Gulf of Mexico, and tickle Pensacola's toes. Now it looked like it was going to zag and come east.

Ron figured being a weatherperson was maybe even

better than being a fake roofer. A weatherperson simply said a lot of stuff. If it came true, they took the credit. If it turned out to be false, they blamed some dumb computer model.

They never actually did anything or fixed anything.

And they never had to climb any damn ladders.

"Why Orlando? What's wrong with some place closer? If you listen to the news or read the papers, you can see that bad guys are always disposing of their victims around here. We've ocean, canals and swamps. That's what makes South Florida your perfect location."

"Yeah? So if all these bodies are disposed of so great, how come you're reading about them in the news? Means somebody, the cops, must've found them, right?"

"Maybe." That was as far as Ron was going to go towards saying that the realtor could be right. "That doesn't answer the question. Why Orlando?"

"Because that's where I know the perfect place to leave Miro's body."

"And where's that?"

"You ever hear of the Orange Blossom Resort?"

"No. Should I have?"

"Strange told me about it. Seems the place is abandoned and Strange Scrap, Inc. is going to blow it up or tear it down or whatever it is that they do. They're scheduled to do the job ASAP, too."

"And you want to dump Miro there?"

"That's the plan. We'll drive him up there tonight. We can be in Orlando in three hours."

"Less, if we push it."

"Let's not *push it* and get stopped by a state trooper with a corpse in the van, okay, Ron?"

"Yeah, yeah." If that happened, he'd fall apart for

sure.

"Like I was saying, it'll be the middle of the night when we arrive in Orlando. That couldn't be better. Nobody will be around at that hour. We'll find some spot in the middle of the biggest deserted building we can find on the property. It's perfect, really." Todd chuckled. "Let Strange blow Miro up and bury his remains someplace."

"Yeah, what you call your poetic justice." Ron pulled onto Congress Avenue, windshield wipers whacking. "Could work, I suppose."

Todd ran his hands along his denim jeans. "It will work." While he talked, Todd typed on his smartphone. Todd rattled off the Orange Blossom Resort's address. "Put that in your GPS."

"The van doesn't have GPS."

"How did I not know that?" Todd furiously stabbed the address into his smartphone's map app and hit Go. "There, all set."

"Maybe I oughta go home and change clothes, too." Ron looked with envy at Todd's clean, dry clothes.

"Okay, but do you really want to show up at your house with a corpse in the back of your van?"

"Why not? Elaine will never know."

"And if for some crazy reason she decides to look inside your van?"

Ron fumed. The joker was right. That had been known to happen. Sometimes the woman got it into her head to grab something out of the van, like the time she'd left her collapsible umbrella in the glovebox.

Sometimes, although Elaine denied it, Ron was sure she only snooped around in the van to see what he might have been up to that day, what he had eaten for lunch, or to try to find any cash she suspected him of endeavoring to hide from her.

Worse, she could read him like a book. If he went home, she'd take one look at his face and know something was up.

He'd spill his guts. Better if she didn't know what he'd done or what he was doing.

"Fine. But I gotta call her first. I can't not show up. She'll worry."

Despite the roofer's convoluted words, Todd got the gist. "Fine. We'd better gas up, too."

"You're pitching in."

Ron pulled into a service station and parked in front of a gas pump. He hopped out, not wanting to talk in front of the realtor.

"Make it quick," urged Todd. "Every minute counts." He dug out his wallet and handed the roofer a twenty.

"Yeah, yeah." Ron took the money and slammed the door in Todd's face. He thought about what he was going to say for a minute while sticking the nozzle in the gas tank then dialed Elaine.

"Hello, dear," he began when she picked up. "I wanted to let you know the job is going great. In fact, Mr. Strange is so happy that he's invited me to spend the night in his guestroom so I can get an early start in the morning and wrap this thing up."

There was a lot of skepticism—Elaine knew damn well what a poor tradesperson her husband was— screaming, and even a little imploring shooting into his listening ear.

When the noise abated, he said, "I'll be home soon as I can tomorrow." He said good night as quickly as he could. Elaine mumbled something that sounded an awful lot like "good riddance."

Frowning, Ron shoved his phone in his pocket, paid the attendant at the window, and climbed back in the van.

With Hurricane Oscar about to bowl through South Florida, he hoped Elaine remembered to board up the windows at the house and her hair salon.

44

Bending palm trees, nothing more than dark sticks with fuzzy tops in the night, bowed and capered to the storm. The weather wizards claimed the Orlando vicinity to be safely out of the hurricane's path, but that didn't stop the strong and ceaseless wind swirling.

Rain fell only sparsely and would make it easier to drive and easier to work. Yet, this would make it harder to cover their tracks when they were finished, realized Todd.

"This is it," announced Todd. "Pull over."

Ron looked around, not that he could see much in the dark. "Orange Blossom Resort? That's a laugh. I wouldn't be caught dead in this dump."

Todd laughed.

"What?" Ron furrowed his brow.

"Think about it," said Todd. "Wouldn't be caught dead? Miro?" He jerked his thumb towards the rear of the van where Miro had been stretched out for the last three-plus hours. A circumstance Todd found discomfiting. How did hearse drivers handle it?

"Oh yeah." A smile broke through the tense and worried mask Ron had worn on his face the past few hours. "That is funny."

Orange Blossom Trail, officially US Highway 441, had seen better days, at least along this strip. The Orange Blossom Resort's neighbors included crack houses, cut-rate motels, strip joints, vacant lots—vacant if you didn't count the litter, a mix of everything from auto parts, beer cans, liquor bottles, busted grocery carts, rusted out washing machines, dryers, refrigerators and ovens enough to open a flea market appliance store, to discarded furniture—and bargain stores with bars on all the windows.

"No wonder the resort went belly up," remarked Ron.

A big neon sign bearing the resort's name stood pitted at the edge of the road. Vandals had shot out most of the lettering.

"This place gives me the creeps," Ron said. The central building, parallel to the road a couple hundred yards back, rose six-stories. Equally tall wings that extended for hundreds of feet behind flanked the main building. Ron pictured a dirty, muck and rainwater filled swimming pool back there in the middle somewhere.

Which only reminded him of Miro again. Was he going to be hounded by Miro the rest of his life, Ron wondered?

"Look," said Todd, pointing to a dangling vacancy sign. "There's a vacancy."

Ron moved carefully into the huge parking lot. The headlights revealed a sea of cracked and buckling blacktop. Waist-tall weeds pushed through every which way. Black and yellow striped caution tape circled the property. A large Caterpillar bulldozer sat perched atop an open trailer, strapped down by heavy chains.

Ron stopped in front of a wide sign nailed between two wooden posts. They both read it.

Danger. Do Not Enter.

Scheduled For Demolition by Strange Scrap, Inc., Detroit, MI.

"Go around the back," ordered Todd. "Let's get away from the street."

"Right."

The van bounced across the parking lot and into the shadows on the far side. "Why don't I pull up to that building and we roll him out?"

"No. Better stop here," said Todd. "You'll break the caution tape."

"So what?"

"So somebody might notice and wonder why it's broken. Better we leave everything undisturbed. Move up as close as you can get. We'll carry him the rest of the way."

Ron complained but complied. Both men hopped out. Ron yanked open the back doors of the van. He waved his hand in front of his nose. "Is it my imagination or is Miro beginning to smell?"

"That's you," Todd replied. "That's your own fear you're smelling."

Ron had been sweating nonstop since nailing Miro. Not that Todd could blame the guy but he did stink.

Todd grabbed one end of the black underlayment—the end with Miro's feet sticking up—and pulled.

Ron waited for the other end to show up and took hold. "Why do I have to carry this end?"

"What's your problem?" grunted Todd, feeling exposed despite the camouflage the darkness provided and the fact that they were around back of a deserted building.

He was getting that feeling of being watched again.

"It's his head. It feels weird."

"Deal with it."

Moving sideways with the corpse dangling between them, they headed towards the deserted buildings, stumbling and cursing the weight of their load and the uneven asphalt.

They had to set the body down to get him under the fluttering caution tape then hoisted him back up. Ron insisted on taking the feet this time.

Huffing and puffing, they entered a dark breezeway between two dilapidated buildings and stopped.

"Let's put him down here and take a look around," whispered Todd. "Keep your eyes open. We need to find some place where the body won't be discovered if a worker decides to take a last look around before they blow this place to the ground."

Ron nodded and let go.

Thunk.

Todd winced. "Did you have to drop him?"

"What's he gonna care?" Ron wiped the sweat from his brow.

Todd pulled out his smartphone and turned on his flashlight app. Ron followed suit.

"This is so spooky," Ron said, his hand shaking as he aimed his phone light this way and that.

"Relax, Scooby. There's nobody here but us."

45

Spools of warning tape strung all around, along with Strange Scrap, Inc. signs placed every 50 feet or so, greeted Christie as she rumbled slowly into the deserted parking lot with the headlights off.

"Well, well. Isn't this interesting," Christie mumbled, hands tightly gripping the steering wheel as the car bounced beneath her, reminding her of the bouncing pony ride at her niece's sixth birthday party.

The van turned into the shadows and disappeared from sight. She followed at a distance. If they saw her, they'd probably speed off.

From the far corner of the weedy parking lot, half-hidden by some old portable storage units rusting and buckling under the stress of Florida's weather, Christie stopped and watched from the comfort of the Honda.

Christie turned off the car's motor. She could have been a spy or a detective. Following these two had been easy. So many people were heading north, trying to avoid the impending hurricane, she supposed, that they never even noticed her practically on their tail.

Not that she imagined they would even suspect that somebody might be following them. Why should they? And the truth was she wasn't sure why she was following them.

She simply couldn't stop herself. She had this vague sense of opportunity. She just hadn't pinpointed what that opportunity was going to be yet. But she could smell it. It was out there.

And it wasn't ho-hum.

It was shazam!

George called twice while Christie followed the men to Orlando. She hadn't bothered to answer. She ignored her phone as it sang its tune once more.

"Screw you, George," she said, glancing at the phone, seeing his number and shoving it back inside her Hermes purse. A gift from George. "Better yet, how about I *don't* screw you?" She giggled.

Christie keenly watched as Ron Patton and Todd Jones moved again, backing their van close to one of the empty buildings. The men hopped out and removed Miro's bundled up corpse.

The pair disappeared from sight. Where were they going? What were they going to do next?

There was only one way to find out.

Leaving her purse on the car seat, she cautiously opened the car door and gently shut it behind her. With the agility of the dancer that she was—she'd studied ballet and modern dance in school—she ran across the crumbling parking lot without breaking a sweat or becoming short of breath.

Being a part-time spokesmodel and on-call girlfriend and living in a fancy hotel with a world-class fitness center, Christie kept herself in tiptop shape.

Christie heard lots of grunting and scraping noises coming from somewhere. This evoked images of the Seven Dwarfs toiling deep in some mine. The precise location of the racket was hard to pinpoint, with sound bouncing all around.

She tiptoed, mindful of the debris scattered on the

walkways. This resort really was a falling down dump. Perfect fodder for George.

Broken glass crunched underfoot. She winced and waited but no one came to see what had caused the disturbance. No one had heard.

She moved again. Weaving in and out of musty, decaying rooms, Christie followed the telling clanking and banging of her prey. Some minutes later, she noticed vague lights emanating from the central building.

Her heart jumped.

Tightly gripping the edge of a crumbling wall, ready to run if she needed to, Christie peeked around the corner.

Ron Patton and Todd Jones lurked inside.

Glowing smartphones lit the scene. The two men moved as if on a dimly lit stage. And Miro's shrouded corpse sat centerstage on a patch of filthy, litter-strewn and mold-eaten carpet.

Ron and Todd dragged sheetrock and timber across the floor.

Christie clenched her jaw, not daring to breathe or move.

Todd said something though she couldn't make out the words. A moment later, both men lifted Miro's shrouded corpse, lowering him into the ground.

They proceeded to cover the corpse with everything they could lay their hands on, lumber, busted furniture, sheetrock, a broken chandelier and more, kicking years of dust into the air of the enclosed space as they worked.

Christie's cough echoed eerily around the deserted rooms like a vocal ghost.

"You hear something?" said Ron.

Todd paused. "Nope. Let's wrap this up." He tossed a pine board onto the pile—Miro's tomb.

"Thought I heard something."

"Rats, probably."

The thought of rats scurrying around his feet was enough to get Ron moving.

Christie choked back a second cough. She melted into the shadows as the two men wrapped up their task, wound their way back to the van and climbed inside.

Christie squeezed through a hole in the bathroom wall of a long-abandoned hotel room. She crept up to the front window with its view of the parking lot. Soft, warm rain fell. An owl hooted in the woods skirting one side of the parking lot.

The corrosion of the wall-mount air-conditioning unit tucked beneath the window was so catastrophic that the face of it crumbled as her knee brushed against it.

Christie peered out the shattered window at the men in the van.

A minute later, they rolled away. Mission accomplished.

Christie let them go. She wasn't going to follow them now. She had seen enough.

She smiled, returned to the Honda and made a telephone call.

Prince Charming answered on the second ring. He had a real name, a civilian name, Peter something... Peter Albert, that was it.

Christie preferred to call him Prince Charming. So much sexier, so much more romantic—in a Gothic romance sort of way. A romantic story sort of way. Not a romantic let's-have-sex sort of way.

It wasn't like she had sex with him or anything.

Well, they had had sex. But that was way back in high school. They were younger and more impulsive then. Now they had their futures to think about.

Like she was thinking about hers now.

As for sex, Christie and Prince Charming agreed that, if they were going to have sex, it ought to be with somebody who mattered, somebody who could help their careers.

Peter Albert's grand ambition was to be an actor too. That was how they'd met and grown closer. Christie and Peter had been members of the high school drama club. Both had bit parts in the junior year production of Romeo and Juliet.

Both thought they should have been the stars.

Christie was working mostly as a spokesmodel with the occasional print ad gig thrown in. Peter was Prince Charming. Literally.

Peter got the role of Prince Charming at Disney World in Orlando over two years ago. Not his first choice as a career move, but he loved every minute of it, from the costume he got to wear, to the awe and admiration of the kiddies who came to see him.

But he wanted more. He wanted to star in movies, Broadway, maybe even his own YouTube series.

Christie envied him that and wished she could have portrayed Cinderella. Despite her best efforts to win the part, the mean old casting agent told her she looked more like a witch than a princess.

Life was so unfair.

"Hello, Prince?"

"Christie?" a sleepy voice answered.

"Am I calling too late?"

"No, what's up? Where are you?"

"I'm at an abandoned motel or something called the Orange Blossom Resort out on Orange Blossom Trail."

"You're in Orlando?"

"Uh-huh. And I need my Prince Charming." Christie swatted at a pair of mosquitoes who had decided to join her in the Honda as she climbed in.

"Sure. What do you need?" Peter yawned but sounded far less sleepy now.

"Meet me here as soon as you can." She gave him directions. "I'll explain when you get here."

"Got it. Give me about twenty minutes," Peter said. "I'm down in Kissimmee, remember."

"Wear dark clothes and comfortable shoes. Bring gloves, if you've got them."

"I've got some extra pairs of Prince Charming gloves lying around the apartment. That do?"

"Yes."

Technically, the Prince Charming costume, and all pieces of it, were to remain on Disney property at all time. Peter Albert wasn't much for technicalities. Unbeknownst to his bosses at Disney, he picked up a little extra cash on days off dressing up as Prince Charming for children's birthday parties. More often than not, Cinderella joined him.

"Can't you give me a hint what's going on, Christie?"

All alone in her car for no one to see, Christie smiled. "Let's just say we are going on a quest, my prince. If we succeed, the future will be ours."

46

Ron was relieved to drop Todd Jones off at his condo
—that man rubbed him the wrong way—and get home
to his own bed. He rolled up to the house and left the
van half sticking out in the street because some stupid
palm tree had fallen across the driveway.

Elaine, who has the ears of a bat, stood waiting for
him at the door in her pale blue bathrobe. Hideous pink
roses festooned each patch pocket. Gave him a headache
every time he looked at them.

Of course, Elaine herself sometimes caused the
same headache. By the look of her, this might be one of
those times.

Elaine looked a wreck. Even her hair was a mess and
Elaine's hair was never a mess. Not good for her image
as a hairdresser, she always said. "It's about time. What
kept you so long?"

Elaine had been up all night listening to the storm
do its Big Bad Wolf thing, threatening to blow the house
down around her. Hurricane Oscar had come and gone,
and left a bit of a mess in his wake. That mess included
their house.

"I thought you were going to board up the house?"
complained Ron, on seeing the debris spreading from
the living room to the dining room. Two green
coconuts, now lying side by side under an end table like
a couple of errant bowling balls, had screamed through

the living room window in the night, shattering the glass and Elaine's favorite table lamp, which had fallen just as surely as the head pin in the deadly accurate sights of a PBA pro bowler.

"Timmy is at summer camp," said Elaine, in no mood for Ron's sass. Timmy was the next-door neighbors' sixteen-year-old kid.

"What was I supposed to do? Tell me that. You had the hammer. You had the van. What was I supposed to do?"

"Great, just great." Ron trampled through the wreckage. "This is going to take days to clean up." He flipped the light switch in the kitchen.

"Power's out," Elaine said, a day late and a dollar short.

"I can see that." Ron picked up a fallen kitchen chair and slumped into it. No electricity meant no hot water, and no hot water meant no hot shower. And no hot coffee.

"So what are you doing home anyway?" Elaine wanted to know. "I thought you had to finish the work today? I thought your new best friend George Stratton was putting you up in that fancy mansion of his? Probably had his gourmet home chef prepare you breakfast in bed."

"Well, you see—"

"I must've called you a dozen times. You don't answer your phone now?"

"Huh? Oh, battery died." Ron hoped she didn't check. Didn't ask for proof. He'd let all her calls go to voicemail. He'd drain his phone battery before she got her hands on his smartphone and caught him in a lie.

"About the roof, Strange said to forget it on account

of the hurricane."

"Was it bad up there?" asked Elaine. She dumped some instant coffee straight from the jar into a sort of clean mug, added tap water, grabbed a spoon from the utensil drawer, and stirred the result around until it was the color of mud. Mud with flecks of brown. "You want some?"

"No, it wasn't too bad. And I'll pass on the coffee. There must be someplace open that we can get something hot to drink."

"That's funny," Elaine picked up a second chair and joined him at the table.

"What's funny? Wanting something hot to drink?"

"No. I was checking the news on my phone and they say the hurricane damage was worse over in Fort Lauderdale."

"You don't say."

"I do say." Elaine gave her husband that look. That look that all husbands dread.

Ron scraped his chair back. "I'm going to bed. I've gotta have some shut eye."

"Yeah, you do that," said Elaine, eyeing him warily. "Because you don't look like you slept so good at all. Funny, considering you must've been sleeping on a king-sized bed with about a thousand and one thread count satin sheets covering it. Fluffy white pillows filled with goosedown cradling your skull."

Ron paused at the end of the hallway. Was she never going to let this go? He hadn't slept a wink. He'd driven all the way to and from Orlando, not trusting that too-slick-for-his-own-good real estate agent behind the wheel of his van. If anything happened to the van, he'd be out of work. Such as it was. "Noise of the hurricane kept waking me up."

"I'll bet it did," mumbled Elaine. Her radar told her that something was up. What it was, she simply couldn't figure out.

But she would.

Elaine took a sip of cold coffee, spitting out the bits that hadn't dissolved.

Ron would sleep and she would clean. Wasn't that the way it always seemed to go?

Well, this time she was going to clean, all right, but she sure as hell wasn't going to be quiet about it. In fact, if they'd had any electricity, she'd have cranked up the vacuum cleaner and run it around in the bedroom for kicks.

Throwing open the hall closet to grab the broom and dustpan, Elaine heard a phone ringing. She recognized that ring. It was Ron's. How could she not? He'd programmed in his favorite song, Dire Straits' Money For Nothing.

"Dead battery, my ass," Elaine cussed. She dropped the wooden broom, taking joy in hearing it clatter to the floor.

Elaine marched out to the van to take a look around. That idiot husband of hers had been up to something.

Maybe the van held some clues.

47

Todd stepped from the quiet, neat and uncluttered, utterly elegant corridor outside the door leading to his condo and inside to a nightmare.

His home, his refuge, his once upon a time bachelor pad, stood a wreck. A cacophonous wreck.

The blue plastic kiddie wading pool filled with pine shavings that should have been hidden away in his mother's room now occupied the front foyer. Mr. Squeals used the pool as his litterbox.

Todd's foot landed in moist pine shavings. "Shit!"

Literally.

"What the hell is this doing here?" he shouted. He had to shout because of the racket. The racket consisted of a blend of bleating potbellied pig, smoker's cough hacking mother, and the sounds of artillery fire coming from the surround sound stereo system connected to the big screen TV on which The Dirty Dozen was airing.

Oddly enough, Todd noticed—peeling off both socks and tossing them directly into the trash can in the kitchen because he was never, ever going to wear those socks again no matter how clean his mom got them in the wash—the Rolling Stones were nowhere in sight. The Rolling Stones were nowhere in sound.

If there was something good to come home to, that was it. The pinball machine was gone.

However.

"What the hell is the patio furniture doing in my living room?" A wobbly stack of outdoor chairs and tables spilled across whatever open space there had once been. Pools of water crept from the sliding doors to the sofa.

Rosalind Jones used one of the loungers as an extended footstool. Mr. Squeals stretched out on another, watching the movie. Apparently a Lee Marvin fan.

"Mom." No reaction. "Mom!" Still nothing. Todd blocked the television.

"Oh, hi, baby. Have a nice trip?" Blissfully, she dialed down the volume without him asking.

"I had a great trip. But what the hell have you been doing since I left?"

"Watching TV mostly. Did some Pilates. Mr. Litchfield said to say hi."

Todd grunted. Litchfield lived up one floor and over. That gave him a great view of Todd's patio. That meant that every time his mother sunbathed topless on the deck or did her Pilates-in-the-raw routine—which he'd begged her a thousand times not to—Litchfield took in the sights.

Todd sank onto the sofa to the left of his mother. Wearing the same outfit she'd had last night. "Where's Irina?"

"Painting. That girl's been locked in that office of yours painting up a storm. You ought to do something nice for her."

"I know."

"You want some?" she patted his thigh and held out her cigarette.

"No, Mom." He twisted his neck around. "Why is the

outdoor furniture inside?"

"Had that storm last night. Hurricane Whatchamacallit."

"Oscar."

"Whatever. That furniture of yours started bouncing around so Irina and me figured we'd best bring it inside. That a problem?"

"No, Mom. Thanks." He looked around. "Any coffee?"

"Half a pot in the kitchen. Bring me a refill?"

"Sure." Todd moved to the kitchen, poured himself a cup of coffee and refilled his mom's. Returning to the sofa, he asked, "Is there a reason that porker's potty is next to the front door?"

Rosalind looked towards the door. "We had to move it somewhere, didn't we?"

"Why?"

"Because Irina and me, we knew how much the pinball machine was bothering you."

He sipped. The coffee was hot and sweet. "And the pinball machine is where?" At the bottom of the Intracoastal, hopefully.

"My room. Kinda tight in there so Mr. Squeal's potty had to go. Smart putting it near the door, don't you think?"

Todd sat mutely, staring at the TV as some soldier got himself blown up trying to take down a rooftop antenna. One more reason to stay off roofs.

"Took quite some doing. We had to get Carlos to help us, but we—"

Todd settled his mug on the lounger and hung his head. He said something he never thought he'd hear himself say. "Bring it back."

48

George woke up, ran his fingers through his thin beard. Grunting, he rolled off the bed and squeezed his pudgy feet into a pair of fleece-lined slippers.

"Get off my robe, damn dog." George yanked at the robe on the floor that Cuddles was using for a blanket.

The dog yelped, moved grudgingly, and disappeared with a clack-clack-clack of his nails across the stone floor. Off to find his mommy, Imelda, no doubt.

George reached for the custom-made draperies, feeling the warmth of the sun through the heavy fabric, grateful and amazed that he had survived his first hurricane unscathed. He was lucky that way. He'd always been lucky.

George slowly peeled back the purple drapes. "What the hell!"

His pristine patio and lawn were an explosion of pink. As far as the eye could see. Pink.

"My roof!" Clenching and unclenching his jaw and both fists, George Strange strutted to the bureau and whipped out his gun and holster. He hastily belted it around his waist over his robe and went out to have a word with the bastards who had done this to him.

"Where are Patton and Jones?" George barked the question at Imelda and Esme, seated together in the breakfast nook. Neither appeared disconcerted or upset even though the landscape outdoors was an alien landscape consisting of every possible shape and size of pink clay shards. Like snowflakes, no two were alike. Cuddles' head poked over the table, eyeing two toasted multigrain English muffins.

"What's wrong, Georgie?" Imelda paused, in the middle of buttering half a muffin.

"What's wrong?" George gestured wildly. "You can't see what's wrong?"

Imelda deigned to raise her brow but not too much. That could lead to premature wrinkles.

"My roof is wrong!" George bellowed.

Cuddles cowered under the table.

"Where's Bogs? Where's Miro?"

"I haven't seen them. Have you, Esme?"

"Sorry, sir. No." The dark circles under Esme's eyes contrasted starkly with her conservative white housedress.

George waved his hand at the two useless women. What he needed was Bogs and Miro.

And the heads of those two clowns whom he'd ordered to make his roof right thrust on poles he'd plant on his front lawn to warn off any future salesmen who dared step foot on his property.

Throwing open the front door, eyes angling towards the roof, he didn't see the tubby bellied man with the receding hairline who was in the process of pasting on a smile and knocking.

"Oof!" The tubby-bellied gent tumbled off the porch, slipped into a rosebush and cursed.

"What are you doing here?" George roared, one hand on his Colt. Dying to pull the trigger on somebody.

The man dragged himself up, plucking the mulch from his trousers. There was nothing much he could do about the thorns in his thigh, although he did try, yanking madly at them and wincing in pain.

He reached into the coat pocket of his off-the-rack brown suit. Because, despite the heat and humidity, he had shown up at the doorstep fully suited, like a knight in armor ready to do battle. Only his was a battle of another sort.

"Larry Goldstein," the tubby gentleman stated, finally getting around to introducing himself and trying not to look too nervous as George aimed some wicked looking weapon in his now pale face. "My card." He extended the hand holding the business card but George chose to ignore it.

"What do you want, Larry Goldstein?" George planted his feet shoulder width apart. The damn Colt had a hell of a recoil and some instructor or another had told him once that keeping his feet planted this way would help compensate, keep him from flying backwards and looking stupid. "And why shouldn't I shoot you?"

Larry Goldstein gulped. "Well, sir, I couldn't help noticing your roof." He gulped again, like the frog that swallowed the fly. Was Florida running out of breathable oxygen? "I mean, kinda hard not to notice your roof, what with it mostly lying on the ground. Sir," he hastened to add.

George narrowed his eyes at Larry Goldstein and tightened his finger around the trigger. "You trying to be funny, mister?"

"No, sir. If you'll just look at the card." He dared to extend his hand a second time. "If you'll only let me explain."

Larry Goldstein waved his business card in front of

George's face and couldn't help noticing how the barrel of the gun seemed to follow, like a moving target. He was careful to keep the card away from his head and heart.

"You have thirty seconds to explain why Mr. Colt here shouldn't give you a third eye." George was more than a little grumpy. "I don't mind telling you, since I'm going to kill you anyway, I had too much to drink last night, mister."

"Hangover? Ah, happens to us all, sir. In fact, I know a little cure for that, you see—"

"Shut the hell up. I'm not finished. Being loaded led to me letting myself get railroaded by Imelda, that's my wife, into paying fifty grand for some crummy painting that wasn't worth a tenth that price, all in the name of some charity I never heard of."

"That's—"

"Then I wake up this morning and discover that some damn hurricane has blown my brand new roof off!" George paused for a much-needed breath. "Any last words, mister?"

Cowering, Larry Goldstein held out his business card. One last valiant effort. "Larry Goldstein, Independent Insurance Adjuster, fully licensed, accredited, and bonded?" He steeled himself for whatever would come next. Was his life insurance policy paid up?

George's gun hand wavered. He really wanted to shoot somebody. On the other hand, he smelled money. He liked money.

George ran his eyes across the business card. "Stop shaking. I'm trying to read!"

"Sorry," Larry Goldstein gulped a third time, this

time like he was swallowing the frog that swallowed the fly. He used his left hand to keep his right hand steady.

"What's all those initials after your name?"

"Those are my accreditations, sir. Mister...?"

"Strange."

"All the initials?"

"No, my name. George Strange."

"Right, hello, Mister Strange." Larry Goldstein visibly relaxed. His sphincter relaxed too, not that George could see that.

"You gonna help me get a new roof, Goldstein?" George lowered the Colt.

"Are you kidding? This one is a slam-dunk. Look at this place!"

"I am looking at this place and I do not like what I'm seeing."

"Trust me, George. Is it okay if I call you George? With my assistance, we'll file a claim that will not only cover the cost of a new roof, any structural damages, plus cleanup of all this wreckage, but we just might finagle enough extra out of your insurance company for you to buy yourself a new boat! Ha-ha."

George holstered the revolver. "Goldstein, I like the way you think."

"Thank you, George."

"Are you trying to tell me you just happened to be in the neighborhood?" George hadn't quite let go of all his suspicions.

"No, sir. I came out first thing this morning. Once it was safe. I live in the area. Well, not this area. A little too rich for my blood. Hee-hee. Out in the suburbs. Wilton Manors, actually."

Larry Goldstein tugged at his tie because the knot

had seemed to be getting inexplicably tighter by the minute ever since he'd arrived. "After a hurricane like this, any storm really, I go looking to see who I can help out."

"Well, isn't that neighborly of you."

"I feel it's my duty. We have to help one another, don't we?"

"Absolutely, so tell me again—exactly how you are going to help me?"

49

Dressed in baggy jeans, a short-sleeve denim shirt and hiking boots, Bogs knocked on Miro's door. "Miro? You awake, kid?"

No reply.

Bogs turned the knob and stepped inside. His nephew wasn't in his room. In fact, Miro hadn't slept in his bed last night. The bed was undisturbed and Esme never made up the beds before ten.

Bogs poked his head in the en suite bathroom just in case.

Nada.

"Probably out scouring the property," grumbled Bogs, who'd had little sleep what with entertaining Esme and being entertained in a whole other way by the fast-moving hurricane that swept over them in the middle of the night.

Fortunately, the estate had its own generator, so they hadn't lost power.

"Probably looking for injured animals to put out of their misery. Or uninjured animals to inflict some injury on," continued Bogs, who enjoyed talking to himself more than he enjoyed talking to other people. He loved his nephew but the kid was slightly skewed to the demented side.

Bogs exited through the side door into the garage. Miro's Chevy Suburban sat in its usual spot near the wall. He pushed the button next to the door to raise one of the overhead metal doors.

"What a lousy mess," he remarked, as the door lifted to reveal the carnage the storm had left behind.

Wreckage smeared the driveway. Roof tiles mostly. Plus, branches, leaves and other debris that the hurricane had dragged up the coast with it and left behind in its wake like so much no longer needed baggage. Two queen palms had fallen across each other near the mailbox—a pair of star-crossed lovers in a dying embrace.

He saw no sign of the roofer or the realtor. Or their vehicles for that matter. Not surprising, considering.

A black Camry sat out on the street. He didn't recognize it. Moving around the side of the house, he found half the patio furniture in the pool. The other half rested in various parts of the yard.

Surprisingly, the fishing boat bobbing on its moorings, seemed to have fared well. Boarding the boat, Bogs called out, "Miro? You out here, kid?" The stateroom was empty, the Hatteras deserted.

Standing at the water's edge, Bogs scanned the river. The only vessel in sight belonged to the Coast Guard. One or two persons were visible in their backyards, all busy picking up garbage or simply gawking at the damage the hurricane had inflicted on their luxury properties.

Then Bogs noticed the roof and reality sunk in. He'd seen the busted tiles on the lawn, sure, but hadn't until this moment realized what it meant. He'd figured a few might've blown loose or they'd come from the pile stacked at the end of the garage.

What he hadn't figured was this.

"Holy shit." Where there had been only yesterday pristine pink tiles there was nothing but bare plywood. "Big George is gonna have a cow."

More rubbish, mostly vegetation, clogged the swimming pool drains. Bogs grabbed the pole with the leaf net attachment and pulled some off the two drains, emptied the baskets of the weirs as well. He'd leave it to the pool tech to fish the furniture out.

Something red at the bottom of the pool near the deep end caught his eye. Using the leaf net, he scooped it up and dumped it out. A Swiss Army knife.

Calloused fingers fondled the wet red-handled knife. It looked like the one he'd given his nephew on his thirteenth birthday. The Huntsman's model.

What the hell was it doing at the bottom of the swimming pool?

Lifting a ladder that Todd and Ron had forgotten on the grass beside the garage, Bogs leaned it up against the roof and climbed.

Walking slowly to the highest peak, he cupped a hand over his eyes to block out the morning sun and surveyed the scene. The world above was all blue skies, white puffy clouds and yellow sunshine. The world at his feet was nothing but mayhem's leftovers. "Miro! Miro!"

Clambering down the ladder, Bogs went looking for Big George. He found his boss standing behind his desk in his office dressed in his bathrobe and carrying his Colt .45. Some harmless-looking guy in a brown suit sat across from him.

"Sorry to intrude. Got a minute, Big George?"

"What is it, Bogs?"

"I'm looking for my nephew. Have you seen him this

morning?"

"No, can't say that I have." Gathering up the bottom of his robe, George sat.

"Okay, I'll let you get back to what you were doing." Bogs turned to go.

"Wait. Bogs."

"Yes?" Bogs turned at the door. "What happened to Patton and Jones yesterday?" Turning to Larry Goldstein, George explained, "Patton's company, Ronald's Roofing, is the one I hired to replace my roof. Jones sold me this house."

"It's a great house, George," Larry Goldstein was quick to say.

"Yeah, yeah. Still, they were supposed to fix my roof. Leaked like a damn PT boat riddled with machine gun fire *after* he'd replaced it!"

"Sorry to hear that," Larry commiserated. "I know some excellent roofers. Don't you worry, sir. Forget about them. Let me handle this. Your next roof is going to be hurricane proof. Guaranteed for life."

"It had better be." George fondled the staghorn grip of his revolver. "Because you're guaranteeing it with *your* life."

Larry Goldstein smiled, looked to the creature named Bogs to confirm that Mr. Strange was making a joke. No such confirmation was forthcoming. He squirmed.

"About Miro," said Bogs.

"What about him?" George snapped, anxious to get on with the business at hand.

"I can't find him anywhere on the property and the Suburban's in the garage."

"Hell, Bogs, he's your nephew. You deal with him.

I'm kinda busy here."

"Yes, Big George." He couldn't tell Big George how he'd last seen Miro last night up on the roof with Patton and Jones. How would that make him look? Very bad. Big George had left him in charge of Patton and Jones, and making sure that they did the roof right. He'd pawned the task off on his nephew.

Now the roof was shattered and smeared as far as the horizon. Was George going to let him forget that he'd failed? What price would he pay for his failure?

More importantly, where was Miro?

"Anything else?" George demanded of Bogs.

"No, Big George."

"Fine. Tell Esme to bring me and Mister Goldstein some coffee. How do you like your coffee, Goldstein?"

50

Night fell. Rain poured. Power was spotty. The house was hot as hell. Elaine barely spoke to him. Morning came. Wearing yesterday's clothes, Ron stepped outside and walked up and down the sidewalk, commiserating with his neighbors.

The rumor spreading through the neighborhood grapevine claimed there was a Burger King open out on US 441.

That meant hot food and hot coffee. Ron volunteered to go check it out. Elaine volunteered to stay home and not care.

Ron went to his van. Since returning from his Orlando adventure, it remained parked halfway in the street with its butt sticking out because he hadn't gotten around to removing the palm tree lying in his driveway and the tree hadn't removed itself, nor had any Good Samaritan neighbor with a chainsaw done it for him.

Lazy bunch of bums.

Ron bounced his keys in his hand then squeezed the door handle and pulled. The door creaked open. Ron hopped inside and hunted for the key to the ignition.

His peripheral vision flashed him warning signals. Ron twisted his eyes to the right.

"What the hell?!"

A nasty black shotgun, butt down on the footwell,

barrel aiming upward, leaned against the passenger seat. From barrel to butt, a distinctive green camo sling hung loosely.

Miro's.

Ron's body turned into an ice sculpture and his heart threatened to burst. He glanced out the windows. Saw nothing out of the ordinary. Across the street, Old Man Willard was mowing his lawn with a push mower in his skivvies. But he always did that. Everybody was used to that.

Ron found a breath and took it. Miro's shotgun. Last seen when Jones stuffed it in with the corpse.

Before disposing of the body for the final time at the abandoned Orange Blossom Resort, Jones had removed Miro's personal effects, wallet, et cetera, and promised to dispose of them separately.

He'd watched Jones shove the shotgun between Miro's legs. Together, they'd bundled the corpse up. Covered it with a ton of trash.

Ron rubbed his eyes. Lack of sleep?

Open eyes.

No, the shotgun was still here with him inside his van. For all the world to see. How had the shotgun gotten here? Who had placed it in his van?

More importantly, why?

Ron's face fell into his hands, smothering his words. "This can't be good."

A rap on the driver's side window sent his head into the ceiling. "Shit!" Falling to earth, he rubbed the top of his head and swung around. "Bogs!"

With superhuman powers he never knew he possessed—the speed of Flash and the instincts of Spider Man—Ron's right arm shot out, knocking the shotgun towards the floorboards. Meanwhile, his left hand jerked to the left, yanking the door handle and throwing the door open.

Bogs jumped back.

All in the same move, Ron bounded from the van, slammed the door shut, and bent to help Bogs up from the pavement.

"Sorry about that, Ron apologized quickly.

"What's wrong with you?" Bogs dusted off his jeans. "You act like your van's on fire."

"Van?" Ron glanced towards the van and back again. "Yeah. Thought I smelled smoke. My mistake. Somebody must have been smoking inside." Ron stepped away from the van, forcing Bogs to follow.

Had Bogs seen the shotgun? Had he recognized it?

Was he, Ron, about to get his head blown off? With Old Man Willard and the rest of his crummy neighbors as witnesses?

"Speaking of people," Bogs folded his thick arms across his thick chest. "I'm looking for Miro." His nephew hadn't shown up at all yesterday and there was still no sign of him this morning.

"Miro?" Ron couldn't keep the nerves from reaching his voice.

"Yeah. He's not answering his cellphone, hasn't slept in his bed the last two nights. In fact," Bogs said, with what might have been suspicion, "I haven't seen hide nor hair of him since the night the three of you were up on Big George's roof."

"Oh, yeah." Ron wiped the sweat from his brow with his arm. "Hell of a night that was. How did the roof hold up?"

"It didn't."

"What?" Ron's body, which had only slightly begun to thaw in the Florida heat, began to refreeze.

"It's lying all over the lawn."

"It is?"

"Every bit of it."

"Oh." Ron gulped. Swallowed his tongue, got it untangled and said, "Is Mister Strange mad?"

Bogs' big fat smile said it all.

"Shit."

"Yeah. So tell me what happened on that roof."

"Happened?"

"Yeah. Did Miro say anything? Like where he was going afterward?"

"No, not that I can recall." Ron saw a way out and said, "He and that realtor, Todd Jones, they talked more than I did. I mean, I was busy trying to get that roof straightened out. Jones mostly talked while I was swinging a hammer. Probably his fault the roof came crashing down. No help at all."

"Sure. So you don't know where I can find my nephew?"

"Has he got a girlfriend? Maybe they're shacked up somewhere."

"Not local."

"Oh. Sorry." Ron shook his head slowly side to side. "Wish I could help."

"Sure you do." Disappointed, Bogs returned to his F-150 and climbed aboard. "Say hi to Elaine for me," he said through the open window before driving off.

Ron promised he would.

Grabbing a few breaths, he steadied himself and reentered his van. The shotgun tilted to the side, barrel pressed against the opposite door. He noticed something white sticking an inch out of the top of barrel. A scrap of paper rolled into a cylinder.

"What the—" Trembling fingers slowly lifted the paper from the barrel of the shotgun. He read.

I KNOW WHAT U DID

51

Ron raced to Port Lauderdale only to be told by some woman—who looked an awful lot like Stevie Nicks, that singer from Fleetwood Mac—and her pet pig, that Todd was in his office downtown.

She gave him the address and he sped off.

Ron had plenty of time to think. The first thing he thought was that Todd Jones was setting him up to take the fall for Miro's death—he refused to label it a murder. It was an accident. Accidents happen. Isn't that what they say?

Besides himself, only Todd Jones knew what happened to Miro. Only Todd Jones knew where the body was buried.

Only Todd Jones could be responsible for this.

The question remained—and he had no answer—what was the guy up to?

Well, there was one sure way to find out. And if he had to use Miro's shotgun to get the answer, then he damn well would use it.

The second thing Ron was thinking about was getting out of the roofing biz. Despite the hurricane and subsequent low hanging fruit—what with all the subsequent roof damage—he was beginning to feel that it was time to make a change. Maybe get into the flooring biz. People were always needing new hardwoods, carpets or luxury vinyl plank—LVP was really hot right now. And with the hurricane and constant Florida storms and turnover in homeowners, he couldn't lose. He could probably write a half-dozen quotes a day. He'd clean up.

And keep his feet on the ground.

After he sorted out Mr. Real Estate Man.

52

Behind the sleek European, custom-built curved teak desk with carbon fiber trim and raised tempered glass top, Todd listened as Mr. Brezhinski talked over the phone.

His turn to speak, Todd said, "Yes, sir. The project is coming along very nicely. I think you will be pleased with the results."

"Wonderful," said Brezhinski. "The question remains, however, will Constantine be pleased?"

"I'm sure of it." From what Todd had seen of Irina's work, they had nothing to worry about. They may not fool an expert, but they'd fool Alexander Constantine. That was enough.

"Excellent. Constantine is making noises. Nasty noises. We've already pushed him past the agreed upon date."

"I realize that, sir."

"What you may not realize is that he's now applied for building permits for four hideous houses to be built on my land." Brezhinski Senior refused to think of the Intracoastal properties as anything but his land. "The sooner we can come to terms, the better. Would another week be too much to hope?"

Todd frowned, stared at his initials on the wall behind his desk. He'd paid a local artist six hundred bucks a letter for the gold-leafed TJ, a symbol of his success. Even at those times when success was nowhere to be seen.

"I'll see what I can do."

"Thank you. I'm anxious to add the Magritte to my collection. If there is anything else you require, do not hesitate to ask me." Brezhinski severed the connection.

"Mister Jones?" The office receptionist, a fortyish divorcee trying to make ends meet while raising two boys, hovered at the edge of his desk.

"Yes?

"Someone left this for you, Mr. Jones." Priscilla's fingers held a plain white, letter-sized envelope. She extended her hand. "Said it was important. Urgent."

"Thank you." Todd took the envelope. He turned it over. Blank on both sides. "Who did you say gave this to you?"

"Well, I didn't say. That is, he didn't say."

Todd frowned. "What did he look like?"

"To tell you the truth, he looked like Prince Charming." Priscilla retreated to her reception desk.

"Did he say what this was in regard to?" Todd called from across the room.

"No, he only wanted me to promise to give it to you the minute you got to the office. Which I did, except you were on the phone when you got to the office, so I'm giving it to you now." Priscilla turned to answer an incoming call.

Todd picked up the carved Brazilian cherry wood letter opener shaped like a snake with fangs, a gift from a client. He sliced open the envelope.

WILL CALL U AT 1

Todd checked his watch. Less than half an hour from now.

53

Todd Jones Realty occupied prime office space on Las Olas Boulevard in downtown Fort Lauderdale. Between the posh condo and the classy office location, Ron could see that the real estate business was good to Jones.

Ron waited impatiently for a red and yellow tour trolley to get out of the way, then pulled up to the curb in a No Parking Zone.

After wrapping Miro's shotgun in a tatty old tarp one of Juan's gang had left behind at the job site, Ron burst into Todd's office.

"Good afternoon, sir. Welcome to Todd Jones Realty. How can I help you?" Though the guy walking in off the street didn't look like the type who could afford one of their properties, Todd had taught Priscilla not to judge a potential client by his or her clothing. This fellow's clothes looked like he'd been sleeping in them since Spring Break.

"I need to talk to Jones," explained Ron.

"If you'll have a seat. I'm afraid Mr. Jones is engaged at the moment." Moments ago, Priscilla had connected Todd with a seller's agent to talk a deal on a two-bedroom condo. "Would you like to speak with one of our other agents?"

Adam Rector was on floor duty, although nowhere in sight at the moment. "Adam's probably in the breakroom." Priscilla gestured towards a blue leather sofa under the front window. "If you'll have a seat."

"I don't want any Adams."

"You don't?"

"Not even John Quincy. I want Todd Jones."

"I see. Perhaps I can offer you something to drink while you wait?"

Ron was in no mood to cool his heels. "Listen, lady, I can see him right back there yammering on the phone. I'd recognize the back of that fat head anywhere."

Ron waved his hand. The tarp slid to the floor revealing the shotgun he'd been concealing. "Oops."

Priscilla threw her arms in the air. "Take all my money! Please, don't shoot!" She tossed her purple purse in Ron's face.

"Hey!" Ron blinked in pain. His eyes watered up.

"Patton?" shouted Todd, swiveling in his chair. "Call you back." He dropped the phone. "What the hell are you doing? Get over here."

Ron, abashed, watched helplessly as Priscilla flew past him and out the front door with her hands in the air.

"What the hell are you doing bringing a shotgun into my office?"

Priscilla ran across the street, turned the corner and disappeared.

"I'll have you—" Todd gaped at the black shotgun. At the camo gun sling. "Is that?"

"Yeah," snarled Ron, coming to his senses and moving closer. Lowering his voice because a young man in a blue suit who could only be Adam was gawking at him from a doorway in back, he said, "It's you know who's shotgun."

"Everything okay, Todd?" Adam refused to stick

anything further than his neck out the breakroom door.

"Yes, everything's fine, Adam. I've got this. You can go back to whatever you were doing." Which was probably nothing. The kid hadn't sold a single property all month.

Todd climbed to his feet, staring at the weapon in Ron's hands. "What are you doing with it?"

"That's what I'd like to know." Ron slammed the shotgun down on Todd's desk. "So why don't you tell me? You trying to get me in trouble, hotshot? Because if you are..."

Todd threw up his hands. "Hold on, hold on. Sit down." He poked the gun with a finger. "Is it loaded?"

"How the hell would I know?" Ron sat.

Todd went to the reception desk, retrieved the tarp and draped it over the shotgun. Out of sight but not out of mind. Definitely not out of mind.

Todd pulled up his chair. "So, you drove to Orlando and removed Miro's shotgun. Mind telling me why?"

"I did no such thing. I'm figuring that's exactly what you did. Probably hoping the police would find it. Probably hoping Bogs would find it. What? Did you send him to my house this morning hoping he'd see me with the shotgun, put two and two together, and take me apart?"

Todd steepled his fingers. None of this made sense. Ron Patton walks into his office and begins babbling. Drugs maybe? A sheen of glaze and rows of red capillaries scarred the roofer's eyes.

Nonetheless, the cold, hard fact remained that he had the dead man's shotgun lying on his desk.

"Start at the beginning, Ron."

Gripping the sides of his chair, Ron explained. "I

got in my van this morning and there it was. On the passenger side of the cab."

"Damn."

"Yeah." Ron pushed his hands along the side of his face. "The next thing I know, Bogs is rapping on the van."

"What did he want?" This tale was getting worse and worse.

"He's looking for Miro, of course. What the hell else would he want?"

"Okay, okay. Relax," Todd said.

Ron snorted. "Relax! Easy for you to say. Oh, and there was this." He fished around in his pocket a moment and came up with a slip of paper. He tossed it across the desk.

Todd unfurled the slip and read, "I know what u did." He frowned. "Who sent this?"

"You is what I'm thinking."

"Think about it, Ron. Why would I send you a note? I know what you did. I know what *we* did." Fingers drummed the glass desktop. "No, there's something else going on. *Someone* else."

"You mean somebody who knows what we did?" Ron glanced over his shoulder. "Who? What do they want?"

Then the roofer had an inspired thought. "Hey, you don't suppose it could be Miro himself? I mean, maybe he isn't really dead and now he's out to get even, scare us, hurt us, maybe."

Todd rolled his eyes. "Miro is dead," he whispered insistently. "We both know that. Stone cold dead."

"Yeah, I guess so," admitted Ron. "He did seem pretty stiff."

"Exactly." Todd leaned back in his seat. "You must have told someone and now that someone is, I don't know, out to blackmail you."

"Us," corrected Ron. "And I didn't tell a soul."

"Not even your wife?"

"Especially not Elaine." If he told her he'd killed somebody, she'd kill him. "What about you?"

"No one."

"So what do we do now?" Ron wiped his perspiring hands across the tarp.

"I have something to show you that is beginning to make sense. Sort of."

"Oh?"

"This was delivered to me here at the office a short time ago." Todd slid open a desk drawer and showed Ron the blank envelope and the obscure note inside.

"I don't like this. I don't like this at all," Ron crumpled the note in his trembling fingers.

"I don't either," admitted Todd. "But there's no going back now." He glanced at his watch. "Prince Charming should be calling any minute now."

"Prince Charming?"

"That's how my receptionist described the guy who dropped the note off."

Priscilla burst through the front door. "That's him, officer!" She waved an accusing hand in Ron's direction.

54

Ron's head zipped around.

Two Fort Lauderdale Police Department officers and that goofy receptionist stood inside the entrance. Okay, it was only one officer, but he was big enough to occupy the space of any normal two people.

Todd jumped to his feet. "Priscilla, what's going on?"

Todd and Ron's eyes snapped to the rumpled tarp and the secret it held. Both knew better than to let their gazes linger.

"Don't worry, Mister Jones. I brought help. Go ahead, arrest him!" The receptionist shoved the bewildered cop forward.

"Arrest who?" Ron blinked. He knew exactly who. That was the problem. Should he run?

The officer took a few steps. He wasn't smiling. Then again, he hadn't pulled his gun. "Everything okay, here? This woman reported an armed robbery." His voice sounded like it had come from the bottom of a wooden barrel. His thick accent said Jamaica.

Office Bunyan, twelve years on the force, had been enjoying a smoothie at his favorite frozen juice bar on Las Olas Boulevard when Priscilla spotted him in the window and insisted he follow her back to Todd Jones Realty. Only to see two men having what appeared to be a gentlemanly conversation.

"Hold on. No need to arrest anybody, Officer." Todd

approached the FLPD man in blue. "Bunyan, is it?" he said, reading the man's name on his uniform. "My friend here came by to say hi—"

"He threatened me with a shotgun!" blurted Priscilla, cowering behind Officer Bunyan.

"Now, now, Priscilla, calm down," Todd said softly. "Ron brought the shotgun to show me. I asked him to bring it. I'm thinking of taking up hunting," he said to Officer Bunyan. "I know it's a little out of fashion but..." He gestured a what-can-you-do with his shoulders and arms.

"Can I see it?" Officer Bunyan asked.

"Of course." Todd turned to Ron who had remained stubbornly seated. "Show him the shotgun, Ron."

Officer Bunyan stomped across the floor. Ron whipped off the tarp. The officer lifted the shotgun to his shoulder and sighted across the floor.

"Loaded?" asked Officer Bunyan.

"No, sir, Officer. I haven't had a drink all day," Ron said quickly. "Sober as a judge."

Big Blue dipped his eyebrow in Ron's direction.

"He's talking about the shotgun, Ron." Todd said.

"Oh." Ron said sheepishly. He declined further commenting because he had no idea if the shotgun was loaded or not. However, they might soon find out.

"What's going—eeep!" Adam peeked out just long enough to get caught in the barrel's line of fire. He disappeared once more.

"Not bad." Big Blue laid the gun gently atop the tarp. "Might be able to bring down a small deer with her but nothing bigger."

"I'll keep that in mind." Todd dared a hand on the officer's massive shoulder and gently directed him to the door. The smartphone in his pocket picked a stupid time to ring.

"Phone's ringing," said Big Blue, eyes swiveling to Todd's pant pocket.

"Right." Was it Prince Charming? He slapped his pocket, wishing it would stop. "I'd better take it. Thank you so much for stopping by, Officer." He held open the front door. "If you ever are in the market, please come see me. I give all first responders a reduced commission."

Big Blue took his cue and exited.

"Gee, sorry, Mister Jones." Priscilla scooped her purse off the floor and reached for her makeup kit. Her hair was a fright.

Todd waved her off and rushed to answer the call before it went to voicemail. "Hello?" He moved back to his desk. "Yes, this is Todd. Who's this?"

"Who is it?" Ron whispered anxiously. "What do they want?"

"Quiet! No, not you." Todd glared angrily at Ron and mimed for him to zip his lips. "Go ahead. What was that?" Todd pulled a face. "How much?"

"What?" Ron pressed his hands into the desk. "They want money? How much?"

Todd turned his back on the roofer. "Sorry. I don't know. That's a lot of money. One second." To Ron, Todd explained, "They want one hundred thousand dollars. Fifty from me, fifty from you."

"Fifty grand!" Ron shouted. Dialing it down a notch after getting a weird look from Priscilla, he said, "Tell 'em no way." Ron leaned back in his chair, crossing his arms.

"Okay," Todd said to the speaker on the other end of

the line. "You've got a deal."

"Not with me he doesn't," hissed Ron angrily. "I've worked too hard for my money to be cheated out of it by some hustler, some lowdown lousy blackmailer."

Todd gestured towards Priscilla.

Ron frowned.

"Right. Forty-eight hours. We'll be expecting your call." The blackmailer disconnected. Todd dropped his smartphone on the desk.

"You're out of your freaking mind if you think I'm giving anybody fifty thousand dollars. Even if he is Prince Charming!"

"What choice do we have, Ron?" Todd returned to his seat, speaking quietly. "Our blackmailer knows what we've done."

"You sure?"

Todd fingered the barrel of the shotgun. "You have any doubts?"

"No," Ron admitted. "But what the hell! Fifty thousand dollars!"

"Quiet." Todd waited while Ron fought to collect himself. "Listen, I have an idea. I don't relish the thought of parting with fifty grand any more than you do. I think we can handle this."

"So why give in?"

"To buy us some time."

Ron scraped his teeth across his lower lip. Wondering how soon he could get out of here and maybe get to the Bahamas. Away from all this madness. "Time for what?"

"First? We've got to move the body again."

"Again? Uh-uh." Ron's arms waved wildly, cutting through the air like spastic windmill blades. "No way, no how. No matter what you say, I am not, repeat *not*, touching or going anywhere near the you-know-what ever again!"

"Fine." Todd folded the tarp across the shotgun. The damn thing made him nervous. Was it loaded? He still didn't know.

"I mean, can you imagine what kind of shape it must be in now? In this Florida heat?" Ron wrinkled his nose. The thought of the smell alone was practically making him gag now.

"I said forget it, Ron. Go about your business. Do whatever it is you do. Leave this to me. I have a plan."

"Is it as good as your last one? You know, the one where we hide the—" The roofer glanced at Priscilla, happy to see she was on the telephone. "Body and nobody was ever going to find it?"

"You just do what I say. I'll call you when everything's in place."

"You'd better know what you're doing, Jones. Otherwise, that cop out there is going to haul both our asses to jail." Ron stumbled to his feet. Shaky knees led him to the door.

"Remember," Todd grabbed his arm. "Don't go anywhere near the you-know-what. In fact, don't go anywhere near Orlando."

Ron laughed. "You couldn't catch me within a hundred miles of that place."

Except that someone already had. Caught them both.

That was a chilling and sobering thought.

Todd left the office. Sometimes he found more privacy on a busy street than he did in his own office. Under the awning of a day spa, he looked at his smartphone, pulled up his list of contacts and made a call.

Circumstances like this required certain resources, an understanding of the vast gray area between right and wrong, avarice, a bit of cunning that verged on the sociopathic, a special discreet touch, and a rare but definitive flair.

"Hello, Nick."

"Who's this?"

"Todd, Todd Jo—"

Nick hung up.

"And so begins the dance." Todd smiled and redialed.

55

Steps away from Todd Jones Realty, Danny Boy's Pub has been a Las Olas fixture since the early 1980s.

"Hey, Todd," greeted Patty, swinging past with a black tray littered with empty beer bottles and glasses. "Your cop's at the bar."

Patty was a Nordic knockout with long legs and a trim behind. Yellow hair cascaded down to tanned cleavage. A black skirt and frilly white blouse completed the look. A look meant to attract the eyes and the tips.

"Last stool. Near the wall."

Todd squinted into the distance.

"I'm glad he doesn't come here a lot," Patty said. "Scares away the customers."

"I see him. Thanks, Patty. Bring us a pitcher when you get a chance, will you? And bring him the whiskey chicken and a basket of buffalo onion rings."

"Sure. And you?"

"I'll do a couple of chicken parm sliders."

"You got it." Patty departed with a green-eyed wink.

Todd worked his way down the crowded bar and plucked Nick's wrinkled sports jacket from the empty stool beside him.

Women's beach volleyball airing on two of the three flat-screens mounted above the bar held Nick's attention.

"You're late," grumbled Nick, his eyes never leaving

the screen. It wasn't everyday he got to eyeball hot chicks in bikinis.

"Who's winning?" Todd asked.

"Do we care?"

"Guess not."

Nick slowly lifted his beer mug and glugged, wiping his lips with the side of his index finger.

Todd hadn't seen Nick in ages. He hadn't changed much. Probably never would.

Nicholas Durham, detective, Broward County Sheriff's Department, working the Major Crimes Section of the Criminal Investigations Division.

A jowly, pale-faced Greek-American with a salt and pepper crewcut, Nick stood a couple inches shorter than Todd. He had a pug nose and large skin pores. A lone brown mole clung to his left ear like a walnut-shaped earring.

Nick was in his late thirties and not happily married. Dark and morose were the colors of his soul.

Todd and Nick had met by chance. Or was it fate? To call theirs a friendship would be a stretch but there were times when they could be quite useful to one another.

"What is it this time?" Nick growled. "Got a parking ticket you need fixed?"

"Let's take it over there." Todd indicated a booth that had come available.

Resettling themselves, Todd began. "Let me tell you a story."

Nick laughed. "This ought to be good."

Patty served them and brought Nick's hideous checkered sports jacket over from the bar. Todd spun his tale, leaving out nothing, emphasizing the important parts—like how it was Ron Patton who'd clumsily, if accidently, been responsible for the death of Miro Frankowski up on Strange's roof.

Polishing off the remnants of his whiskey chicken, Nick twirled the last of his onion rings around on his thumb. "Some story. A real doozy. Even for you."

The two men had been through a lot together, most of it seamy—the kind of things you don't want a light shined on. "So now your blackmailer wants a hundred grand or your gooses are cooked."

"That's about it."

"To paraphrase the great Oliver Hardy, that's another fine mess you've gotten yourself into."

"I'm glad you see the humor in this," Todd said sourly.

"Now's the moment of truth." The thumb stopped twirling. Nick chomped down on the onion ring, tugging with his teeth until it broke free. He inhaled it, chewing slowly, talking with his mouth full. "What is it you want from me?"

"Before I answer that, let me add one more thing."

"I'm listening."

"I did not tell Ron everything," Todd confessed.

"Such as?" Nick hoisted the empty pitcher. Patty shouted that she'd bring another over in a minute.

"Such as I know who the blackmailer is. Her name, at least. Christie Campbell, spokesperson for Strange Scrap, Inc."

"Strange as in this George Strange fella you were telling me about?"

"The very same."

"Mind telling me how you know this?"

"Because I googled her number. She's all over the place on social media. Nice looking, too." He held out his phone.

"She's a looker, all right. You think she and George…"

"Oh, yeah. Wouldn't you?"

Nick chuckled. "Still, your blackmailer, Christie, is none too bright. She should've used a burner phone."

"Yeah. But she was bright enough to figure out what happened to Miro and to get her hands on his shotgun."

"Where's this shotgun now?"

"Still in the office. Wrapped in a tarp beneath my desk."

"And you told your pal Patton none of this? About Christie Campbell being the one behind the extortion?"

Todd nodded.

"Why?"

"I didn't think it pertinent."

Nick grunted. "I know you. That's your way of saying you've got another angle. An angle that might not be in Patton's favor."

Todd merely shrugged. "It's because of that incompetent roofer that I'm in this mess in the first place. Whatever happens to him now is his own fault."

"And now you want Uncle Nick to make it all better."

"Let's say I could use your expertise."

Nick went silent a minute. An empty beer pitcher left, a filled one took its place.

"You tell quite the tale, quite the tale. The thing is," Nick said, leaning back against the booth, "you left out the most important part."

"What's that?"

"Todd, Todd, Todd. You disappoint me. Smart as you are? The most important part is…what's in it for me?"

Patty stopped at their booth to see if they'd like anything else. Surprisingly, Nick passed on dessert.

"Okay, take your time, boys." Patty slid the bill next to Todd's plate.

"Thanks, Patty." Todd dropped a credit card on the table and she disappeared with it.

Nick waited, expressionless.

"Okay, here's the deal. Christie demanded fifty grand from each of us. But that's not going to happen. I'm not giving the woman a penny. I know who she is. What's she going to do? Who's she going to tell without me ratting on her? It's a stalemate."

"And?"

"And Patton doesn't know that. Strange paid Patton a quarter of a million dollars for that lousy roofing job." Todd talked over Nick's long, low whistle. "He is going to give fifty thousand of that to the blackmailer. At least, that's who he thinks he's giving it to."

"Who is he giving all this lovely money to?"

"You."

Nick smiled.

"You help me and the fifty thousand is yours."

56

"All of it?" Nick appeared suspicious.

It would be hard for anybody who'd met him to miss the fact that Todd loved his money.

"Every last penny."

"That'll work," Nick replied. Easy money had a way of cheering him up. "By the way, that guy that followed you into the bar—"

"What?"

"Beefy guy in the denim shirt."

Todd swung his head around for a look.

"He can't keep his eyes off you. Maybe he thinks you're his type."

Todd stiffened. "That's Bogs."

"What's a Bogs?" All three men were staring at one another now.

"He works for George Strange."

"What's he want?"

"I think we're about to find out," Todd said as Bogs slid off his barstool and came, beer in hand, to the booth. "Hello, Bogs. Can I help you?"

Bogs nodded to Nick. "I'm looking for Miro. Have you seen him?"

"Not since we finished working on Strange's roof."

"Yeah, some job you did."

"Tell that to Patton."

"I did. I also asked him if he'd seen my nephew."

"What did he say?"

"Same as you."

"There you go then. Sorry I can't help you."

Bogs pressed his fingers against the table. "I can't help wondering what Patton was doing at your office."

"That's easy. As a real estate agent, I've often got clients with properties who are looking for roof repairs. Ron stopped by to fill out some paperwork so I could add him to our referral list."

"Him? Bogs appeared justifiably incredulous. "I wouldn't trust 'em to shingle Cuddles' dog house!" Bogs turned his hard eyes on Nick. "Who's your friend?"

Nick stared him down. "Todd doesn't have any friends."

"Yeah," Bogs chuckled. "I can believe that." He stuck his hand in the right pocket of his jeans and slammed a Swiss Army knife down on the tabletop.

"Any idea how this ended up at the bottom of Big George's swimming pool, Jones?"

Todd suppressed a shudder of fear. "No. It's not mine."

"No, it isn't. It's Miro's."

"Are you sure? Don't all Swiss Army knives look the same? Maybe one of the other roofers dropped it or the hurricane blew it in."

"I gave it to Miro on his thirteenth birthday."

"Maybe he went swimming with it and it fell out of his pocket," quipped Nick.

Bogs snatched up the knife and whipped open the long blade. He stuck its point within a hair's breadth of Nick's neck. "You've got a smart mouth, friend."

"I told you, Bogs." Nick shook his head slowly side to side. To his credit, he never flinched. "Todd doesn't have any friends. I, on the other hand, have a special friend, this loaded thirty-eight aimed at your balls." He tilted his head in the direction of his lap.

Bogs saw the gun in Nick's hand, half-hidden under a checkered sports jacket. He smiled and pulled back his hand. Closing the blade, he said to Todd, "If you had anything to do with my nephew's disappearance, it's your balls you're going to have to worry about."

Bogs turned and shouldered his way out of Danny Boy's.

"Memorable parting words," Nick said, putting his weapon away.

"Memorable guy."

"Where's the rest of this Miro's stuff?"

"All his personal effects, everything I could find in his pockets, I tossed." Actually, he'd saved them all and then hidden away in his condo. One never knew when an extra driver's license or credit card might come in handy.

"Good. That's good." Nick rubbed his hands together. "First thing we gotta do is get rid of that body properly."

"You have any ideas?" Todd demanded.

"You got a boat, right?"

"Yeah, I don't use it much." Todd's 1995 Sea Ray 380 Sundancer, picked up secondhand, sat in dry dock at a state-of-the-art facility next to his Port Lauderdale condo.

"You're going to use it now."

"What do you have in mind?"

"Sharks gotta eat too, right?"

"Right."

57

Watching the giant blue plastic sheets go up on his roof, George looked on with satisfaction. That Larry Goldstein was one all right guy. Especially for an insurance man.

He hadn't shelled out a cent of his own money. Larry Goldstein was taking care of everything, well, him and the insurance company he was in negotiations with. George suspected they'd be suing Ron Patton's ass but so what? The idiot had it coming.

A crew of ten men scurried like rats along the rooftop, mindless of the height. His wife had retreated to their Detroit place, taking Esme with her, not wanting to deal with the noise and commotion going on here at the house.

George had been calling and calling Christie to no avail. She was still registered at the Ritz—which he was footing the hefty bill for—but she never answered her door. The snooty hotel staff claimed not to have seen her. "Hey, Bogs!"

Bogs shuffled over.

"You hear from that useless nephew of yours yet?"

"No, Big George." Miro's disappearance had taken its toll on him. He was tired and tense. "I don't get it. There's no sign of him and he doesn't answer his phone."

"Probably goofing off somewhere, doing drugs or a

woman or both."

"He wouldn't do that," insisted Bogs, not quite contradicting his boss.

"Since he's not around, I need you to go stake out the Ritz. When you find Christie, and I expect you to, you tell her to hustle her butt on over here."

"Yes, Big George."

"And you can tell her that Imelda's up in Detroit, so she can pack her bags and join me at the house."

"Right."

"No point wasting good money on a hotel when I've got all this space. Off you go!" George shooed Bogs away.

With Miro missing and needing Bogs here in Fort Lauderdale, a crew from Detroit had driven down for the Orange Blossom Resort demo job.

Everything was set. Today they'd be setting up the charges. Maybe he'd go up to Orlando tomorrow with Christie and watch them blow the place to kingdom come. She liked seeing things go boom practically as much as he did.

58

"Look at us," said Nick, cranking up the radio, blasting a Hank Williams, Jr. song. "A couple of partners in crime. Off on our first road trip."

"I'll be sure to mark the occasion in my diary," replied Todd.

Todd Jones and Nick Durham drove north to Orlando under cover of darkness. Nick commandeered a twenty-year old Volvo 240 station wagon left to rot in a county impound lot. It was long and low and as aerodynamic as a bag of bricks. Nick sat behind the wheel.

For its age, the car seats were remarkably comfortable. Most important, Nick was quick to point out, there was plenty of room for a body to stretch out in back. He'd stolen a body bag from the morgue for the job— heavy-duty plastic, leak resistant, with nylon reinforced handles.

"This baby's even OSHA approved!" Nick had told Todd with a laugh because he found it funny that health and safety could possibly matter to a dead body.

It was nearly midnight as they rolled along Orange Blossom Trail behind a pickup truck hauling a horse trailer that left in its wake a stench of wet hay and muck.

"This is it?" Nick stared through the windshield at the busted resort sign. Light rain blurring his vision.

"Yeah, better keep moving," suggested Todd. Several vehicles sat on the property that had not been there the previous visit. A light was on inside one of them, a pickup truck.

Nick did so, only coming to a stop in the unpaved parking lot of a no-name mini-mart about a half mile up the road from the Orange Blossom Resort, its ramshackle buildings visible as dark hulks down the road.

"You told me this place was deserted."

"It was," replied Todd. "They must be getting ready to demo." He'd explained to Nick how Strange Scrap, Inc. was due to bring the place to the ground. "It looks like they've got security to keep an eye on things."

"Those *things* could include sticks of dynamite planted strategically throughout the buildings. One wrong step and boom!" Nick clapped his hands together loudly.

"So we tread carefully."

Nick grunted. "Any other way onto the property?"

Todd gave the question some thought. "I think there might be an access road on the far side. You've got that woods there along the perimeter and I seem to remember a small road near some storage containers and trash bins."

"That'll do." Nick forced the old Volvo to move. It jerked then slowly picked up speed.

It took about twenty minutes, crisscrossing the smaller streets until they found themselves popping up behind the resort. A half-dozen deer jumped in front of the Volvo.

Nick killed the headlights. "Looks simple enough."

"Let's get this over with." Todd tugged on his door

handle. "I'll get out and guide you around all the potholes and crap. We can't take a chance using the headlights. Whoever's in that pickup out front might notice."

"Okay. Pay damn good attention. We can't afford for anything to happen to the car. Especially once we get the dead guy inside." Nick ran a sweaty palm over his sweaty forehead. "The things I do for a lousy fifty Gs."

"You've done worse," Todd reminded the detective, giving the door a kick when it refused to budge.

"Not so fast." Nick yanked him back.

"What?"

"That." Nick pointed. An SUV running with its bright lights stabbing the darkness and fog lamps aglow came around the far corner of the property, moving in a wide, slow circle.

"Damn."

"Yeah. Plan B. We leave the car here and go the rest of the way on foot."

"That means carrying the corpse all the way back here. That's a hundred yards or more. Easy."

"You got a better Plan B?"

The SUV rolled off. Todd and Nick hopped out of the Volvo, went around to the rear hatch and removed the two pairs of gloves and pickaxes they'd purchased at a Walmart on the way up.

"It's over here. In the main building," said Todd, leading the way.

Both had dressed in black for the occasion and ran hunched across the uneven pavement. Nick uttered a string of curses.

Approaching the building parallel to and furthest from their target, they skirted the swampy swimming pool, a breeding ground for mosquitoes and the source of a horrific stench. The resort's long room wings hid the two men from view on all sides.

Unless there was a security man wandering around the premises, they would be safe from discovery.

Todd breathed a sigh of relief. Nick coughed the cough of a man who smoked too much, drank too much and exercised too little. "Quiet," urged Todd.

"Relax." Nick leaned against the pickax. "Nobody here but us ghosts. Where now?"

"Up ahead. We can get in through those busted doors. "

"Right." Nick balanced the wood-handled pickax over his shoulder and followed Todd. "I cannot believe you morons thought this was a good spot to dump a body."

"It seemed like a good idea at the time," Todd said in his own defense. "They are demolishing this place."

"And when they find an unidentified male body in the rubble? What did you think they'd do then? Sell it for scrap?"

Todd clenched his jaw. Said nothing. He didn't like being criticized. He didn't like being wrong. He didn't like being made to look stupid.

The worse thing was, Nick was right. He'd been stupid.

The stupidest thing was referring Ron Patton to George Strange. How nice it would feel to rip the roofer off. Payback for all the trouble he'd caused him.

"In here." Todd struggled over several fallen boards. Rats—or could it be bats?—skittered and scuffled in the blackness. He pulled out a thin flashlight. "Got your flashlight?"

"Sure." Nick coughed once again. He dug into his pocket, came up with a duplicate flashlight and shot its beam across his immediate surroundings. "Damn well stinks in here." He waved a hand in front of his face.

"Yeah. What did you expect? This place has been sitting here rotting for years, I'll bet."

"I was thinking more along the lines of eau de rotting corpse," chuckled Nick.

"Thanks for sharing that lovely thought."

Nick chuckled once more.

Todd twisted slowly in a small circle, getting his bearings. "I recognize that counter. He's over this way." Stepping around the scattered debris, he worked towards the spot where he and Ron had laid Miro's remains. "This is it." He waved his light side to side. "Huh."

"What?" Nick came to a stop beside him, picking at the crap at his feet with the tip of the pickax. "Problem?"

"I'm not sure. Just doesn't look right somehow."

"What's to look right?" Nick pushed Todd aside, anxious to be done and out of this place. He didn't like closed, dark spaces. Especially ones that were falling down around his ears. Slipping on his gloves, he started throwing the larger chunks aside. "Don't just stand there, lend a hand."

Todd drew on his gloves and shoveled smaller heaps of garbage over his shoulder. Soon they were both coughing and trying desperately to cover their noises.

Two bright beams of light shot through from behind them.

"Shit." Nick ducked and pulled Todd down beside him. "It's the SUV."

"Think somebody heard us?" Todd's chest pounded.

"How could they? We weren't that loud." Nick spat flecks of dirt from his lip to the ground.

"Maybe we should go."

"Give it a minute," Nick said. "If one of those SUV doors open, then we hightail it."

After an excruciating couple of minutes, the headlights retreated as the vehicle backed up then drove off in search of other potential late night prey.

Todd and Nick redoubled their efforts, taking turns holding the flashlight while the other dug through the rubble.

Nick, dying for a drink and sweating like he'd been told there would be no tomorrow, stood clenching the flashlight in his fist next to Todd when the realtor cursed. "What's wrong?"

Standing knee-deep in a small depression now partially cleared, Todd numbly stared at the hole. He watched a fat cockroach burrow itself into a crack in the floor. "He's not here."

"You sure?" The beam of the flashlight danced across Todd's feet. Nick laughed.

"What's so funny?" Todd didn't like this one bit.

"There's nobody home. Get it? No *body* home?"

59

Todd hurled the pickax into the darkness, listened with satisfaction as it struck something hard and clattered to the ground.

What did it matter? Even if somebody found the pickax, he'd been wearing gloves. An ax is an ax.

And a dead body's a dead body...

"Give me a hand." Todd extended his hand and Nick pulled him out of the shallow hole. Black muck coated his shoes.

"I guess our Christie is not as dumb as we thought she was." Nick pulled out a pack of cigarettes and lit it from a wrinkled book of matches he'd lifted from the Seminole Hard Rock Casino.

"No, I guess not. What do we do now?"

Nick took a moment to enjoy his smoke then said, "We negotiate."

Todd nodded. "I thought you quit smoking."

"I quit a lot of things. If I didn't restart a few of those things now and again, I'd have nothing left to quit." He sucked noisily on his Camel. "Then where would I be?" He coughed. "Besides, I blame your mom."

"My mom? Not that I don't blame her for plenty myself, but why are you blaming her?"

"Last time I saw her she insisted I take a pack of Camels."

"That's my mom, generous to a fault. Emphasis on

the *fault*."

"Let's get out of here." Nick threw his pickax into the shallow depression. "Unless you'd like to stick around and see this resort blown to smithereens."

Todd started back the way they'd come. Nick tossed his cigarette and followed.

"You're not going to put that out?" Todd paused, watched the red tip of the cigarette glow in the darkness. He thought about the sticks of dynamite scattered throughout.

"What's it going to matter? This place is toast anyway."

They moved on. A chorus of frogs and insects provided the soundtrack.

"How did she do this?" Todd wondered aloud, breaking the joint silence as they neared the Volvo. He tore off his gloves and tossed them in the back of the station wagon. The body bag sat there like a deflated balloon. A reminder of his deflated confidence and burst plans.

Things were not moving his way.

"Christie must have had help. She couldn't have moved the body alone. Too heavy for one girl."

"Right. Prince Charming," said Todd.

"Who's Prince Charming?" Nick started up the Volvo and reversed down the bumpy road, headlights off.

"That's what I'd like to know." Todd slammed his fist into the dashboard. "That and where Miro's corpse went."

60

Ron laid in bed thinking.

Elaine slept beside him. Hair in curlers. Toes cold as popsicles.

Florida Power & Light had managed to get the power up and running in their neighborhood but the tiny fifteen-year-old room air conditioner mounted in the bedroom window provided more noise than it did comfort.

Sweat oozed from every pore of his body.

He stared at the popcorn ceiling, deep in thought.

Deep in dark thoughts. Dark thoughts that made him angry—at himself and Todd Jones.

Todd is tricking me, Ron decided.

There really is no blackmailer. And the more he thought, the more he convinced himself. That lousy realtor wasn't helping him, wasn't fixing things. No, that lousy realtor was out to get him. Out to screw him.

The only blackmailer was Todd A-hole Jones. That was why Jones hadn't let him listen in on the phone call with the so-called blackmailer. Jones had probably set the whole thing up, told a friend of his to call and pretend to say some crap while Jones fed him what he wanted him to hear.

It was all a hoax, a put-on.

Ron slammed his fists against the mattress.

Elaine stirred, rolled onto her side.

Todd Jones was out to rip him off for fifty thousand dollars!

Ron slipped quietly out of bed, careful not to wake his wife. He scooped his clothes off the chair where he'd tossed them and collected his shoes from the closet.

Shutting the bedroom door behind him, he dressed in the kitchen.

He'd show Todd Jones a thing or two.

What would he do? What could he do?

Ron knew one thing. He couldn't sleep. Tiptoeing to the front door, he fished his car keys from the candy dish on the console table and exited.

A starry sky, straight out of something that crazy dead dude Van Gogh might have painted, greeted him. The van sat parked at the curb. He climbed inside.

Ron didn't know how or why the idea came to him. It simply had. Out of the blue. Like a bit of magic or a miracle sprung out of the air as he planted his butt on the warm vinyl seat.

Snap of the fingers and there it was. The idea. The BIG IDEA.

He was going to kidnap Stevie Nicks, aka Todd's mother. He'd turn the tables on Todd. That turnip thought he was so smart. Ron would show him. He'd show him who was smart.

Ron started the engine, a smile blooming on his haggard face.

He'd kidnap the lady. Hold her for ransom. One hundred thousand dollars, that's what he'd demand. Add that to the quarter of a million he'd already pocketed (less expenses) and he'd be rich, filthy rich, beyond his or even Elaine's wildest dreams.

But he'd need a plan. He'd need to do it, snatch her,

when Todd wasn't around.

Leaving the quiet, sleeping neighborhood, Ron headed east to Port Everglades, almost as if on autopilot.

Sitting at the far edge of the Port Lauderdale Condominium Towers now, Ron shut off the engine.

Time to reconnoiter. Moving in the shadows, following a row of rustling palm trees, he worked his way to the resident parking garage. All was quiet. He stepped around the automatic gate arm and into the parking structure. With only a couple of small levels, it didn't take him long to discover that Todd's Audi was absent.

Ron scrambled back to the van. He pulled Todd's business card from his wallet. Stared at the column of phone numbers. The realtor had given the card to him when he was in his office. Todd told him to call only in case of an emergency.

The last telephone number was listed as the home number.

Did he dare call? Why not? He could always hang up. No harm done. No warning flags raised.

He dialled. A woman's voice answered, a voice ravaged by years of smoking and drinking. He pictured the woman he'd met when he'd come by before searching for Todd. An aging hippie smelling of pot and perfume.

"Hello? Hello?"

Ron cut the connection.

Jones was out. Probably. His mother was definitely in.

Goosebumps rose on his arms.

Maybe he'd do it now. Snatch her now and get it over with. What was he waiting for? Todd could come home any minute, any second, and he'd lose his chance, his big opportunity. Do it now he told himself.

And he would.

Ron started up the van and headed north on Federal Highway looking for some place open. It didn't take long. He pulled over in the brightly lit parking lot of the Sav-A-Bunch Discount Mart. Using his smartphone, he googled the Port Lauderdale Condominium Towers. Several phone numbers popped up. One for the community homeowner's association, one for security, and another for the lobby.

Ron dialed the number for the lobby. "Hello, Todd Jones here," he said, trying hard not to sound like himself.

"Yes, sir?" replied a bored voice. Pulsing Latin music played in the distance.

"I'm expecting a guest soon. A Mister..."

"What was that? Who'd you say?"

Ron bit his tongue. No, he couldn't say Patton, could he? No, he couldn't have the guy at the desk remembering his name. Just in case. In case something went wrong.

"A Mister Archibald's coming." Ron had given a man named Archibald a quote on the roof of his duplex last week in Coral Springs. "I have to make a call. Send him straight up when he arrives, would you?"

"Of course. Sure thing, Mister Jones."

Ron hung up. "That was way too easy." He ran inside the Sav-A-Bunch, purchased a roll of duct tape, a length of nylon rope, a box of black plastic bags and a prepaid smartphone with a service card. The girl at the checkout looked at him funny.

"Some hurricane, huh?" Ron said, paying cash for everything. "Still cleaning up the mess. And my phone is kaput."

"Tell me about it." She handed him his change.

"Thanks." He jingled the coins in the palm of his hand.

"Want to hear something funny?"

Did he have a choice? No, probably not. "What's that?" Ron asked, anxious to be going, get this done before his courage failed.

"My house burned to the ground."

"Wow, that is tough."

"That's irony. Here we get a frigging hurricane and all that rain."

"Nine inches, I heard."

"Storm knocks a fifty-year-old oak tree through my roof and into my kitchen. Starts an electrical fire and whoosh!" The clerk threw her arms in the air. "Up she went." Her brows pinched. "Or is that down she went?"

"That's a real bummer." Ron scooped up his two plastic sacks of supplies, resisting the urge to give her his business card, reminding himself that he was definitely out of the roofing business.

He dropped a quarter and a nickel in the tip jar nestled between the credit card scanner and a clear plastic bucket filled with tubes of 99-cent lip balm.

61

Back at the no-name mini-mart—doing a brisk business for this hour of the night—Todd asked Nick, "What do we do now?"

Nick yanked a beer free from its six-pack collar, popped the lid and savored the cold, bubbly rush. "Let's call her."

"Christie?"

Nick handed Todd a can. "Yeah."

"Thanks. She's supposed to call me tomorrow." Todd opened the beer and sipped. "It's the middle of the night."

"Element of surprise," said Nick. "Look at that hooker over there. Shameful."

Todd glanced at the woman in question. Dark skin, long tresses, teal hot pants and a crinkly tube top. She chatted up every man that went inside the mini-mart. She'd chatted him up too. So far, no takers.

"Go ahead, call her."

"What should I say?"

"Wing it," suggested Nick. "You're good at that sort of thing."

Todd did.

A sleepy voice answered the phone. "Hello?

"Hello, Christie Campbell. Todd Jones here."

"Oh!" gasped Christie.

"Put it on speaker," whispered Nick.

Todd hit the speaker icon and Christie's voice filled the cabin. "Mind if I call you Christie?"

"How-what-what do you want?" Bedclothes rustled. A click signaled that she'd turned on a bedside lamp.

"I wanted to talk to you about this whole nasty blackmail business," replied Todd. "I'm surprised at you, Christie. A pretty woman like you, smart, talented, spokesperson for Strange Scrap, Inc. Not the sort of thing a person like you ought to be involved in."

Nick sniggered, guzzled his beer and reached for a second can.

"I don't know what you are talking about," Christie said, gathering her strength, struggling to sound firm, something she'd learned in acting class. "You've called a wrong number."

"Oh no. I've got the right number, Christie. I've got *your* number. And if you think you're going to blackmail me out of fifty thousand dollars, you've got another thing coming."

"And it isn't going to be good!" snarled Nick.

"Who was that?" gasped Christie.

"My muscle," improvised Todd. Nick was correct. He really was good at this sort of thing.

Christie's sobs surprised them both.

Todd softened his tone. "Listen, Christie. I know you didn't mean any harm. This isn't really something we can talk about on the phone. Certain things should be said in a more secure situation. I'm sure you know what I mean."

"Yes," her voice barely audible, she sniffled.

"Let's meet," suggested Todd. "Christie, listen to me," he said, smooth as dripping honey, "I believe we can help one another."

"We can?" Christie's voice held a smidgen of hope.

"Yes, we can. We'll meet. We'll talk about it. Would that be okay?"

Silence followed.

"If not," bellowed Nick with a smile and a wink that only Todd could see, "heads will roll!" The detective crushed the empty beer between his hands.

"Eep!" squealed Christie.

"Nick!" Todd said. "Relax, Christie. I'm going to help you."

"You are?"

"Yes, I am. You help me and I'll help you. Deal?"

"Yes. I-I think so."

"Good." Todd breathed a sigh of relief. Things could work out yet. "Tell me where you are. I'll come to you." It wouldn't do to have her at the condo or office. Strange might see. Bogs might see. Too many people might see.

"I'm home."

"And where's home?"

"Detroit."

62

"Archibald. Here to see Todd Jones," Ron Patton said with a confidence he wasn't feeling. In fact, he was feeling rather queasy. His stomach twisted around like he'd swallowed a bad burrito.

The night deskman at the Port Lauderdale Condominium Towers paid little heed to the sloppily dressed man in baggy jeans and a rumpled blue T-shirt. He'd seen worse. South Florida was casual central. The only thing that caught his eye was the name Ronald's Roofing silk-screened on the face of the dude's shirt.

"Go on up," he said, half an eye on the visitor and the larger part of his attention on his Twitter account.

Ron headed to the nearest elevator, shopping bags in hand. As the car started moving silently upward, he checked the upper corners of the elevator. No security camera installed. No eyes in the sky keeping watch on him. At least, none that he spotted.

Good.

So far, so good.

He reached into one of the shopping bags and ripped open the box of big black trash bags. The idea was that Jones' mother would answer the door, he'd throw a bag over her head, then bind her up with rope and tape. Take her down in the service elevator. A joint like this had to have a service elevator. The kind of folks that lived in castles in the sky like these didn't want garbage stuck in their noses when they rode the elevator, or furniture deliverymen and other such riff-raff clouding up the atmosphere.

If there was no service elevator, he'd be forced to march her down twenty-two floors of steps. The stairs emptied out into a side lot. He'd spotted it during his recon.

Ron hoped the old lady was up to it.

He hoped he was up to it.

The elevator doors slid open to reveal a deserted hallway, chilly and quiet. He found Todd's door and pressed the buzzer. No response. He tried a second time and followed up with a rappity-rap on the solid mahogany door.

The door inched open.

A deep grunt caught Ron's attention. He looked at his feet. A wriggling, hairy black snout appeared. "What the hell?"

"Can I help you?"

Ron jumped. Was the pig talking to him?

The door scooted open and Stevie Nicks, in silk tiger print pajamas, glass of amber scotch in hand, said, "Oh, it's you. Come on in."

Ron slipped the loose garbage bag into the shopping sack and followed. "Nice place you've got here." Damn realtor lived like a king. Maybe he'd up his ransom demands.

"Care for a glass?" she held her own crystal glass in question.

"No, thanks." Actually, he'd kill for a drink right now. His knees shook and his hands trembled. "Well, maybe a small one." Simpler to ask for one than to actually kill her for it.

Rosalind Jones smiled and crossed to the bar. She poured him his drink and carried it to him. "You find my son okay?"

"Oh, yeah. Thanks again." Ron gulped the scotch down. This was the good stuff.

"My, my." Todd's mother grinned. "Another?"

"Okay, but last one." Ron followed her to the bar this time. The pig cut between his legs, tripping him up and spilling him across the rug. "Oof!"

His empty glass flew across the room.

"Don't mind Mr. Squeals." Rosalind scooped up his glass and wiped it off with the tail of her pajama top. She handed him his refill then stooped to scratch Mr. Squeals between his ears with her long pointy fingernails. "I think he likes you."

"Lucky me." Ron picked himself up, balancing his scotch in his hand. He hoped she didn't notice the sarcasm. Was that a pig hair stuck to the inside of his glass and was that another floating in his drink?

"He likes his hard stuff too," she said, pouring the pig a scotch neat. "Although my son frowns on me indulging him."

She placed the glass gently on the floor. Mr. Squeals squealed with delight and noisily slurped the potent brew. Nudging the empty glass with his snout, he then pressed up against the bar with his front feet and snorted repeatedly.

"Now, now, no begging. One's all you get. You know drinking too much this close to bedtime give you nightmares." She curled her fingers under his belly and gave him a pat. This elicited a grunt of approval.

Mr. Squeals fell to all fours and squawked off like a pissed off teenager.

"Let's ignore him," said Rosalind.

"Sure, Mrs. Jones." Ron said. *With pleasure* was what he was thinking.

Ron smiled. Thinking, *do it, do it now.* "Where is Todd anyway, Mrs. Jones? He around?"

"No. And you can call me Rosalind," Rosalind Jones pulled a pack of Camels from the upper front pocket of her pajamas and lit a cigarette with a marble lighter that made its home on the coffee table. "He had to go to Orlando."

Ron's fingers tightened around his glass. Orlando. Miro's corpse. What the hell was the bastard up to?

"Did he say why? I mean, just curious is all."

"Business. That's all I know." She sucked in some smoke, blew it out. "You know Todd. It's always business with that boy. Never any time to have fun."

"Yeah, he's a hustler, all right."

"Are you in real estate too?"

"Not exactly."

"Roofs?"

"What?" Ron nearly spilled his drink. Was Jones' mom psychic as well as psycho?

"Your shirt." She tapped him on the chest.

"Oh." Ron smiled weakly. Shit. Stupid, stupid, stupid of him to wear one of his work shirts to a kidnapping.

"How about a game of pinball?" Rosalind rested her glass on the tabletop and powered up the machine. The Rolling Stones welcomed her with Sympathy For The Devil.

Her fuzzy-slippered feet—zebra stripes clashing horribly with the tiger stripes—kept time to the music.

What kind of lunatic asylum was this guy Jones living in? he wondered. Pigs and pinball machines in his living room?

Wow. Elaine was right. We do all have our own crosses to bear, Ron realized.

Ron also realized that he may not have to resort to any rough stuff to kidnap Jones' mother. Crazy as she was, he might just get her to agree to come with him with no fuss or strong-arming at all.

63

Elaine woke with a start. Her hand went reflexively to her left. Feeling for a familiar lump.

A lump that wasn't there.

Her fingers explored the rarely visited territory.

No Ron.

Bathroom?

Elaine strained to listen. Nothing. If he was peeing, she'd hear it. Always did. Even over the clackety-clack of the window air conditioner.

As much as she hated to speak because it would only wake her up more, she whispered, "Ron?" She pulled the sheet up to her chest. "Ron? You out there?"

Wide awake now, Elaine went in search of her husband. She expected to find him in his skivvies, couch potatoing on his favorite chair—until that nice man Bogs had sat on it and now Ron refused to go near the thing for some reason she couldn't understand—so couch potatoing on the sofa, munching chips, drinking beer, watching the soft porn tapes he didn't think she knew he kept stashed in a toolbox in the garage.

But Ron wasn't here. "Ron's not here," she said to the warm and empty living room. She pulled back the edge of the curtain. His van was nowhere in sight.

Ron wasn't in the kitchen either. No surprise with the van gone.

But her handbag was and her smartphone was

inside the handbag. At least somethings were where they were supposed to be.

Slumping into her chair, she punched her husband's face. His face icon, not quite as satisfying as his real face at this precise moment, but his smirking, high-def image would have to do.

"Excuse me," Ron said to Elaine, setting his glass on the cling-clanging pinball machine. Mick Jagger crooned some jibberish about satin shoes and plastic boots. Ron reached into his back pocket for his personal smartphone. Elaine's face appeared and while it was only a digital photo, it scared him. Uh-oh. "Hello?"

"Where the hell are you? Are you in some bar? It's the middle of the night. One minute you're in bed and the next—"

Time for some fast thinking. Surprising even himself, Ron blurted, "Hey, Todd, buddy. We were just talking about you."

"About me?" Elaine pulled at her hair curlers.

"We who? Why, me and your lovely young mother. That's right, Rosalind. Yeah, what a coincidence, I'm here right now. Yeah," chuckle chuckle, "at your place."

"Who is Rosalind?" Elaine demanded.

"Hi!" shouted Rosalind, her hands never leaving the buttons of the pinball machine, flappers flapping. Bells and gongs, belling and gonging.

"Is that Rosalind?" Elaine voice rose a notch. Things weren't great with her and Ron but they were married for crying out loud.

"What's that, Todd? Oh, sure. I can do that," Ron forged ahead.

"What's that boy of mine up to?" Rosalind demanded.

"Ronald Patton, you get home right now or so help me..." Elaine had learned that it was always best to leave a threat rather vague. Anything Ron could imagine would likely be far worse than what she'd really do to the jerk.

"Sure, I'll take care of that right away. Promise. Gotta hang up now."

"Now listen here, you—" Elaine didn't bother to finish her thought—and it was a good one too—because her idiot husband had hung up on her.

"That man's going to have some explaining to do," she told the refrigerator.

She pulled out the bucket of cold leftover chicken and grabbed a passionfruit cocktail-in-a-can to wash it down with while she devised new and improved ways to torture her husband.

64

"High score!" Rosalind threw her hands up in the air. "Whoo!" She spun like a ballerina. "Sure you don't want to play a game?" She elbowed Ron. "Maybe see if you can beat an old lady?"

"I'd love to," Ron said, "but Todd told me to tell you that he wants you to pick up some papers at his office for him and fax them over to him. Like you said, that kid of yours is all business." Would she question why Todd asked him to relay the request rather than call her direct?

"Sure. Can do."

Nope. She wouldn't question it for a second. If he'd told her Todd wanted the fax sent to the Moon to the attention of little gray Lunatics, he doubted she'd have questioned that either.

"I'll get my keys."

"You don't have to do that. How about this? I'll drive you over and bring you back after."

"Are you sure? I don't mind driving. A little fresh air drive with the windows rolled down might help clear my head. Don't tell Todd I said this but drinking and smoking have a way of clogging me up, knocking my chakra out of kilter."

"I won't. Promise." Besides, he was pretty sure Todd knew exactly how unclear-headed his mother was.

"Well..." Rosalind ran her finger along the inner lip

of her glass and sucked her finger.

"I insist. What would my buddy Todd think of me if I let his dear mother run around town in the middle of the night all by her lonesome? Unescorted."

Rosalind switched off the pinball machine. "I'll get my coat." Turning outside her bedroom door, she asked, "Can Mr. Squeals come? He just adores car rides. You got a convertible?"

"Sorry no. I'm afraid I only have room for one." What would Elaine think if he brought home that satanic looking porker? "He can come next time, I promise."

"You are so sweet. Why can't all of my son's friends be as sweet as you? Be right back."

"Take your time," said Ron. After she was out of sight, he went straight to the kitchen. Finding a Todd Jones Realty notepad in a kitchen counter drawer, he scrawled out a note for Jones.

$100,000 or you'll never see your mom again.
Will be in touch.

Satisfied, Ron taped the ransom note to the refrigerator with a strip of tape from the spool of invisible plastic tape he'd found in the same kitchen drawer.

"Ready when you are!" called Rosalind.

Ron was ready. Everything was falling into place.

The only remaining bump in the road was Elaine. Hopefully, she'd understand.

65

"I don't understand," said Elaine, weary and worried. "You kidnapped her? This nice lady? You kidnapped her?"

"I told you, Elaine. I had to do it. It's for our own good." It had gone so well too. Way, way better than his original plan. First he'd conned Rosalind Jones with the fake phone call from Jones.

Once in the van, he'd said he had to make a stop first before heading to her son's real estate office. That stop being his house.

Rosalind could not have cared less. She cranked up an FM station playing a lot of eighties hits, including a ton of Fleetwood Mac and zoned out. She sang along, riding in the van, oblivious to all else.

He hadn't needed the extra smartphone, the tape, the rope or the garbage bags. He could've saved himself nearly fifty bucks in expenses.

The trouble hadn't started until he'd arrived home. That trouble hadn't come from Rosalind. No, she walked right up to his house. Said she was happy to go inside and meet the wife.

The trouble, that had all come from Elaine.

"Todd Jones, her son, he's out to get me. Get us," he added, waving his hand between the two of them for emphasis.

"The way this is going, there is not going to be any

us," hissed Elaine. "Just a you. A you with your sorry butt in jail. I mean, charging folks a few hundred bucks for the privilege of giving them ridiculously high quotes for their jobs—"

Turning to Rosalind, Elaine said, "You should hear some of the crazy quotes he gives people for roof replacements."

"You don't say?" Rosalind chewed on a chicken leg, extra crispy and ice cold. Just the way she liked it. "Too bad Mr. Squeals isn't here. He would love this chicken."

Back to Ron, "Doing that, that's one thing," Elaine said. "Kidnapping, that's a whole other thing, Ron. A whole, whole other thing. Who's Mr. Squeals? You got him tied up someplace too?"

"Forget Mr. Squeals," said Ron, losing his patience. "He's nothing. He's a pig. It's Jones we've got to worry about. He's framing me for murder, Elaine."

"A pig?" Elaine looked at Rosalind Jones for guidance.

"A pig," agreed Rosalind, smacking her lips and reaching for a chicken thigh. "Potbellied. You got any slaw?"

Ron paced the muggy little kitchen, hating its ancient linoleum floor and laminated particleboard cabinetry. Jones' condo was all expensive marbles and exotic woods. "A murder I didn't do," he reminded himself and Elaine.

Elaine snorted.

"I'm telling you, it was an accident. I told you a hundred times. The nail gun went off in my hand. It was an accident. Miro fell off the roof. Another accident. That damn nail gun's defective. I ought to sue the manufacturer, that's what I ought to do!"

"Yeah, you do that. Go see some fancy downtown Miami lawyer, tell him how you accidently shot a man full of nails, knocked him off the damn roof and into a swimming pool to make sure he drowned in case the nails and the fall didn't kill him, then hid his corpse in an abandoned hotel and you, you Ronald Patton want to sue the manufacturer for damages!"

"I don't know, Elaine, Ron does have a certain point," Rosalind offered. "Maybe you're being too hard on him."

"Yeah, Elaine," said Ron, quick to grab at any straw, even a straw coming from the crazy lady who dressed like Stevie Nicks and had a potbellied pig for a best friend. "You're being too hard on me."

"You've got to give them the benefit of the doubt, that's what I always do with Todd."

"That's all I'm asking, Elaine." Ron pulled at what little hair he had, wishing it was more.

"Fine. What's next, Mr. I'm-Giving-You-The-Benefit-Of-The-Doubt. Whatever that means," she added with a grumble, feeling ganged up on.

"Sorry about this," Elaine told Rosalind. "Sometimes Ron gets these crazy ideas..."

Rosalind nodded, yawned. "My boy gets the same way." She finished peeling the orange Elaine had offered her earlier, plucked a section loose and bit into it. "Mmm, goes good with chicken. So now what happens?"

"Yeah, Ron." Elaine yawned too. Yawns really were contagious. "What happens next?" She gave him a look that said she figured he had no idea what happened next.

Of course, he didn't. Not exactly.

Then he had another brainstorm. He called them brainstorms. Elaine, smart mouth that she was, liked to call them mini-strokes.

Ron fell into the empty chair between the two women—stuck between a rock and a nut case. "We turn the tables on him." He jerked the table sideways.

"Hey!" shouted Elaine. "You're spilling my drink!"

"Sorry." Ron released the kitchen table. "Anyway, Jones comes home, sees the note—"

"You left a note?" Elaine inquired.

"Yeah, of course. A ransom note."

"That's nice," Rosalind said. "I wouldn't want him to worry."

Ron pinched his nose. There was a monster headache inside his cranium dying to get out. "He reads the note and we negotiate. Now, what do we have?"

His wife opened her mouth to speak, no doubt something sarcastic so he didn't give her the opportunity. "What we have is we've turned the table on Jones. He thinks he's coming back from Orlando to blackmail me somehow with a dead body but instead I've got his mom here. If he wants her back, he's going to have to back down. And meet our demands."

"You keep saying *our*, Ron. I keep telling you, I want no part of this." Elaine's right foot hadn't stopped bouncing for six minutes straight.

"How much am I worth?" Rosalind Jones wanted to know, helping herself to a lime mojito in a can chilling in the fridge.

"A hundred grand," Ron said proudly.

"Wow." Rosalind popped the tab on her drink and guzzled, reminding Ron of the noises that potbellied pig of hers made when it drank.

"A hundred thousand dollars?" Elaine's mouth hung open.

"Sure." He turned to Mrs. Jones. "Your son can afford it, can't he?"

"I suppose so. Business does seem to be going rather well these days." Rosalind slapped the table with her palms. "I have an idea. How about if we fly down to Jamaica?"

"Jamaica? Sounds good to me," Elaine agreed, seeing dollar signs bouncing on the blue Caribbean waters while rum-colored young men in board shorts oiled her from head to toe on the beach.

"What for?" Ron needed to know.

"Because I've always wanted to visit. It looks so pretty on all those travel shows."

"Yeah, but—"

"You could tell my son you're holding me for ransom in Jamaica. Tell him that if he wants me he's going to have to come and get me."

"And bring the ransom," Elaine added.

"Of course," agreed Rosalind. "Pick someplace nice, with an outdoor restaurant and a bar overlooking the beach—"

"And a swimming pool," injected Elaine, her vision growing stronger by the minute.

"We are not going to Jamaica."

"Pity I forgot to pack a bathing suit," Rosalind said.

"Don't you worry, honey." Elaine patted Rosalind's hand. "You can borrow one of mine."

66

After hanging out in the Orlando airport for several long and tedious hours, Todd and Nick boarded a morning flight to Detroit. Both were aching and tired.

"I'm glad you're coming with me," said Todd, buckling in. Things could still get ugly. And messy.

"I've got to earn my fifty grand. If I leave the job to you, you might screw everything up. Then where would I be? Fifty grand poorer, that's where I'd be."

Nick tossed his lightweight jacket into the overhead bin and slammed it shut. "Besides, I wouldn't miss this for the world. You know how boring a cop's life can get?"

Nick stuffed the remains of a bag of cherry licorice into the back pocket of the seat in front of him. "Not to mention, I could use a couple days away from the wife."

Nick and his wife, Trish, got along better the farther apart they were. As they took to the sky, Todd told Nick about Irina's cousin expecting him to marry her.

Nick laughed. "That's hilarious." He grabbed Todd's arm. "And it isn't just the alcohol talking." The detective had several preflight drinks to calm his jitters. He hated flying.

"What should I do?" Todd asked Nick as the titters died down.

"Buy a tux and order a big wedding cake." Nick squeezed Todd's upper arm. "Can I be best man?"

"Funny."

Nick waved for the flight attendant. "This calls for champagne. You're buying."

"I always am," replied Todd, shutting his red and bleary eyes.

A couple hours later, Detroit loomed below. City of Todd's birth. He pressed his face to the windowpane. "I haven't been back in years. Not since me and Mom moved to Florida."

"What about your dad?" Nick asked.

"Disappeared when I was a kid."

"That's tough."

Todd merely shrugged. He'd grown accustomed to it.

"So have you told your mom about this whole marriage thing yet?"

"No. I haven't had the chance. What with everything else going on."

"What do you think she's going to think? I mean, she's a woman. Women love all that marriage shit."

"Mom is crazy about Irina."

"What about you? You crazy about her?" Nick grinned.

"Maybe." The plane circled in the air, sliced through the tall clouds. Skyscrapers and lakes Erie and St. Claire shimmering in the distance.

"What about that other chick you were seeing? Blue eyes, black hair. Looked like a supermodel. You were crazy about her."

"Holly. That's all in the past now."

"Then here's to the future," Nick said, slugging him in the shoulder. "And the future Mrs. Todd Jones!"

"Let's not get ahead of ourselves," Todd replied. Marriage, to anyone, was the furthest thing from his mind. "First and foremost, let's make sure there is a future."

The pilot announced that he was beginning their descent.

The Great Recession had hit Detroit especially hard. The city had been in bad enough straits before the recession. He'd heard things were getting better now.

Oddly, one of the things he remembered most, outside of his own childhood, about Detroit was the time a passenger jet had gone down in the late 1980s. Of the 149 passengers and 6 members of the flight crew, only a 4-year-old girl had survived. He'd never forgotten that and sometimes wondered what it felt like to be her.

The jet bounced against the runway and, for a second, Todd wondered if history was going to repeat itself. His fingers dug into his armrest. But the big jet settled down and rolled to the gate without incident. Within minutes, he and Nick were disembarking.

"First class all the way. That's the way I like it, uh-huh, uh-huh." Nick pressed his knuckles into the small of his back and rubbed. It had been a crowded flight but going in business class had eased the pain. "So what do you think Christie's doing in Detroit?"

"Sulking, plotting. We'll find out soon enough." Todd handed the rental car agent his driver's license and a credit card.

"You think she might have carted Miro's corpse up here?" Nick said.

"Not so loud," warned Todd, as they marched down the skybridge.

Nick ignored the warning. "Maybe she's got him stashed alongside Jimmy Hoffa somewhere. Maybe under Tiger Stadium."

"That was torn down years ago. The Tigers play in Comerica Park now."

"Yeah, yeah. I knew that." Nick picked at his wrinkled, overripe shirt. "Maybe we could stop and pick up a change of clothes and a toothbrush first." Nick sniffed his armpits.

"We can do that once we hit the city."

Todd and Nick had no luggage, only the clothes on their backs. The Volvo was sitting in long-term parking at Orlando International Airport. Picking out a silver sedan from the selection of rentals, they climbed inside.

Todd's phone rang. He looked at the number and frowned. "I've got to take this."

"Sure," said Nick, taking off his shoes and rubbing his feet.

"Good morning, Mister Brezhinski. This is a surprise," Todd said.

"How is our little project coming along?" Mr. Brezhinski asked without preamble.

"The painting? Great, as far as I know. Is there a problem?"

"Constantine is the problem. He wants that painting ASAP. He thinks I'm leading him on, stalling, for sinister reasons all my own." A deep chuckle followed. "How soon can we deliver?"

"I'm out of town at the moment," Todd answered. "Let me check. Give me till this afternoon. Hopefully, I'll have some good news for you then."

"I expect you will. I'm counting on you."

"Yes, sir. Trust me, you'll be pleased with the results."

The two men said goodbye after Todd repeated his promise to call back in a few hours with an update.

"What's up?" asked Nick. "You taken up painting? Like Picasso?"

"A little favor I'm doing for Brezhinski." Todd started the car's engine.

"Not dealing in stolen art, are you? I mean, you do know that's illegal."

"Come on, Nick. Would I do anything that wasn't one hundred percent on the up and up?"

Nick grunted. "Right. I'd hate to have to bust you."

"Or coerce me into paying you to keep your mouth shut so I don't end up in a cell somewhere?"

"What can I say? I'm civic minded." Nick answered with a shrug. "Prisons are awfully overcrowded."

67

Todd entered the coordinates for Christie's place into his smartphone, settled the phone in the cubby under the dashboard, and drove out of the garage and into a dirty gray sky. "Twenty miles to the Book Cadillac."

"What kind of person lives in a hotel?" Nick wanted to know, picking through the radio stations, deciding nothing was listenable and shutting it off.

"You heard Christie. Strange has a penthouse in the same building. I guess he likes to keep her close at hand."

"From the pictures I've seen of her on the Net, I can't say I blame him." Nick settled back and closed his eyes.

When he opened them again, downtown Detroit loomed above him.

Built in 1924, the Book Cadillac, self-named after the Book Brothers, claimed to be the tallest building in Detroit and the tallest hotel in the world at that time. It held a prime location on Washington Boulevard at its intersection with Michigan Avenue, and close to the Detroit River. The Book Brothers' vision was to turn this area into the Fifth Avenue of the Midwest. It hadn't turned out to be quite the success they had imagined. The brothers lost the hotel during the Great Depression.

Through good times and bad, ownership changed hands many times, and the brick and limestone Neo-

Renaissance edifice in its current incarnation, circa 2008, boasted thirty-one floors, with the top eight floors belonging to private residents such as the one George and his wife called home.

Leaving the car with the valet, Todd and Nick strolled up to the second-floor lobby, all white ceilings, white floors and thick brown-clad columns. A few potted plants sprinkled around the brightly polished interior let guests know that nature still existed, if only just barely and well-contained to prevent its spreading.

An impeccably dressed middle-aged woman standing at the ready at one of several check-in counters waved the men over.

Todd booked them a couple of rooms for the night then asked the clerk to call up and announce their arrival to Christie Campbell.

They rode the elevator in silence, ignoring the looks of a short Asian woman in her fifties with dyed blonde hair and a dog that looked surprisingly to Todd like George Strange's dog, Cuddles.

Exiting the elevator, Todd rapped on Christie's door.

"Who is it?" came the voice on the other side. A voice he now recognized as being Christie's.

"It's me, Todd—"

The door opened before he could finish.

"I know who you are. I recognize you." She opened the door wide and let them in. Her own room, a club-level suite had a commanding view of the Detroit River.

"I don't recognize you though." She was staring at Nick. People often did.

"This is Nick. He's with me," Todd explained.

"The pleasure's all mine." Nick bulldozed his way in and across the room. "Some digs." He gazed out the window. "Some view." He pointed. "Is that Canada over there?"

"I think so," Christie told the detective. "Anybody want anything? I haven't eaten all morning."

"Coffee would be great," Nick said from the window. "Same here."

"I'll order some." Christie called room service from a tabletop phone beside a plush club chair, ordering a pot of coffee and an assortment of croissants, fruit and muffins.

"What do you mean you recognize me?" Todd asked, following Christie to a dark sofa.

"I was watching you." She folded her legs under her. A tight pink leotard hugged her lower half. A white sweatshirt hung loose from her shoulders.

"Watching me?" An uneasy tingle shot up Todd's spine.

"Yes. At George's house. Then again at the Orange Blossom Resort." Christie toyed with her ponytail, chewing the end of it until she realized what she was doing, blushed and stopped.

"You followed us." Suddenly it all became clear to Todd. "You saw what happened on Strange's roof. You saw Miro get killed." That explained the feeling he'd had of being watched. His intuition had been correct.

Christie nodded. "I saw Ronald Patton, that's his name, right?"

Todd nodded.

"I saw him shoot Miro. Why'd he do that?"

"Because Patton knows as much about nail guns as he does roofs."

"Oh." Christie didn't seem to care much one way or the other. "Anyway, I saw Miro fall off the roof. Then you both fished him out of George's pool and carried him to the van."

"It was an accident," Todd insisted. "After that, we wanted to cover our tracks."

Christie's bare shoulders moved up and down. "I don't care. I hated Miro. Always spying on me for George."

Nick chuckled. "Man, I wish I'd been there to see that. You and that lousy roofer. Sounds like you two performed a real Keystone Cops routine. And you," he said to Todd, "Mister Doesn't-Like-To-Get-His-Hands-Dirty, trying to repair a roof in the first place."

Nick snorted and went to answer the rap at the door. "That was quick."

"Then I followed you to Orlando," Christie continued softly to Todd.

"And watched us hide the body."

"Impressive," said Nick, eyeing the young woman with newfound respect. He rolled the room service cart to the sofa and fell into a chair, helping himself to coffee and pastry, carefully avoiding the fresh fruit.

"Where is our lovely corpse now?" Nick wanted to know between mouthfuls. "In the closet? Under the bed? And how did you manage to get him there?"

"I had help."

"Prince Charming," Todd said, pouring coffee for her and then himself.

"What?" Christie said with surprise. Her hand shook, spilling coffee on the sofa. "Damn." She rubbed at the wet stain with her palm.

"Your friend," continued Todd. "Prince Charming."

"You know about him?"

"I told you, I know everything," lied Todd. "For

instance, I know about you and George."

"Listen, I'm not saying I'm proud of it but a girl has to do what a girl has to do. Besides," she toyed with her fingers, "it didn't start out that way. George, Strange Scrap, offered me a modeling gig. Things just sort of got out of control from there."

She stabbed a slice of cantaloupe with a small fork and pushed it into her mouth, chewing slowly, sullenly.

"What's your beef with him? Looks to me like he treats you right." Nick said, pointedly taking in the fine finishings of the apartment in the sky and the girl's expensive clothing, diamond-stud earrings and hundred-dollar haircut.

"He's mean. He lied to me. Like I said, he even had that punk Miro keeping tabs on me for him. Bogs, too."

"Sounds like you've got anger issues," Nick grinned, folding a croissant in two, mindless of the crumbs falling on the tops of his shoes. He bit into the flaky pastry.

"Anger issues?" Christie's blue eyes burned. "I'd like to blow up Imelda. That's what I'd like to do!"

68

"His wife?" Todd said. She really did have anger issues.

"Give me the corpse and you can consider it done," Nick replied quickly.

"Not his wife, his boat." Christie shot Nick a troubled look.

"A boat?"

"His stupid fishing boat."

"Oh." Nick appeared surprised. And a bit disappointed.

"Why the boat?" Todd asked.

"George promised to rechristen the boat in my honor. But I saw that stupid boat. He put you-know-who's name on it."

"Don't tell me, the wife's?" Nick said.

Christie's blue eyes narrowed and her face hardened on hearing that word. "She's staying here now," she said, her gaze drifting upward.

"In the hotel? I thought I recognized her coming up," Todd said.

Nick snapped his fingers. "The dog lady in the elevator."

"Probably her," seethed Christie. "I can't stand the woman."

"Okay. I get that," Todd replied. He had a hunch the feeling was mutual to say the least. "But there must be some better way of getting back at him. Her. Both. Something more rewarding."

"Such as?" Nick wanted to know.

"I've got it." Todd beamed. "How about offering him the deal of a lifetime on a rare painting?"

"Again with the painting?" Nick appeared skeptical.

"What kind of painting?" Christie asked, picturing something featuring Cinderella and maybe rainbow-colored unicorns.

"A painting worth a million bucks."

Nick whistled.

"Why would I do that? Besides, I don't have a painting like that. If I did, I'd sell it myself and have all the money I need."

"No. You don't. But I do. A Magritte to be exact."

"What's a Magritte?" both Nick and Christie chorused.

"Henri Magritte is, was, a world-famous artist. His paintings can fetch into the millions."

Nick whistled appreciatively.

"And you've got one of his paintings?" Christie's eyes grew greedily.

"He's got a fake, that's what he's got," Nick told her.

"That's right." Nick always was good on the uptake. "It's a forgery. But that's not what you're going to tell George."

"I'm not?" She blinked. Lost and confused.

"Here's what you are going to say," Todd explained. "You're going to tell George that it's a very expensive painting that you, Christie, are going to claim your recently deceased grandfather bequeathed to you."

Christie's puzzlement continued unabated. "My grandparents are alive and well."

"I'm guessing George doesn't know that, right?"

"No. He doesn't give a hoot about my family. Knows nothing about them. Mom and Dad hate him."

"As I suspected." What parents would want their daughter seeing a married man, let alone one twice their daughter's age?

"So you tell him Grandpa recently passed, left you the Magritte in his will. You'll tell him you have no idea what it's worth but that a dealer offered you, I don't know, a couple hundred thousand for it. I'm guessing he'll outbid our dealer."

"You really think so?"

"I'd bet on it," said Todd. "And I know just the dealer." Irina's cousin Stalin would be glad to oblige.

"You really think George will believe it?"

"He'll want to believe it," Todd assured her. "He's a greedy bastard."

"True."

"I've only got one question," said Nick, sliding his empty coffee cup from hand to hand across the tabletop.

"What's that?" Todd asked.

"Can I still blow up the boat?"

69

Growing drowsy as the last couple of days and nights caught up with him, Todd stood and paced the thick carpet. "If you are so mad at Strange, why blackmail me and Patton?"

"For the cash, of course," explained Christie. "I want some money of my own. Not the puny allowance George doles out. Strings attached, I might add. He's so stingy. And him with his millions."

"Sounds like a real jerk," Nick replied.

"Peter and I—"

"Peter?"

"Prince Charming. We have plans to go to Los Angeles. The money will help tide us over until we become stars."

"Movie stars?" asked Nick.

Christie said without hesitation, "TV stars would be okay, too. Even YouTube stars. Some actors are making tons on the Internet."

Todd suppressed a smile. Christie had a lot to learn about life. "This Peter is your boyfriend?"

"No, a friend. We know each other from high school."

"I see. Was this blackmail his idea?"

"No, the idea was all mine. I couldn't very well blackmail George. He might figure out it was me. He'd dump me for sure. Then where would I be?"

Christie crossed her arms. "Peter didn't know a thing about it until I asked him to help me move the body from where you'd hidden it."

"That explains the case of the missing Miro," Nick put in.

"What about you, Todd?" asked Christie, joining him at the window, laying a hand on his arm.

"Excuse me?"

"What do you want?" Her fingers did a little dance on his forearm, causing his little hairs to join in.

Nick's eyebrows went up in question, his eyes fixed on Todd, waiting to hear his answer.

"Easy. You give me the body, I give you the painting." He had to put an end to this whole Miro episode. Get Bogs off his back.

Nick nodded. "Not quite what I was expecting," he mumbled. "But sounds fair." He clamped his hands over his knees. "So, Christie, where's Miro? Got him a room here at the hotel?"

"Nick, I don't think—" Todd's phone rang in his pocket. He pulled it out and glanced at the screen. "It's Irina. I'd better take this."

Christie returned to the sofa and poured a second cup of coffee. Nick focused on the pastries.

"Hello, Irina. I was going to call you later to ask about the project. Because I heard from Brezhinski and —"

"Todd! Listen! You must listen to me now!"

"Huh? Okay. What's up?"

"It's your mother, Todd. She is gone."

"What do you mean gone? You mean dead?"

"No, I mean she is missing. She was here last night. We had supper. I was up late finishing painting. This morning she is gone. Her bed not slept in."

"Christ," swore Todd. This was no time for his mother to disappear. "Relax, Irina. She's probably run off to see some rock concert. Check the Internet. See if any of her favorite bands are playing anywhere in the area. Trust me. That's where you'll find Mom. Camped out at some festival. Listening to music, getting high."

"Yes…okay." Irina sounded uncertain. "Then how do you explain the note?"

"What note?"

"The note I find taped to refrigerator."

"I don't understand. A note? Mom wrote you a note? Did she say where she was going? When she would be back?"

"No. I do not think it written in her hand. Plus, the note says you must pay money if you want to see her again. Lots of money."

"Mom wants money?" She always wanted money but this was a new angle, and a stretch even for her.

"No no no. You not understand me. Ooooh. This so hard."

"Okay, okay. Take your time."

"Kidnapper take her, Todd. Kidnapper take her."

"Kidnapper? Seriously? Somebody kidnapped my mother?" Todd asked, incredulous. Why would somebody kidnap his mother? It was crazy. It was ludicrous. "Seriously?"

Of all the bad luck. Why couldn't they have kidnapped the pig?

"Yes, my Todd." The words streamed out in a flood. "He took her and she is gone and I do not know what to do and I know I shouldn't call you because your work is important but I am so worried and—"

"Whoa, whoa. Slow down. Breathe, Irina." Todd had never heard Irina sound so agitated before. He'd never heard her sound agitated at all. "Let's start over. You're sure you got this right? I mean, no offense but your English isn't the greatest. Maybe Mom left the note as a joke."

"A joke, Todd?"

Had his mother moved out? Gotten an apartment of her own? Taken that four-legged pork chop with her?

No, that was too much to hope for. Besides, Mom had no money of her own and she hadn't asked him for anything out of the ordinary recently. Unless this so-called ransom note was her way of raising the cash for first, last and a security deposit on an oceanfront condo.

"This is what I do not know, Todd. I do not think a joke. Not funny. The note says she is gone. Gone!"

"Okay, okay. Mom left a note saying she was gone. Did she say when she would be back?" What had gotten into Irina?

He heard her gulp and take a long breath.

"The note, Todd, it says—Wait, I read it to you. It says 'one hundred thousand dollars or you'll never see your mom again. Will be in touch.'"

"I don't get it."

"The note is here Todd. Ransom note. I find it taped to refrigerator this morning when I come to make breakfast. Rosalind gone. Only me and Mr. Squeals here."

"Ransom note?" Todd went rigid as the reality of the situation hit home. "Mom's really been kidnapped?"

Nick shot up from the sofa.

Christie gasped.

Todd's fingers tightened around his smartphone.

"Who? Who would kidnap Mom?"

"It is Ronald's Roofing man," Irina said.

"Ron Patton?" Anger flooded Todd's eyes. "How do you know?"

"I call the desk downstairs. Ask about Rosalind. The man on duty overnight. He remembers man in Ronald's Roofing shirt visiting. Your mother goes with him. But I do not remember seeing such a man, Todd. I-I was working on painting…" Sobs smothered her words. "I-I am so, so sorry. This my fault."

"No, no, no. Irina, listen. This isn't your fault. Calm down. Mom's fine. Trust me." If anything, Ron was in trouble. Mom could be a handful at the best of times.

"What's going on?" demanded Nick. "Somebody snatched Rosalind?"

"Yeah," Todd said. "Why couldn't he have kidnapped Mr. Squeals instead?"

"Who's Mr. Squeals?" asked Christie.

"Todd's kid brother," Nick said with a grin. "His mom's favorite."

"Very funny." Turning his attention to the distraught Irina, Todd said, "Listen, everything is going to be fine. I'm flying home today."

"I call police?"

"No, no police," Todd said firmly. "We can handle this. Besides, I've got Nick here with me. He is the police, remember?" She knew Nick.

"Yes, this is good. You come home soon?"

"Very soon. Soon as I can. What about the work?"

"All finished. That is why I did not notice your mother missing. I work all night. Everything done. I want you to be happy, Todd." She sniffled. "I am so sorry. If I had been paying attention…"

"Then the bastard might've kidnapped you too," concluded Todd. "And I wouldn't want that to happen."

"You would not?"

"No. No, I would not." Todd had startled himself. Did he really have feelings for Irina? "We'll talk about this later. I'll call you when I've booked my flight. Give you all the details."

"Flight?"

"I'm in Detroit. Nick and I have business here. I'll explain later. I've got to go."

"Yes, Todd."

"If you hear from Mom or Ron, let me know ASAP."

"Yes. Promise."

"Great. Hang tough. I need you to do me one more favor."

She blew her nose. "Yes?"

With Christie and Nick listening avidly, Todd explained to Irina that he had some personal effects belonging to Miro Frankowski hidden away and where she could find them.

"Who is this Miro person?"

"I'll explain later, when I see you. Right now, the important thing is that you overnight the credit cards to those friends of yours, Yulia and Nico. Tell them to start spending, charging to the credit cards."

"Charging, Todd?"

"Hotel rooms, food, clothes. Whatever. Do you think they'll agree?"

"Yes, I think they do. But why they do this?"

"I need certain people to believe that Miro is alive and well and living in Antwerp at the moment." That would get the heat off him. At least, for a time. If anything, it would confuse and stall Bogs.

A long silence followed. He heard the sounds of continued sniffling. "Irina? Are you there?"

"Yes. I do this for you. Right now," she vowed. "I have another thought, if is okay?"

"Sure. What?"

"Why not Yulia and Nico create email account for this Miro and contact these certain people you call and tell them he is all right? Would not that help?"

Todd laughed. "Irina, I love you! That's a wonderful idea!"

Irina gasped.

Nick's brow shot up.

"This is so sweet," Christie said, hovering close and hearing everything. "Hello, Irina! Can't wait to meet you!" she shouted into the phone. "I can give you all their email addresses, if you want them!"

"Yes? Hello? Who this?" Irina asked.

"Don't worry," Nick bellowed. "It's Nick. Sit tight."

"Sit tight, Irina." To Nick, Todd said, "We have to get back to Fort Lauderdale right away. We have work to do. You too, Christie."

"Ooh, this is like a movie," Christie stage whispered in Nick's ear. "I wonder if we could pitch this to a Hollywood producer."

"Good idea," Nick said, wrapping a hand around Christie's waist. "Tell me, who do you see playing me?"

Todd knew Irina was right. It must be Ron Patton. Who else could it be? Trying to squeeze some money out of him. "Two can play this game." Todd marched to Christie's bedroom, shutting the door behind him. "Sorry about all the commotion."

"Yes, Todd. Is okay. You are in trouble. Rosalind in trouble. Irina help."

"I know." They went over the plan once again and rang off.

Todd pressed his back against the door, thinking of the enormity of what he'd done, what he'd said. Was he going to have to order a big wedding cake?

70

Rosalind Jones spent the night in the Pattons cramped guestroom. The double bed was double lumpy. The AC barely worked and sounded more like it was coughing up blood rather than trying to produce cold air.

And the so-called guestroom was more of an extra-large storage closet holding everything they didn't want or no longer needed but couldn't bring themselves to part with.

This included two stacks of warped LPs Ron had been hauling around since the nineties, a blue electric Fender Mustang guitar Ron had been meaning to learn to play by listening to all those warped LPs, and tons of old beauty salon equipment—including a couple of antiquated perm stations that looked like some alien brain-sucking devices that every UFO driver worth his/her/its salt carried with him/her/it when visiting Earth and probing earthlings—that Elaine hadn't been able to give away, let alone sell.

Happy to be out of the stuffy and overcrowded bedroom, Rosalind shuffled out to the kitchen, following the scent of scrambled eggs, toast and coffee. A nice relief from the smell of dust and dampness rising from the forty-year-old carpet.

"Good morning," said Elaine, hair in curlers, body in pink and blue kitten PJs. "Coffee?"

"Yes, please." Rosalind helped herself to a seat at the kitchen table.

Ron joined them, helping himself to a full plate of eggs from the warm skillet on the stove and two slices of good old American white bread slathered in butter.

"You know, for a couple of kidnappers, I think you and Elaine are really quite lovely." And stupid. They hadn't tied her up or even locked her door. And being a single-story home, she could have easily escaped out the bedroom window anytime she liked. She wasn't that old and frail.

Stupid, real stupid.

"Thanks," said Ron, taking a tentative sip of the coffee Elaine had brewed up in the drip machine. Each day was an adventure in regards to Elaine's coffee brewing talents. Today's brew wasn't half bad. Then again, it was only half good. "Sorry to put you through this. But your son left me no choice."

"Todd can be rather stubborn at times. But he's mostly all talk. He really is a good boy."

"I'm sure he is," Elaine said, joining them at the kitchen table. "Why do you suppose he wants this poor dead boy's corpse, Rosalind?"

"Really, I have no idea. Maybe he wants to give the child a proper burial. Maybe his conscience was getting to him, digging at him. Did you ever think of that?"

Elaine frowned. You could see she was thinking that that did make as much sense as anything else. "Yeah, Ron, honey, did you ever think of that? *Before* you kidnapped this sweet lady?"

Ron's cheeks glowed. "No, I didn't. And that's not what he's doing. He's out to get me." Turning quickly to Rosalind, he added, "No offense, ma'am."

"None taken. You're upset. Maybe a nice trip, a little vacation would do you some good. I know a vacation always does me wonders."

Ron banged his fork against the table. "I already told you, we are not going to Jamaica."

Rosalind shrugged. "Just a thought." She unfolded a paper napkin and let it flutter to her lap. She'd been forced to don a simple yellow housedress of Elaine's. Mrs. Kidnapper had been kind enough to lend her some clothes. Not at all her style but at least they were fresh and clean. No shoes though, her feet were too big. "What happens now?"

"I'll give Jones a call. Get the ball rolling."

"You call him and he'll know it's you," reminded Elaine. "Assuming he hasn't figured that out already."

"For your information, Elaine, I have a smartphone I bought from the Sav-A-Bunch. No way Jones can track the call back to me. And I'm going to disguise my voice."

"Clever," admitted Rosalind. Not so clever the night before though when they'd strolled out of the condo building right under the nose of the night duty man. Todd was probably on his way here now.

"Tell me you're not going to drag out that lame Cary Grant impression of yours," Elaine said to her husband. To Rosalind, she said, "You ought to hear it, or rather you're lucky if you don't have to. Ron thinks he's some sort of suave Golden Age movie star. Sounds more like the chimpanzee in all those old Ronald Reagan movies, if you ask me."

Rosalind tittered.

"Nobody *is* asking, Elaine," Ron said through a very tight jaw.

Elaine stuck her tongue out at him.

"Getting back to business, if you don't mind." Ron cleared his throat, hoping to symbolically clear the air. "If things go to plan," Ron said, wiping the remaining half-slice of toast across his plate, "we'll set up the money drop and Rosalind here will be home in time for dinner."

"What about in the meantime?" Elaine pressed.

"What do you mean? Meantime what?"

"I've got a beauty shop to run. My customers count on me."

"So?"

Elaine bent her head in Rosalind's direction. "What's Rosalind going to do all day? I'm going to work and you're going out to play Mister Kidnapper."

"I could watch TV. I saw a set in the other room. Do you have cable or satellite? Either will do."

"Neither," said Elaine, giving Ron *the look*. "Ron's too cheap."

"Not even Netflix?" Rosalind appeared astonished.

"We've got an antenna on the roof," explained Elaine. "At least, we did until Hurricane Oscar decided it didn't look so good up there and sent it on its merry way."

Ron frowned, seethed, sweated, throbbed. Who knew holding a lady hostage could pose so many problems? The sooner this was over with, the sooner life could get back to normal.

Ron locked eyes with Todd's mother. "You promise not to go anywhere? Call anyone?"

"Scout's honor," promised Rosalind, raising her hand and shooting him the peace sign.

Elaine said, "Guys, that's all well and good but don't you think this is the first place Jones is going to look?"

More frowning on Ron's part. "Fine, we'll keep her at the beauty shop."

"Oh no, you won't," replied Elaine. "I don't want some SWAT team swooping down on me and my customers. Business is bad enough as it is."

"The beauty shop sounds fun," interjected Rosalind. "I've been meaning to get a new look." She fluffed her hair. "Honey, do you think you can get me some of those whatchamacallits, extensions, make me look like Stevie Nicks, all permed up, circa 1978 when Fleetwood Mac was out playing their Rumour's tour?"

"I suppose. If I saw a picture."

"I can show you on the Internet," Rosalind said with a tinge of excitement.

71

Ron scraped back his chair and stretched out his back. All this prattle was making his head hurt. He needed air. "Okay then, it's settled. You two ladies will spend the day in the beauty shop. I'll give Jones a call around noon."

"Why wait?" asked Elaine.

Ron grinned. "Let him sweat a little. It'll do him good."

Ron slipped on his shoes and went out the front door and into a wall of sunshine.

He squinted and looked at his van. He threw open the garage door and rooted around in the clutter until he came up with a scraper and his stenciling kit.

Ron was changing the corporate name on his van from Ronald's Roofing to Ronald's Flooring Specialists when who should pull up to the curb? None other than George Strange's personal henchman himself, Bogs.

Bogs hopped down from his truck and Ron could've sworn he felt the earth move under his feet.

"Good morning." Ron glanced quickly at the house, hoping Elaine and Rosalind didn't choose that inopportune moment to come outside so they could leave for the beauty shop.

What would Bogs think?

Ron set the can of spray enamel he'd been using to blot out the Ronald's Roofing lettering down on the concrete driveway. "What brings you here?"

"Still looking for my nephew. You seen him?"

"Sorry. Not hide nor hair. Besides, why would I? Not like we're friends or anything."

Bogs grabbed hold of Ron's collar and lifted him off the ground. "You bad mouthing my nephew?"

"N-no!" blurted Ron, struggling for breath.

Bogs dropped him.

Ron straightened his shirt. Three buttons had come loose and lay on the ground. "Ask Jones."

"I already did that. He said to ask you."

"I'll bet he did." Anger spread across Ron's face.

"What's that supposed to mean?"

"It means I think there might have been some bad blood between Jones and Miro. In fact, I'd bet on it. You ask me, that Jones is nothing but trouble."

"Erg-um," grunted Bogs.

Unsure what the grunt meant, good or bad, Ron grabbed the can of blue spray paint and shook it wildly. He set the can down, taped up some letters with painter's tape on the side of the van, picked up the blue paint, shook it some more, and started spraying.

Ron hoped Bogs didn't notice how badly his hand shook.

Bogs sniffed as if he enjoyed the scent of spray paint. "Ronald's Flooring Specialists. You gonna start botching people's floors next?"

Ron let the comment slide. To respond would be to open himself up to nasty remarks and possibly some even nastier bruises.

Ron sprayed. Bogs watched silently for a while then left without another word.

As Bogs' truck rumbled down the residential street

for all the world to see and hear, Ron, trembling, set the can of blue spray paint down next to the van's front tire.

Looking at the side of the van, inspecting his work, he swore. More blue paint surrounded the stencils than did blue paint fill the stencil letters. Some squirts stretched as high as the roofline. He'd have to start over. Repaint this entire side of the van.

Elaine and Rosalind stepped outside, arm in arm. They stopped and not so much admired his work as gawked at it.

"You missed a spot," snickered Elaine, leading Rosalind to her Toyota.

Watching them go, Elaine's Toyota retreating down the street, Ron hurled the can of blue spray paint at the car. "Miss this!"

The can flew through the air, end over end over blue-capped end. Ting!

"Uh-oh!" Ron flinched. Sonofabitch. He'd actually managed to strike Elaine's car. Right smack on the trunk too. For a fleeting second, he was feeling practically proud of himself.

Then brake lights popped on.

Elaine stuck her head out the window.

Ron ducked and ran towards his backyard, keeping close to the hedge that both he and his next-door neighbor refused to trim because each man insisted it was on the other's property.

72

After the bombshell news of Todd's mom getting snatched by Ron Patton, the Detroit trip had been cut short. Christie and Todd booked a direct flight to Fort Lauderdale.

Nick hopped on a plane in Detroit, off the plane in Orlando and into the borrowed Volvo station wagon left slow cooking in the long-term parking lot of the Orlando International Airport.

Todd claimed business class was full and made Nick fly coach. That meant no priority seating and gourmet meal. Nothing but a teensy bag with maybe four peanuts inside. To top off his misery, he'd had to pay for his drinks.

It was nearly dark now. Nick's stomach reminded him that he'd had no dinner. It was tempting to stop at one of the joints in the airport but they were overpriced and he wanted to get his hands on Miro's remains ASAP. He'd eat better after he had the body tucked away.

Christie had given him Prince Charming's phone number, though he figured he had this guy's number already. Not his telephone number maybe, but he'd seen dozens of Prince Charmings in his line of work.

Handsome female magnets. If Peter Albert hadn't been in Christie's pants, that didn't mean he didn't want to be. Why else would he help her hide a dead body?

South Florida was full of guys like him. Plenty of

them claimed to be real princes from countries you never heard of and could never check up on the existence of.

These lotharios hobnobbed with the Palm Beach crowd hoping to bilk the rich old blue hairs out of their fortunes even if it meant getting them out of their clothes and into their beds to do so.

In that sense, Peter didn't fit the mold Nick had stuck him in. Christie had no real money, only her sugar daddy, George Strange, did. Were the two working a deeper con? It seemed unlikely, unless this Prince Charming had a lot more smarts than the girl.

Pulling into the South Cell Phone Lot off Access Road, stomach tetchy from lack of sustenance, Nick dialled up this so-called Prince Charming. Peter answered on the first ring and gave him directions to his place down in Kissimmee, an apartment overlooking Lake Tohopekaliga, better known—and pronounced and spelled—by the locals as Lake Toho.

Nick found the apartment complex easily enough. He stopped the car to look at the large lake and the expansive outdoor park bordering it.

A body could get lost in that lake. But he and Todd had other plans, nothing solidified just yet, but they were hoping that Miro would serve some better purpose in death than he had in life. Make himself useful.

They just weren't sure how that was going to manifest itself yet. Taking the body out in Todd's boat and disposing of him in the Atlantic was out. Todd had taken that off the table. The sharks were gonna have to go hungry.

Nick pulled into the three-story Kissimmee-Toho Garden Apartments parking lot and angled the Volvo between two guest slots.

He stepped from the Volvo, happy to be out of the car because the AC sucked. Not that the heat and humidity around here was much better. But at least the air was fresh.

"Hey!" shouted a voice from above.

Nick looked up. "I'll be damned." Some guy looking like Prince Charming right out of a children's picture book was waving to him. "Peter?"

"Yeah. Come on up."

Lights glowed in the stairwell. Mosquitos flowed in hungry clouds. Nick swatted at them as he plodded up the stairs, arriving breathless, in a bundle of sweat. The two men shook hands. "You couldn't rent a ground floor apartment?"

"View's better up here."

"If you say so."

"Come on in." Peter Albert led the way into his apartment, a Minimalist's dream come true with sparse midcentury modern furniture and white walls. Twelve-inch taupe tile ran in every direction as far as the eye could see.

Not exactly the kind of place Nick expected to see a prince living in.

Framed photographs featuring Peter decked up as Prince Charming, holding various poses against various backdrops, held centerstage, or center-wall, that is, above the blue sofa on the longest wall.

Peter's unprincelike civilian clothes consisted of khaki shorts showing off a pair of calves that made it look like he biked forty miles a day—all uphill— a Mickey Mouse T-shirt and yellow flip-flops. And still he managed to look like Prince Charming. Must be the haircut, Nick decided.

The detective plucked a banana from a bunch holding down a gold plate on the kitchen counter. Snapping the soft fruit down in two bites, he tossed the peel in the kitchen sink. "Sorry." He smacked his lips. "No supper."

"Make you a sandwich? I've got some peanut butter and there's some leftover roast beef in the fridge."

"No, thanks. Beer will do." Nick opened the refrigerator and helped himself to two bottles, one of which he grudgingly handed over to the prince.

Seated in a white chair near the patio overlooking the swimming pool, Nick sucked on his beer like it was mother's milk.

Peter sprawled out on the sofa. Making himself at home. Which he was.

Over their Michelobs, the two men got down to business.

"So," Nick wanted to know. "Where is the body?"

Peter grinned. "Would you believe, we've got him on ice in the Magic Kingdom."

Nick laughed and hoisted his beer in a toast. "Disney on ice. I'll bet old Walt never envisioned that."

"Nope, I'll bet he didn't." Peter rose. "Christie tells me you're in a hurry. Shall we go get him?"

Nick hesitated. "You think it's safe? Shouldn't we wait till the middle of the night or something? When there aren't a million guests wandering around the park?"

Peter shook his head. "No, it's okay. He's underground. In one of the big freezers."

"Underground? Freezers?"

"The park is crisscrossed with tunnels and rooms.

It's a real subterranean world. Filled with workers, like me. Everything and everybody that the park does not want Joe Public to see."

"Like the garbage bags stuffed with dirty napkins and soiled cups of overpriced soda?"

"Exactly." Peter grabbed his keys from a dish at the bar-height kitchen counter and jingled them in his hand. "Come on. I'll show you."

They took the station wagon because Nick wanted to grab the corpse and go. Like Prince Charming had said, time was of the essence.

As dark was settling in, Nick swung into an employee parking lot at Peter's direction.

Peter said, "I gotta tell you, I'll be glad to get rid of the body."

"Yeah, I guess it wouldn't do for Mickey or Minnie to stumble across him."

Peter laughed. "No, that it wouldn't." He shook his head. "The things I do for Christie."

"Speaking of Christie," Nick adjusted the AC vent so the not-so-cold air struck him in the crotch. It was better than nothing. Definitely better than opening the windows. "What's up with you two?"

At least he had new clothes. Todd sent a personal shopper out while they were at the Booker Cadillac to buy them some new shirts, pants, underwear and socks.

Nick felt like a new man. Every single article of clothing was worth way more than he'd normally spend on an entire outfit, maybe even his entire wardrobe. No matter, it was Todd's money.

"What's up?" Peter asked in regards to Nick's question. "How do you mean?"

Peter waved to a guy dressed like a giant chipmunk.

At least, Nick assumed it was a guy. Who knew?

"You don't mind her being George Strange's arm candy?"

"Sure, I mind. She could do better."

"Like you?"

"No. I mean, we've slept together. But we're better as friends. I mean that Christie could do better. She could really make something of herself."

"Like a movie star?"

"Maybe. Somebody's got to be a star, am I right?"

"When you put it that way, you're right." Nick swung into an empty parking slot and killed the motor.

Guiding Nick past the guards and into a world of employees only with the flash of his Disney ID card, Peter led Nick to a cramped elevator. They rode it down into the bowels of the Magic Kingdom.

Nobody gave Nick much attention although several folks said hello to Peter as they wandered down several well-lit tunnels.

"In here," whispered Peter. He carefully looked around, decided the coast was clear and led Nick into a hellishly cold freezer filled floor to ceiling with cases of overpriced food for the park's hungry masses.

Behind a pallet in a shadowy corner, Peter paused. "Here he is." He kicked the side of the pallet.

"Where? I see nothing but boxes. You didn't chop him up into little pieces, did you?" If so, he had a newfound respect for the prince.

"Nah." Peter started moving boxes from the pallet to the floor. "Give me a hand."

Moving boxes of frozen burger patties out of their way, Nick discovered a long black bundle hidden in the middle. "So this is the famous Miro I've been hearing so much about, huh?" He leaned closer. "Doesn't look like so much trouble now, does he?"

"Believe me, he's been trouble enough," Peter replied.

"It's like one of those Egyptian pyramids you read about," Nick quipped. "With some dead, forgotten pharaoh's tomb secreted away in the center."

"Yeah, I guess it is."

"Let's get him out of here. I'm freezing my balls off in here."

Peter and Nick hauled the body off the pallet. It wasn't easy. Miro was cold and stiff. The tarp stuck to the pallet and sounded like skin being ripped off bone as they tugged to free it.

"Not the most agreeable work," muttered Nick.

"Tell me about it. Nobody but Christie could get me to go along with something crazy as this."

"Right," huffed Nick, cold clouds spewing from his mouth. "Cheer up. If everything goes to plan, you and her are gonna get a nice payday out of this."

"Yeah, she told me. It'll be a bit of a bummer leaving this gig, but I'm looking forward to L.A." Peter slapped his arms for warmth. "Especially after today."

The two men laid the frozen stiff on the ground.

"How do you plan to—"

"Shh." Nick clamped his hand over Peter's mouth and held a finger to his lips.

The sound of whistling carried across the space. Muffled steps approached.

"Disappear," Nick whispered to Peter, motioning him to take cover in a nearby dark corner.

A gangly man in a black Goofy hoodie with the cowl pulled over his eyebrows stepped around the corner. "Hey," he laid a hand on his heart. "You about gave me a heart attack, man." Strands of red hair leaked around the edges of his loose hood. "You supposed to be here?" He raked his eyes up and down Nick, who was clearly underdressed for the freezer in a thin, short-sleeve pale yellow cotton shirt and khakis.

"Picking up some ice cream." Nick grinned.

"Ice cream?" The fellow took a step back. "You got some ID on you, Mr. Ice Cream?"

"Of course. Wouldn't leave home without it." Nick eased his wallet out from his back pocket. He flipped it open in the man's face. "See?"

The man leaned in for a look. Nick's empty hand reached around the man's neck. He twisted sideways, locking his arm around the man, elbow under chin. He squeezed and the man sank to the floor.

"Wow, how'd you do that?" Peter wanted to know, popping up from his hiding place.

"Learned it in the Boy Scouts."

"He's not dead, is he?"

"Nah. Only napping." Nick grabbed the sleeping man under the armpits and dragged him to the other side of the pallet where he'd remain out of sight until he came to and figured out how to stand again. "We better move fast. When our friend wakes up, he's gonna sound the alarm," cautioned Nick.

"Yeah." Peter's face for the first time showed worry lines.

"Careful kid, you'll get wrinkles."

"What?"

"Never mind," Nick replied. "How were you planning to get our special package out of here without being seen or causing suspicion?"

"Same way me and Christie got him in."

"Which is?"

"We'll grab one of the electric golf carts and drive him straight out one of the tunnels. Right to your Volvo. Anybody asks, it's some of my wardrobe."

"That's some wardrobe."

"Hey, a prince has to dress right, know what I mean? Besides, I often carry wardrobe and props out of here for the extra gigs I pick up."

"Moonlighting? I get that." Moonlighting was a time-honored tradition among cops. "Tell me," said Nick, anxious to get out of the Arctic setting, "you don't mind dressing up the way you do?"

"Like they say, a man's gotta do what a man's gotta do."

"Even if that man's gotta wear tights?"

73

It was dark as Todd and Christie landed at the Fort Lauderdale International Airport. They'd caught an early evening flight. A squall had appeared out of nowhere, according to the pilot, and touchdown had been a little rough.

Irina retrieved them, pulling up to the terminal minutes after Todd texted her to announce their arrival. Christie rolled a Louis Vuitton carry-on and Todd carried a leather overnight bag he'd picked up in Detroit for his dirty laundry. He tossed both bags in the rear seat.

"Any news?" Todd asked as he helped Christie into the back then climbed into the Audi beside Irina.

"Nothing," replied Irina. "I do as you ask. Miro Frankowski's credit cards will arrive in the morning."

"And Yulia and Nico?"

"They know what to do and they are happy to do this for you. Especially Nico," she said with a grin. "He tells me to tell you hello and that he misses you."

"Who's Nico?" Christie asked from the backseat.

Todd blushed. "Never mind." Turning to face Christie, he said, "You know what you've got to do?"

"Uh-huh." She popped her peppermint gum. She'd been chewing since they'd boarded the flight. She claimed it kept her ears from popping. But all that loud smacking rattled Todd's ears and got on his nerves.

"Great. We'll drop you at the Ritz-Carlton. You call Strange, tell him you're back in town."

"Yeah, yeah. Back from Grampy's funeral. Sorry to leave so sudden like, blah blah blah. And, oh, Grampy left me a…a…" Christie wrinkled her nose. "What did you call it?"

"A Magritte. Henri Magritte. Man On A Blue Sofa. Remember that, it's important."

Christie smiled. "I'm committing it to memory. Bizzit." She pressed her index finger to her forehead. "Bizzit. There. All done."

Todd and Irina shared an eye roll.

They dropped Christie off at the Ritz's well-lit entrance. "Remember, tomorrow it's showtime!" Todd called out as she pranced away.

Christie turned and waved. "My first starring role! I can't wait!"

"Neither can I," mumbled Todd. But for a lot of different reasons.

"Let me tell you about my day," Todd began once they were safe and secure in the condo. It was so quiet, so peaceful, so roomy without his mother around. Serene, that was the word. Maybe he should insist Patton keep her another day.

At least, it would have been serene if Mr. Squeals hadn't come running to the door to greet him with his snotty, wet snout, leaving silver trails up and down the lower half of his brand new designer slacks.

"Pour you a drink?" Irina asked from the bar. She looked sexy in a subtle sort of way in a flowing black dress that fell to her ankles and platinum open-toe sandals.

"Absolutely. Let's take them out on the balcony. I

could use some air." The flight from Detroit to Fort Lauderdale had been confining. He threw open the sliding glass doors.

Mr. Squeals followed them out. Todd eased the pig back inside with his foot and slid the door shut. The look of disapproval on Irina's face led him to open it again. "Come on out, you oversized canned ham."

Mr. Squeals snorted, hopped up on his lounge chair and settled in, sniffling softly. Smelling horribly.

Todd sipped his vodka. This was the good stuff. A gift from Irina's cousin. She'd added a drop of orange flavoring to their drinks. "Ron Patton called me today. He tried to disguise his voice." He chuckled twice. "The idiot doesn't realize I'm on to him."

"The kidnapper?" Irina stiffened. "You spoke with this man? Your mother she is okay?"

"Yeah, I mean, I'm sure she's fine. I didn't speak with her. He says she's fine. I've no reason to assume she isn't."

"When she come home?"

Todd shrugged. "Tomorrow."

"Tomorrow, yes? For sure?"

"Guaranteed. Ron insisted on making the exchange today. I insisted we do it tomorrow."

"Why you do this?"

"To gain time. Come up with a plan of action."

"You pay this man?"

"Hell no." Todd polished off his drink. "Want another?"

She held up her glass. "I still have this one."

Todd went for a refill.

When he returned, he sank into his chair, doing his best to ignore Mr. Squeals. The beast had rolled over on his side and was begging to have his ugly belly scratched, wiggling his stumpy legs, trying to draw attach to himself. "You are such a ham," Todd said in a not-so-friendly tone. "Pun intended."

"You have this plan, Todd?" Irina lovingly massaged his neck. She could sense that he was stiff and tired.

"Oh, yeah." Todd kissed her. "And none of it would be possible without you." He caught the light woody floral scent—a mingling of cedar, jasmine and saffron—under her ear. He'd bought her a bottle of perfume in Antwerp. Something new and she'd been delighted.

A tear tumbled from Irina's right eye. Todd gently erased it with his thumb. "Marry me?"

74

It was the witching hour and an old Volvo station wagon hurtled along the Florida Turnpike, a road one had to pay for the privilege of driving on.

The Volvo's driver had opted to shell out the bucks rather than take I-95, which could be trafficky at times, filled as it was with bad drivers, truckers running late and state troopers in search of prey.

Very few witches, truckers or troopers moved along the road now. So there was nobody to see the Volvo slowly detour to the right, over the shoulder and into the weedy canal that snaked along beside the turnpike mile after lonely mile.

Not even the driver of the Volvo saw this. Because he was sleeping.

But he slept no more.

Nick's eyes bulged. A black wall came straight at him. The ground shook. Lights bounced in every direction. The moon laughed at him.

UFO abduction? was the first thought to jump inside his jarred brain.

A second later he was flying. A second after than he was splashing.

Nick's head banged against the steering wheel loosening several teeth. Blood flowed from his nostrils.

Miro, swaddled in the tarp that was itself swaddled in a topnotch body bag, now dangled over the front seat.

"Shit."

This was no UFO abduction. He wouldn't be going on any all-expenses-paid vacation to Planet Kryptoid, where the alcohol flowed freely and all the alien babes fought for the chance to see what sex with an Earthling was like.

No. He'd run into a goddamn irrigation ditch.

Nick grabbed the Volvo's door handle and pushed against the door. It wouldn't budge. He put all his weight against it. No movement. He slammed his shoulder into the door and it inched open a crack. Water rushed inside. Cold, dirty water. "Shit shit shit."

Grabbing his pistol, Nick hammered at the driver's side window with the butt end, shattering the glass. He climbed out, sloshed through the muddy bank, falling on hands and knees into something prickly.

Nick swore. His brand new clothes were ruined. Sopping wet, stained with blood—ironically his own —goop and detritus. A gaping hole had opened up under his right armpit, allowing easy access to every malnourished mosquito within a million miles.

Breathing heavily and swallowing mosquitoes by the mouthful, he stared at the teetering Volvo. Its big old nose angled downward. The good news was that it hadn't sunken any further than the height of the tires. The bad news was that there was no way in hell he was going to be able to extract the vehicle.

Not without help.

And who could he call? When he had a corpse in the back, well, in the front now, but the point remained— who the hell could he call?

He'd be lucky if some stupid Good Samaritan, or worse, some state trooper, didn't show up to see if he was all right and offer to lend a hand.

People could be annoying that way.

He dragged himself out of whatever the hell bush was so damn prickly and into another bush that instantly made his hands and arms itch like hell.

Trudging up the slope to the road, he cast his eyes about. The shadowy, blurry rectangle up ahead served as a beacon. He walked heavily to it for a closer look, having to duck back into the dense thicket as a pair of semis hauled passed going ninety.

Safe to move again, Nick plodded closer and stared at the sign by the glare of his smartphone—miracle of miracles it was still working.

West Palm Beach 22 miles.

He slid the phone into his wet pocket. Now he knew exactly, well, sort of, where he was. Now he knew who to call.

75

Ron cursed. "What a lousy day," he complained, seated at the kitchen table between the two yammering women. One being his wife, the other his kidnapping victim. Neither of whom seemed to give a hoot about him or the day he'd had. *Look at them*, he fumed, seated across the table. *They act like they're best friends and I'm chopped liver.*

To top it off, he'd had to order a family-sized bucket of chicken with all the sides, at his own expense. Why was he forced to spend money feeding Todd Jone's mother? She was supposed to be a prisoner, for chrissakes!

Instead, she was getting the royal treatment.

He squeezed his fork. "I tell you, no offense, Rosalind." They were all on a first name basis now.

"Yes, Ron?" Rosalind drove a spoonful of mashed potatoes and gravy into her mouth.

"That son of yours is a real prick."

"Ron!" scolded Elaine, shock exploding on her face. "You watch your tongue! That's no way to talk at the table." She shook her head in disappointment. "And in front of our guest, too. Shame on you." She waved a butter knife back and forth in front of his nose. "Really, Rosalind. I am so sorry. Seems like I can never apologize enough for this guy."

Stab went the knife in Ron's direction. Ron flinched.

His chair scooted backward and bumped the wall.

This irritated him all the more and not just because Elaine was berating him in front of people. Again.

No, because he shouldn't have been banging any wall. His seat, his normal seat, was over there, facing the stove. But no, Rosalind had somehow claimed it as her own.

"All I'm saying," Ron said, scootching back to the table so he could finish his dinner, "is that I called Jones to arrange the meet, the drop, the whatever you call it —"

"Exchange?" suggested Rosalind, who was tickled pink with her new hairdo. She thought looked exactly like Stevie Nicks now. Well, Stevie Nicks wearing her, Rosalind Jones', skin.

"Yeah, exchange. And what does he tell me? He tells me he can't do the exchange today. He tells me it's got to be tomorrow. Today is inconvenient, he says."

"And you've told us that a hundred times already, Ron," complained Elaine. She was on her third glass of chianti and smoking a Camel. Elaine never smoked. Rosalind had gotten her started. "Let's talk about something else. You line up any flooring estimates yet?"

"Maybe he had a showing today?" Rosalind suggested, slurping down a serving of peas. "Too bad Mr. Squeals isn't here. He loves his fried chicken, extra crispy, just like this."

Elaine stuck her nose in the box. "We got plenty left. Let's wrap some up in foil. You can take it home with you. Reheat it."

"Ooh, that would be lovely."

"Anyway," Ron forced the conversation forward to something that actually freaking mattered. "Speaking of home, we set the exchange up for tomorrow."

"What time?" both ladies chimed.

"Two o'clock."

"Oh, dear," said Elaine. "That won't do."

"Why not?" Ron's eyebrows sunk as low as they could go.

"I've got a lot of customers tomorrow."

"So?"

"Rosalind offered to handle the manicures for me. I'm double booked."

"So undouble book," Ron snapped.

"Why should I change my schedule around to suit you, Ronald Patton?" Elaine rose in anger. She snatched her wine glass, which had started life as a jelly jar, and tossed down what was left of her drink. Rosalind offered her a generous refill. Especially generous since it wasn't her wine. She hadn't paid for it. "That's always the way it is with you. I'm supposed to change my schedule just so you can go play at whatever it is you have half a mind, and a brain, to!"

"Now, now." Rosalind eased Elaine back down into her kitchen chair. "Let's be civil. No need for words we're going to regret."

"Too late for that," snarled Ron, whose stomach was churning with mashed potato, corn nibs and six pieces of spicy extra-crisp chicken. Three wings, two breasts and a drumstick. Sounded like he'd eaten an alien, not a chicken.

"How about this," Rosalind suggested. "Instead of making your exchange, you go meet Todd, collect your money and then you let me go." Her hand fluttered upwards. "After the manicures are done, of course."

"Not bad," Elaine said, looking with admiration at

her new best friend.

"That way, I can stay and help Elaine as long as she needs me."

"Won't work." Ron shook his head side to side. "He's gonna want to exchange the money for you." Although why, he could no longer imagine.

Rosalind's index finger tapped her chin a moment. "I know, you tell him to call me. I'll tell him everything is hunky-dory. That he should give you the money and I'll see him back at home real soon."

Ron wanted to know, "You think he'll buy that?"

"Of course," assured Rosalind. "My boy would do anything for me."

Ron supposed that much was true. Jones did put up with her and her damned pig. He knew better than to say that aloud. Forks and knifes could easily turn into implements of murder and mayhem.

So, instead, he said, "I suppose that could work."

76

Todd was pissed. Nick was calling him in the middle of the night. And he wasn't calling in the middle of the night to report good news. No, he was waking Todd in the middle of the first good night's sleep he'd had in days to report bad news.

He was calling to report his screw up.

After listening to Nick make up excuse after excuse, Todd promised to get back to him and hung up.

He wasn't relishing a run up to Palm Beach at three in the morning, and wasn't sure what he could do about the stupid situation Nick had gotten himself —and, by extension, Todd himself into, considering Miro Frankowski's very cold, very dead body was inside that Volvo now stuck floating in some ditch along the Turnpike.

What to do?

The only person Todd knew who'd possibly be up and about at this hour was Surfer Steve. The kid kept all sorts of crazy hours.

And knew all sorts of crazy people.

So when Todd explained the situation to Surfer Steve and asked him if he knew anybody who might be able to lend a hand in getting him out of this mess, the kid was quick with the answer.

"Misty," he answered quickly. He was wide awake, sprawled out in the game room, getting high, immersed in an online multiplayer fantasy involving dragons and damsels. And getting higher.

"Misty?"

"Cool chick. Owns a fleet of Big Chill ice cream trucks."

"What?" The noise coming through the phone was overwhelming. "Please, turn the stereo down, Steve!"

Silence followed.

"Can you here me, dude?"

"Yes." Todd turned away from Irina, asleep in the bed beside him. "Is this Misty the best that you've got?" he whispered. "Because what I could really use is somebody with a tow truck. Did I mention Nick got the car stuck? Drove into a canal or something?"

"Yeah, what a rush that must've been."

"Steve—"

"You talk to Misty, bro. She'll put your guy on ice. No problem."

"What about the car, Steve? You know anybody?"

"Can't you leave it there? What do you want some old Volvo for? Let her go to her watery grave."

Todd blinked. "You're right. I only need the stiff. Thanks, Steve."

"You want me to call Misty for you?"

"Good idea. She might not talk to me. Talk to her then give her Nick's number and he'll guide her to his location."

"Excellent, dude."

"Steve, you're sure she's discreet?"

"Are you kidding? Dad uses her sometimes to haul weapons that he doesn't want to necessarily go through regular channels."

"She's a gun runner?" Who was Todd getting himself

mixed up with now?

"Dude, I would not say that to Misty's face. Hang in there. I got this."

With those less than reassuring words, Surfer Steve disconnected.

77

"Sonofabitch," Nick said, climbing the embankment and goggling. "He really did send an ice cream truck. Whoa."

Nick slammed to a halt.

The girl climbing out of the boxy white vehicle decorated with colorful ice cream bars, popsicles, cones, and frozen sundaes was stunning—thirtysomething and something to look at.

"You must be Misty," Nick approached the redhead.

"And you must be the doofus who ran a Volvo into a drainage ditch."

Nick blushed. "Name's Nick. And there were extenuating circumstances." He had a whole story planned about the drunker truck driver who swerved in front of him. He began. "You see, there was this—"

"Save it." Misty planted her hands on her well-formed hips. "Fell asleep at the wheel, right, Nick-o?"

Three cars rushed by, blowing her hair around her head, vibrating the air between them.

"Let's get this body of yours moved before anybody gets curious."

"Or stops to order an ice pop?" Nick cracked a grin.

Misty headed down the incline. "This way?"

Okay, so she was lacking in the sense of humor department.

Nick hurried after her. "I got the package over here."

He pointed to a mound covered with shrubbery he'd ripped from the earth.

"Sure you don't want to simply toss him back in?"

"No, I need him."

"You sure? The gators would be happy to dispose of whoever you've got in here." She toed an exposed section of underlayment in the approximate location of Miro's feet.

"You really an ice cream truck driver?" Nick hurried to lend a hand as Misty tossed the bits of shrubbery and weeds off the body and into the slow-moving, wide ditch.

"Why do you ask?"

"Well, you don't seem very bothered about moving a dead body, for one thing."

She stopped, looked long and hard at Nick. "Steve tells me you're a cop."

"That's right."

"Okay, cop, you don't hear me asking you why you got a dead body lying around out here at the side of the Turnpike, do you?"

Nick shrugged.

"And you don't hear me asking why you don't appear bothered about moving that dead body either, do you?

"No—"

"Then how about we cut out the questions? In fact, how about if we cut out the talk altogether and get this little package of yours moved out of here and into the back of my truck?" She slapped her temple and a mosquito the size of a titmouse became a mosquito flapjack. "Because this character is beginning to reek. And you—" She directed a finger at Nick. "Already do."

Nick resisted the very strong urge to pull out his

ankle pistol and shoot her. She was too damn pretty. And he needed her.

They secured the soggy bundle that was Miro Frankowski in the freezer compartment of Misty's Big Chill ice cream truck.

"Time for phase two," Misty said, climbing in the truck, slamming her door shut and urging Nick-o to hurry up and do the same.

"What's phase two?" Nick asked.

For an answer, Misty inched the ice cream truck slowly down the embankment, gunned the engine and bumped the Volvo into deeper water. Again, bump! Again, bump!

Gurgle gurgle.

Water filled the Volvo.

Nick gazed at Misty. He was pretty sure he was in love.

78

Ron was apoplectic.

That asshole Jones was a no show.

Ron stood for over an hour out at the far end of Anglins Pier, the meetup spot he'd chosen in Lauderdale-By-The-Sea for the exchange. Anglins Pier's been a South Florida fixture for over fifty years. Surely, even that jackass could find the spot.

And did Ron have his hundred grand? No. He did not. What he had was a stupid sunburn. And he'd had to pay to go out on the pier—seven bucks for admission, plus frozen bait and rod rental because he wanted to blend in with the other losers fishing in the inky foul depths.

He'd carefully selected a pair of cut-off denim shorts, rope sandals and a pink T-shirt that had blown into the yard after the hurricane. The straw sombrero and moustache from the Sav-A-Bunch Discount Mart completed his disguise.

The black moustache melted, leaving black rivers down each side of his chin, to be soaked up by the pink T-shirt.

What had happened to Jones? Had he balked? Decided his mother wasn't worth the hundred grand? Maybe Jones had seen that his mother wasn't on the pier and come to the conclusion the exchange was off.

If that proved to be the case, Elaine and Rosalind

were going to hear about it. And how. This whole thing had been their dumb idea.

"Should have done things my way!" Ron hurled the rented rod over the side of the pier and kicked what remained of his bait into the water to join it. The fish could have everything.

Splash!

He was going right to Hair By Elaine. From here on out, he was going to do things his way.

Women be damned.

Climbing inside the sweltering newly-christened Ronald's Flooring Specialists van, snarling at the parking ticket thrust under his windshield—a gift of the city for having overstayed his welcome—Ron's personal smartphone belted out Money For Nothing.

Ignoring the parking police lady in her little electric cart idling at his rear bumper, Ron snatched his phone from the dashboard and stared at the screen. Todd Jones calling.

"What the hell." Ron fell back against his blistering seat.

The overzealous parking police officer banged a knuckle against his window. "Pay or go!"

"Just leaving!" Ron backed up quickly, nearly taking her nose off with the sideview mirror.

He eased into traffic, driving one-handed. "What do you want, Jones?" Ron was getting an unsettling feeling. Why was Jones calling him now of all times?

"I'm glad you ask, Ron. What I want," said Todd, "is one hundred thousand dollars. Large bills would be nice. Easier to carry."

"What the hell are you talking about?" Ron leaned on his horn. Some tourist in a minivan refused to turn on red. "Turn already, moron!"

"Having a bad day, Ron?"

"You still there? Because I'm hanging up now."

"I wouldn't do that if I were you."

"Well, you aren't me and I ain't you, so—"

"Not if you want to see Elaine again," Todd went on cooly.

"What's that?" A bead of sweat popped up in the middle of Ron's forehead, slid down and salted up his right eyeball. He pulled into a 7-Eleven.

"A hundred grand, plus the safe return of Mom, or you'll never see your wife again."

"Um, you know about that?"

"About my mom? Yeah, Ron, I know about that. Next time you decide to kidnap somebody, how about wearing a shirt that doesn't display the name of your company on it."

"Shit."

"Yeah, and you're in it deep. Your only way out is to give me my money."

"A hundred grand? For Elaine?" Ron asked in disbelief.

"Same as you asked for Mom. Couldn't be more fair."

"So we trade, Elaine for Rosalind. Assuming you've got Elaine in the first place. And I'm betting you don't."

"No deal," Todd said.

"What do you mean no deal?"

"I mean no deal, Ron. I've got expenses."

"Listen, Jones, I don't know what game you think I'm playing, but I'm serious here, if I don't get that money, your mom could get hurt—"

"Trust me on this, Ron. Mom's fine. It's Elaine you've got to worry about."

Ron wiped his arm across his face. It was so damn hot in the van. He cranked the AC to its max.

"Like I said, this is simple. I've got her and if you want her back you'll pay me the hundred grand."

Ron laughed to suppress his fear. "You're nuts. Are you forgetting I've got your dear sweet mother? What a load of hooey this is. You really are full of it, Jones. You've got balls. I'll give you that."

"Do you have my mom, Ron? Do you? Because if you drive to your wife's beauty shop out on Oakland Park, I think you'll see that it's locked up tight. Seems Elaine and Mom left work early."

"I don't believe you." But Ron sort of did.

"One hundred thousand dollars, Patton. Midnight tonight. We can meet on the pier. You know where the pier is, don't you? Wear your clown costume."

"Clown costume?"

"You know, the cheap straw hat and cheesy moustache."

"Listen, Jones—" Ron stopped when he realized he was talking to dead air.

79

"Nick, this is a surprise." Rosalind Jones tapped Mrs. Elmwood on the shoulder. "This is Nick, dear, a friend of my son's."

Mrs. Elmwood smiled, careful to keep her fingers extended because Rosalind was in the middle of giving her the best manicure she'd ever had in her whole life. And that was saying something. She'd been getting weekly manicures for nearly forty years.

"Help you?" asked Elaine, scissors dangling from her thumb.

"This is my friend, Nick," explained Rosalind.

"Speak with you a minute, Rosalind?" Nick sneezed.

"Coming down with something?" asked Rosalind.

"Nah, must be all the chemicals." This beauty salon smelled worse than a chemical factory. Which, if you thought about it, it sort of was.

He followed Rosalind past a woman snipping another lady's hair and through a pink drape into a cluttered storeroom.

"What's up, Nick? Come by for a trim?"

Rosalind helped herself to a Danish, offered one to Nick.

"No, I came for you. Todd sent me." Nick inhaled the Danish, licked icing off his fingers. "You got any soda in here?" He popped open a brown minifridge and peered inside. Seeing nothing but bottled water, he kicked the door shut with his toe.

"So soon? We had a deal."

"What deal? With who?"

"I promised Ron and Elaine, mostly Elaine, that I'd help out here at the salon this afternoon. I was planning to come home later."

Nick couldn't resist a grin. "Plans have changed. You've got to come now."

Rosalind frowned. "Elaine isn't going to be happy."

Nick helped himself to a tube of shampoo from an open cardboard box on a shelf. He slid the tube into his pocket. The shampoo claimed to smell of cedar and cypress. More importantly, it purported to lessen gray hair. Couldn't hurt to look a little younger.

"That's not the half of it." Nick pulled back the edge of the curtain dividing the storeroom from the salon. "That Elaine there?"

He directed his gaze at the woman standing at the cutting station near the window. Her hair was dark brown streaked with platinum, held behind her head with a purple ribbon.

"Yes."

"Ron's wife?"

"That's right."

"Okay." Nick pocketed a second tube of shampoo, stuffing it in his opposite pocket to balance things out. "Let's go." He pushed through the curtain divider with Rosalind dogging his heels.

Elaine dropped her scissors in a jar of alcohol. "What's going on?"

"Nick's here to pick me up. Giving me a ride home," explained Rosalind.

"So soon?" Elaine adjusted her customer's bib.

"'Fraid so." Rosalind made a sad face.

"But what about my manicure?" Mrs. Elmwood demanded, fingers splayed, eyes pleading.

Nick towered over Mrs. Elmwood, lifted her left hand. "Looks good to me. Nice job, Rosalind."

"Thanks."

"You've got a knack," Elaine said. "A real knack."

"Thank you." Rosalind retrieved her purse from the empty cutting station she'd been using to stash her things. "Nice meeting you Elaine. You too, Mrs. Elmwood," Rosalind waved goodbye.

"You, too, Rosalind. Come back and see me sometime. I can give you those highlights we talked about."

"I will and thank you again for the haircut and the perm." Rosalind Jones flounced her Stevie Nicks doo with her free hand.

"How about next week, Rosalind?" pleaded Mrs. Elmwood. "Can I make an appointment? How does Tuesday at one sound?"

Nick helped Mrs. Elmwood to her feet even though she was unprepared for it. He handed her the red purse at her feet and shuffled her to the door, one hand on her bony shoulder. "She'll call you."

"But I haven't paid," argued Mrs. Elmwood, half in and half out the door, one hand in her purse reaching for her wallet.

"My treat," replied Nick. Not that he intended to pay for the manicure. Or the shampoos in his pockets.

He turned around. Rosalind and Elaine hugged farewell.

"Forget the goodbyes, ladies," interrupted Nick. He pointed at Elaine. "You're coming with us."

"You mean?" A trace of something resembling a smile showed on Elaine's face.

"That's right. We're kidnapping you."

"Kidnapping me?" Elaine and Rosalind shared a look.

It wasn't a look of fear or dread. It was the kind of over the moon look two girls get when their folks tell them they get to have a sleepover. "Okay, give me a minute to lock up."

"You got it." Nick turned the sign in the window to Closed.

80

After dealing with Ron Patton, Todd carefully packed up the Magrittes, laying them out on his bed and wrapping them in thick plain brown paper. Tying them up with string.

One for Brezhinski to gift to Aristotle Constantine, one for Christie to sell to George Strange and the third, the real one, for Brezhinski. He'd deliver that one himself.

Brezhinski would be pleased. Stalin would be pleased.

Todd would be richer. And very pleased.

Irina was keeping him out of the office turned art studio, insisting she had a surprise of some sort for him later.

"The paintings look great, Irina."

"You really think so?"

"I do." Todd kissed her on the cheek. "You nailed it. Trust me, Brezhinski is going to be very, very happy."

Irina had done a hell of a job.

"Thank you. I walk Mr. Squeals now, okay?" Irina insisted the brute was lonely, missed his mommy and thought stretching his legs, stubby as they were, might make him feel better.

"Go ahead. I've got this." Todd didn't care if she was right or wrong. It was nice having the pig out of the way while he finished working.

This whole forgery business might be worth pursuing. South Florida's filled with greedy art collectors who wouldn't ask once or think twice about buying a painting of murky provenance. He might broach the subject with Irina once things settled down.

Christie showed up at the condo right on time. Todd gave her her copy of the Magritte.

"Now it's up to you to sell it to George. Don't settle for too little. An authentic Magritte is worth a small fortune."

"Don't you worry," Christie said. "I'm going to squeeze him for every penny I can."

"That's my girl."

Todd saw Christie off, then he and Irina, back from her pig walk, took the real Man On A Blue Sofa and the copy for Aristotle Constantine, loaded them into the trunk of the Audi, and drove to Brezhinski's estate.

81

"Sorry, it's a little crowded in here," Nick said, squeezing Elaine and Rosalind onto the benchseat beside him.

"I don't mind," said Elaine, twisting her head around. "Never rode in an ice cream truck before."

"Me, too," said Rosalind.

"So does this kidnap victim get a free ice cream?" Elaine asked.

"Sorry." Nick put the clunky Big Chill truck in gear and rumbled out of the strip mall. "No flavor that you'd like."

Miro Frankowski's frozen corpse was taking up most of the retail space at this point in time. It had been nice of Misty to let him borrow the truck a little longer. That girl was sweet.

"Where are we going?" asked Elaine. "Or should I say, where are you going to stash me?"

"Todd and Rosalind's place," explained Nick.

"Oooh, that's wonderful!" exclaimed Rosalind, smushed up against the passenger side door. "We can play pinball and you can meet Mr. Squeals."

"Don't worry, Elaine," Nick said. "You ladies can hang out at the condo till around midnight. Then I'll drive you home."

"Then can I have my ice cream?" Elaine teased.

"Sure," promised Nick. It was the least he could do

considering what he was going to give her husband.

82

Ron rattled up to Hair By Elaine—a hole had sprung up recently in the muffler but he was too cheap to fix it. He slid into a slot in front of the plate glass window. The first thing he noticed was the Closed sign. Elaine never closed during business hours. And the lights were out.

Elaine's Toyota sat out at the edge of the parking lot in its usual space. The magnetic signs on her car doors letting passersby know that she was open for business.

Which she wasn't.

Ron realized his goose was cooked.

"Hey." The manager from the dry cleaners next door poked his head out. "You got a card?"

"For what?" Ron wanted to know.

"The man pointed to the side of the van. "We need the floor replaced. I'm thinking vinyl. Somethin' durable."

"And I'm thinking take a hike," snapped Ron. "I'm kinda busy here."

The man shot him a bird of the one-finger variety and went back inside.

"Stupid sonofabitch." Ron felt like punching somebody. Better yet, he felt like taking his nail gun and shooting a whole bucket of nails into Jones' ugly hide.

The stupid defective nail gun was another reason he was in this mess. Lying in back of the van, just waiting to point the finger of guilt at him.

Could those nails he accidentally shot into Miro be traced back to his nail gun and subsequently him?

He was going to have to ditch it someplace. Maybe drop it off the end of the pier later when he went to retrieve Elaine.

Ron drove home slowly, in a daze, trying to find some way out of this jam. Thinking of nothing.

The only person who could help him come up with something was Elaine. And she'd been snatched.

Or had she?

Realizing he hadn't tried her number, he did so. Straight to voicemail. "It's me. Call me back."

He knew she wouldn't.

"Fine. You'll get your money," Ron muttered, pulling into his driveway. Hoping beyond hope that Elaine would be inside waiting for him. Knowing she wouldn't be.

He opened the door and called her name.

Nope.

Crap.

Still, things could be worse. The bank finally freed up the funds. He'd stashed most of it in a safe deposit box for quick access. He and Elaine would still have plenty of money left after paying off Jones.

And he was never going to let her forget how much he'd paid to get her back.

That should put an end to her nagging forever. A hundred grand ought to buy that much—even at today's inflated prices.

Ron retrieved the safe deposit box key from his underwear drawer, fixed himself a chicken sandwich on rye because a fella's gotta eat, then drove to the bank.

83

"I like this one." Irina fingered an antique diamond ring. "You think is too much?"

"Ah, a lovely piece," replied Stalin, lifting the ring from the velvet display. "Came from the Highland Beach estate of a lovely woman whose father had built a chain of shoe stores. Sadly, their fortunes went downhill after his passing. The woman has no business sense at all. And six ex-husbands who'd been happy to spend her inheritance. Let's try it on." Stalin slipped it over Irina's ring finger.

"I love it," whispered Irina.

"A perfect engagement ring, I think, yes?" Stalin's eyes moved from Irina to Todd.

Irina's eyes moved to Todd. "You like?"

"Yes. It suits you." The pale ring against her pale skin was perfect. Not too flashy. Understated but elegant. Just like her.

Irina kissed Todd. "I think so too."

"Sold!" beamed Stalin. "Figuratively speaking, of course, my gift to you." He could afford to be generous. "Todd has succeeded beyond my expectations."

"Somebody at the door, boss," boomed the Latvian gatekeeper.

George and Christie stood shoulder-to-shoulder outside the locked door, half-blocked from sight by the Latvian, who could have blocked out the moon if he'd a mind to. A shaft of sunlight bounced off George's head.

"Here they are," Todd turned away quickly, not wanting to be seen. "Show time."

"You two lovebirds wait in back." Stalin wiped his hands down his silk shirt. "I'm going to enjoy this." He ordered the Latvian to open up.

Christie had phoned ahead to let Todd and Stalin know that she was bringing George down to get the Magritte appraised.

This was a good sign. It meant George had swallowed the bait. Accepted that the painting was an authentic Magritte.

All Stalin had to do now was confirm Man On A Blue Sofa's authenticity and Christie would get her money.

Todd already had his money. Brezhinski was a man of his word. Todd got every penny he'd been promised. Plus, Brezhinski hadn't minded when Todd explained that Irina had been the artist who'd created the forgery.

In fact, he'd been so impressed, he'd offered her a commission to paint a mural for his office lobby on Federal Highway in downtown Boca Raton.

Christie, dressed in a scoopneck Minnie Mouse T-shirt and tight black shorts, dragged George in by the arm.

George slummed it in a pair of wrinkled seersucker pinstripe shorts and a polo shirt. Dark sunglasses the size of dessert dishes took up half the real estate on his face. Not a good look. No surprise since the pair belonged to Imelda but they were all he could find.

George shot his eyes over the muscled Latvian unlatching the door for them and unashamedly gawking at Christie's breasts while he did so. "You sure this is the right place, doll?"

"This is it, George. Come on." Christie carried the painting. She had removed the string and paper wrapping at his house. He practically drooled over the Magritte as she unveiled it.

On the drive up to Boca, George coddled it in his arms like a baby kitten, secure in the big back seat of the Bentley, letting Christie drive his precious car—which he never did—rather than relinquish the painting.

His usual driver when required, Bogs, had flown up to Detroit hoping to find a lead on Miro there. George planned to dock Miro's wages for every day he'd missed. Make him beg for his job back too. That would teach the squirt to blow him off.

"Help you?"

"I'm Christie and this is George Strange," Christie carried the Magritte to the counter and set it down.

Stalin smiled. "Ah, so this is the item in question. Magnificent. Magnificent."

"You really think so?" George whipped off his sunglasses and stared at the painting. Personally, he thought it was uglier than one of his demo sites, uglier than his Aunt Helen and she had a face that kept the squirrels out of her yard.

It was what the canvas was worth that mattered, not what it looked like. As far as he was concerned, that was what collecting was all about.

"I do." Stalin pulled a jeweler's loupe from his pocket and stuck it to his right eye. "How do you come by this?"

Christie repeated the story she'd given George, as written by Todd. "Grandpa Henry passed away suddenly. I knew he was loaded but imagine my surprise when he left me this." She twisted the frame so the man on the blue sofa faced Stalin.

"That Grandpa Henry," said George, drooling over the painting. "What a guy." Imelda was going to love this. She was going to love him for this. And for getting such a deal on it. At a quarter of a million bucks, he was practically stealing it.

That made this all the more satisfying.

Maybe she'd agree to let him hang it in his office where he could show it off, boast to all his business associates about what a deal he'd gotten.

"Definitely an original Magritte. I stake my reputation on this." An ivory-handled magnifying glass appeared in Stalin's left hand. He peered through it at the painting. That cousin of his really could paint.

"You sure you know your stuff? I mean, no offense," George said, one eye on the large Latvian who, in turn, had his eye on him—or was he eyeballing Christie's chest again? "But this is a pawn shop." What kind of reputation could this thug have? He gave desperate people pennies on the dollar for their crap.

Stalin rocked back on his heels, twisted a very large, very obvious diamond pinkie ring on his finger. "I give you two hundred thousand for it myself. Today."

"I don't know," Christie pouted, fingered the edge of the weird painting. "I was hoping it would be worth more than that."

"You understand, of course, that this would be a cash deal. A cash deal between the two of us. No need to tell Mr. Taxman." He ran his fingers over his lips, figuratively sealing them. "Trust me to be very discreet. I have one or two clients who might be interested in this. They, I promise you, are discreet too." Stalin picked up the painting. "So, we have a deal, yes?"

"Now just a second there, buddy." George grabbed

across the counter for the Magritte. "We only came for a professional appraisal, not for you to try to nab it for yourself."

The Latvian took a menacing step in their direction but a subtle nod from Stalin returned him to the front door.

George snatched the painting from Stalin's hands. "Come on, Christie, doll. I already agreed to give you two-fifty if it was real." He snaked an arm around Christie. "This guy says it's real. So, fine. Two-fifty it is. And that's all cash too. Plus, I'll give you six more commercials this year." Her rate was four grand per commercial shoot.

"I want twelve." Christie yanked the painting from George and clutched it to her bosom.

"Twelve commercials?"

"Did I say twelve, I meant twenty." Christie batted her lashes.

George frowned. "Fine. Twelve."

"And a Boxster?"

"A box of what?"

"A Porsche. A Porsche Boxster." She'd look great cruising around the L.A. Hills in a brand new Boxster convertible. "A red one. A convertible."

"Two-seventy-five!" blurted Stalin, getting into the spirit of things. And wanting to stick it to George. Make him pay through the nose. "And ten thousand dollars store credit. Anything you like."

"Wow." Christie did a turn. "You've got a lot of neat stuff." She sidled along the counter. "How much is that Patti the Platypus?" She pointed to a purple creature kept in a clear plastic case up on a shelf.

"Hmm, a very rare 1993 edition, one of the original

nine Beanie Babies," Stalin explained. "As you can see," he pulled the stuffed toy off the shelf and displayed it, "she is in excellent condition and still has her Ty hangtag."

"Okay, okay. Let's cut the crap." George tugged at his shorts. "Two-fifty, twelve commercials and a Boxster." The damn painting was worth triple that.

"Convertible."

"Yeah, yeah. Let's have it." George wriggled his fingers.

Christie released the painting into George's hands. The plan had worked like a charm. Men really were idiots.

And she really was a great actress. She'd be a movie star yet. George's money was going to help make it happen.

Then she'd never have to see him again.

He could have sex with his wife for all she cared.

84

When Carlos called Todd from the Port Lauderdale Condominium Towers lobby to tell him his ride was waiting downstairs, Todd kissed Irina and his mother goodbye, told Elaine it had been nice meeting her and went down alone in the elevator.

He expected to find Nick waiting for him. He wasn't expecting the ice cream man. Todd glanced at Carlos who merely shrugged and held the lobby door open for him.

"I wasn't expecting the ice cream man." Todd walked around the Big Chill truck. "What's wrong, Nick? You couldn't find anything that stands out even more than this?"

"Consider the big picture," Nick said, walking beside him. "Who's gonna be suspicious of the ice cream man? Let alone be looking for a dead body in the back of an ice cream truck. Which," he added softly, "there is."

"I suppose you have a point." Todd popped open the passenger door. A bit unsettling to think of Miro chilling in back but what other choice did he have at this point?

All this was Miro's own doing. Well, his and George Strange's and Ron Patton's. He was the one now having to clean up the mess. As usual.

"Nice of Misty to let you borrow it."

"I paid her a grand."

"A grand!"

"Well, you paid her a grand. That is, I promised you'd pay her."

Todd decided to let the matter slide. Money was coming in like the tide. "Fine. Let's get this over with. It's after eleven. Ron should be on his way to the pier to meet Surfer Steve. The house will be empty."

"I think she likes me."

"Who?" asked Todd.

"Misty."

"You're married."

"Sometimes you can be a real spoilsport. Besides, me and Trish are separated."

"I didn't know." Trish had the dubious honor of being Nick's spouse.

"Well, separate beds. It's a start."

"Uh-huh."

"Did you bring the shotgun?"

"It's in my office downtown. I didn't want the thing lying around the condo. Think of the damage Mom could do."

This earned him a chuckle from Nick.

"We'll pick it up on the way." Todd settled back, clipped on a cherry red seatbelt. The interior smelled like one of those strawberry éclair ice cream bars he used to gobble up as a kid on his way home from elementary school. "I can't wait to get Elaine out of the house. More permanent guests I don't need."

"Steve knows what to do?"

"Yep. Even Steve can't foul this up. He's coming by here for Elaine anytime now. I gave him Ron's description and told Ron my guy would make contact. He wasn't happy I wasn't coming but what choice does he have?"

"Not a single damn one."

"Exactly."

"What if this weasel reneges? Refuses to pay?"

"He won't, trust me. You know Surfer Steve, he'd be happy to shoot him. He's gun crazy. It's in his genes."

"Good. I didn't go through all this shit for nothing. Fifty gees of that ransom belongs to me."

"You'll get it. And I'll be happy to get Elaine out of my hair." He'd left Elaine and his mom slurping martinis shoulder to shoulder on the sofa, binge watching James Bond films—currently caught up in You Only Live Twice.

"Oh, that reminds me," Nick began.

"What?"

"Just a sec—" Nick leapt from the truck, ran around the back, popped open a freezer and extracted a box of Neapolitan ice cream, chocolate, strawberry and vanilla. "Run this upstairs for me, will you, mac?" He thrust the premium ice cream at Carlos.

Todd stuck a ten-dollar bill out the window.

"Thanks, Mister Jones." Carlos took the ten and the ice cream and ran to the elevator.

"What was that all about?" Todd asked Nick.

"I sort of promised Elaine some ice cream when this was over. I wasn't sure what flavor she liked." He cranked up the motor. "I figure you can't go wrong with Neapolitan."

They zipped off, picked up the shotgun from the real estate office and drove to Ron and Elaine's house. "Nearly midnight. Perfect," Todd said taking a look from the curb at the sad, decrepit Lauderdale home.

Todd chose dark slacks and a black T-shirt for the

occasion. Nick dressed like the ice cream man, a white Big Chill uniform, matching white hat and white shoes. Pastel blue trim and a logo of red, white and blue ice cream scoops on both hat and uniform jacket did nothing to add flair.

"You're going to stand out like a sore thumb," complained Todd.

Nick tugged at his white jacket. "I wanted to blend in, get in character."

"You look like a character, all right." Todd eased open his door. "How do you want to do this?"

The street was quiet but who knew who might be watching from one of those dark windows. Todd distrusted suburbanites.

Piles of debris crowded the street on both sides. The work of Hurricane Oscar, which the homeowners had diligently hauled to the curb. Trucks would haul the mounds of trash out west to the dumps near the Everglades to join the mountains of trash rising like a new range. Flocks of gulls circled and picked through the smelly heaps for treasure.

"Let's recon." Nick hopped out of the Big Chill truck and plodded up the driveway. Just another ice cream man making a midnight delivery.

85

"You got my money?"

"You got my wife?"

Surfer Steve and Ron Patton faced off, nose to nose, at the end of Anglins Pier, which wasn't as far out in the ocean as it used to be because Hurricane Irma took a bite out of it back in '17 and nobody had gotten around to rebuilding yet.

Dim metal lights hovering like flying saucers atop slender metal poles illuminated the kidnapper's assistant, the kidnapper's mark, and the stalwart eight gentlemen and one gentlewoman chatting idly and lazily casting and tugging at their fishing gear, gazing into the darkness, not giving a damn about the two antagonists because there were fish to catch.

These lights also illuminated the myriad night creatures that found such lights enticing. These creatures considered the antagonists nothing more than curiosities at the least and food sources at best.

Steve wrinkled his nose. These fishing people smelled worse than their slimy bait resting in rusty buckets and plastic containers on the equally slimy boards of the pier.

"Money's in the cooler." Ron hoisted the green six-pack-sized cooler he'd brought along for the occasion.

"Let's see."

"Fine." Ron turned his back to the pier and cracked

the cooler open an inch.

"Yeah," muttered Surfer Steve. "That's what I'm talking about."

Ron pushed the lid shut. "So where's Elaine?"

"Yoo-ha! I think I caught a pompano!"

"Elaine?" Ron gaped.

A woman hollering some six yards down the pier and tugging on a fishing pole sounded a lot like his kidnapped wife. However, she sounded like she was having way too much fun for a kidnap victim. Was this his wife?

Where were the ropes? The gags?

"Elaine, is that you?" Ron scurried down the pier and joined his wife.

"Oh, hey, Ron." Elaine beamed. "Look." Grunting, she hoisted up her borrowed rod. "Is this a pompano or is this a pompano?"

"That's yer pompano, all right," pronounced an old gent in a navy rain jacket and white canvas sneakers. A burled pipe stuck out the corner of his cracked red lips. Intelligent eyes swept over the twisting eighteen-inch fish, greenish-gray sides turning to silver and a sloping forehead. The compressed body and small mouth gave the pompano a cartoonish appearance.

Fisherfolk applauding. "Nice catch," said several.

"Elaine, Elaine." The fish slapped its tail in Ron's face. Wet, cold and painful. "What the hell!"

"Huh, what?" Elaine reached for the thrashing pompano. "What happened to your face?"

"I got sunburned standing around here all afternoon waiting for you and Jones to show up, that's what happened to my face. And it still hurts like hell!" More now that he'd been fish slapped.

Ron was exhausted. Worn out. It had been a long and arduous afternoon and evening as he stressed waiting for this time to come when he would be getting his wife back and handing over all that hard-earned money.

This was not the way he'd pictured the exchange going.

"You ought to put some aloe on that. You look like a boiled lobster."

"Never mind my face! Ouch!"

The dumb pompano slapped him again. Who knew a stupid fish could pack such a punch? And with its tail fin, no less?

"Do I smell alcohol on your breath?" Ron asked Elaine. "Have you been drinking?"

Elaine was too busy talking to the fish to talk to her husband. "Come here, you!" she launched her hand at the moving target that called itself a fish.

"Elaine!" Ron grabbed a serrated fishing knife lying atop the wood railing and cut the fishing line. The pompano flopped to the deck.

"Oh no, you don't!" Elaine dropped the fishing rod and scurried after the fleeing fish. "My fish!"

Ron grabbed her shoulders. "What are you doing? You're supposed to be kidnapped."

"I was." Elaine pouted as the pompano dove off the side of the pier, returning to the safety of its watery world.

Ker-splash.

"Now look what you did." She gave her husband that look that told him he was in trouble.

Ron wasn't buying it. "What I did? What I did? I saved your life is what I did. I just paid your goddamn ransom. One hundred thousand dollars!"

That got the attention of the nearest fishermen.

"That's right," said Steve. "Almost forgot. If you don't mind." He reached for the cooler. "I'll take the bait. Pun intended."

"Oh no, you don't." Ron pulled out of reach. "I'm not paying." He had his wife. He had his money. "And there's nothing you can do about it."

"Uh, Ron." Elaine tapped her husband's shoulder.

"You stay out of this, Elaine," ordered Ron. "I'm tired of being pushed around. Let's go home." He grabbed her arm and pulled.

Surfer Steve stepped in their path. "Is he always like this?" he asked Elaine.

"'Fraid so," confessed Elaine. "Ron, you really should keep your end of the bargain."

"My end of the bargain? What bargain? Jones is trying to extort money from me. From us. He kidnapped you."

"Are you forgetting you kidnapped Rosalind, his own mother?"

Ron frowned but only for the briefest second. "I still blame Jones for all this." Glaring defiantly at Surfer Steve, he said, "You tell Jones we're even. That's it, even. Done."

"Not till you turn over that cooler."

"You want it? Try and take it." Ron planted his feet.

"Uh, Ron, I wouldn't—"

"You stay out of this, Elaine. I got this. If this punk thinks—"

"Have you met Tiny?" asked Surfer Steve.

"Tiny?" sneered Ron. "Who's that? Another of your doped up surfer dude friends?" The kid dressed and looked like a preppie Rostafarian, baggy shorts, hemp sandals, purple Hawaiian shirt and silver neckchain featuring a marijuana leaf charm.

"Meet Tiny." Surfer Steve slid an automatic pistol from his board shorts. The small gun barely filled his hand. "Brez Bulldog .380. I know it's small but, believe me, it can put seven holes in anything, including you. Real popular. Dad manufactures these by the bajillion."

"Hey, I got one of those," one of the fishermen bragged to his buddy.

"Dad?" Ron's lips had gone as dry as the Sahara.

"Steve's dad is in the arms business."

Ron decided this would be a good time to smile. Make friendly. "You don't say?"

"I do say."

Ron shot his wife a dirty look. "Here you go. Sorry about the misunderstanding." He handed Surfer Steve his beer cooler 'o cash.

"All forgotten, dude. You two have a good night." Steve slipped the Bulldog into his pocket. When his hand came back out it held a short wet joint. "Smoke before you go?"

"No, I don't think so." Ron's open hand fluttered between them. All he wanted to do was get home to the comfort and security of his own home. "It's late."

"Sure, maybe some other time," said Elaine, earning her a queer look from her husband.

"Okay." Steve dropped the joint in his pocket. "See you around. Thanks," he added, hoisting the cooler in the air.

"Bye, Steve!" Elaine waved. "Thanks again for the ride in the Ferrari." This earned her a second queer look from her husband.

"No problemo!" Surfer Steve replied without turning around.

"And I love the ponytail!" This earned her a third queer look from you-know-who.

Surfer Steve's free hand grabbed the ponytail hanging on to the back of his head and gave it a wag.

Elaine turned to her husband. "Think we could buy a Ferrari with some of the money we have left, dear?"

Ron wasn't thinking about buying Ferraris. Ron was considering his wife and considering that maybe he'd made a mistake.

"A red one?"

"Get in the van, Elaine." Soft as the sound of a fluffy white snowflake falling on a fluffy white sheep's butt, he added, "Before I change my mind."

Crossing the Intracoastal Waterway bridge back to the mainland, Ron hurled a paper sack out his window. The car behind him leaned on its horn. A voice shouted "litter bug!"

"What was that?" Elaine had to know.

"Nail gun."

Elaine gasped. "Won't you be needing that to do flooring jobs?"

Ron's look sliced her into two halves.

"Oh, right." He never actually did any jobs. Elaine oozed down in the passenger seat wondering if she would see Rosalind again.

86

Todd and Nick cut through the weedy overgrown lawn between houses. Automatic lawn sprinklers called chick-chick-chick from the back neighbor's lawn.

"Not a creature was stirring," whispered Nick. The screendoor uttered a solitary squeak as he pulled it open.

"What a mess." Todd took in the dirty patio. "This place isn't so much furnished as it is littered. You suppose the hurricane did this?"

"Looks more like a lifestyle choice to me. The frame's still up." An aluminum structure built to hold the screen panels crisscrossed the patio. Some sections of screen limply spilled over the sides. Other sections were gone. Probably to Georgia. "Somebody call 1-800-JUNKME."

Nick examined a narrow door leading into the house from the patio on the far side. "Opaque glass, must be a bathroom." He jiggled the knob. "Everybody forgets to lock their bathroom door."

Todd and Nick slid inside and scouted the house out by the light of their smartphones.

"Home sweet dump." Todd was not impressed by what he saw. Low ceilings, outdated kitchen, cramped living room, threadbare carpets and tired linoleum.

Todd looked in the puny master bedroom. Deep red walls and dark satin curtains. The flatscreen television balanced atop the dresser was nearly as wide as the bed across from which it sat. A framed wedding photo of Ron and Elaine grinning and hugging on a cruise ship stood on a night table. Ron's eyes seemed to follow Todd as he crossed the bedroom.

"What do you think, Nick? Bury Miro in the backyard or simply tuck him in Patton's bed?"

Nick chuckled. "Nah, I can't do that to Elaine. It'd give her nightmares."

"So what then?" Todd looked at his watch. "We haven't got all night."

"Follow me. I've got an idea." Nick waved. Todd followed the detective back to the screened in patio. "What do you think?"

"The pool?" A typical thirty by fifteen foot rectangle took up most of the patio. But this was where typical ended. Forget clear blue waters. This swimming pool was filled with something ugly and green and smelly. "Care for a dip?"

"Stinks worse than the morgue in a power outage. This isn't a swimming pool. This is a cesspool," Nick noted. "And I'm thinking Miro might enjoy a nice refreshing dip."

Todd broke into a grin. "I like it."

"Thought you would. It's like poetry. Let's go," said Nick, starting back to the Big Chill ice cream truck to retrieve their package. "You fish him out of one pool, plop him in another."

Seeing that the street was deserted and nobody was peeping out their windows, so far as they could tell, Nick threw open the big freezer compartment where he and Misty had loaded Miro. A blast of cold air splashed across Nick's face. "Damn, that's cold." Nick grabbed the stiff underlayment and tugged. "Give me a hand here."

Todd propped his arms under the body as Nick slid Miro the rest of the way out. Todd got stuck with the head end. Nick held the feet.

"Is it me or is Miro putting on weight?" Nick grunted as they moved awkwardly through the darkness with the body.

"Must be all that ice cream," Todd whispered.

"Yeah." They struggled up the lawn.

"Not much further now." Todd kicked the screendoor open with his foot and struggled through the doorway. He paused at the edge of the pool. "Ready? On the count of three."

"Screw that. My back's killing me." Nick tossed Miro heels over head. A dull splash was quickly followed by a gurgling and bubbling noise that sounded like some kraken was having trouble digesting his Happy Meal.

Frogs croaked in protest and a cloud of angry mosquitoes swarmed their heads.

"Let's get out of here." Nick led the way.

"What about the shotgun?" Todd stopped at the corner of the garage.

Nick paused. "Right. Shit."

"Toss it in the pool?" Todd's phone chirruped. He quickly fished it out of his pocket. "It's a text from Steve."

"And?"

"And he's made the switch, got my money." Todd quickly sent a reply to Steve.

"Our money. Don't forget half that ransom is mine."

"Right." Todd switched his phone to vibrate and settled it in his back pocket. "Our money."

"Elaine and her hubbie will be home soon." Nick swatted a moth, wiped the guts on his uniform.

"Misty isn't going to like that."

"Damn." Nick spat on his thumb and rubbed his trousers.

"You're going to owe her a pair of pants."

"She's gonna have to take this pair off me first," Nick said with a mischievous grin.

"Wait here." Todd ran to the ice cream truck and returned with the twelve-gauge shotgun.

"What are you planning to do with it?"

"Reunite Miro with it. He was obsessed with this thing." Todd hefted the heavy shotgun in his hands. "Never went anywhere without it." He moved to the patio with Nick at his side. "Why deprive him of it now."

Todd extended the hand holding the shotgun over the murky open sewage pit Ron Patton called a swimming pool.

"Wait." Nick laid a hand on Todd's arm.

"What?"

"I hate to see a good piece like that go to waste."

"It isn't going to waste. I'm hoping the police finding this weapon in Patton's pool will put another nail in his coffin." Todd's brow went up. "Not having second thoughts about framing him, are you, Nick? Getting soft in your old age?"

"No way. In fact, him going to jail might be the best thing to happen to Elaine in a long time. She can do better."

Todd flipped the shotgun into the pool, watched it disappear. "She couldn't do any worse."

87

Ron felt the tension leaving his shoulders as his house came into sight. "Home sweet home." Yeah, there were heaps of stinking, rotting debris everywhere, but still, this was home.

Elaine had been unusually silent most of the drive.

"You okay?" Ron asked.

"Tired."

"They treat you rough?"

"No, just the opposite." Elaine's lip turned downward. "I wonder how Rosalind is doing."

"Forget Rosalind, forget Todd Jones, forget anybody whose last name is Jones," Ron barked, slowing to turn into the drive. "Hey, look at that."

"What?" Elaine pulled herself up in her seat.

"Ice cream truck." Ron pointed a finger to the left. "Across the street there. In front of the Hendersons' house."

"So?"

"So maybe Henderson finally got off unemployment and got himself a real job." Ron snugged the front bumper of his van up to a pile of tottering garbage, put the vehicle in park and shut off the engine. "About time. Never seen such a lazy layabout."

Elaine threw open her door and rolled her eyes. "Let's go to bed."

"Good idea." Ron jiggled his keyring. He was pissed

J.R. RIPLEY

about all that money he'd given up but, all in all, things still looked pretty good. Plus, he had a chunk of change left over from the Strange job. The shoddy work he'd done had been destroyed by Hurricane Oscar. Good old Hurricane Oscar. Who said hurricanes were a bad thing?

The cherry on the sundae? Todd Jones was out of his life. Miro Frankowski was gone forever.

Life could get back to normal. Maybe he'd print up a few flyers. Stick 'em in mailboxes. Drum up some flooring business. He probably couldn't command as high a fee for flooring quotes as he had got away with for roofing quotes, but even at ninety-nine bucks a stop, he could make a pretty decent living. For a while anyway.

That was all that mattered.

Ron followed Elaine through the front door and kicked off his shoes.

Life may not be great but life was good.

88

Crouching together behind the front of the Big Chill ice cream truck, Todd and Nick watched Ron and Elaine arrive home and disappear inside their house.

"Now?" Nick asked, slurping up the residue of his Jolly Rancher snow cone.

"Let's wait half an hour or so. Let him get real comfortable. That will make it all the sweeter," replied Todd, who'd swallowed his Choco Taco in three bites. Ice cream got sticky and messy if you took too long to eat it. "Then you can make the call." He yawned then tapped Nick on the shoulder. "Home, James."

Nick crumpled up the paper snow cone and tossed it in the general vicinity of an open trashcan.

They climbed in the truck and drove to Port Everglades.

"When do I get my money?" Nick stopped in front of Todd's condo building. The place was quiet and deserted but for the guy seated at the desk inside who barely glanced up at them.

"We're meeting Steve for breakfast tomorrow at Lester's. He'll bring the money. Nine thirty." Lester's Diner on State Road 84 was a Fort Lauderdale landmark.

"I'll be there. Make sure my money is too."

"Don't trust me?"

"Not in this lifetime."

Todd grinned and climbed down from the truck. He

slapped the door. "Good night, Nick. Don't forget what you've got to do."

"You kidding? This is the fun part."

After dropping Todd at home, Nick would make an anonymous call to the police from a public telephone at the airport.

Ron and Elaine would be getting some unexpected late night guests.

By Nick's estimate, six squad cars filled with his uniformed and well-armed comrades would soon descend on the Patton residence. Lights would flash and blaze. Sirens would waken and annoy Ron's neighbors.

The leader of this pack would hold a search warrant in one hand, and a grappling hook in the other.

Miro was about to make an encore appearance.

89

Ron gulped down a beer in the kitchen, burped and struggled out of his shirt and pants, dropping them on the floor and kicking them into the corner near the washer/dryer combo—making life easier for Elaine.

Elaine had already retired. He found her in bed, strawberry-scented goop on her face, eyes closed. One of those little book light thingamajigs dangling over a romance novel.

"Who reads that crap?" Ron crawled into bed beside her. Leaving on his socks and boxer shorts.

Elaine always wore flannel PJs. No matter what the weather. Wore it like armor.

All he'd done for her and still no thank you. "You got anything to say?" Ron asked.

"Yes, be quiet. I'm trying to read," Elaine snapped, holding her place on the page with her finger.

Ron swore under his breath and turned out his lamp. He pulled the covers up, twisted and turned. Buried his head in his pillow.

Distant sirens grew louder, stronger, angrier.

Ron rolled onto his side. "You hear that?"

Elaine considered, more concerned with what Derek and Amy were going to do next now that her boyfriend was out of town and she was falling heavy for her sexy new neighbor. "Must be a fire someplace nearby."

"Yeah, guess so." Ron reburied his face in his down-filled pillow.

BANG BANG BANG

"What the hell?" Ron shot up.

"Sounds like somebody at the door." Elaine balanced her book across her chest. "Go see."

BANG BANG BANG

"Probably Old Man Willard again. Idiot."

"Now, now. He's old. He gets confused."

"So? Does he always have to confuse his house with our house?"

BANG BANG BANG.

"Shit!" Ron kicked off the covers. "Will this day, will this nightmare never end?"

"Put some clothes on."

"Forget it." Ron stomped off to the front door, wrinkled boxers, droopy socks and flabby belly. It was only Old Man Willard after all. Spent his life in his skivvies. And let all the world and his neighbors know it.

"Maybe now we've got some money we can move into a better neighborhood," Ron mumbled, reaching for the doorknob. "Yeah, Willard, what do you—"

Ron blinked. A wall of police officers ringed the front door. A swarm of police cars filled the streets. His neighbors, including Old Man Willard standing at the end of his driveway in his skivvies, gawked.

"Ronald Patton?" A stern-faced and mustachioed police captain thrust a paper in Ron's startled face. "Search warrant."

"Search warrant?"

"You know a Miro Frankowski?" The captain waved and his men spread out. Two burly officers burst through the front door past him.

"Miro?" Ron squeaked.

"You have the right to remain silent."

Ron did so.

90

Aristotle Constantine was happy. He'd foisted those lousy submerged Intracoastal residential lots of his off on that prick Yevgeny Brezhinski. He'd even gotten a valuable Magritte in the deal. How sweet was that?

Puffing a cigar, nestled in his forest green leather chair in the study of his modest eighteen-thousand square foot Greek-inspired mansion on the Intracoastal, he admired Man On A Blue Sofa.

"What a work of art," he muttered through the cigar clenched between his teeth. Maybe he'd mount it over the fireplace in the living area facing the water and his sixty-three foot yacht. All visitors would see the masterpiece the minute they entered the room.

Sure, the painting was a bit surreal...was that the word? A guy with a banana stuck in his face. But artists were a crazy bunch.

Constantine cocked his head. What was that in the righthand corner? He rose, crossed to a cherry wood desk, removed a pair of tortoise shell reading glasses, popped them on his nose and crossed to the easel holding his newest acquisition.

Aristotle Constantine leaned closer, glasses sliding down his nose. Was that? He kept a gold-trimmed magnifying glass next to an antique globe on one of his shelves. He picked up the magnifying glass for assistance because his reading glass prescription was far too weak. He zoomed it in and out, struggling with the focus.

Was that a pig? Its beady black eyes and hairy snout peeking out around the corner of the blue sofa?

Indeed, it was. Inspired by her friend Yulia's tale of Chagall's habit of including cats in his compositions, Irina had decided to include Mr. Squeals in her own work. Why not? Who'd notice, after all?

Certainly not Aristotle Constantine. Well, he noticed but it seemed normal to him...that is, if normal was the word to be used regarding any of Magritte's work.

Aristotle Constantine chuckled, blowing acrid smoke over his head. Yep, he thought again, artists really were a crazy bunch.

91

Up on the twenty-second floor of the Port Lauderdale Condominium Tower, Todd, Irina and Rosalind gathered in the living room. Todd and his mother occupied the sofa.

"I have surprise," announced Irina, standing behind the sofa, rubbing the back of Todd's neck.

"I've already had one surprise today," Todd said. The bill had arrived for the new refrigerator that his mom had taken the liberty of ordering. Good thing the money was coming in because the way his mom spent it, he'd be in trouble if it didn't. He had two additional mouths to feed, three counting Mr. Squeals—and he literally did eat like a pig.

"What is it?" Todd asked politely. Life was as good as it got. Surfer Steve had done a great job for him just as he'd done a great job for Brezhinski.

Nick had gotten his share of the ransom money and was talking about using it to buy a Big Chill franchise as a side investment. Todd was sure it was more a ploy to insinuate himself further into Misty Kirkpatrick's life and/or pants.

But that was Nick's problem, not Todd's. Well, it was more Misty's problem than anybody's, but Todd had a feeling the lady could take care of herself. And Nick.

Ron Patton was in jail pending his trial for the murder of Miro Frankowski. He'd be spending all his money on his defense. Todd had heard the guy had wisely argued with his defense attorney against getting out on bail until the trial.

Word on the street was that Bogs was intent on saving the Florida taxpayers the needless expense of keeping and providing three square meals a day to Ron Patton for the next ten to twenty years.

Of course, Ron's court-appointed defense attorney hoped to get the murder charge reduced to involuntary manslaughter. That would cut Ron's potential stay in a state facility down to something in the nine to fifteen year range.

As for getting married, well, things could be worse. Truth was, Todd was getting used to having Irina around.

"Wait here." Irina, dressed in an ankle-length white summer dress, ran to Todd's office. She'd been keeping Todd out, insisting he could have it back only when she said so.

"Here I come," said Irina a minute later from the door to the office. "Close eyes, everybody."

Todd reluctantly shut his eyes.

"This is so fun." Rosalind slapped her palm across her face. "I love surprises!"

Irina leaned a four by six foot framed painting on the sleek mantel of the modern wall-mounted gas fireplace across from the sofa. "Okay, open!"

Todd threw open his eyes. "It's—"

"It's beautiful! I adore it!" Rosalind clapped her hands against her cheeks. "Isn't it wonderful, Todd?" Her smile hung from ear to ear.

"It's, um, yeah, wonderful." Todd felt his heart skip a beat or three.

"I surprise you, no?" Irina leapt on Todd's lap and kissed him hard.

"You surprise me, yes."

"Is early birthday present for you, Rosalind."

"Call me Mama, baby."

Irina blushed. "You like?"

"I love." Tears ran down Rosalind's face. "I'll treasure it forever. Mr. Squeals! Oh, Mr. Squeals!"

Todd's mother clapped her hands twice and the pot-bellied porker came running in from the balcony where he'd been preheating.

"Look, Mr. Squeals." Gripping both sides of the pig's face, she aimed his devil eyes at the painting. "It's you!"

And it was. An oil portrait of Todd's mom and Mr. Squeals seated on his sofa. Practically lifesize. The workmanship was incredible. The subject matter? Unspeakable.

"What do you think, Todd?" Irina asked. "You are so quiet."

"Unbelievable." All he'd picked up for his mom's upcoming birthday was the Fleetwood Mac LP collection and a new phonograph she'd been shamelessly hinting about.

Irina pinched Todd's cheek. "Don't worry, my love. I have surprise for you too!"

"That really isn't necessary," Todd said, fearing the worst. Could there be anything worse? "One surprise is enough." For a lifetime.

The doorbell chimed.

"Too late. Surprise is here!" Irina jumped from his lap and ran to the door. She threw it open.

Todd gaped.

A familiar gangly young man in baggy, cuffed red

shorts, pink muscle shirt and open-toe leather sandals stood at the door. His door. The a-man's-home-is-his-castle door.

"Nico is here!" Nico Bechem's grin was wide and his moustache looked like he'd dipped it in olive oil.

"Yulia too!" A woman waved behind Nico's shoulder.

"So thank you for inviting us, Todd! Come give Nico a kiss and a hug!"

Todd managed to rise halfway to his feet. "How-how..."

"How long?" Irina patted Todd's hand.

"We stay until wedding," Nico answered for her.

Only then did Todd noticed the luggage hanging from Nico and Yulia's hands.

"Come see my portrait—our portrait," Rosalind added, seeing Mr. Squeals weaving and bobbing excitedly between the two new guests. "My daughter-in-law-to-be painted it for me!"

"Of course." Nico and Yulia squeezed into the living room. "Take these, please." Nico handed Todd his suitcases.

Yulia dropped her two pieces at his feet, planting a kiss on each of Todd's cheeks. She wore brand new flip-flops that slapped the marble floor as she walked and a bright yellow T-shirt she'd bought in the airport gift shop.

The gaudy shirt's message: Welcome To Florida the Sunshine State, spelled out in cartoony letters and palm trees, taunted him.

"Oops!" Nico stopped, snapped his fingers. "Almost forgot. Here's your tip!" Nico turned around and pinched Todd's butt cheek.

Did it hurt? Hard to say.

Todd was too numb to feel anything at all.

Hi, thanks for reading!

If you enjoyed this book, please support me by sharing your positive review online and on your favorite social media platforms. Trust me, ever little bit helps.

And, don't forget, if you like NAILED IT!, please check out FIVE MINUTES and FIVE MORE MINUTES, for further adventures of Todd & Co.

Thanks again!

J.R. Ripley

J.R. Ripley (Glenn Eric Meganck) is also the national best-selling author of A Bird Lover's mystery series, the Maggie Miller mysteries, the TV Pet Chef mysteries (writing as Marie Celine) and other novels. He is also a critically-acclaimed singer/songwriter.

Visit GlennEric.com and connect with JR at Facebook.com/JRRipley & @JRRipleyAuthor.

ABOUT THE AUTHOR

J. R. Ripley

 Hi, thanks for reading!

If you enjoyed this book, please share your positive reviews online and on your favorite social media platforms. Every kind word helps.

And, if you like NAILED IT!, please check out FIVE MINUTES and FIVE MORE MINUTES, for further adventures of Todd & Co.

Thanks again!

J.R. Ripley (Glenn Eric Meganck)

National best-selling author and critically-acclaimed singer/songwriter. Visit GlennEric.com for more info.

BOOKS IN THIS SERIES

Todd Jones Comic Thriller

Nailed It!

TBD

Five More Minutes

Five more minutes.

That was all the woman standing outside his floundering business, Todd Jones Realty, wanted. Just five minutes. What could go wrong? Surprisingly, everything. And that's what Todd Jones is about to learn when he allows the enigmatic Caterina Kadlec to enter his office. He's hoping that her wealthy client, and the big fat commission he'll earn, will be the answer to his prayers. Unfortunately, Caterina has other plans and those plans include grand larceny.

As for the murder, well, sometimes things don't go as planned, do they?

Nope, they sure don't. And that's what Todd is also about to learn and learn the hard way. No matter, Todd always has plans of his own and has no qualms about implementing them. Because when it comes to ethics and morality, it's all a gray area as far as Todd is concerned. To complicate matters, his girlfriend has left him. Again. And his live-in mother, who already insists on keeping an annoying pet pig named Mr. Squeals, has invited a homeless Russian woman to take up residence, thus kicking him out of his home office.

If it wasn't for downhill, it seems Todd's life would have nowhere to go. And he's going to have to do something about that...

Five Minutes

Got five minutes? Well good, here's what Nick Lucas' amazing Five Minutes is all about...

Todd Jones is a hotshot realtor in Fort Lauderdale, Florida. He's got a hot girlfriend, too. The trouble is that Todd is a real bad judge of character, especially his own. Todd's got himself tangled up worse than an old fishing line balled up in that long forgotten tackle box in the garage. Let's enumerate.

One of Todd's biggest clients is mad because the property Todd talked him into buying is underwater—literally. A screwy surfer dude with a recreational drug habit and a millionaire gun manufacturer for a father has got some not-so-friendly dealers on his tail. Todd's mother has shown up and wants to live with him. And she's brought her pet pig. And, oh, yeah, there's this little problem Todd is having with one of his best friends, Dr. Doug Freeman. Todd has been sleeping with Doug's wife. Okay, so maybe he shouldn't have. He'd be the first to admit that it may have been an error in judgment on his part. He is a bad judge of character, remember?

And that leads us to Todd Jones' biggest problem. Dr. Doug has found out about Todd's philandering and is aiming a pistol at Todd's forehead even as we speak. Todd has five minutes to live. Maybe less if his girlfriend finds out about his cheating ways.

Nick Lucas' FIVE MINUTES starts at a brisk boil and never lets up until the last sentence is laid down in this gripping comic thriller about a man whose life has taken a quick and nasty turn for the worse. And goes downhill from there. . .

www.ingramcontent.com/pod-product-compliance
Lightning Source LLC
Chambersburg PA
CBHW030551020726
47494CB00005B/1563

* 9 7 8 1 8 9 2 3 3 9 4 6 1 *